Ribbons of Death

Edita A. Petrick

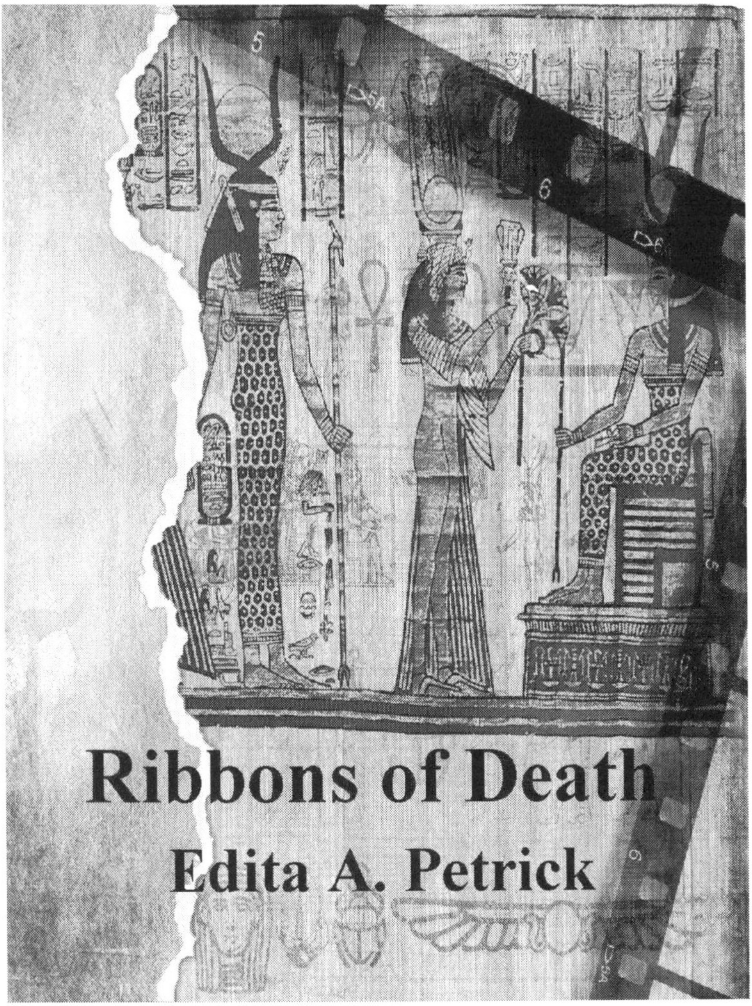

Cover Art:
Michelle Crocker

http://mlcdesigns4you.weebly.com/

Publisher's Note:

This is a work of fiction. All names, characters, places, and events are the work of the author's imagination.

Any resemblance to real persons, places, or events is coincidental.

Solstice Publishing - www.solsticepublishing.com

Ribbons of Death
by: Edita A. Petrick

Prologue

Cairo
February 1
Eid-Ul-Adha (Day of Sacrifice)

The last hundred-pound note Gahiji gave to the Has-Al'Sharim Food Service driver saw him as far as the restaurant's utility room. The bribe earned him the privilege of sitting on a rickety wooden crate and waiting for the kitchen help to come and sign for the delivery. He stifled an urge to wring his hands, even though he felt like praying. He wasn't a beggar, for God's sake. He was an Egyptologist with a PhD from Oxford that sat as proudly stiff behind its glass and mahogany frame as the day it was awarded to him, deservedly. But in spite of his prestigious doctorate degree, he'd spent decades serving bureaucrats with inflated egos and empty heads. Today, he was a phone call away from bankruptcy.

He knew this was his last chance in his ten-year long quest to talk to Nicola Moses.

The billionaire was having a power lunch with the Cairo General Manager of IBM and a bevy of other business flunkies in the screened-off portion of Papillon Bleu, the 'grassroots' Lebanese restaurant located in the middle-class section of Sa'afayeen, just a stone's throw from Cairo's still very popular camel market, Imbaba.

Finally he got a break. Moses had only two bodyguards standing in attendance while the rest of his security fleet sat outside in cars parked on the road rightfully claimed by camels and donkeys. Years of tireless pursuit of Moses and a hundred-pound note bribe had gotten him a stone's throw away from the man. What now?

He couldn't afford to create a scene in the man's favorite 'roots' eatery.

"Has everything been off-loaded?" a voice said

from behind him.

He turned around to see a man in a white waistcoat and black trousers bearing a cork-bottom plastic tray with a stack of fluffy paper serviettes.

"Yes. I'm just waiting for someone to sign the invoice." A surge of panic tightened his throat.

"I'll sign for it. Where is it?" the waiter asked.

"Ah, my partner is just getting it from the truck."

"Well, come and get me when he returns," the waiter said and turned around to leave. It was now or never.

"Excuse me," he called after the man. The waiter turned around.

"Would you be so kind as to deliver a note to a patron having lunch in this restaurant?" he asked, careful not to appear anxious.

"What kind of note?" the waiter asked.

He smiled, rose and motioned at the stack of paper serviettes on the tray. "May I...?" He fished out a pen from his chest pocket, gingerly removed the top serviette and looked around for a writing surface.

"Here, use the tray," the waiter suddenly offered.

Gahiji thanked him and sat down on the crate. The paper was thin and ripped easily.

"Take a couple to make it easier," the waiter advised.

Again, he thanked him, cut the stack in half, then patted them down to make a compact surface, though it was still difficult to write. Holding the paper surface with his thumb and forefinger, he quickly drew an outline of a cartouche and filled it from the top, starting with an inverted ankh symbol. The original cartouche was "misplaced" on a shelf in the "non-performing" exhibits storage room in the museum. Only one person knew exactly where to find it, since he had also put it there. He drew two birds, back to back. It suggested strength and a shift in power brought about by such destruction. Moses had built his business empire on his father's dual entrepreneurial venture as a Beirut restaurant owner and wine merchant. The meaning behind the duality of the chick-bird-glyph would not be lost on him.

"It's not a curse, nor threat of any kind," he said, seeing the man's suspicion-narrowed eyes, when he took back his serving tray.

"What is it then?" the waiter asked, frowning.

"A business note — a proposition, that's all," he said and on impulse added a symbol for wealth that could also mean price or demand for ransom. He hoped the billionaire's knowledge of hieroglyphics was as good as his own, or he might never see the light of day.

"I'd appreciate it if you delivered it to Mr. Moses," he said, quickly flipping out his wallet from the hip pocket on his coveralls. All he had left were two twenty-dollar US bills from a conference trip to Los Angeles. He'd meant to use them to pay for lunch with Stella Hunter in Hollywood's Dragonstar Restaurant, but the American mythology expert ignored his gallant attempt. She slapped her credit card down on the waiter's tray as he passed by their table before he could even open his wallet. Later on, whenever he thought of changing the currency back to Egyptian pounds, the memory of the woman's insult washed over him, and he couldn't touch the bank notes. She grimaced whenever she thought he wasn't observing her. Ironically, he knew she thought he was a crackpot, talking about the Peacetaker's existence today, in modern times, even though all her research supported precisely that kind of outcome. Now, he wondered whether it wasn't fate that prevented him from changing the bills.

"Thank you," he said, taking both bills and handing them to the waiter. "That's for any inconvenience I may have caused you." He knew he had chosen wisely when, five minutes later, the waiter returned to guide him through the back corridor into the screened-off portion of the restaurant that was reserved for the most valued patrons.

He handed the first bodyguard who blocked his path his business card.

"Dr. Fineas Gahiji, Assistant Director, Cairo Museum of Antiquities," the security man read flatly. His boss didn't react. Moses simply stared at the cartouche drawing on the napkin, tapping it here and there with his index finger.

Every Meridian hotel had a life-size painting of its owner hanging in the place of honor in the lobby. Just last month, Gahiji attended the Antiquarian Society of Egypt's annual conference in Cairo's Meridian Obelisk. The hotel was a flagship of Moses' Mediterranean hospitality industry. The founder's portrait loomed over the curved glass-and-Brazilian mahogany reception station, its magnificent size dwarfing the human attendants serving on the floor. The word 'minions' had sprung into Gahiji's head as he cautiously glanced back and forth between the owner's life-size image and his staff.

In person, the billionaire was even more menacing. His dusky skin was so tautly stretched across his high cheekbones that the two round whitish spots gave an impression of the bone about to shoot through the skin. He was sixty-five but his hair was jet black. Gahiji doubted that anyone who worked for Moses had ever dared to question the miraculous absence of white powder that was a herald of old age. It might have even been a genetic gift. The black color further hardened his dark eyes beneath his widow's peak hairline into menacing tools of control. Newspapers, in particular, liked to talk about the "visual power" the billionaire had when delivering one of his speeches during the launch of yet another Meridian Industries subsidiary.

Such rubbish, he thought, whenever he read the drivel in the papers.

Now, trying to contain the shivers, he breathed as

quietly as he could and watched the head of jet black hair move ever so slightly up and down as Moses scrutinized the drawing. Moses was not just a generous patron of the Cairo Museum but also a scholar and antiquities collector. However, he didn't just collect myths and legends. He collected their sources, and it was a poorly-kept secret that many such sources disappeared shortly after having been "discovered" by the billionaire. That's why Gahiji had to be very careful how he presented his find.

"I've heard of this legend. In fact, I've heard many versions of it. Egyptian is the best version, of course. You have found this wretched creature?" Moses asked without raising his head to look at him.

"Yes, Your Excellency," Gahiji said, trying not to show the relief that flushed through him.

"So our mythology still has the power to rule the world from the shadows," Moses said.

"As you said, Your Excellency, this particular legend appears in several ancient civilizations and has been correlated on a global basis. It is not only the Egyptian...." He trailed off because he realized that his audience was not interested in the myths and legends weaving their tales through the ancient tapestry of global civilizations. Moses was only concerned about what such legends could do for his interests.

"Have you tested the creature's powers?" Moses asked and lifted his head.

Gahiji's breath caught in his throat. The man's eyes must have fired a bolt through his heart. It was the only way to explain the stabbing pain in his chest.

"Somewhat," he said without confidence, and then hastily added, "That is, I have not tested his powers completely, Your Excellency. I wanted to reserve that privilege for his new owner."

Moses' lips curved upward in a smile that was difficult to interpret. "Do you have a function in mind that would convince me to pay your price?"

"A 'White Candle' women's march at the Cairo's stadium, sponsored by the Egyptian Women's Cinema Association and Cairo University female students. The event is scheduled to start the first Monday of the new month, at noon. The organizers expect about five hundred women and children to march around the stadium, carrying burning white candles, singing and chanting peace prayers and incantations." It was a huge risk to answer in such detail, but he wanted to show Moses that he had not just picked something on the spur of the moment but had long planned it out.

"My wife and daughters, together with Mrs. Ferris and her three little girls, are scheduled to participate in the peace march," the billionaire said, tilting his head to one side and staring at Gahiji.

"Perhaps it would be wise to convince Madame Moses and her daughters to withdraw their participation for health reasons," Gahiji said, holding his breath. He wasn't sure what Moses wanted. It was difficult to read him.

"But not Mrs. Ferris and her children?" Moses asked, his voice thick with irony.

"But of course, Your Excellency, the American Ambassador is your friend. His wife and children should be advised to withdraw…."

"Leave that to me. I shall be the bearer of bad news when and if it's necessary," Moses said sharply.

Gahiji bowed his head. "As you wish, Your Excellency. Who shall you assign to conduct the demonstration?"

"You, of course," the billionaire said, soft laughter churning in his throat.

Gahiji recoiled. "But…but there will be chaos, mayhem. I may perish in the carnage…."

Moses burst out laughing. "My dear Dr. Fineas Gahiji, never, ever forget that as long as there is breath in the man, he is capable of producing an idea. I'm sure you'll figure out something that will see you walk out of the stadium alive. Besides, aren't you the master of this creature of mayhem and destruction?"

Gahiji took two quick cleansing breaths. "If I am to be the one to run the test, then I'm afraid I need to renegotiate my compensation." He almost closed his eyes because if Moses had him shot, he didn't want to see the gun.

"But of course," the billionaire said. "I perfectly understand that insurance premiums rise in tandem with danger. You will have twenty million dollars, U.S. currency, deposited into your bank account in the Cayman Islands twenty-four hours post successful demonstration of the creature's powers. And I do mean to see everything in that stadium the legends claim."

"Yes, Your Excellency," Gahiji said and bowed his head. "But there is just a small matter…"

Moses didn't let him finish. He nodded at one of his bodyguards, who turned around and left the restaurant. Gahiji was just starting to worry, when the security man returned with a small cedar box. He opened it to show Gahiji that it was filled with crisp new one hundred dollar U.S. bills, then snapped the lid shut.

Gahiji accepted the box. He bowed to Moses and then quickly walked out, pressing the box to his chest. A man carrying a carved cedar box would not be suspicious. The market was full of stalls with tables heaped with such trinkets.

He walked toward a bus stop, wondering what would be a right bribe for all those factions he had to tip to let him carry out his plan. He didn't want to tip a hundred if ten would do.

Chapter One

Cairo
March 2,
Day of Aashurah - 10th day

The French reporter, Pascal Giroux, called when Carter was already en route, heading for the airport.

"*'Allo, Cartier. C'est Giroux.* I have an event that may be of interest to you, *mon ami,*" the newsman said.

Carter glanced out the window. The blue Novotel neon roof sign and square white pillars of the hotel flashed by. He was practically at the airport. Last night, when he sat with Pascal in Il Giardino's pool bar, sipping Glenlivet and watching the sunset transform the pyramids into giant orange tents, the reporter complained about Cairo's quiet news scene.

"*Cartier*, are you there?" Pascal asked in his cigarette-scarred voice.

"I'm here, Pascal, but *here* is a taxi, heading for Cairo International."

"*Ah, c'est mal.* I have an interesting proposition — attending an event."

"Why didn't you tell me last night? I would have tried to change my flight."

"It wasn't *fait accompli*. I just got the word that it's a go. When is your flight?"

"Leaves at noon," Carter said, reshuffling the priorities in his head. His Delta flight for Istanbul, if on time, was to depart two hours from now. Did he have time to drop by Pascal's 'event' and what would be the consequences of taking a later flight?

Hurmutz wasn't waiting for him at Ataturk International. The agent had begged Yassine to give him a week off to go stay with his dying mother, who wasn't expected to last more than two to three days. Hurmutz had spent a year establishing five 'exit' points that would pass the Lebanese restaurateur's scrutiny. Dying mother was his third excuse in two years of working for Joseph Aziz Yassine. Carter didn't have to be in Istanbul today. Tomorrow would do just fine.

"The event is scheduled to start at noon," Pascal said, sounding chagrined. "A 'White Candle' women's march at Cairo's stadium, sponsored by the Egyptian Women's Cinema Association and Cairo University female students. The organizers expect about five hundred women and children to march around the stadium, carrying burning white candles."

"Sounds very tranquil and very dangerous. Are you sure you should be there, Pascal? You, of all people, should know that any demonstration in Egypt these days is just a preamble to a civil war. Is the French press covering it as a favor to Human Rights Organization or…?" Now Carter understood why last night the event still wasn't *fait accompli.* The last time there was an actual demonstration in Egypt was in '81 — triggered by El-Sadat's assassination and instantly an Emergency Law was put in place banning all demonstrations. And since those good old times, there had been no demonstrations in Egypt, only bloody riots and skirmishes with the police at the cost of many lives.

"We're covering it not only because it's the first legal demonstration with legitimate permits, *mon ami,* but also because this morning the Egyptian government asked us to record a testimony that will show all those other news reports about the police trampling demonstrators' human rights with batons, rubber sticks and gas grenades to be malicious propaganda," the Frenchman said, his voice thick with sarcasm.

Carter laughed. "Ah, so you're actually being bribed by the government to make a goodwill video so Egypt can hoodwink Europe and North America. Now, I understand just how very legal it is. But why would this demonstration march be of interest to me?"

"You're an *Americain,* no?"

Carter held the cell phone away from his ear, staring at it with suspicion. Was Pascal indulging his French sense of humor or had he started his breakfast by sipping Crème de Menthe instead of coffee?

"I thought you had figured that out for yourself six years ago when I took you to a Dodgers' game in L.A.," Carter said dryly and once again held out the cell phone to avoid the Frenchman's laughter.

"I forgot, *mon ami.* You *are* leaving, so you probably didn't have time to open up your laptop and check the news, but Madame Ferris and three *petite Mademoiselles* will be marching in the first row."

"Are you serious? Our Ambassador's wife and her daughters are part of this protest?" That was something an American businessman, even on a brief visit to Cairo, should know. Diplomats' families did not participate in peace marches on foreign soil. It had to be Mrs. Ferris. She didn't endear herself with the security back home, and she was probably stressing them out twice as much in Cairo.

"Peaceful march, not a protest. *Mais oui.* Madame Ferris delivered a fiery speech at the Ghazir Club's luncheon last month, demanding human rights for women and families throughout the Arab world. She illustrated her point as delicately as a sledgehammer when she showed her affluent audience the Kirkuk video of a women's shelter, revealing not only the living conditions of Iraqi women but also the body of one of the shelter's organizers, slashed to bloody pieces."

"Wasn't it a French newswoman who produced that documentary video?" Carter asked, wondering what else the *Agence-France Presse* award-winning journalist would dangle before him as the carrot that would make him relent and reschedule his flight.

"It had to be a woman, *certainment,* but nationality plays little part in news gathering. Ambassador Ferris is proud of his independent wife, but the embassy security and the *Americain* soldiers are much stressed out by her outspoken nature. It makes their jobs very difficult. There will be some tall burka-clad women marching to the left and to the right of Madame Ferris and her little daughters."

Carter chuckled. Pascal could be once again indulging his peculiar sense of humor but it wasn't such an outrageous consideration to maintain security around the Ambassador's wife and daughters. American soldiers and security officers in Middle-Eastern drag would be actually a clever solution. But the newsman still hadn't told him why an American environmental consultant should be interested in a women's peaceful protest march?

Carter had spent five days in Cairo, changing suits and donning fresh white shirts just to make small talk and sip coffee with bureaucrats who held the key to unlocking any number of large contracts for the Sinai development project. Relocating three million people away from the densely populated Nile Valley was certainly an expansive endeavor and one that saw many North American companies send representatives with proposals on how to do it efficiently and effectively in the shortest time possible — for a price, of course.

Global Environics, out of Toledo, Ohio, featured in Carter's documents as his employer and his place of residence. His business card was elegant but simple — black and white with a gold-braid trim and seven green leaves, for good luck. His passport endorsed him as Timothy J. Carter, Senior Vice-President, Technology and Solutions. His mother would be proud. Then again, his mother, if she was alive, wouldn't recognize anything, least of all the name on her son's passport, because it wasn't the one she gave him.

He glanced at the taxi driver. The man sat unusually

tall, holding a cigarette in his right hand, but Carter did not see him take a puff. The taxi was no longer moving, which meant they were already parked at the strip near the airport. When the taxi picked him up, the driver wanted fifty Egyptian pounds for a trip to the airport. Carter gave him twenty at the start of the trip. Obviously, the man was enjoying eavesdropping on his passenger's conversation while waiting for the rest of his fare.

"Pascal, this peaceful march sounds interesting, but I've already shook our Ambassador's hand and wished him political luck while he promised to support American business involvement in the Sinai project."

"You then do not wish to see Madame Ferris and her burka-clad Marines bear white candles and sing?"

"Marines? Don't you mean DSS? Diplomatic Service Security is usually the ones who provide protection for the embassy personnel on any outing. I thought you were just generalizing – soldiers. Are you sure it's our Marines?"

"*Mai oui, mon ami,* normally it is the members of DSS, but this time the usual protocol has been *augmentée.*"

Carter frowned. Change of protocol, especially security protocol was never done on a whim. Somebody, somewhere had to be really stressed out by Ambassador's outspoken, free-spirited wife. Maybe because children were involved....

"*Mon ami*, it is not every day that you get to bear witness to burka-clad Marines, marching with white candles," Pascal said, tipping his head to a side.

"It sounds like a newsworthy item, Pascal, and I'm sure the pictures will win you another journalistic prize but—"

The Frenchman interrupted him. "Madame Ferris and her *petite filles* will be marching in company of Madame Bianca Moses and her two college-student daughters."

"Ah," Carter breathed out, understanding in a flash why the newsman had called him in the first place.

"The demonstration's organizers are from various women's organizations but the secret sponsor who has purchased the use of the stadium, much police cooperation and good will, not to speak of the press coverage, is none other than Nicola Moses. I learned this just an hour ago."

"Where should I meet you?" Carter asked, this time glaring at the smoking taxi driver to at least prompt him into opening the window.

"Outside the stadium's main gate. Look for a white van with wide-open doors and men with cameras on their shoulders."

"See you there, and thanks," Carter said and flipped the cell phone closed. "Toss out that cigarette and start the car," he told the driver. When the taxi picked him up the driver asked him in English for his destination. Carter had no need to dazzle the man with his linguistic skill. On this business trip he was an American businessman and that's just what he wanted the world to see.

"I'll give you twenty pounds in addition to the thirty I still owe you to take me to the Heliopolis stadium," he said.

The driver opened the window and flicked out the cigarette. "Fifty and the thirty you owe me."

"It's a ten, fifteen-minute trip. Twenty," Carter maintained dispassionately.

"Half an hour, maybe more," the driver said.

"I'm sitting in a Benz, not a donkey cart. Twenty-five, and the thirty I still owe."

"Sixty-five," the driver said, starting the car.

"A total of sixty and not a *piaster* more," Carter said.

"Tip," the driver said, rubbing his thumb and forefinger together.

Chapter Two

Pascal grabbed Carter's shoulder just as Carter stopped by the white van of the *Al-Hurra* TV Station. The English equivalent of the Arabic name, 'The Free One' was stamped on the van's side in bold black letters.

"Where is your van?" Carter asked, wondering as he turned his head left and right. The stadium looked as if it was under siege by a fleet of blue and white vans and cars equipped with light strips mounted on their roofs. The entire Cairo police force seemed to be eager to supervise this event.

"*France Presse* has earned the honor to be one of a handful of news agencies allowed to record this celebrated event from inside the stadium," Pascal said, pulling him away from the *Al-Hurra* van. "As they say in America, we are on the green carpet."

"I don't think that's exactly the American saying, but I know what you mean." Carter chuckled.

"You will be my right-hand man," Pascal said, motioning for Carter to bow his head so he could put the France Presse pass threaded on a light steel chain around his neck. "Does your French still work?"

"*Mais oui*," Carter said, grinning. "But I think it'll be safer if I just keep my mouth shut. I don't look French." His ancestry was Irish, Greek and Norwegian.

"A Frenchman these days can look like Inspector Clouseau or your Executive Officer in the White House, *mon ami*. You have nothing to worry about. I also have rather worrisome news," Pascal said as they fought their way through the crowds surging toward the main entrance. Carter realized that while the Egyptian government wanted the foreign press to call the peaceful march a rally, it was really more of a media spectacle. The presence of Mrs. Ferris and Mrs. Moses would give the march its political support, but five hundred women dressed in black robes and bearing lit white candles would certainly amount to a performance rather than a political statement.

"What's the worrisome news?" Carter asked when they finally made it to the field where a dozen news vans were parked in a circle. The Agence-France Presse van sat next to the BBC News dark blue sport van.

"The organizers issued apologies on behalf of Madame Moses and her daughters. They won't be able to take part in the march," Giroux said.

"Why should that be worrisome?" Carter asked.

"Moses has purchased the use of the stadium for the demonstration. He has purchased the most excellent security available — the entire Cairo police force — and yet, his wife and children withdraw at the last minute because…" His voice trailed off.

"What did the organizers say is the reason they won't attend?"

Giroux pursed his lips. "They didn't say. That's what is worrisome. They just told us that Madame Moses sends her apologies to the members of the foreign press."

"But you think it's because her husband doesn't trust all the excellent security he's purchased?"

"I am a newsman, *mon ami*. I wonder when I hear news without explanation. Is it good or bad?"

"Maybe Mrs. Moses got sick or maybe she has a family emergency. There could be any number of reasons—"

Giroux interrupted him. "*Oui*, there could, but the true reason would have to be so compelling that Madame Moses and her *filles* would risk dishonoring a cause that they ardently support and thus risk their own reputation and standing within their elite community, not to speak of the global community of their sisters."

"They're just women, Pascal, and this is an Arab world, in case you haven't noticed," Carter said. "Here the application of honor is reserved for men only."

"Not so, *mon ami*. Bianca Moses is an Egyptian delegate to the International Women's Human Rights Organization. When the press reports that she has cancelled her participation at the last moment, it will reflect very poorly on her — and on her husband's political ambitions."

Moses didn't have political ambitions. He just wanted everyone to think he did. His ambitions were much darker than mere politics. But, that was one topic that Carter couldn't discuss with the Frenchman right now.

"I'm sure you'll eventually find out the reason for the cancellation and will be politically correct in interpreting it for your audience," Carter said, looking around because the stadium seats, while by no means crowded, already held a respectable audience. He wondered whether Moses had also bought a few hundred spectators to give the spectacle more dignity. Five hundred women holding lit candles and marching around the stadium was, after all, not a powerful demonstration, more like a large social function for affluent women. Mrs. Ferris' presence would certainly make the march newsworthy, and her burka-clad Marines....

He shook his head. How did James Bowen Ferris end up with a wife like Melisenda Neron? Ambassador Ferris was short, bald and, though a very capable diplomat, utterly devoid of humor. He'd gripped Carter's hand in a firm but brief handshake, asked the obligatory questions about his business appointments and when his secretary handed him a small white note, he read it, gave it back to her to shred and invited Carter to join him for lunch. For nearly two hours, Carter sipped sweet Egyptian wine, sufficiently tasted every dish the waiter placed in front of him to say he had eaten, and briefed the Ambassador on the disturbing rumors that had started to seep into the intelligence community about Nicola Moses.

"But you say none of these allegations can be

substantiated?" Ferris said when Carter paused to let the diplomat digest the information.

"No," Carter said, opting for brevity because he sensed that unless Ferris heard such information on television, or the President himself phoned to confirm it, the Ambassador wouldn't attach much weight to it. Moses had probably been funding various Middle Eastern terrorist groups since he made his first million. But the need to track down terrorist financing didn't come into the spotlight until after the September 11 attacks.

"Then, I'm afraid I can't withdraw my support of the cultural bridge that Moses proposed," Ferris said.

"The atmosphere may not be right yet back home, sir, for such a bold move as Mr. Moses' cultural good will tour. American people have a long memory—"

Ferris interrupted him. "American people would benefit from seeing the Middle Eastern people's cultural expression as it comes through the various arts and crafts. It's what they have in common, as people of this planet."

Carter pretended to be occupied with something that looked like a nervous doughnut but he could only prod and poke the jelly ring so long without Ferris interpreting his silence as an insult.

"Mr. Ambassador," he said, abandoning his effort to discover the pedigree of the confectionery. "I'm just a messenger. I've delivered what I've been commissioned to do. Folks back home are very uncomfortable with the idea of a traveling exhibition that is expected to raise money for several charity organizations, all of them conveniently grouped under the umbrella of the United Middle Eastern Meridian Relief Fund."

"The Meridian Obelisk Corporation is certainly large enough to have its own charity foundation," Ferris said.

Carter cleared his throat. "Sir, don't you think that's a little like a terrorist owning stock in all the global ammunition factories?"

"I don't follow your analogy, Mr. Carter," Ferris said.

Carter wondered whether the man would be able to follow the 'wolf in sheep's clothing' analogy but kept such sentiments hidden behind a bland smile. Back in Washington, his boss, Saunders, told him that there was only one thing wrong with Ferris — the man had no imagination whatsoever. He was an accountant with a PhD from Harvard. The ten years he served as an economic advisor in Washington should not have catapulted him into ambassadorship anywhere, least of all Egypt.

Giroux said that Ferris was proud of his activist wife but embassy security worried about her outspoken nature and her public involvements. If Ferris wasn't worried before, he sure as hell worried now, witness the change of security protocol – DSS replaced by Marines as the security detail. But if Ferris was so spooked now, why allow his wife and daughters to participate at all?

"*Pardon?*" Pascal said, and Carter blinked to banish his reflections.

"I was just thinking, Pascal, about something you said on the phone. Embassy security is worried about Mrs. Ferris and her daughters taking part in this march but her husband is still allowing her to…?"

"The security men are paid to be worried all the time," Giroux said, tapping Carter's forearm. "They're starting the march, *mon ami.* Look," he invited, pointing at the stadium's entrance where the first rows of black-clad figures bearing candles already appeared.

Carter glanced toward the main gateway and immediately focused on three much smaller figures, skipping ahead of the crowd behind them. The news crews started to jockey for positions, running across the field to capture the first wave of solemnly moving women.

"Pascal." He stopped the Frenchman who also

wanted to rush after his cameraman. "Why wouldn't Ferris be worried about his wife and daughters participating in this event?"

"Because *Monsieur* Moses not only reassured him of the security he has arranged for the event, but his own wife and daughters would be marching...." His voice trailed off.

"But Bianca Moses and her daughters withdrew from participation at the last moment," Carter reminded him, his voice hardening. "Which means Melisenda Ferris and her children shouldn't be marching here either."

The Frenchman considered what he said then shrugged. "You spook easily, *mon ami*. This is a festival of lights, a spectacle," he said, waving at him and running after his camera crew.

"I'm paid to get spooked by things a hell of a lot less significant than this spectacle," Carter murmured, moving after the newsman. For some reason, his eyes wanted to remain fixed on the three little girls dressed in long black gowns, skipping ahead of the marching women.

Chapter Three

Carter didn't know their names but knew their ages — eleven, nine and eight. Because of the long black gowns, they looked much younger to him. The eleven-year-old was a head taller than her sisters. She measured her steps as if pacing the distance. Her sisters tried to keep up with her and ended up skipping alongside, the white candles in their hands bobbing up and down.

Carter smiled and turned his head to look at their mother, walking about five feet behind them, holding a candle in one hand while moving the other like a conductor, no doubt to slow down the singing pace of her marching companions. The news crews kept running along the field, setting up their shots, since their focal point would be the wife and children of the American ambassador. Carter felt that Melisenda Ferris would be annoyed with such tactics. In her eyes, every one of the women marching in the procession was equally important.

Some of the marchers wore traditional burka, but most had settled for long black gowns and didn't bother with hijab. If anything, Carter felt that many of the women might have arrived at the stadium directly from a hair salon, because he saw quite a few elaborate hairdos. Well, Pascal did say that one of the organizers was the Egyptian Women's Cinema Association, and actresses had to maintain their public image. The six burka-clad marchers who formed a crescent around the Ambassador's wife stood literally head and shoulders above the rest of the crowd. The Marines and security officers would certainly have tales to tell back home, after completing their tour of duty at the embassy.

When the first rows of women entered the stadium and started to sing, the spectators tried to join in, but without a conductor to synchronize the effort, the sound bounced around the stadium. Eventually the crowds gave up and let the women sing their sisterhood song. He couldn't distinguish the words. The echo in the stadium was awful. Then again, that's not what the stadium was built for. During soccer matches or baseball games, the sound would come from the speakers while the wide megatron screens would show replays or close-ups of the game. Why didn't Moses purchase that service too? He'd bought just about everything else.

Carter walked on the green turf, not to keep pace with the marchers but to stay within sight of Melisenda Ferris and her children. Twice, he bumped into reporters and cameramen covering the march and was met with curses. One of the reporters even threw a punch at him but missed when Carter, startled by such hostility, leaned to a side. The police formed what looked like a navy blue fence along the stadium's periphery. He wondered whether they came dressed in their riot gear and carried fat bamboo rods because Moses requested it or whether they came prepared for something more than a peaceful march.

The fact that Moses' wife and daughters withdrew from participation at the last moment bothered him more than it should. Pascal said this was an organized event that the government wanted to capture on video to show the world the fiction underlying the plethora of news reports about Egyptian police brutality. There were probably just as many police at the stadium as there were marchers and yet…

He was frustrated at not being able to define what it was that he feared. When a cameraman obstructed his way, he pushed the man aside and increased his pace to catch up to the front rows that moved halfway down the stadium's track. He turned his head in time to see a man's fist obviously aiming to hit him from behind.

"Sorry," he said, ducking out of reach. "I need to keep up. I'm security," he improvised, because the newsman's face was split in a vicious sneer. The cameraman seemed to react more to the sound of Carter's voice than the actual words and lowered his hand. The young man shook his head as if he wasn't aware of what he was doing then mumbled something in Arabic, replaced the camera on his shoulder and moved down the grass strip.

Very odd. Newsmen, regardless of their nationality, weren't usually that touchy or sensitive. If anything, they were the ones subjected to the commonplace pushing, shoving and jostling. And that hatred-distorted sneer...weird. For a few seconds, it had looked as if the man wanted to rip out Carter's jugular with his teeth.

Moving more carefully so as not to push or shove anyone, Carter caught up to the front rows of marching women. The eleven-year-old had squeezed herself between her mother and an accompanying woman, but her two younger sisters continued to skip ahead, using the candles like wands.

Suddenly, even as Carter spotted Giroux, a few feet ahead talking with his cameraman, Melisenda Ferris left her slowly moving companions and rushed, bird-like, toward her two younger daughters. Her tall burka-clad companions immediately elbowed their way into the front row.

The mother reached to grab her eight-year-old's hand, obviously intending to reprimand her for using the burning candle as a wand. The little girl yanked her hand out of her mother's grasp and viciously stabbed at her mother's face with the lit candle. Melisenda Ferris screamed in pain and horror and covered her face with both hands.

Two Marines threw off their headdresses, revealing military crew cuts, and rushed toward her. For some reason, they stopped just short of reaching Melisenda, who staggered around with both hands pressed to her face. Instead, they turned and attacked those who followed behind. In seconds, the black-clad formation of marchers fractured as the police rushed in, their riot shields held in front of them to push the bodies out of their way. Their bamboo sticks marked their aggressive movement through the crowd. The marchers in the distant rows were still singing but soon their voices were drowned out by screams, cries and gunshots.

Carter failed to immediately react. Maybe it was because the scene felt so unreal. His mind was still struggling to comprehend what caused a peaceful women's march to fracture in a matter of seconds into a full-fledged riot. The image of the blonde child viciously poking a lit candle at her mother's face was so powerful that Carter felt displaced by his surroundings.

The pressure of bodies colliding had vanished. Something swished by his face. He reacted by trying to move to a side and was shoved backward. The riot shield kept hitting him in the face and chest. He tasted blood but strangely, felt no pain. Then, suddenly, hands fastened around his throat. He gripped them, all the while focusing on his attacker's face.

A high-pitched scream broke his concentration. A woman rushed at him, screaming and clawing at his face. There was nowhere to push her. He knocked her hands away. Another pair replaced them. He gripped someone's head with both hands. He was caught in a living mass of heads, hands and weapons, striking anything they could reach. A sharp blow to his kidney made him let go of the head. A blade swished across his eyes. He blinked and used his knee to kick its owner away. Suddenly, a flash of excruciating pain shot through the roof of his mouth and into his brain. He screamed.

And, as if the sound was anesthesia, the pain disappeared. What replaced it was anger and hatred, flushing into his limbs. He wanted to grip throats and crush windpipes. His knee kept jerking, rising to deliver punishing kicks. The enemy was everywhere. Everyone had to die.

He threw himself against a wall of writhing bodies, punching, kicking and tearing at flesh and clothing alike. A body slammed into him, and he found its throat pressed against his face. The urge to bite into it and keep on biting overwhelmed him. The smell of human sweat mixed with blood made his nostrils flare. The anger he had repressed for years surged through him like electric current. *Kill, kill them all! Tear them to shreds for what they've done to my Emily.*

Emily! The sound of his daughter's name was sharp, like a gunshot. His vision cleared, and he found himself looking down at the bloodied face of his sixteen-year old daughter, resting between his massive hands, waiting to be crushed. It was what he wanted to do when the morgue attendant slid her body out of its cold resting place. To take her rigid face between his hands and squeeze out all that nonsense teenagers carried in their heads. Peer pressure, the need to fit in, belonging to the in-crowd, being skinny, taking drugs, drinking — all garbage. He couldn't show the anger that coursed through him at the morgue, couldn't give his hatred its rightful direction but he could now....

Jesus Christ! What am I doing? His reason returned as if someone gave him an antidote shot to counteract the madness and the medicine was cleaning his blood of the virus.

He parted his hands and stared at the bloodied face receding from him as its owner fell down, the body settling on the ground slow motion. The people to the left and to the right of him staggered around, grunting and crying, however, when he raised his head, the pathway ahead was covered with bodies. Some were still moving, trying to crawl, but most lay still. What the fuck had happened here — and why?

A scream ripped through the air. He spun around in time to see a black flapping shape rushing at him. The last thing he remembered was a woman's horribly distorted face and open mouth, yawning like a cave.

Chapter Four

Sunburst, Montana
May 2
Birth of Prophet (Peace be upon Him)

Carter's Delta Airlines flight landed at the Great Falls International at three o'clock in the afternoon, two hours late because upstate Montana was experiencing unusual spring weather — a snow blizzard driven by forty miles per hour winds.

"I haven't seen snow here in May since…well, I guess since I was in grade school," the young woman behind the service counter of Hertz Car Rental said, shaking her head and sighing. Carter thought she looked as if she still had many teenage years ahead of her, so grade school couldn't have been a distant past, but he kept his sentiments hidden behind a tired smile. She had already stared at him, transfixed, as he approached her counter.

He pre-empted her question by stroking his scarred cheek and saying, "It's just as they say, most accidents happen at home. I was building a shelf in my garage and fell off a ladder. Tools and wood tumbled down, right on my face. Doctors told me I have to wait a while before they can smooth it out."

He knew it was the right thing to do when she blinked and nodded, understanding. The right side of his face looked pretty ugly. The puckered purple seams and a rosette-shaped scar took up most of his cheek. Under his black turtleneck, his throat, where the bamboo rod had pierced, looked even worse than his cheek.

The doctors at the Bethesda Medical Center told him that he'd have to wait six months, maybe longer, before they'd attempt to smooth out some of the scar tissue with plastic surgery. Even his boss, Saunders, kept repeating "I'm sorry, I'm sorry," when he first saw him, so

Carter knew the effect his injuries had on people and strove to stem their curiosity and apologies with creative explanations.

"It must have hurt a lot," the young woman said, rubbing her cheek.

"It did," he said matter-of-factly. "But the pain's gone. Now I just have to wait until the doctors can make me pretty again."

She laughed and busied herself with the paperwork.

"Hope you brought a parka," she said when she finished assembling the forms and put them on the counter so he could start filling them out. She immediately turned around and started pointing at the display board behind her where he saw a dozen sets of keys hanging on cup-hooks. She kept reaching for a set of keys and changing her mind just as quickly. It only reinforced his impression of youth — and immaturity.

"You need good brakes," she mused.

"Absolutely," he agreed, hoping it would speed up her decision, regretting that he'd left the choice of vehicle up to her.

"And good windshield wipers or you won't get far in this weather."

"Aren't your fleet cars fairly new?" he asked, wondering whether he shouldn't have chosen one of the other car rental agencies at the airport.

"Explorer!" she exclaimed, snatching a set of keys off the hook. "It has ABS, and it's just come back from servicing," she said, obviously ignoring his question.

"Will it get me to Sunburst before midnight?" he murmured, checking whether he had filled out all the boxes and categories she'd checked out on the rental agreement.

"Are you going to cross the border to Alberta?"

"Only if I miss Sunburst in this weather." He smiled, pushing the form toward her.

"I was just asking, because if you're going to

29

Canada, you'll need more insurance," she said, holding up the keys and jingling them, indeed like a mischievous child.

"I'm not going to Canada." He held out his hand, palm up, to receive the keys.

She finally gave him the keys. "Go through that door." She leaned across the counter and pointed to the right. "You can wait in the lounge until Pete brings the Explorer. It's black," she said, sounding pleased.

He thanked her, smiled and hurried away because he feared that if she continued to chat, he'd slip and say what was on his mind. When it came to dealing with young people, it would only be sarcastic.

According to the map he'd studied on his laptop when still in flight, Sunburst was just over a hundred miles north of Great Falls. In decent weather, he could make it in less than two hours. But, in a blizzard, he'd be lucky if he arrived in time for dinner.

He looked at the dashboard clock when he took I-15 north. It was almost four o'clock. Two and a half hours later, he swore he'd not look at the clock again until he saw the Exit 389 for Sunburst. He broke his own promise just after Shelby. It was almost eight o'clock and though the blizzard had simmered to only an occasional gust-driven swoosh of slushy snow, driving was treacherous. There were portions of the Interstate where he couldn't do more than twenty-five, and long stretches of highway where he felt he was the only adventurous idiot out today. He drove another half an hour in darkness, figuring he had covered much of the twenty-six mile distance between Shelby and Sunburst and made a vow to pull into the first gas station that came along.

It proved to be a two-pump establishment with the whimsical name of Tickle Gas.

He didn't see a sign anywhere to tell him what type of service he should expect – full service, self-serve or nothing – so he waited in the Explorer. When, after a couple of minutes, no one came out, Carter shook his head to banish his fatigue, grabbed the parka on the front seat and got out.

The man in the steel wire-mesh cage was attuned to something other than a customer at the pumps. He sat on a high stool, pink earplugs sticking out of his ears, eyes closed and humming what sounded to Carter like a church song, broken now and then by, "Amen."

He hated to interrupt what could be a worshipping session but he had to get to Sunburst — tonight. He rattled the wire mesh just enough to get the guy's attention because he didn't want conflict. He needed directions.

"Well, I'll be...." The man opened his eyes and took the earplugs out. "I didn't think anyone would be out there in this weather. You all right, mister?"

Carter knew what the last question was about and offered his "home-accident" explanation.

"I'm not much of a handyman." The man shook his head, chuckling. "Guess that's why I'm still pretty." He rubbed his stubble-covered face, grinning at Carter. "Don't mean nothin' by it, you know...."

Carter assured him that he didn't take offence. If anything, levity was welcome, after a grueling drive. He then asked how far it was to Sunburst.

"You're here," the man said, spreading his arms wide. "Hard to see the town lights in this weather but the town's just down there. Head the way your car's nose is pointed for about quarter-mile then make a left onto Nine Mile Road. You'll be heading east for about another quarter-mile then make a left on North Railroad Ave, then hang a right on 1st St. South and you're dead center of town. Where you headin'?"

"I don't have an address, but Sunburst's not a big town. I'm looking for Stella Hunter's house. Do you—"

The man snorted so loudly Carter thought he was trying to sneeze. "Never thought I'd see her up here again.

Came last spring for Hazel's funeral, stayed couple of hours and off she was again. Didn't have the decency to see folks off…wake was still going and she ups and leaves."

"So, you know Dr. Hunter?"

"Doctor? Hrumph, she's a teacher. Teaches at some fancy school out east, Michigan or something."

"Yes. She's a professor at the University of Michigan, but she's on sabbatical. Can you tell me how to get to her house?"

"Can't miss it, mister. It used to be a decent color house when Hazel, her aunt, was still alive. But, like I said, no sooner Hazel's gone and Stella finds out the house is hers, she comes up here last summer and starts tearing down walls. When folks asked her why she was ruining a good house, she said she needed open space. As if the rooms she grew up in suddenly weren't good enough for her. Folks were pretty ticked-off to see all that rubble that used to be Hazel's kitchen cupboards being tossed into the big dumpster up front. And then, when she's finished tearing down walls, what does she do? Well, she paints the outside of the house — yellow. Looks like a Bird of Paradise. You can't miss it, mister, even in this weather. When you get to 1st St. South, head on until you see an elementary school then hang a left and there you'll see it, right at the end, shining like one of them yellow canaries."

"Thank you," Carter said, realizing he'd stirred up a hornet's nest. "Would it be too much of an imposition to fill up the Explorer. Or, is this a self-serve?" he asked, just in case he asked the unthinkable.

"Hell, no!" The man spat on the floor. "I'd have been out there if you'd have honked, which is what most folks who pull in to gas-up do."

"I didn't want to be rude," Carter said, moving aside so the man could open up the wire cage and get out.

"Nothing rude about honkin'," the man muttered as he squeezed by Carter, heading outside. "What that woman did to Hazel's house is rude."

Ten minutes after he pulled out of Tickle Gas, Carter saw Stella Hunter's house. It was just as the gas station owner said. The yellow-painted siding managed to shine even through the battery of snowflakes. In daylight and particularly on a sunny day, it had to glare, indeed like an exotic bird's plumage. He parked the Explorer in the driveway, as close to the carport as possible and cursed his lack of foresight for not also bringing higher boots, because the pathway leading to the verandah was piled high with snowdrift. Obviously Stella, like the rest of upstate Montana folks, wasn't ready for the unusual spring weather.

He tried to avoid the snowdrifts by skip-hopping around the higher ones, but after slipping and almost falling, he gave up and bravely trudged to the porch, holding his briefcase to protect his laptop. He climbed up the stairs and when he stood on the porch, stomped his feet, listening to the dull echo coming from the hollow wood beneath.

He rang the bell but didn't hear any sound, not even a buzzer. Oh well. He sighed and reached to open up the storm screen door so he could bang on the door. It was locked. He didn't want to bang on the glass or the screen portion of the door and pushed the doorbell several times in quick succession. He still didn't hear any sound, but just as he was turning to see if there was a window he could rap or rattle, the yellow-painted door opened. The front portion of the foyer was dark but there was some light in the background. He saw a shape of what had to be the house owner still holding the door with one hand.

"I'm not signing anything, do you hear me? If the fucking bastard wants to serve me his shit, he can come and serve it himself. So just take your clipboard or whatever it is you have and get the hell out of here," said a woman's voice with crackling hostility.

He had four pages, single-spaced, of "background history" on Dr. Stella Hunter. He knew exactly what her hostility was about.

"I'm not a process server, Dr. Hunter. My name's Carter. I'd like to talk to you about your work — your book, actually," he said, putting his briefcase on a bent knee. He opened it and took out her book, then closed the briefcase quickly before he lost balance. He held out the book to her so she could at least see that he was telling the truth since she didn't believe in turning on the porch light, either.

"My last book-signing was three years ago, in a campus bookstore at Michigan," she said inhospitably. "So, you're a bit late for my autograph."

"Dr. Hunter, I really need to talk to you. I've come all the way from Washington—"

She interrupted him. "Oh, swell, you're a bureaucrat, probably from Internal Revenue. Those are the only idiots who'd drive out here in this kind of weather. Tax people have nothing on me, do you hear me? And I haven't even signed the divorce papers, so we're nowhere near the division of property or alimony corral. Not that I want anything from the fucking bastard that's not rightfully mine."

"I'm not from the IRS. I do contractual work for the government."

"A government contractor? My, why does that sound so ominous? So, you're from one of the law agencies — which one?"

"I work on contract for the Department of Justice, but I've done contracts for other law agencies."

She made a throaty, displeased sound. "So, where is your badge? Flash me something that will make me fall down to my knees and beg for mercy."

"You could say I'm a law officer without a badge," he said, wondering whether she was going to let him freeze out here on the porch, since the wind had picked up again and the temperature was dropping so fast he felt the cold sting his cheek.

"Ooh, now I'm really nervous. What is it that the CIA doesn't like about my book? It's been out for nearly four years. Surely they would have found whatever they consider objectionable the first week the book came out?"

"May I come in?" He decided to be blunt because the fear of frostbite made him contemplate ripping the screen door off its hinges.

"And, if I say no, will you go away?"

"No. I must talk to you. It's very important." Just when he thought she'd slam the door shut, she leaned forward and turned the deadbolt on the screen door.

He hurriedly opened the door in case she changed her mind and decided not to offer his hand for a greeting until he made sure the door closed behind.

Once inside, he stuck out his hand. "How do you do, Dr. Hunter?"

She didn't take it but only because she stepped to a side to flick a switch. Bright light flooded the space around him, momentarily blinding him. She took his hand, shook it firmly and let go.

"How do you do, Mr. Carter, government contractor? Now you know why I keep my lights shut. The electrical contractor I hired last summer was an idiot who put all the lights on the main floor on one switch. I'm not even sure whether it's dangerous. Come on in. I'll turn on a couple of lamps. The hack did manage to give me five outlets, thank God."

She shut off the lights and his eyes, just getting used to the bright illumination, became once again blinded.

"What time did you leave Washington?" she asked from the shadows. Then he heard soft clicks that produced mellow lighting from a couple of table lamps.

"This morning," he mumbled, putting down his

briefcase and looking around for something to sit on to remove his boots. His feet inside the boots were dry but his jeans were soaked to his knees.

"Did you fly to Great Falls and drive from there?"

"Yes."

"Had anything to eat lately?"

He raised his head, holding back a grin. "Not really. I didn't want to pull off the Interstate in case I couldn't find my way on to it again."

"We'll eat, then you can shower me with praises about my brilliance as demonstrated by that fine piece of work — my book," she said.

He took off his parka, hung it on a doorknob because he didn't want to open the door in case it proved not to be a closet, and straightened up. Even in the mellow light of table lamps, he could see what the gas station owner was talking about. The entire first floor had been gutted. He couldn't see even a partition, never mind a wall. But the open space wasn't yawning like a hall or a cafeteria, because she had cleverly portioned off the space with furniture, bookcases, desks, and potted plants hanging down from the wood-beamed ceiling. He saw shadowy outlines of what had to be her office-workspace, with two computer monitors. The front windows had white shutters, now closed, and plants hung in front of them, nestled in planter-holders. The far wall to his left had a fireplace that provided warmth as well as low-level lighting that would no doubt be welcomed by those sitting on the couches or wingback chairs. The mellow lighting wouldn't let him see the fabric pattern, but everything he could make out was either bright yellow, lime green or glowing pink.

"Over here," she said from the far end of the house.

As he walked down what must have once been a hallway but was now a walkway defined by a peacock-blue carpet, he deliberated which 'injury' story to tell. Should he give her the 'garage' version or the 'broken glass' version?

She'd ask or at least keep glancing at his face until she'd leave him no choice but to explain. Eventually, he would tell her the truth. Would she be insulted then, considering he'd first given her a lie? He decided to wing it.

By the time he arrived in the kitchen, outfitted with white cupboards, a yellow glazed countertop and pine nook, she had set the table with dishes, cutlery and food.

"Don't worry. We're not going to have a candlelit dinner," she said and reached over the back of the pine bench to turn on a high-intensity study lamp. He stared at her for five seconds then, involuntarily, raised the book he held in one hand and turned it over, looking at her picture on the dust jacket.

She laughed. "I'm no longer the polished scholarly matron, the serious academic that you see. Scrimmaging on the marital battlefield will knock the academic stuffing out of you."

He thought it was more like a shift in personality, and a sudden realization that she had spent years defining herself not just in dry academic terms but also as the wife of the Dean of Literature, working at an Ivy League university. For more than fifteen years, she taught medieval and early modern studies while feeding her passion for mythology like women in medieval times would nurture an illegitimate child, out of the academic eye. When she finally found the courage to reveal her years of personal research, her colleagues scoffed at her "fanciful hobby" as a work of mediocre fiction and questionable fact. Coming out of the closet with her passion for mythology was not the only factor contributing to the dissolution of her marriage. But since the union had been ailing, the negative publicity coupled with her colleagues' ridicule gave her husband the reason to distance himself, and his career, from his 'delusional' wife.

The woman spooning peas and mushrooms on to his plate, next to the roasted chicken leg, was a far cry from the esteemed Dr. Stella Hunter, a professor, wife and mother to three teenage children. She obviously had gained weight, but her plumpness was healthy and robust. She wore a lime-green loose sweatshirt and washed-out khakis. Her bright orange hair rivaled Medusa's. He doubted she wore makeup up here in Montana, where she came to live with her aunt and uncle at the age three, when her missionary parents died of yellow fever. Even though she was forty-five, two years his senior, she had the look of youth and vitality that would suggest much younger.

"I don't have pop, just iced tea," she said.

"Iced tea is fine," he hurriedly replied.

"Put that briefcase down and come sit down. Let's eat." She waved him over to the bench. Though she didn't spend much time looking at him, being busy with the meal, he knew she noticed his scar. Was she really that oblivious or was she that overly polite that she preferred not to ask the stranger eating in her house what happened to his face?

"So how many guns do you have in it?" she asked, when he put the briefcase down on the high-backed pine bench.

"None," he said, chuckling, realizing this was a good time to get the uncomfortable issue out in the open. "I wasn't shot in the face. This is the result of a recent accident."

"You ought to be more careful shaving," she quipped and busied herself with her food. She didn't lift her head from her plate until it was clean and the bones were neatly piled on a serviette beside it.

She waited for him to finish, collected the dishes and said she'd make coffee.

"It's the only way to talk with a government contractor, over coffee," she said, carrying away the dishes.

He put her book on the table and occupied himself rehearsing opening lines in his head.

She didn't give him a chance to start.

"So which parts of the book interest you and, more important, why?" she asked, pouring coffee into the cornflower blue mug she had set before him.

"Your knowledge of mythology is impressive," he said, fixing his coffee.

"Thank you, but you're avoiding my question."

"How long did it take you to research all...that stuff?"

"Hmm, let's see. I'd say I began my research when I was six years old. Back in '76, my aunt gave me a book for Christmas. It was the *Greatest Greek Myths and Legends*. I guess you could call that the genesis of my fascination and research."

"So nearly forty years of research became compacted into a 386-page book. I'm impressed."

She stared at him for a long time, then said, "I have a feeling, Mr. Carter, that you already know the answer to any question you're going to ask me."

He shook his head. "No."

"But you did your homework before you came up here, right?"

"Somewhat," he admitted.

"So, you know everything there is to know about me, including my messy marital situation?"

"That's not why I'm here."

"I sure hope not, because I'd toss you out, socks and all. Why are you here?"

"I'm interested in the facts buried in the myths and legends featured in your book."

"Facts? You've come to the wrong professor. If you're interested in facts, then you should go see Dr. Mullins, he's an archeologist at the Kelsey Museum back in Michigan."

He put his hand on top of her book. "*Myths and Legends: The Ribbons of Truth*. That's the title of your book, and I've read it, cover to cover. You've correlated many legends across various ancient and even modern-day cultures. You've explained why some of these so-called myths and legends keep surviving, what drives them, what gave them birth and what keeps them living. There is one particular legend that interests me. It talks about a being capable of sowing discord amongst people wherever he walks. Death trails him but never catches up to him because he's a product of the underworld. I want you to tell me more about this being because you're the expert who has taken 'myth' out of mythology."

She groaned. "Oh, my God, are you for real?"

"Does that mean you don't believe in your own work, the product of your research?"

She rowed a hand through her hair, closing her eyes and shaking her head. "Taking 'myth' out of mythology was just good publicity shit. A catchy jingle that Cynthia, my publisher, liked so much she insisted it appear on the jacket cover. It gave the ad people something to work with for their press release."

"So you don't really believe in your work," he insisted, keeping his voice flat. He saw she was already frustrated and didn't want to make her angry.

She raised her head and slowly let her eyes creep open. "Look, Mr. Carter, I'm a professor of medieval studies. I teach cocky teenagers who can drive a saint to distraction with their sarcastic and often crude comments on any academic subject, not just those that end in 'ology', but even the most obnoxious class loudmouth hasn't had the nerve to ask me what you just did. Of course I believe in my work, but we're discussing myths and folklore, not mathematics. There are no absolutes, just intuitive interpretations of the people and their culture that came before us."

"In that case, wouldn't you say that if a certain myth keeps appearing in different cultures throughout the centuries, it validates its legitimacy as something more than just a mere myth?"

She put her hands on the table, fingers splayed as if she wanted to leave an imprint in the wood. "The point I was trying to make with my book is that no matter what environment we live in, no matter what our cultural and religious beliefs, and no matter when we've lived, we all tend to think alike. We all share the same dreams, entertain the same hopes and aspirations, and we all speculate about and fear the ultimate unknown — death. Our cultural practices may differ. Our food may be different. Our skin color may vary and we may say our prayers in many different languages but in our dreams we become one voice, one color, one language and one beating heart. Do you understand what I'm talking about?"

"Yes. And, it's precisely this unifying aspect that forms the backbone of your book that interests me," he said, picking up his cup and sipping coffee even as he watched her face.

She shook her head again. "Mr. Carter, just because a certain local legend can be cross-correlated through many cultural references and keeps reappearing at irregular intervals throughout history doesn't mean its origins are rooted in facts. Myths and legends are products of people's imagination. That's the unifying factor that defines us as one human tribe."

"On page three, in your foreword, you say that many myths and legends have a strong component of truth." He tapped his index finger on the book lying beside his coffee cup.

She laughed. "Component, Mr. Carter, means that some real event or need motivated people's imagination to spin the legend or fashion a myth. When the ancient Egyptians needed to explain how the fierce sun came to be in the sky, their imagination created a god able to take on a form of goose. As a goose, Geb or Keb laid the egg from which the sun was hatched. Geb was the third divine king of the earth."

"Do you read hieroglyphics?" he asked, watching for her reaction to the sudden change of topic.

She slid her hands along the table until they fell into her lap, out of his sight, and pursed her lips.

"I have a reason for asking." He hastened to reassure her that he wasn't just obscenely curious about her academic credentials.

"I don't doubt it," she said dryly. "Yes, I can. When I was young and still impressionable, I spent a year at Oxford, acquiring the skill. Naturally, the British are the only experts in all global languages, dead, alive and dying. Why do I have a feeling that you already knew this before you asked?"

He didn't reply but opened his briefcase, took out a plastic bag and carefully slid out a white paper serviette and a folded sheet of paper.

"This is an imprint of the original inscription." He pushed the serviette toward her. "And, this is a more practical tracing of the inscription on the napkin. It can be handled without tearing." He opened the sheet and smoothed it out, then put it next to the white tissue square.

She leaned forward and studied the serviette without touching the fragile tissue and then took the piece of paper and held it in one hand while drumming the fingers of her other hand on the table.

"Who drew this cartouche?" she asked sharply, not looking at him.

He ran his finger across the book and waited until she put down the paper. He turned the book around, opened the cover and pushed it toward her. "I believe you autographed it for him," he said, wondering whether she'd ask about the smudged brown fingerprints on the page.

Chapter Five

"Fineas Zahur Gahiji." She spoke the name with familiarity, without the usual stumbling pronunciation that he came to expect from his countrymen. "We finally met in person about year and a half ago. He cornered me at the Wasserdown Conference in LA, practically dragged me to the Dragonstar restaurant and all but dusted my chair for me to sit down. I only went to escape Franmore...."

He interrupted. "What?"

"Not what, who. Dr. Leandra Franmore, my British-born American esteemed colleague. She did part of her undergraduate work at Princeton. She's my foe."

"Foe?" he echoed. The last time he heard anyone use the word was in high school, and Mrs. Cruickshank, his English teacher, was giving the class a quiz on Shakespeare.

"Enemy — in military terms. I keep forgetting that you're a government contractor and don't speak the same business English that I do. Dr. Franmore was the first to condemn my book and my years of research as 'fanciful and frivolous foray into a field that falls outside of my specialty.' Other than overdosing on alliteration, she said in her review that I had 'overshot' my academic reach and as a result killed the lay reader's interest. Her alma mater's Cambridge, and she has a Ph.D. in medieval history with keen interest in mythology."

"Ah, you share the same hobby that's outside of your academic field," he said to show he understood.

"Her book was only half-finished when mine came out. She blamed me when her publisher balked and withdrew the offer to publish it. I only saw a couple of articles she published in a British magazine, excerpts from her unfinished book, and most of it sounded like she copied it out of the Old Testament or some sorcerer's *grimoire.*

She was more into potions and antidotes to ancient curses than true mythology. I heard she resigned her position at Cambridge and went to work in a museum. I think she's writing a book on castles now. I managed to avoid her at the conference, but she finally caught up to me just as Gahiji was waving my book in my face. I opted for the lesser of two evils and agreed to have lunch with him just to escape Dr. Franmore.

"Once at the restaurant, I read the entire menu, as a hint that I was trying to ignore him, but when I had to put it down because there wasn't anything else to study on its page, he was still waxing poetic about the fantastic coincidence of our surnames meaning the same thing. Gahiji means hunter in Arabic, and wasn't that an omen. He kept pressing this book to his chest, as if it was a treasure. Is he still alive?" she asked, lifting her head and staring at him with a closed expression he couldn't read.

He pursed his lips to hold back the smile. She was very intuitive, far more than she'd let anyone believe. She knew exactly why he was here and his purpose, but for reasons of her own wanted to get rid of him quickly and chose the easiest way to do it — by pretending that her book was merely a commercial product, written for monetary gain. That there was no substance to her research other than to stir up a controversy that would be excellent for sales. Well, it was his turn to play the game.

"Why would you ask that?" he asked, frowning and shaking his head.

"Dr. Gahiji didn't care much about me autographing the book," she said. "That was just a gesture on my part. He first contacted me ten years ago, wrote a letter — one academic to another. He was an assistant curator at the Egyptian Museum of Cairo. His expertise wasn't as much mythology as he was obsessed with a particular myth." She tapped the sheet of paper. "This one."

"As you said, it's just a myth. Nothing deadly," he

said, pretending not to understand where it was leading.

She motioned with her head at the open book. "Those brown smudged fingerprints have to be Gahiji's, and the brown stuff's blood. If I had to express why I wrote the book in percentile terms, I'd say that thirty percent motivation goes to Gahiji. Ten years ago, he wrote in his letter that he was excited because he was very close to finding this." She tapped the cartouche. "Do you know what it means?"

Well, it was no use playing the game anymore. "It was translated as a 'troublemaker' or 'mischief-maker' but it can also mean someone who delights in causing hardships, wreaks havoc, or creates chaos."

She shook her head. "No, it's a lot worse than that. You must have consulted the experts who panned my book. This is a cartouche bearing a title rather than descriptive meaning. Actually, it's more of a functional name — the Peacetaker."

"That doesn't sound so bad," he said.

"I thought you said you read my book — cover to cover."

"I did, but I'm not an 'ologist."

She laughed. "Oh, I keep forgetting. You're a government contractor. I'm still not sure which government you run contracts for."

"The friendly government," he said, chuckling.

"Well, that means it can't be ours," she deadpanned. "Is Dr. Gahiji still alive?"

He shook his head.

"Did you kill him?"

He glared at her. "Of course not. He died last March 19th, a victim of a hit-and-run accident. According to the Cairo police report, he walked across the street, holding this book," he gently tapped the open cover, "and didn't see the light had turned red."

"How did you get hold of the book, then?"

"A friend of mine who works in Cairo visited him in the hospital. He lived two more days before succumbing to his injuries. Gahiji gave him the book—"

She interrupted. "Let me guess — Fineas gave your friend a message for me and asked him to deliver this book to me since your friend was an American — another government contractor, I presume."

"All right," he said, pressing his back against the hard wooden bench. "Gahiji never recovered consciousness. My friend saw the book on his bedstand and took it."

"Government contractors aren't supposed to steal, especially from the dying," she said, smirking.

"My man was following Gahiji and saw what happened. His account is significantly different from that of Cairo's police. Gahiji carried your book but he wasn't reading it as he walked. He was run down by a large black Benz. My man's also trained to notice details — like license plates. The car that ran down Dr. Gahiji was a fleet vehicle registered to the Meridian Obelisk Corporation."

"Ah," she breathed out. "Nicola Moses."

He stiffened his back and pursed his lips. "How do you know that?"

She shrugged. "Fineas talked about him during our lunch at the Dragonstar. He said he'd been trying to see him for years but the billionaire had a wall of security and staff around him that he couldn't penetrate."

"What did Gahiji want from Moses?"

"Sponsorship, funding — what else?"

"Funding for what?"

"He wanted Moses to bankroll his search for the Peacetaker."

"Gahiji was looking for a mythological deity?"

She stared at him with something akin to pity. He couldn't decide whether it was a look of disgust framed by pity or regret framed by bitterness at having let him in the house in the first place.

"I'm wondering about your reading skills. Maybe literacy doesn't mean the same thing to government contractors as it means to me. The Peacetaker's not a mythological deity or any other kind of lore figure. If indeed Gahiji discovered such a person, he would be a very real, very physical modern-day young man."

He motioned at the sheet of paper. "But this cartouche—"

She didn't let him finish. "This cartouche is something that keeps popping up throughout history, mostly ancient Egyptian history, but I believe the last genuine historical record found dates to about 600 AD. As a museum assistant curator, Fineas went out on field trips. I'm sure he was conscientious enough to attend to museum business, but I wouldn't be surprised if he didn't sneak in a side trip here and there to pursue leads on his passion — the Peacetaker cartouche. According to what he told me in LA, in eight years he managed to document forty-one references to the Peacetaker. The earliest one dates to the third millennium BC. That's the time of Cheops and the great pyramid."

"And you found a corresponding reference in Babylonia, a Sumerian legend dating to the times of King Etana of Kish," he said, tipping his brows upward.

She was silent for a long time then said, "I should just throw you out, but then I'd probably have a ton of your colleague-contractors, swooping down on this quiet Montana town in noisy choppers, flashing all kinds of threatening badges at me — CIA, FBI, Homeland, NSA, DEA for all I know, and folks in this town are already weary of me as is. They never liked me even when I was a child, growing up here."

"I read your book but I'm not an expert."

"What you're saying is that you only remember parts that serve your purpose," she said, smirking at him.

"Something like that," he admitted. "So what can you tell me about this Peacetaker?"

"I'll tell you about the Peacetaker legend. In many ways it's unique because it doesn't involve a deity, although if you take the Osirian legend as the primary source, the Peacetaker was a product of revenge sought by the god of chaos, Set, against the moon god, Thoth, because the latter healed Horus after Set tore out his adversary's left eye. In Greek mythology, Set is an equivalent of the demon-god, Typhon," she said and launched into the story.

According to the Osirian legend, the war between Horus and Set lasted eighty years. During this time, Set gouged out his opponent's left eye, and in retaliation Horus tore off Set's foreleg and testicles, castrating him. When Thoth's intervention restored Horus' sight, castrated Set became livid since no one rushed to restore his manhood. He waited until the second full moon in the same month then reshaped his aardvark-like head into human form and tucked his long forked tail between his legs, then wrapped it around his waist and went for a stroll through a village where he knew a woman was going to give birth that night.

He stopped outside a hut and listened to the woman's screams. When he ascertained she was about to give birth, he entered the hut, made everyone inside fall asleep, then carried the cot with the woman outside under the light of the Blue Moon. He delivered the boy-child, cut the umbilical cord with his teeth, then raised the crying infant as a mock offering to the full moon and howled for as long as the baby kept crying. When the exhausted newborn fell asleep, Set licked the blood off the baby's body and put him on his mother's chest. Satisfied with the grueling night's work, Set changed back to his curved snout and square-tipped ears appearance, freed his tail and walked away, no doubt twirling his tail with satisfaction.

"And that's how the Peacetaker was created," she finished, flashing him a quick smile.

"That's it? That's the revenge?" What she said was a simplified and personality-colored version of the legend's origin that featured in her book.

She laughed. "As far as demons go, I have to agree with you. Set wasn't one much for grand revenge ceremonies even though he was also supposedly a god of thunder."

"In your book, on page 123, you said he cursed the child and all his descendants to be warmongers, particularly on the night of the full moon when the villagers would normally hold celebrations and pay homage to the moon-god."

She brought her hands out, put them on the table and clasped them. He watched her knuckles grow white as she kept tightening her hold.

"Come on, Dr. Hunter, I want the fact component of the myth."

"What's in the book, Mr. Carter, is a politically correct euphemism. Set saddled the child with a curse that would see all celebrations of the moon-god scrambled or quickly dissolved into skirmishes. Essentially, his curse stripped Thoth of his worshippers."

"What's a politically incorrect version?"

"Set cursed humanity for all eternity."

"How so?"

"In 1980, John Friedrich, the American-born great-grandson of one of the German archeologists who did excavations at Ur around 1914, was settling his father's estate in upstate New York and found three clay tablets, filled with cuneiform writing. He made tracings and consulted experts at the Smithsonian on a premise that if these proved to be valuable he would donate them to the museum. Well, the experts translated the three tracings as the Babylonian version of the Peacetaker legend. Friedrich allowed them to date one tablet but when the results showed it dated to the fourth millennium BC, he quickly reneged on his offer to donate it and — this is just a speculation — probably sold them on the black market to a collector because he left the country shortly afterward. The Smithsonian still has the three tracings but they're very sore about not getting the valuable artifacts. The Babylonian legend is almost identical to the Egyptian version except it has a different god cursing humanity in perpetuity. The child born as the Peacetaker is an equivalent of Pandora 's Box — containing only the plague. As he walks amongst the people, the Peacetaker literally devours all peace in his vicinity."

"Devours?"

"Absorbs, drains if you will, leaving raw human nature. He strips the thin veneer of civilization we all wear and reduces everyone to his primal state. As children, we're taught to be tolerant and to share. If we're raised in a particular religion, that factor will further coat us with goodliness and love of thy neighbor. But all these layers of civilized behavior are just clothes we were taught to wear. Underneath them, we're still apes, swinging clubs and bashing each other. The Peacetaker doesn't just take off our civilized veneer, layer by layer, he rips it off as suddenly as if we were sandblasted. The result is an indescribable surge of anger and fury, flushing through us with such force that our minds aren't able to react fast enough and trip safety breakers. We resort to reacting by primal instinct — kill or be killed — our survival and supremacy via conquest of others, weaker ones."

"What if a person's temperament is such that he's meek and seldom if ever angers?" he asked.

"I dare you to find even one person in our country who's not angry about something, no matter how well he keeps such anger and disappointment hidden or in check. Everyone's vulnerable. Where the Peacetaker's power is concerned, there's no such thing as mild or meek — much less saintly."

"Everyone?" he echoed, still trying to sort out what she said so far.

"Even the Pope must have been annoyed once or twice in his lifetime at some of his advisors," she said. "I don't think there's a human being in the world who doesn't have at least a drop or two of anger in his emotional reservoir. And it doesn't have to be just anger. It's any negative feeling — envy, regret, avarice, and disappointment, even pessimism. If you take a rattle away from a baby, he screams. What do you think he's feeling?"

"We're not talking about legends any more, are we?" he asked quietly.

She sighed. "I don't know."

"Oh, I think you know that we're talking about a pervasive legacy that has survived into the modern age."

"The fact that a version of the Peacetaker legend can be found in almost every culture that we have is not just significant but disturbing," she said. "A pervasive legacy — well, it's pervasive all right, but I don't think legacy's the right way to describe it. A child who's born with the power to strip a man's veneer of civility by simply being there is not a cultural or religious *legacy*. It's more like a Devil's sledgehammer smashing every single one of the Ten Commandments with a single blow."

"How would a child who possesses the power to seed murderous frenzy in people be able to survive in any clan, group or even a family?" He finally asked what had been bothering him even as he'd read her book. She had documented the sources of the legend in academic terms and correlated it across many ancient civilizations but stopped short of explaining how this cursed child functioned while growing up to become the man capable of unleashing the worst of human nature everywhere he walked.

"The best explanation of how the Peacetaker functions comes from the third century AD, in China, during the period of the Three Kingdoms. In my terms, that's practically an eyewitness account. During this period, Buddhism came to China from India. Lao Deng, a Buddhist monk, wrote three scrolls describing the 'grooming process,' as he called it, of the human demon that walked barefoot and bare-handed through the temple of Shan Tien. Before he was out the door, the monks were already at each other's throats. One monk lived long enough for Lao Deng to reach him and tell him the story. The local warlord sent his accountant to the temple to audit the monks' revenues so he could determine how much tax they owed him. The monks pointed out that as holy men, they were exempt from taxes. The warlord, not wishing to risk a curse or retribution if he stormed the temple, sent the Peacetaker to walk amongst them. Apparently, the warlord had groomed the young man from birth but kept the nature of his powers secret. Do you want more coffee?" She stopped her narration and then, not waiting for his answer, rose and went to make a fresh pot. When she returned, she poured both of them a steaming, fragrant cup of coffee and resumed her story.

Lao Deng was an educated man. In his studies, he'd come across five historical accounts of the Peacetaker's use and function. He donned the robes of a traveling singer and storyteller and made his way to the village *shuchang,* the local storyteller house. The first night he only sang songs of the Three Kingdoms and told tales of heroic exploits but on the second night he craftily began to weave his knowledge and understanding of the Peacetaker function into his stories. Soon enough, his audience started to correct him, thus giving him valuable input. Having good grasp of his countrymen's mentality, Lao stopped corrupting his story just before the crowd would start to pelt him with rotten vegetables, and invited the loudest members of his audience to 'correct' his stories — in exchange for secret recipes of herbal medicines he'd gathered on his travels.

Three days later, when Lao Deng left the village, he had enough information on the 'grooming process' that transformed an otherwise ordinary young man into a demon to fill a dozen silk batik or rice paper scrolls.

According to Lao Deng's story, the child with Peacetaker powers would be born in the year when the bouquet of white fire began to move across the sky. He suggested this event happened about once every hundred years.

"Considering that Halley's Comet has been known since about 240 BC and probably even before then, it's probably the event that heralds the birth of the Peacetaker in Chinese version of the legend," she said. "Strangely enough, ancient Chinese who were otherwise very precise people, couldn't pinpoint the birth event closer than this. During the year when Halley appeared in the sky, the village midwife would keep a watch over her expecting clients.

"Although Lao Deng wasn't able to pinpoint the child's birth down to a week or even a month, he was detailed in describing the testing and awakening processes. Depending on the size of the village, there could be a few dozen children born in the year when Halley made its appearance in the sky. However, people also believed that the year of the "white bouquet of moving fire in the sky" favored birth of female children, so the women would try hard to avoid conceiving during that period. As a result, fewer children would be born during the year of Halley's passage and only male children would be tested."

"Why test only male children?" he interrupted. "The Peacetaker curse applied to the descendants of the original male child. Surely there would be at least a few female descendants?"

She kept staring at him, alternately sucking her lower lip and biting it as if trying hard not to burst out laughing. When the silence grew uncomfortably long, he cleared his throat and said, "I realize that no matter what the culture and civilization, its historical path barely recognizes a woman as a member of human tribe, never mind documenting her footsteps through time, but we're talking descendants here."

"Actually, women made quite a few inroads in ancient Egypt, especially if they were born into royalty, but for once, stereotyping and discrimination play no part in the matter. Set was one of the gods of the underworld as well as master of chaos, but even he was steeped in basic genetics. A woman's emotional make-up precludes her from being seeded with the Peacetaker powers simply because the woman has traditionally played the part of the Peacemaker. Testosterone fuels aggression and that defines the warmongers as members of the male tribe - exclusively. Remember, Set was castrated by Horus and the Peacetaker curse was a two-fold revenge against his nephew, and Thoth who healed him."

"Horus was Set's nephew?"

"Set was brother to Isis, who was a mother to Horus. This is a relatively simple familial lineage compared to some of the other deities."

She took a sip of coffee then resumed Lao Deng's story. "Since fewer children would be born in the year of Halley's passage, the village midwife might deliver at most one or two male children. When the boys reached the age four, they would undergo the first test.

"In China, the activator was usually a piece of jade carved into the likeness of the white bouquet of fire in the sky; sort of a star with a fan-tail. In Egypt, it would be the crescent moon made from hammered gold. The African tribes used ivory carved into an idol, or polished obsidian. In the Indian culture, it would be *ainul hirrat*, the cat's eye, placed inside a soft-leather pouch and carried by the Peacetaker. Whatever the amulet, it would be placed around the child's neck, or tied to his wrist or even strapped around the ankle, then the boy would be sent on his walk, while the council of village elders stood by, observing."

"They'd send the boy to walk amongst the village people?" he asked, feeling that he missed something or misinterpreted what he'd so far heard.

"They may have been simple folk, superstitious, but they weren't stupid. They'd send the child to walk in a fenced area filled with the most placid or timid creatures they could find — rabbits, chickens, even mice. Lao Deng's scrolls claim the local warlord tested the boy in a pen filled with baby rabbits, with spectacular results. The child had hardly finished his transit of the pen when the rabbits started attacking each other. But there are rules, because even a god can't spin a curse without adhering to some set of rules."

"The Peacetaker can be 'activated' for the initial test at age four, but not again until he reaches full maturity at age eighteen," he said, keeping a straight face and watching for her reaction. She didn't disappoint him.

"Out!" she said, hand raised and pointing at the door.

"Page 324." He pointed at the book.

"That information doesn't figure in my book. Out!"

"No, but the book's owner felt it was important enough to include it so he wrote it on the margin, on page 324."

She made a throaty, growling sound and flipped through the pages. When she saw the scribbled entry, she calmed down.

"I'm not testing you," he said, feeling he owed her an explanation. "I'm still trying to wrap my mind around these myths and legends that seem to be spun on a solid platform of physical reality. The last passage of Halley's Comet was in February 1986, so, we're looking for someone who was born in 1986 which would make him twenty-eight today – I don't know, that sounds a bit too old for me. I would have said that twenty-five would be the cut-off point for youthful idealism—"

She interrupted him. "Excuse me, *looking*? Did you say looking, as in now-time real occurrence? Are you out of your fucking mind?" She half rose, leaning over the table and shouting her last word practically into his face.

He put his hands on her shoulders and applied pressure, forcing her to sit back down.

"Is Halley's Comet passage the absolute requisite for Peacetaker's arrival…his birth?" he asked.

"No. That's what figures in Chinese legends. They were fixated on Halley's but other sources, Egyptian in particular, have just one celestial condition that heralds the arrival of Peacetaker – the occurrence of two full moons in a month or monthly Blue Moon," she said.

"Gahiji was Egyptian, so he'd apply the Egyptian rules, which means the child would have been born under a Blue Moon. Today, he would be between eighteen and twenty-five tops, which means he'd be born between 1990 and 1997. How many Blue Moons do you think there have been since 1990?" he asked as if he already forgot her threatening outburst.

"Oh, let me consult my Farmer's Almanac. I'd say three or four. Are you insane?"

He fingered his scarred cheek, knowing it would draw her attention. "I was, for what seemed like a microsecond and eternity at once. Do you have a VCR or perhaps a DVD player?"

"Both. A combination player, actually. Are you insane? The lore and legends may contain a grain of truth, but even Fineas wasn't wholly convinced that the cartouche he saw chiseled into a stone on an ancient well in Berenice pointed to the modern-day existence of the Peacetaker."

"Is that where Dr. Gahiji found this?" He tapped the piece of paper with the cartouche tracing.

"The modern-day reference — yes," she snapped

then continued more evenly. "While the well was ancient, that particular stone was a relatively new addition. The stone was chiseled to fit the gap in the wall. Gahiji said that the tooled edges were hardly weathered. The cartouche was freshly carved too. He estimated it to be no more than ten, fifteen years old. He said that in '98, one of his field trips took him to Berenice, about 160 miles east of Aswan. It used to be a bustling port in ancient times. The city existed for more than nine hundred years, from Ptolemaic times — about 250 BC to around the fifth century AD, the Roman occupation.

"There was a group of archeologists, out of UCLA, working on defining the ancient spice route between India and Egypt. I don't know why Fineas was there but, according to what he told me in LA, a group of them went for a stroll through Arab Saleh, the desert village that now incorporates Berenice, and that's how he spotted what he termed to be his most exciting find. He came back the next day, photographed the stone cartouche and had a chat with the local nomads. He couldn't find any male children born in the years of the Blue Moon and spent the next year finding out all he could about the people who'd moved in-and-out of that area. We've had seven Blue Moons between 1980 and 1998. Then he started checking on merchants who might have either picked up sheep or goats, or delivered in Arab Saleh, but I stopped listening, just like I'm going to stop listening to you now."

"I do want you to stop listening because I want to show you something. Where did you say that VCR was?" He rose, taking his briefcase and looking around.

"Where it would be of most use — underneath the TV," she said acidly, nodding in the direction of what he initially thought to be a particularly small microwave oven.

"Is that a 19-inch screen? I don't think I've seen one in the last ten years."

"Twenty, and remind me to tell you sometimes

57

what the old Egyptians did to the guests who insulted them in their own home."

"Sorry," he murmured and went to put his briefcase on the coffee table. He'd brought a videotape and a CD, just in case progress hadn't caught up with Montana. In the photograph on the back of the book's dust jacket, she looked like someone who'd use a TV only as a teaching tool, because to use it for entertainment would be frivolous. The woman who let him in her house looked nothing like Dr. Stella Hunter of the *Ribbons of Truth* fame — and controversy. She reminded him of a rumpled Bette Middler and proved to have just about the same kind of personality — witty, sharp and temperamental.

He loaded the CD, pushed the button to close the drive and turned to see where she kept her remote control. She was not just highly intuitive but a mind reader.

"In my hand," she snapped, pointing it at him.

"Play."

She saluted with her free hand and clicked the remote. He backed up to stand beside her because he knew what was coming.

There was no preamble, no warning. The sound and image burst into the wall-less room at the same time, startling her into dropping the remote. He was ready and caught it before it hit the floor. The footage of the carnage in the Cairo Stadium in Heliopolis back on that fateful day in March was only four minutes long, because that's all that could be salvaged and spliced from the various pieces of recording equipment strewn around the field. Initially, the Cairo police refused to let the members of the foreign press, who'd rushed to Cairo for the grim purpose of identifying bodies of various members of their staff at the makeshift morgue in the Military Academy Stadium, reclaim whatever recording equipment was salvaged.

But the global leaders, calling on the Egyptian President to express their shock and deliver condolences, also slipped in a reminder that the rest of the world should see the results of what was no doubt a terrorist attack on a government-sanctioned peaceful rally — of women and children no less. The four-minute footage was all that could be put together from fragments of the British, French, Canadian and Spanish news crews' equipment. The US news crew rental Dodge van got a flat tire five hundred feet away from the car rental place. By the time the cursing driver ran back and managed to get a replacement van, drive it to where the disabled van stood, transfer all the equipment and head for Heliopolis, the police had closed off all the major routes to the stadium. The three crewmembers, plus the reporter and the cameraman, literally owed their lives to Cairo's car rental agency's poor vehicle maintenance.

The footage of murderous madness, interspersed with screams, cries, shots, sirens and sounds of breaking — bones and equipment — had finished, replaced by the blue of the video mode screen. He clicked the remote and shut off the TV. He knew she'd not ask to see the footage again. She was tough, but even he deliberated for three days before watching it again.

"What you saw started as a peaceful candlelit march of some five hundred women and children, on March 2 of this year, at the Cairo Stadium in Heliopolis. The police were there only as ornaments since it was a government-approved rally. Our ambassador's—"

"I know," she interrupted, voice hollow. "I've read about it and saw a five-second fragment of flailing limbs and gnashing teeth. Melisenda Neron and her three daughters perished in the mayhem. I think Ambassador Ferris is still secluded somewhere on his family estate in Massachusetts. The American people are shocked by the tragedy that struck, as you said, the least likely event to suffer such violence."

"What would you say if I told you that the hidden

sponsor of the event — the one who purchased all the excellent security in form of the entire Cairo police force and the stadium facilities — is Nicola Moses?" he asked, thinking he'd have to wait a long time for her answer.

"I wouldn't be surprised," she replied almost on the heel of his words.

"Why not?"

"Because Fineas said Moses had political ambitions. Sponsoring a peaceful march would be just the kind of soft profile event that would give him the right political glow," she said.

Gahiji had probably lied to her since he would have to know that the man from whom he sought funding was a different breed of Middle Eastern businessman — a terrorist's banker. And since Gahiji wanted Moses to bankroll his search for the Peacetaker, he'd have to make his sales pitch to the billionaire attractive, along the lines that would make Moses not just agree to bankroll the curator's fancy, but salivate at the prospect of what he could do with such a person if Gahiji found him. And the odds were that Gahiji had found such a person because he was now dead, run down by a car from Moses' corporate fleet.

"I'm sure you have at your disposal all kinds of government analysts, Mr. Carter," she said evenly. "So, was it a terrorist attack?"

"If you'd have asked me that an hour ago, when I stood on your porch, I'd have said: I don't know."

"What do you say now?"

"I think Dr. Gahiji found a Peacetaker, here and now, in modern times. I think what happened at the Cairo Stadium was a sample demonstration for Nicola Moses of what Dr. Gahiji's find was capable of doing."

"No!" She recoiled in shock. He saw her dismay was real. "No, no," she kept shaking her head, "Fineas was obsessed with the Peacetaker legend, but he wasn't insane.

He wasn't a homicidal maniac, a mass murderer. He was a scientist...he would have never...." Her voice trailed off.

"Are you sure?" he asked. "You may have corresponded for ten years, but you only met the man once."

"He wanted to validate the Peacetaker legend but not for monetary gain," she maintained.

"Maybe so," he said, even though he thought she was wrong. "But the way Dr. Gahiji validated the legend was not only by finding such a young man but also activating his Peacetaker powers with an amulet, bringing him to the stadium and marching him around, then leaving quickly before or just as the mayhem started to break out. He did it to show Nicola Moses that whatever sum of money he'd asked for the young man was well justified."

"I can't believe Gahiji would be capable of such a horrific act," she murmured but with a lot less self-assurance.

"Bianca Moses and her two college-aged daughters were scheduled to march in the white candle rally, alongside of Melisenda Neron and her children. However, Mrs. Moses withdrew her and her children's participation at the last moment, sending her regrets via emissary."

"Do you know that for sure?"

He nodded slowly. "The French journalist who told me that five minutes before the march started died that day on the green." He heard her sharp intake of breath and raised a hand to stroke his scarred cheek all the way down to the still purple seams of flesh along that side of his neck. "I was there, Dr. Hunter, right on the green carpet, as they say in America, and I'm one of the few who lived to remember the onset of murderous madness but very little else."

***

He'd turned off his cell phone and his pager and left them in his briefcase. It would have been rude to have their conversation interrupted by buzzing and chiming. Then again, he hadn't seen a microwave tower on his drive up here so his tools might not be operational. But in the blizzard, it was hard to see anything, even the strip of highway ahead.

"Well, I should be going," he said, reaching for the book to put it back in his briefcase.

"Going? Where, pray tell, would you go at this hour? There's a blizzard out there and it's midnight, in case you haven't noticed and you're in a small Montana town, population 492 at the best of times. Do you think there's a Sheraton or Marriot just around the corner? I sleep up there, in the loft." She motioned at the floating staircase with a wooden picket railing that he thought led up to the attic. "The downstairs is all yours. There's a full bathroom on this floor. That's the door where you hung your parka on the doorknob. I have another full bathroom upstairs. There are three sofas in here. Two are pullout sleepers — the periwinkle blue and the lime-green one. Take your pick. I'll toss you down some bedding linen and a duvet. You have nothing to worry about even if you didn't lock your truck. No one steals in this town because everyone would know it five minutes later and the folks are not into conspiracies."

He thanked her and didn't argue because everything she said made sense.

"Dr. Hunter," he called after her when she'd already handed him an armload of bedding and headed back up the stairs. "Are you working on something…another book or research?"

"No. My sabbatical was not exactly a choice; rather a strongly recommended course of action — by my husband and my lawyers. Sometimes I wonder whether the two camps aren't in collusion. I'm keeping busy up here, updating my resume, searching job ads, things like that."

"I'm sorry. I didn't mean to pry into your private affairs. I just wanted to know whether you could leave here, with me, if necessary."

"Ah, so you think you'll need an interpreter of myths and legends — an advisor. Would that be a salaried position?" she asked, chuckling.

"I'm sure the Justice Department could make some kind of arrangements along those lines — compensation, for a consultant."

"Really? Are you saying that you're an employee of our Justice Department — I'd have thought that your social security number doesn't figure anywhere in our government."

"I'm alive, I work and I pay taxes," he said, nodding at her.

"Glad to hear I'm not harboring a criminal or a spy," she mumbled and resumed her climb up the stairs.

Chapter Six

Washington, DC
May 2
Birth of Prophet (Peace be upon Him)

The organizers succeeded closing the Mall between the Washington Monument and 3rd St. SW, but only because the event was billed as a festival, not a rally that would stream into a protest march up Pennsylvania Avenue, nor as an outright demonstration. However, even before they reached Virginia Highlands, heading NE on 395, Paige heard the radio newscaster say, "…today's demonstration at the Mall." She changed the station and listened. Sure enough, the WJFS newscaster also referred to today's "Fantasy Warriors" festival as a demonstration.

"Agent Smith," her partner and driver said. "If you can't find anything you like on the radio, why don't you shove in a CD? There's a CD case with a decent collection in the glove compartment."

"I'm sorry, Agent Denton, if I gave you the impression that I'm a radio-station surfer," she said evenly, since his tone of voice was also dangerously even. "As of 3:00 p.m. this afternoon, I'm on duty and whatever I do on duty is invariably related to my job."

"Right," Denton said.

When she glanced at him, she saw his clenched jaw, grinding whatever else he may have wanted to say. He'd disliked her from the moment their boss, Saunders, called him into his office to formalize the assignment and assignation. Then again, if an FBI agent was foolish enough to develop a reputation, good or bad, it would precede him and often prejudice those colleagues who might have otherwise carried away a different first impression if not for the fame — or infamy, as was in her case.

64

Denton had been with the Washington office for four years. She was a newcomer, a transfer from Georgia. It was her third reassignment in five years. It didn't help that her Atlanta boss, Vernon Saunders, was also reassigned and became her boss at the Washington office. If anything, Saunders stood to lose the respect of his subordinates by pairing her with Special Agent Kevin Denton, a man who believed that "arrogant" was a synonym for "outspoken."

Saunders sent Denton an email, telling him why he appointed Agent Smith as his new partner. Paige knew that her boss meant it as a pre-emptive move to pave the way for Denton as much as her when the two of them met in his office. Denton summoned everyone in the office by whistling and snapping his fingers, to come and look at the memo. When everyone read it, he raised his arms, and shook his fisted hands at the ceiling, crying, "What have I done to offend thee, Lord...?"

Paige left and spent half an hour in the washroom, calming down. What an asshole! She managed to keep her voice crisply professional when she acknowledged Saunders' instructions but left the handshake offering up to her new partner. He didn't disappoint her. He gave her a slow nod and spoke her name as if reading it off a gravestone. She half-expected him to refuse when Saunders told them what their assignment was, but he settled for tipping his head to a side and looking resigned.

"I know the event is billed as a street festival rather than a rally or a demonstration," Saunders said, "but I want you to be extra vigilant. I'm not interested in pot smoking or even drug deals. If you see such activity, alert the police and let them take care of it. I want you to keep your eyes open for saboteurs, agitators — anyone who might want to incite the crowd into starting a riot."

"Saboteurs and agitators," Denton murmured when they were already in the elevator, heading down to the parking garage. "In a crowd that's going to be wearing fantasy warrior costumes, which means half of the participants will be children."

Paige felt there was more to this seemingly routine duty than just looking out for potential troublemakers. After all, that's what the Washington police were for. They were experts in crowd control, second to only the New Orleans police force.

"Someone who incites a riot or tries to set off a brawl or a street fight may actually be considered a terrorist," she said speculatively.

Denton looked at her with hooded eyes. The narrow look told her what he thought of her attempt to raise their assignment's profile and importance. FBI agents would mingle with the demonstrators if the Bureau received a tip that such gathering might hold one or two undesirable but most-wanted criminal elements, but policing street festivals was normally left to the local authorities.

"Perhaps this is a training exercise, Agent Smith," Denton said as he got in the car. "Back to the grassroots, gentle duty, since the Chief obviously thinks one of us needs to—"

"Cut the crap, Denton," Paige said, pulling on her seatbelt.

"As you wish, Agent Smith," he said and didn't speak again until she started changing radio stations.

They took the 7th street exit, turned north and just before the tracks turned right on to D Street. Denton flashed his badge at the policeman who wanted to direct them into the detour. The cop nodded and then motioned for him to head up to C Street, where the police had roped off parking spots for emergency and other utility vehicles.

They walked up 4th Street NW, uncomfortably close because the street was already crowded with people heading for the Mall. Denton was right about one thing. Half of the people she saw were adults, the other half were children. The adults didn't really get into the spirit of things, because their costumes lacked imagination, whereas all the children were dressed as pirates, ninjas, samurai, gladiators or other fantasy warriors.

Everywhere she looked, there was a sparkle of gold and silver, red and purple, black and white, blazing blue and flashing orange, not to speak of the jewels, crowns and gleaming helmets. And while there was subtle irony in the festival's name — Fantasy Warriors — Paige doubted that the parents tried to explain to their children how it applied to the White House bureaucracy. Various radio stations may have called the event a 'demonstration,' but that was probably a marketing ploy to hold their audience long enough to hear the next advertisement jingle.

"Checkpoint," Denton said, and she raised her head. He held out his cell phone to her, and stomped his foot on the ground. "We'll meet back here in ten minutes. I'm going west. You go the other way. Look around. I'd be happy to tell you what to look for, but I have no idea what's expected of us. If I'm not back here in ten minutes, call me. Do you have my number?"

"Yes, Agent Denton," she said as flatly as she could and watched him move away. He walked with a rolling gait, as if he had just come back from a long voyage and disembarked from a ship. She shook her head and sighed. Were it any other man, she'd have said he buried himself in his part of a reveler. Denton, however, was just wanted to make another statement — insulting her.

She turned and headed east. The children and their parents streamed by her, in both directions. *What exactly am I looking for?* She couldn't help but wonder when five minutes of looking around brought nothing but young faces, painted and decorated with sparkles. Saboteurs and agitators — in this sandbox crowd?

Was this really an assignment or was it Saunders' means to have her bond with her new partner? Even back in Atlanta, her boss had been a great proponent of 'psychological solutions.' Whatever malady struck his subordinates — trauma, addiction, self-esteem, doubt, even inability to make tough decisions — Saunders's solution was psychological counseling, as if that were the mother of all cures for everything that ever ailed a man and his ego.

No. Saunders wouldn't use such underhanded tactics. He may have been addicted to 'psychological solutions,' but he wasn't a bastard. If he said it was an assignment, then that's precisely what it was.

She stopped when an unaccompanied child sidestepped to put himself in her path.

The boy was about seven years old and dressed as an Aladdin character. Whoever chose his costume was not only resourceful but had much imagination. The white Nike slush pants were a good substitute for roomy pantaloons and the red-and-white sneakers with gold stars had just the right touch of exotic flavor, but a bunch of trinkets hanging on strings and fake gold chains around his neck spoiled the effect. The boy's cropped red-velvet vest trimmed with a gold braid worn over a white sweatshirt was large enough to allow him to move his arms, so it was probably an adult's.

"That's a very nice costume," she said, smiling at the child. "Did your mother make it? I'm Paige. I'm a security officer. I'm here to make sure that this party's safe for warriors like you. Where are your parents? What's your name?"

The boy smiled back but remained silent.

She motioned at the elaborately etched leather scabbard attached to the boy's belt. "I hope that's not a real sword in that sheath."

The boy's smile faded, replaced by such a rigid look of concentration she leaned over, intending to reassure him that she was just teasing. The child's hand flashed so fast she perceived the movement only as a blur.

"Surrender your life, infidel, and your sins shall be

forgiven," the boy cried in a clear, high-pitched voice, pointing the weapon at her. He spoke with an accent that was hard to place.

"Jesus...!" she breathed out, staggering backward as the foot-long blade gleamed in the child's hand. The unmistakable gleam of steel and the width of the blade made the short sword a lethal weapon. Her training kicked in but she knew that softer, tolerant approach would yield better results than heavy-handedness.

"That's a fine-looking blade, young man. Sharp, too — and that's the problem. I'm afraid I can't allow you to have it, because not only you but others might get hurt." She motioned for him to hand over the sword. "I'll check it with the duty officer over there," she indicated where she saw the local police had set up a tent for assistance and information, "and he'll give you a receipt for it. Your parents can come and pick it up after the...." Her voice trailed off when the boy thrust the sword at her twice in quick succession. Well, goodwill had limits and these were rooted in safety.

"Give me that!" she ordered, reaching to grab the child's hand. She was trained to expect the unexpected and deal with it diplomatically, but the stupidity of parents who'd allow a child to carry a steel blade grated on her nerves.

"Smith!" The sound of her name, shouted practically into her ear, made her stumble sideways, her hand reaching after the weapon flying upward to help her regain balance. She turned around.

"Denton." She shook her head, relieved and annoyed at the same time. "You won't believe what some parents allow their children to carry," she said, turning to look at the boy who'd moved back a few steps but remained on the scene, facing her with that silent, rigid look of concentration. He no longer held the sword in his hand.

She approached him, saying, "I'm sorry, young man, but I have to take that sword, and I would like to speak with your parents. Where are they? What's your name?"

The boy let her grab the jeweled hilt and pull out the sword.

Even before she completed the motion, she knew something was wrong. The weight she expected to feel with a steel blade was missing.

Denton joined her, nodding at the boy then lifting his head to stare at her. "What's the concern here?" He reached and took the plastic sword from her hand, hefted it then pointed it at the boy and lightly tapped him with it on one shoulder then the other.

"I dubbed thee Sir Lancelot," he said in sing-song then flipped the piece of plastic over and offered it back to the boy, asking, "What's your name, son?"

"Ash...croft," the boy said haltingly, accepting his sword and deftly sliding it back into the scabbard. Paige heard a distinct clink of metal as if the sword once again became the steel blade that had menaced her.

"Is that your first or last name?" Denton asked.

"Does it matter?" the boy asked in accented English but Paige still heard a trace of contempt that was not a product of his accent. For some reason shivers attacked the back of her neck.

"I'd like to know whether I should call you Mr. Ashcroft or just Ashcroft," Denton said amiably.

Paige realized that her partner was "playing" a part in an impromptu fantasy skit and reached to touch his arm to warn him that something was very wrong here.

"It doesn't matter what you call me," the child said, backing away from him, "because soon you'll be dead, like all the infidels." He spun around so quickly his motion was a blur and ran off into the crowd.

"Denton, that kid had a steel blade. It wasn't a

plastic toy. When he pulled it out on me, it wasn't...." her voice trailed off. Even as she spoke, the memories of the Slocum Commune came alive in her head.

She'd said the almost exact same words to the SWAT officer who burst into the farmhouse to find her leaning against the wall, her gun dangling from her limp finger. The eighteen-year-old farm boy who'd pointed a sawed-off shotgun at her lay sprawled on the dirt-littered floor in a pool of blood.

Twenty-four hours later, she sat in a gray-walled room, hands clasped tight on the hard plastic table while Saunders read the lab report. The sawed-off shotgun was a homemade prop. A good one; certainly good enough to fool a ten-year veteran FBI agent into believing her life was in jeopardy...and react according to her training. Saunders tried to make it easier for her, kept repeating that the FBI agents weren't expected to be mind-readers or instant experts able to determine that the sawed-off shotgun pointed at them was a badly made home-spun weapon that might have fired once — to give an illusion of functionality to its maker — but even that one-time-event was probably an accident, not to occur again.

She didn't want his sympathy or his comforting reassurance that she acted in line with the FBI protocol. An eighteen-year-old kid was dead. The bullets that killed him came from her gun. The hand that fired the gun was hers.

A thousand years ago, the honorable thing for a lawman to do would have been to put the offending hand on the wood block and chop it off. Today, the lawmen were expected to use the offending hand to write a comprehensive report exonerating their action and their superior would sign it.

Saunders was a compassionate man, but his patience had limits. He ordered her to undergo psychological counseling and then, upon her own request, transferred her to the first office that had a vacancy —

Washington. Coincidentally, he was already appointed as the new Section Chief in Washington. It made her wonder whether he didn't create the opening to accommodate her.

"Agent Smith, you've got to let go of the past, at least when you're on field duty," Denton's voice remained flat, as if the lack of tone would lessen the gravity of his warning.

"I know what I saw," she said, averting her face so he'd not see she was biting her lips.

"For God's sake, woman, this is a street festival—"

"Demonstration," she cut him off. "The event is a peaceful demonstration, Agent Denton, and that's why we're here on duty, to make sure the demonstration remains peaceful."

"It's a street festival with a fantasy theme," he insisted. "The organizers thought they'd get a better attendance if they billed it as a demonstration, but it's a cultural event, Agent Smith."

"That kid had a real weapon, Denton. It wasn't plastic when he pulled it out on me. You damn near deafened me, shouting in my ear, so I turned away for just one moment. That was enough for the kid to get rid of the blade."

"Oh, well, why didn't you say so before?" he mocked. "Kid's really Aladdin and he's got a genie who helps him hide a lethal weapon and conveniently replaces it with a plastic prop."

"Fuck you!" she spat, turning away.

She heard him snicker. "No, thanks. You're not my type. Then again, that's why they stuck me with you, because you're no one's type…because you like to rush ahead of your partner, eager to snatch all the glory for yourself…."

He was still speaking but she no longer distinguished the meaning of what he said, only the sound issuing out of that arrogant mouth that begged to be smashed. The wave of fury that suddenly rushed into her was so powerful that for a moment everything around her went black. She couldn't catch her breath. Her ribcage felt as if someone had pumped her stomach full of expanding gas. Her vision cleared as suddenly as it dimmed. An overwhelming desire surged into her hands, raising them, fingers crooked like claws. The only place she wanted to see her hands fasten on was the neck of the man who spoke such insults that each word scored the target like a bullet.

"You smug, arrogant, filthy son-of-a-bitch...." She managed to push the words out of her fury-tightened throat even as she lunged at his back.

She dug her fingers into the flesh of his throat and felt an urge to bite down and keep on biting and tearing until her mouth was filled with soggy mulch. It was as if all the primal urges that ever coursed through a human being flushed into her, driving her murderous frenzy, and there wasn't even a shred of reason to stand in their path. Someone was pumping power into her hands to make them squeeze harder and harder as if it was indeed possible for her fingertips to meet in a death-circle. She heard the sloshing and gurgling sounds of an unclogging drain right next to her ear.

For a moment, dizziness assaulted her. Its source seemed to be a swinging pendulum motion applied to the lower part of her body. A pain shot through her ankles when these banged together, but instead of letting go of Denton's neck, her hands squeezed even harder, fingers straining to close the circle. She felt the excruciating pain but her mind ignored the source and kept churning with hatred. If anything, pain seemed to be the fuel driving everything that man ever needed in order to kill his fellow man. Her body fractured into many different battle posts, each one with its own set of orders, each one connected to the central command through its own pipeline. And every order that flushed through it brought another wave of intensity to drive the killing tools.

"Paige, honey, put down that rock," her mother's soft but even-keeled voice came back across the barrier of years compacted into memories. "It's all right to feel angry but it's not all right to let the anger command your actions. Billy's wrong to make fun of your freckles, but is the price of your hurt feelings more pain?" Her cousin, Billy, visiting for the summer at their farm, was a bully who deserved to have a rock thrown at him, even if it hurt him — badly — but her mother believed otherwise. She thought that Paige should learn to love herself until her confidence grew to where silly insults would be dismissed with laugher, not retaliation seeking to inflict more pain.

"Love and acceptance of yourself opens for you the window of forgiveness," her mother said. "But anger is a doorway to hell." Her mother's voice faded as suddenly as her memory disgorged it.

She didn't remember passing out, but the sensation of awakening came on strongly. People were shouting at her, shaking and jostling her to wake up.

"All right, all right." She raised her hand to swipe at whoever was shaking her. A blinding flare sizzled next to her head.

"Jesus, fucking...!" She rolled on her side and struggled to sit up. A body came hurling at her out of a black hole and landed with a thud on her legs. She kicked them free, digging her heels into the turf to move backward until she could stand up. Then suddenly, as if someone had yanked the earplugs out of her ears, a waterfall of sound rushed into her world. She had no comparison for the orgy of cries, moans, screams, shots, and breaking that went all around her.

The sliver of space between her and the body lying on the ground was all there was to her freedom. Everywhere she looked, there was a living wall writhing with human shapes. Like a macabre abstract painting of war, people's hands flashed in a never-ending rhythm of violence, clawing, tearing, beating down upon anything that stood in their path, and yet no one was trying to move in any particular direction.

Her shock-stilled mind refused to accept what the eyes were feeding to her brain. The raging crowd of adults and children around her was composed of maniacs literally trying to tear each other apart.

Where is the cause of this murderous frenzy, a small part of her mind still lined with a shred of reason wondered. What are they fighting over? What set off this riot?

A fist came at her and landed a blow to the left side of her neck. She drew her gun even as she staggered sideways, seeking to regain balance.

"Don't fucking move another step!" Holding the gun in both hands, she pointed it at swaying bodies coming toward her. When her warning didn't stop them, she quickly tipped the gun upward and fired three shots.

The deadly mosaic of threatening limbs stilled for just a moment — then rushed forward.

Chapter Seven

Carter dreamed he was back in the morgue. The moment he stepped into the sterile steel and ceramic room, the cold began to seep into his body through every crevice, every pore. He felt his limbs stiffening as the cold drained his life energy and turned him into an ice statue.

"Carter, Carter, wake up!" he heard shouting, as if someone had been left outside the door and for some reason wanted to come inside.

He shed the cobwebs of the dream suddenly, a legacy of years spent as a Ranger when the Special Operations Forces was still called Operational Command. Back then, he'd learned to close his eyes and catch forty winks while sitting in the belly of a noisy aircraft, wearing a chute and ready to roll at the sound of the sergeant's footfall, which he perceived more than heard, since his instinct never slept. He was with the 5th Group, Airborne, 'working' mostly Northeastern Africa and Southwest Asia — hot places, arid and bleached of living color, save whatever whimsy the natives managed to weave into their robes and headdresses.

"What time is it?" He ran two fingers across his eyes but the darkness wasn't a product of sleep. All he could see was Stella's outline, bending over him, shaking his shoulder.

"Six in the morning. Get up. You've got to see this, hear it. Come!" She grabbed both of his arms and tugged until he sat up on the couch.

"Where?" he asked, marveling at his foresight by going to bed in his jeans and T-shirt.

She thrust something into his hand. The soft knit told him it was his cotton sweater. He struggled into it even as she kept dragging him along by a loop on his jeans.

"Up, to my loft. I have a home theater up there.

You've got to see this on a decent screen. The 19" is an antique. I don't like to keep a real TV down here. I'd end up watching our old home movies and crying."

He ran up the stairs to catch up to her but he could hear the newscaster's voice even before he emerged into space that was perhaps as large as the downstairs so she'd also had to make other modification to the house; the kind the townsfolk didn't know about — yet.

The large Sony screen had excellent resolution. For once, it wasn't something to appreciate. This time there were no camera crews at any of the spots on the Mall where the murderous frenzy erupted, or perhaps the networks weren't allowed to air those shots. But even what he saw — pavement and strips of grass dotted with black plastic mounds, though some of the bodies were hastily covered and the viewer could clearly see a limp hand or a foot — made his stomach tighten.

Last night, a quasi-demonstration, more of a festival or rally, with a fantasy warrior theme in Washington at the Mall turned into a massacre. The bizarre part of the tragedy was that the participants, for reasons that even the networks didn't dare to speculate about, turned on each other.

"The dead number 287, half of them children and an estimate of more than 3,000 injured because the numbers are still coming in from the hospitals," Stella said quietly.

He lifted his head and found her on a sofa, knees tucked and held against her chest.

"Do you know what this means, Carter?"

"That the Washington participants were luckier than those in Cairo, back in March, since that death count was 411, with almost 3,500 injured?"

She shook her head and closed her eyes. "No. I wasn't comparing the numbers. Something much more sinister crossed my mind."

"What?"

"He's here."

***

How do you fight terror that doesn't strike with bombs, doesn't throw grenades, doesn't even discharge a weapon, doesn't hold anyone hostage, doesn't walk into a crowded place wearing a ton of explosives strapped to its chest? How do you fight a myth that simply walks amongst the people and seeds them with murderous frenzy, sets them against each other as if they were primal beasts, competing for nothing more complex than to stay alive?

Carter drove south on Interstate 15, trying to wrap his mind around such speculations without being able to even glimpse a possible answer. Stella sat in the passenger seat, bundled in a parka and wearing a beige ski hat, though when he told her they were going to Washington she said she'd pack "warmer-weather" clothes in her travel bag. He'd already checked his pager and listened to messages, half of them from Saunders, the others from his field operatives. All dealt with the last night's carnage at the Mall.

"Carter, being a government contractor, you have connections, right?" she asked.

"What did you have in mind?" He glanced at her but she sat staring rigidly ahead.

"Last night, I told you about Friedrich and the Babylonian clay tablets he said he'd donate to the Smithsonian if they proved to be valuable." She waited for his nod before continuing. "Well, the tracings of those 6000-year old tablets are still at the Smithsonian. I never saw them. I was only able to get a copy of the translation and even then it was my husband who, after much pleading…anyway, I've never been entirely comfortable with the translation of the tablets. I'm sure the Smithsonian would have contracted the best experts they could find skilled in reading cuneiform writing but often there is more to translation than just excellent skill."

"Intuition," he said, to show her he understood what

she was getting at.

"Yes. For one thing, whoever translated those tablets used the word "warmonger" and that's not even close, though in the context it might be semi-accurate."

"But you're after something else," he said. There was nothing wrong with his intuition either.

She sighed and remained silent for a while then said, "Do you know what it is that I've subconsciously looked for while doing my research on myths and legends, when it comes to the Peacetaker legend?"

"How to stop him?"

She grunted. "That's the easy part. The amulet, whatever its shape and nature, is the true activator. When the man with the Peacetaker powers wears the activator, he's seeding people's minds with madness, leaving destruction and death in his wake. When he takes the amulet off, he becomes a normal person, like you and me. No one could tell the difference."

"But the Peacetaker knows what he's doing even as he's doing it?"

She cracked her knuckles. The sound came like a popgun. "I'm not sure about that, Carter. That's one of the reasons why I want to see those tracings of the original script."

"You can read cuneiform?" he asked. When she didn't say anything he turned to look at her and found her glaring at him. "Sorry," he mumbled, stifling laughter even though he didn't feel cheery at all.

"He may not remember at all what he did, what transpired when he was off and walking about activated with his amulet," she said.

"Do you mean he's not aware of his own powers?"

He caught a movement out of the corner of his eye and figured she was shaking her head.

"I don't think he *is* aware," she said thoughtfully. "But I've never found any evidence in any of the legends, anywhere, to validate such belief. The Peacetaker was created as a tool of revenge. That means he's someone who's meant to be used. Based on this very flimsy assumption, I'd say the young man wouldn't know what his controller is using him for or even why."

"Controller?"

"Definitely, but it's also common sense. If the young man's unaware of his powers, then he must have a controller — in this case a conspirator — who would place the amulet around his neck or tie it to his wrist, telling him some tale why it's necessary and that's the person who's perhaps just as, if not more, dangerous than the Peacetaker."

"I see your point," he said, not sure whether he should appreciate the additional worry her theory revealed.

"In 1928, archeologists uncovered artifacts from a civilization that flourished at the site of a present-day Nigerian village, from about 500 BC to 200 AD. They called it Nok, after the name of the village. That ancient culture apparently possessed skill to smelt iron and make weapons and farming tools. Unfortunately, much of Africa has seen one conflict after another in the last few decades so for a long time after the discovery not much work was done on the Nok civilization. But about ten years ago, the Nigerian government allowed a small multi-national group of archeologists to pick up where their colleagues left off seventy years ago, for a hefty fee, of course. A Swiss national headed the expedition, with a couple of French and Belgian colleagues. They discovered iron tablets with pictorial images; crude, but definitely symbols and images of animals."

"Like hieroglyphs," he said.

"Similar, even though the experts didn't dare to call them language or alphabet. But one of the native workers saw them and told the Swiss leader that he knew what the drawings were about — apparently he was a tribal leader's son and the knowledge or tale has been handed down in his tribe for generations."

"The Peacetaker legend," he said, grimacing.

"The Sleepwalker legend," she said, flashing him a twisted smile when he turned to look at her. "The tribal chief's son earned a hefty bonus for sitting with the archeologists and telling them the modern-day version of the story, which he said has been the same since the dawn of man. Even as late as in his great-grandfather's times, when peace reigned for a long time amongst the tribes and warriors grew lethargic from all the drinking of beer and smoking cannabis, the tribal chief would send a special young man from his tribe to walk quietly through the neighboring tribe's village under the cover of darkness. By sunrise, when most of the tribe members were either dead or dying, having attacked each other, the tribe with the Sleepwalker, would arrive, "discover" the ambush and set off with war cries for whatever tribe the chief would tell them was responsible to revenge their neighbors and the war would be on to occupy all the warriors in the neighboring tribes for some time."

"It's the "Sleepwalker" part that interests you," he said. "Because you don't think that the special young man was sleepwalking."

"Precisely. Two thousand years ago, the Nok civilization knew about such a special young man and the legacy of his "function" was so powerful it survived to modern times. So, I don't think the Peacetaker is aware of anything while he's taking his walk."

"Which means his controller would have to accompany him or at least be in the vicinity to quickly lead him away so he'd not fall victim to the murderous frenzy he'd unleashed," he said.

"Definitely — he wouldn't want to lose his prized tool."

"You keep saying tool—"

She interrupted him. "The Peacetaker is a victim. Those who use him are the real criminals."

While he agreed with her in principle, the reality was that those who used the young man who had such mythical powers would be infinitely harder to apprehend. Carter was willing to settle for eliminating the direct cause of mayhem and then go after his controller or controllers. But precisely because she kept stressing that the Peacetaker was a tool, a victim, he couldn't voice such sentiments.

"Would you kill him if he was here now, right here, sitting next to you?" she asked, her voice a little high-pitched.

"No. I'd make sure he wasn't activated, then take him where no one would be able to use him again."

"Prison," she spat.

"There are places other than prisons where people who hold a real potential for causing harm to either themselves or others can be kept, in comfort."

"It might not be a penal institution and it might even be comfortable and pleasant, but it would be a prison nevertheless because he wouldn't be free," she maintained.

"Did it ever occur to you, Doctor, that this young man, if he exists and has indeed the powers you say, is being used to perform acts of terrorism against the people of United States?"

"The Peacetaker is not a terrorist."

"Perhaps not, but those who control him and use him for their purpose, are."

"I won't let you kill him," she said crisply.

When he didn't reply, she said, "Well, aren't you going to say that if I stand in your way you'll kill me too?"

"We're getting ahead of ourselves," he said dryly. "We're not even halfway to Great Falls yet."

There was silence between them for at least ten miles and then she asked, "Are you married?"

"No."

"Were you ever married?"

"Yes."

"Did you kill her?"

And finally, he was able to laugh, unrestricted and without his chest tightening up on him.

Chapter Eight

In the last three months, Carter had seen so many doctors and had been either wheeled through or, when he was able to walk, shuffled through so many hospital corridors that the impact of the Virginia Hospital Center in Arlington kept him spinning around to make sure he was indeed in a medical facility and not some posh country club. The state-of-the-art hospital that had opened just a couple of years ago even had a cascading waterfall, no doubt providing white noise for the private conversations of staff and visitors, and though he didn't plan to make detours or even brief stops to pick up a newspaper, he had to yield to Dr. Hunter when she tugged at his sleeve then took off — for Starbucks.

She returned with two *grande* lattes and told him that they'd need the "pick-up" of caffeine since they've been on the road since seven o'clock in the morning.

Saunders was waiting for them on the third floor, outside one of the intensive care units. Carter noticed that there were as many people around in white lab coats as there were in police uniform and blue FBI jackets.

"Love these colors," Stella murmured as she padded beside him, sipping her latte. "Pale shades of cream, ochre yellow, washed-out evergreen and dark-blue green accent in door frames. This is a classy hospital," she finished in a whisper.

"Special Agent Vernon Saunders, this is Dr. Stella Hunter." He made the introduction when Saunders was still ten feet away, just to stop her decorator-musings.

"Special Agent, as in FBI, the Justice Department?" she asked, approaching Saunders with an outstretched hand.

"Yes, Doctor. You sound…disbelieving."

"Well, I thought I'd be introduced to another government contractor, the kind who'd be shy to admit he was one of our country's policemen."

Since he stood behind her, Carter made a face at Saunders, who puckered his mouth, no doubt to contain levity, considering the situation, then moved to stand where she could see him.

"Fancy place," he said, looking at Saunders. "But every hospital in a 200-mile radius must be crowded with emergencies."

"It added some travel time to the ambulance," Saunders said, "but I wanted her brought here because this is one of the few completely wireless-enabled facilities. I can use a cell phone here and believe me, I haven't been able to close it since last night."

"How is she?" Carter asked.

Saunders half-turned, staring at the partly open door where two agents kept guard, while another one was visible sitting on a chair inside the room.

"She's not going to make it," he said quietly. "That's the only reason the doctors will let us talk to her. Her parents are in a lounge, just down the corridor. We'll see them later."

"I'm sorry. Paige Smith was with your office down in Atlanta, wasn't she?"

"Yeah, a good agent. A little overly conscientious when it came to application to duty, but I thought she just ran into a bit of bad luck in Georgia. That's why I made an opening for her up here when I was promoted, figured she deserved a break. Maybe it's just as well she won't...make it," he finished almost in a whisper.

"Why? What happened?" Carter asked, also keeping his voice low.

"As best as we can piece together what happened is that she killed her partner, Agent Kevin Denton. I just assigned her to him yesterday, when I sent them to the Mall. According to a preliminary medical report on Denton, she went for his throat and, just to make sure he stayed dead, she...." Saunders' voice trailed off. He ran a hand through his hair, looking around, but Carter saw that the FBI agent wasn't looking for anyone.

"She what?" Carter prompted him to finish.

"She bit right through Denton's jugular. Same shit you saw going on back in Cairo. What the fuck's going on, Carter?"

"I don't know yet."

"When will you know?"

"Gotta be soon, that's for sure. Let's see if we can get some information from Agent Smith." He turned to Stella Hunter. "Maybe you should stay out here...."

She didn't as much look at him as she looked through him then turned to Saunders. "Am I allowed inside, Agent Saunders?"

"Yes, if that's what you want, Doctor."

"I want it," she said and moved ahead. Carter had no choice but to rush after her.

The policeman sitting on a chair rose when they entered the room. Carter stuck his latte into the cop's hand and said to mind it for him. Saunders motioned for the policeman to go outside but said to stay nearby.

The patient's bed was surrounded by monitors. Some were low and portable, while others appeared to be built into the floor. What looked like a jungle of vines hung down from the ceiling. Plastic bags containing liquid of every imaginable color were connected to the patient through tubes stuck in her arms and probably her ankles, too, since he couldn't follow the tubes once they disappeared under the sheets.

Carter had never met Paige Smith in person, but he'd seen her — through a one-way glass when she was being debriefed after the Slocum Commune shooting, down in Georgia. He was one of the 'consultants' on the Slocum case because the patriarch, Pops Newton, developed a sudden passion for Middle-Eastern art and invited two

English art dealers visiting the US to be his 'middlemen-brokers.' While the British art dealers were legit, Carter had doubts about their Turkish contact, and his Lebanese contact, and that contact's cousin — in Baghdad. The Brits acted in good faith, not suspecting they were going to be used as 'mules' for information that had very little to do with art and everything to do with forged US documents and weapons.

The face that stood out of the white background of the pillow was hardly recognizable as human. Then again, he knew only too well what cuts near and above the eyes and blows to any part of the face will do to a person. Only her mouth area seemed uninjured. He tried not to think of why that was.

A doctor came inside. He focused on Saunders, since he probably knew him by now, and told him they had five minutes to speak to the patient.

"Excuse me, doctor...?" Stella walked toward him.

"Alvarez," he said and shook her offered hand.

"How do you do, Dr. Alvarez? I'm Stella Hunter. I just want to ask something. Your patient over there," she nodded with her head at the bed, "is not expected to live, correct?"

"I'm afraid there is nothing more we can do for her," he said.

"In that case, what does it matter whether we talk to her five or fifty minutes, if the information she may give us, no matter how scant or fragmented, may save many lives in the future?"

"There is such a thing as respect for the patient who's dying, Ms. Hunter," the doctor said brusquely.

"The patient is a US officer of the law. As a matter of her job and her oath, she carries an obligation to help prevent needless loss of life. She's worked for years, carrying out her duty precisely according to such directives. It's what she chose — to serve and protect the citizens of this country. This isn't just about our need to know. It's more about her right to pass on whatever information she may possess that will help her fellow agents prevent similar occurrences as what happened last night at the Mall."

"I'll be back in ten minutes," he declared uncompromisingly. "When I return, I expect this room to be empty except for the officer on guard duty."

Carter watched the doctor march out, and when Stella turned around, he gave her a thumbs-up sign before they gathered around the bed.

"I'm not heartless," she told him when she came to stand beside him. "But if this young woman can tell us anything at all, no matter how inconsequential it may seem to her, that would give us a lead on the...person, I don't want to be shooed out just as she speaks."

"I don't think anyone will dare to shoo you out, Doctor," Carter told her. "But I also doubt Agent Smith will be able to do much talking."

Just then, as if she indeed wanted to take Stella's side, Carter heard a chortle and a hoarse whisper from the bed. Paige Smith was conscious but hardly able to speak.

"A...lad...in," she said when he leaned closer.

"A lad in what? A lad in a costume? A lad at the Mall?" he kept asking even as all three of them bend over the swollen purple face and small, almost deflated lips that tried to push the words out.

"A lad...sword...real...real," she whispered.

Carter looked up at Saunders.

"It was a festival with a fantasy warrior theme. Maybe someone had a real sword. I told them to watch for unusual things, saboteurs and crowd agitators." Saunders bent over the agent. "Paige, what started the riot? Who started the fight?"

"A lad...in...real...sword. Anger is...is a doorway to...hell...hell...hell."

"Anger is a doorway to hell," Carter said, looking at

Saunders.

"Anger..." Paige somehow managed to push the word out with sound. "Anger...must not throw rocks. Must forgive...learn control."

"Were you able to pin down the location where the first fight erupted?" Carter asked Saunders.

The FBI agent groaned. "Everywhere. That's what's so confounding about it. Cops down on D Street said that the only people they saw running away from the Mall were around them. Everyone *at* the Mall was running to kill each other. It wasn't a riot and it wasn't a fight, Carter. It was an outbreak of homicidal madness, and everyone at the Mall was afflicted with the plague."

"Paige." Carter leaned over the woman. "Listen to me. Did you see a young man pass by you or did you speak to a young man just before the fight broke out?"

"A...lad...in...a lad in."

"You spoke to a young man or saw him. What did he look like?"

"Real...sword...changed...magic."

Carter looked up at Stella. She barely moved her head but he read in her eyes that he should gloss over the last whispered word. This wasn't the time to air outlandish theories.

"A lad, a young man, had a real sword. Was he light-skinned or dark-skinned?" Carter asked.

"A... lad in... stars... red trim... white sneakers... gold stars."

"What about a moon? Did you see anything moon-shaped, like a necklace or a bracelet?"

"White... red... gold sneakers."

"Did you see a gold crescent moon?"

"Stars."

"All right." Carter cleared his throat. "Can you remember, Paige, if this young man was tall or short?"

"Short...shorter...shortest doorway to hell...."

Stella motioned for him to lean back so she could take his place.

"Paige," she said softly. Carter recognized a mother's voice, talking to her child. He looked at Saunders. The agent blinked back in agreement.

"Paige, honey, did you speak to the young man?"

"Yes... I speak... he speak."

"Did he make sense?"

"Yes... then he said I... die."

"Why did he say that?"

"Sword... real... change... Denton didn't believe... magic."

"Your partner didn't believe you and that made you angry."

"Anger...is a doorway to hell."

"Yes, Paige." Stella reached around the tubes and touched the woman's shoulder then gently stroked it, saying, "Anger is a yawning doorway to hell. That's why we have to learn to be more tolerant of our fellow man, less critical and less aggressive. Did you ask the young man for his name?"

"A... lad... lad... in... stars... Ash... croft. Just Ashcroft."

"That's it. I've kept my word. Now I expect you to adhere to...." Dr. Alvarez said from the doorway.

"Thank you, Paige," Stella said, touching her fingertip to the young woman's hideously puffed-up cheek. "Thank you. We're leaving now and you rest. Good night."

Outside, Saunders excused himself because he had to go listen to his messages. He'd turned off his cell phone when inside the room but now it was time to reconnect with his agency.

"I think we should go talk to her parents," Stella said.

"What can they tell us?" Carter asked.

"Probably nothing," she snapped. "But we should at

least offer our sympathy."

"That was a good thing you did inside," he told her.

"You don't have any children, do you?" She headed down the hallway. He followed, keeping his head down, eyes tracking the floor. He didn't want anyone to see what flashed in them.

"Mr. and Mrs. Smith?" Stella was already heading for a couple in their sixties when he entered the lounge.

"I'm Stella Hunter and this is Agent Carter. I'm so sorry about your daughter," she said and hugged Paige Smith's mother. For some reason, it seemed an entirely natural thing to do for her though Carter was never able to even slap shoulders with strangers.

The Smiths were a normal middle-class couple from Smyrna, Delaware. They were happy when their daughter was transferred to the Washington FBI office because it made visiting her easier. She was their only daughter. There was an older married brother who was on a contract assignment in Japan. He would be arriving shortly with his wife and children, to offer the much welcome support to his parents in their hour of grief.

"Anger is a doorway to hell," Pamela Smith said, rubbing tears that kept welling in her eyes even as she spoke. "I kept telling her that when she was growing up. She had freckles and kids used to tease her about them. She'd want to strike back, throw stones. That's when I'd tell her to learn to be tolerant and to grow comfortable in her own appearance and identity."

They stayed for ten minutes and he let Stella do the comforting talk. He wasn't good at conveying sympathy or expressing grief. His ex-wife had shouted it at him across Emily's open grave at the cemetery. She called him a cold man with a stone heart. He knew otherwise and the cemetery was not the place for grief-driven family squabbles and recriminations.

"I'm not an agent, you know," he said when they

were in the elevator, heading for the main floor.

"I worried that if I'd introduce you as a government contractor they might take you for an electrician," she deadpanned. They walked all the way to the parking lot in sticky silence.

"Find us a decent hotel," she said when they were already sitting in another Explorer, a red one this time, since he didn't park-and-fly, preferring to leave his car in the safety of his double garage.

"What for?" he growled, tired and testy for many reasons. "I live here. If I step on the gas we'll be in my driveway in ten minutes."

"Well then, step on it but slow down when you come to a McDonald's."

"What for? I can cook."

"It's comforting to hear that, but I think McDonald's crowd would be a much better dining company than you will tonight."

"Fine. Then you cook and I'll sleep."

"How long were you married?"

"Eighteen years."

"Spent any of them at home?"

He looked at her, shook his head and pressed the gas pedal.

Chapter Nine

In the morning, Carter called Saunders and asked whether he'd be able to make arrangements for him and Dr. Hunter to visit the Smithsonian. The Mall would still be closed, and so would quite a few businesses, but no matter how much the town would like to observe a couple of days of total inactivity out of respect and in memory of the dead, it was the country's capital. There was the rest of the country to consider. Washington had to not just recover from its tragedy quickly but resume all its functions.

He was surprised and a little dismayed when Saunders said, "The only places open and functioning today in Washington are funeral homes and hospitals."

"Damn!" he swore under his breath then, realizing that Saunders might take it for a mercenary attitude, hastened to explain, finishing, "It's really important, sir."

"Who exactly is it you need to see at the Smithsonian?" Saunders asked.

Carter handed the phone over to Stella. "Tell him who you need to see and what you need to do at the Smithsonian."

Five minutes later, she finished explaining and put the phone back in its cradle.

She'd cooked a breakfast this morning as a peace offering to his last night's quick dinner. He'd found a pre-cooked bag of sauce in the freezer, thawed it while boiling spaghetti and fixing salad. He was gone only a couple of days and always kept his breads in the fridge. A spin in the microwave made the buns fresh again. He'd sliced them diagonally to give an appearance of French stick slices and they enjoyed his home-cooked dinner in polite silence.

He woke up in a better frame of mind than last night. She woke up the way he suspected she always woke up—with a sense of urgency. He told her that he would have to first arrange a possible visit to the Smithsonian and that it might not be possible, considering that the police were still cleaning up the Mall.

Saunders called back before she poured herself a second cup of coffee.

"Are these tracings of clay tablets part of the Egyptian collection?" he asked her.

She shook her head. "The city of Ur was in Babylonia. Even though he doesn't deserve the honor, the museum decided to call them "Friedrich Inscriptions." They're supposed to be on exhibit in the Sumerian wing of ancient Babylonia."

He'd left the mouthpiece free so Saunders could hear what she said.

"He'll call back again," he said when the FBI agent told him that there might be problems.

The phone rang just as she was taking a long sip of coffee. This time he motioned to her to pick it up. A few seconds later her expression told him that perhaps he should speak with Saunders himself and motioned for the handset.

"Like I said," he heard Saunders's voice. "The Friedrich Inscriptions are part of the Old Sumerian traveling exhibit. Dr. Gorman said they're currently on exhibit — at the Royal Ontario Museum, in Toronto. But he said they have copies. Why can't she settle for copies?"

"She needs to see the original tracings. That's all. It's important, sir, it really is."

"Very well. I'll see you when you get back from Toronto. Might be a good idea to drive to Baltimore and take a flight out of there. I don't think Dulles or National are going to be user-friendly. Make sure all your papers are in order. Super clean, understood?"

He acknowledged and hung up.

"I've spent a semester in Toronto, at U of T, a guest lecturer," she said in a misty, musing voice.

"Good. Then you know where we're going." He

expected her to drain her coffee cup, rise and go pack. She did drain her coffee cup but instead of rushing off to pack, poured herself another.

"Carter?"

"It's not going to be easy flying out of these parts today," he reminded her.

"I know. What were you doing in Cairo back in March?"

"Delivering a company business proposal."

"So businessman is your cover?"

"I *am* a businessman. I told you I pay taxes, just like you."

"Why were you at the Human Rights march?"

"I told you that, too. A French journalist, a friend, invited me to attend. I was his guest."

"What was his name?"

"Pascal Giroux."

She nodded as if he'd confirmed the information she already knew. "The Frederic Bastiat Award-winning journalist. He was a cousin of the French President's wife, Madame Meunier. Nicola Moses sent his condolences to the French President and his wife, as well as to the British Prime Minister and Mrs. Blandon on behalf of the British news crew that perished in Cairo. You slept on my pullout couch that night, but I went up to my loft and fired up my laptop. Doing research is, after all, my forte and my passion."

"A lot of good people died in Cairo," he said, forcing his hand to stay down because the moment this topic came up he wanted to touch his scar.

"Yes. I'm sorry about your friend, but my research had other purposes than simply to check out your side of the story. Moses does a lot of business in Europe. The Obelisk Corporation owns a chain of hotels right across Europe, from Prague to Monaco. His Obelisk Marquee in Monte Carlo has apparently eclipsed the Grand Casino in business and luxury."

"Moses is a billionaire. His corporation owns many business interests, in Europe and right here, in our country. That's why he's…" His voice trailed off. She didn't know about Moses' other 'business' interests, the ones with roots in terrorism, and it wasn't something he wanted her to know, either. But he had forgotten about her intuitive talent.

"That's why he's virtually untouchable," she finished his unspoken sentiments.

He remained silent because he couldn't tell her the truth and didn't want to lie to her.

"If Moses was a sponsor of that rally in Cairo—"

He interrupted. "His wife and daughters were scheduled to participate in the candlelight march, so he paid for the use of the stadium and bought all the security his money could buy in Cairo — the entire city police force, for all I know. But his name was never mentioned anywhere as a sponsor."

"He put up his money. That makes him a sponsor. The organizers may have orchestrated the event, but the underlying financial costs were borne by Moses. He is a sponsor," she maintained.

"You'll never get him to admit that to the press," he murmured, grimacing.

"Probably not, but in his part of the world, word of mouth carries farther than any newsprint. Moses didn't keep it a secret that he paid for the security and the use of the facility, which means he wanted everyone to know."

"He has political ambitions," he repeated the popular version of Moses' ambitions.

"Maybe. But if Gahiji succeeded in contacting the billionaire and Moses extended him the funding to look for the Peacetaker, then Moses' motives may be much higher than mere political ambitions. I think we both agree that Gahiji found the Peacetaker. You told me that Fineas is dead, a victim of a traffic accident, most likely orchestrated by Moses. I don't think that Moses had Gahiji killed because he didn't want to pay him whatever sum of money the curator asked for his prized discovery. Once Gahiji gave his demonstration of what the young man's capable of, Moses killed him because he couldn't afford to have anyone else know about the Peacetaker's existence — and what this young man can do."

"Look, Dr. Hunter—"

"Call me Stella. I'm getting mighty tired of Dr. Hunter. And since you probably don't have a first name, I'll continue calling your Carter."

"All right, Stella. I won't pretend that I don't need your help when it comes to this Peacetaker legend, but I'm not going to discuss any other peripheral issues with you."

She laughed. "You don't have to. There's nothing wrong with my reasoning powers. Like I said, I spent half the night surfing the 'net for information about the events of March 2nd in Cairo. Our new ambassador in Cairo is a career diplomat who spent nearly three decades in Washington and in the Middle East, in progressively higher senior positions. He's ten years older than James Ferris and not as easily seduced by the Middle Eastern charm. Henry Dempsey was polite but very firm when he cancelled Moses' insistent push for going ahead with the planned Middle Eastern arts and crafts tour in the continental US. The newspapers quoted him a lot. Even though it hasn't been established that what happened at the Cairo stadium was a result of terrorist action, the atmosphere left in the wake of such tragedy is simply not right for Mr. Moses to go ahead with the planned tour, exhibiting and promoting Middle Eastern arts and crafts throughout the American nation."

"Dempsey slammed a door on Moses' plan to bring over a great number of his countrymen, as organizers, caretakers and exhibitors with the tour." Carter didn't see any danger in discussing what she would have read in historical news issues on the 'net. Then again, he was still not used to looking far ahead to see from where she was going to fire her winning shot.

"An exhibit tour that was to last six months, moving right across the USA, would have been an ideal vehicle for Moses to bring in a special young man, legally and with no suspicions attached to him whatsoever. It would have also given this special young man an incredible mobility across our country. Wouldn't you say so?"

"I said I'm not discussing this topic with you anymore," he said crossly. However, when she continued staring at him, he grimaced and said, "Yes, it would have been an ideal opportunity."

"But Moses gave it up without as much as blinking. He agreed with Ambassador Dempsey and even commended him for being an astute judge of politically sensitive issues. I read many articles in a ton of global news issues on the 'net. Moses thanked Dempsey for safeguarding not only his people's welfare and peace of mind but also for pointing out to the billionaire how ill-timed such a cultural endeavor would have been. What do you say to that?"

"Moses had no choice but to backpedal," he said, suddenly feeling unsure for reason that wasn't quite clear to him.

She laughed. "Come on, Carter. I've known you only forty-eight hours, but that's certainly long enough for me to realize that you know probably everything there is to know about Moses. Just like you did a background check on me, and I'm only a recent interest, you must have spent years studying Moses, learning about the man. So do you know him as someone who would backpedal so easily?"

He leaned back in the chair and stared at her, feeling painful pin-pricks in his cheek and all the way down the side of his neck.

"Well, do you?" she insisted.

He shook his head. "No. He's certainly not someone who'd give up so easily."

"But this time he did. Why?"

"I don't know, but I have a horrible feeling you're going to tell me."

"Oh, I'm going to do more than that. If what happened in Cairo was a demonstration of the Peacetaker's powers for Moses' benefit, then Moses took an awful risk, allowing Gahiji to march his young man around that stadium. If the special young man's power proved to be genuine, by orchestrating the Cairo tragedy, Moses was effectively detonating his chances of pushing ahead with the exhibit tour."

"Maybe he disbelieved that the young man could possess such powers," he offered, feeling upstaged by her reasoning.

"Come on, Carter! Men who have more money than an entire nation could spend in ten lifetimes will never, ever pay for something they don't believe works."

"But Moses didn't pay Gahiji for the prize. He killed him instead."

"He funded the spectacle at the stadium, and I would bet you my tenure that Moses paid Gahiji an obscene sum of money for the prize, and then had him killed but not to recover the money. He removed the only other man who believed in the Peacetaker legend. Gahiji lived for three weeks after the Cairo massacre. He would have collected his money and stashed it away somewhere. I bet you it's sitting in some Swiss account or in the Caymans. During those three weeks, Moses, with Gahiji's guidance, might have even run more tests with the Peacetaker to make sure he understood how it worked. Not on a large crowd but a small gathering somewhere isolated. We're talking Africa here. Who's going to trumpet the news to the world of a dozen nomads or tribal people killing each other in a murderous frenzy?"

"So you're saying that Moses dynamited his own cultural exhibit tour set-up with the Cairo debacle. Why?"

She smiled craftily. "When would you blow up your bridge that you absolutely need to cross over to the other side?"

"When you have discovered another one that's easier to cross."

"The Peacetaker's here. So is whoever controls him. They could have come in on a visitor's visa, or as businessmen or even on a diplomatic passport. My point is that the Peacetaker and those who control him are in our country legally."

"Jesus," he mumbled, feeling vaguely that she wasn't finished yet.

He was right.

"And since he and those who control him are in our country legally, it means they have no reason to hide. I'd say that would make it almost impossible to find him."

"Jesus," he murmured again. She was right. After September 11, passport and visa scrutiny at the ports of entry became almost draconian. These days any foreigner, particularly from any of the Middle Eastern countries, who was allowed entry into US might as well have been tattooed with a white lily on his forehead. The airport customs security was that vigilant and that thorough.

Moses had quite a few business interests in the US, but the country's security agencies kept a close watch on any new personnel arriving from Middle East to work at every business establishment connected to the Meridian Obelisk Corporation. Moses was careful, too. Other than one or two Middle Eastern executives or 'managers-in-training,' he would staff all his US establishments with American citizens. It made it doubly difficult for the security agencies to come after him with something more than mild venom, because he was, after all, a significant employer of Americans. As of last count, the Obelisk-controlled US enterprise provided employment to 16,000 US citizens. Any Congressman who wanted to hold on to his seat in the Senate or House of Representatives would quickly shuffle the right paper to reach the right Chief or Director if any of the agencies showed obvious signs of aggression against the Obelisk hotel or manufacturing industry and thousands of Americans stood to lose their jobs.

"Hand me the phone," he said, motioning at the phone on the counter behind her.

"I've been meaning to ask you something. Is your phone here secure?" she asked, handing him the handset.

He inclined his head and stared at her for five seconds, then said, "These days, hardly anyone would bother bugging phones or listening in. Hell, why bother with such cumbersome measures when they can park a satellite over your head and listen in on your conversation in the bedroom or anywhere in your house."

"Can they really do that?"

"Yeah." He laughed.

"Do you have scramblers in your roof?"

"This house is a Faraday Cage. The walls are lined with aluminum foil and all glass in the windows absorbs radio waves. All electromagnetic emissions heading for this house are absorbed."

"They spent 500,000 dollars at Michigan converting their computer facilities into a Faraday Cage. You must draw an impressive salary."

He hung his head and shook with laughter. When he composed himself, he said, "These days, when you find a protection against one type of technology, no sooner do you install it than someone develops a hammer to smash it. It's gotten to the point where we're back to communicating with code phrases and whistles." He raised a hand to silence her and called Saunders. He asked him to collect and examine all routine reports on those non-US citizen Obelisk employees throughout the country who had been monitored ever since they'd been cleared to work in the US and let him know if anything out of the ordinary showed up.

"It also would be good to track down all visitors, business and otherwise, who've legally entered the US in the last week from priority one countries — and priority two and three as well. I don't think we have to go lower than that," he said.

"Any lower and we'll be checking on the rest of the world," Saunders said and hung up.

Chapter Ten

Arlington
May 5
Ancient Egypt: Festival celebration of the living children of Nut

It took them seven hours to get to Toronto, but just two hours of that was actual flight time. The rest was spent waiting at the Baltimore airport, trying to book a flight that would actually take off. There were no charters available either, or Carter would have taken that route half an hour after he arrived at the crowded airport.

"Imagine what the Peacetaker would do in a place like this." She nudged him in the side as they sat on a bench, watching the flight posting boards. He looked at the constantly flowing mass of people and suddenly a fifteen-year-old memory came alive.

He was part of the US quick reaction force in Somalia. A French missionary and two American Red Cross relief workers were trapped in a compound on the outskirts of Mogadishu. His squad went in to get them out. The snipers in the nearby burned-down building made the rescue mission difficult but not overly intimidating because they were poor marksmen. The terrain posed the greatest danger because of land mines.

The thirty-foot wide clear strip that separated the compound from the rubble-strewn hillside area defining the town limits was the death trap. Half of his squad led the civilians to safety while the other half brought up the rear, providing cover. Everything was going well when suddenly a flock of people appeared amongst the ruins as if a tribe suddenly rose from the dead. He could only afford a quick look but they appeared to be mostly women and children, refugees fleeing the city. Immediately the snipers started firing at the crowd. They didn't need marksmanship to hit a target because the refugees moved in a tight group.

His teammate motioned for him to take up defensive position to the left, while he took a step to the right. Carter heard the telltale crack of a foot landing on death and straightened up, unmindful of sniper fire. His teammate stood ten feet away, frozen on the threshold of limbo. The soldier's eyes screamed at him to run as far away from him as possible. Carter's duty, how he lived and defined himself for nearly ten years, wouldn't allow him to abandon his teammate. He felt as trapped by who and what he was as the ranger whose foot rested on the landmine. The shots and screams of women and children coming from top of the hill finally decided for him, and to this day, he believed that if not for duty calling to him from elsewhere, he would have stayed and died with the doomed ranger. And that's exactly how he felt now, looking at the milling crowds — trapped because he knew only too well what Stella was saying.

She must have sensed that he was struggling with private demons and painful visions because she lowered her voice to a mere whisper. "Any gathering of people in a public place, a lunch crowd or a group of school children on a nature walk in a park — everyone's vulnerable to Peacetaker's curse. No one's immune and there's no protection against the incomprehensible phenomenon that rips off our humanity and reduces us to the level of hungry piranhas in a fish tank. This is a new breed of terrorist, a new form of terror. It's far more effective than parking a car bomb in an underground garage or crashing planes into our skyscrapers. The moment the Peacetaker arrived in our country, it became a corral filled with 295 million victims."

"If you're aiming to cheer me up with these doomsday scenarios, it's not working," he grumbled, because he didn't want to think in such expansive terms.

"All right," she said. "I'll tell you something that will definitely cheer you up. Other than those who control him, you and I are the only people in United States who believe the Peacetaker exists."

He never thought he'd be able to sit next to someone for five hours and not say a word to them but the day proved to be one of those historical milestones.

Finally when they were already in a cab, heading east along Queen Elizabeth Way for downtown Toronto, he heard her sigh. He knew she was going to capitulate and break the silence.

"There's a Four Seasons Hotel just a couple of blocks north of the Museum," she told him. "It's a very nice place and definitely within a walking distance of ROM."

"Fine, we'll camp at Four Seasons," he said and told the driver where they wanted to go.

"Avenue Road and Bloor," the driver said. "It's much nicer than the Travelodge downtown, but also much more expensive."

"It wasn't that expensive when I stayed there," she said hurriedly.

"When was that?" Carter asked.

"Oh, about six, seven years ago."

"Our dollar was trading much higher back then," he said, smirking.

***

The Smithsonian staff had made the appointment for them at the ROM for ten o'clock in the morning. The Museum Director, Dr. Kirsch, had his assistant waiting for them downstairs, outside the turnstiles.

"Dr. Hunter, Mr. Carter." A young woman dressed in a smart burgundy blazer and knee-length gray skirt approached them when they entered the stone edifice and paused after climbing the outside stairs. "How do you do? I'm Elizabeth Marshall, Dr. Kirsch's assistant." She shook their hands and motioned for the guard to open up a side-bar so they could pass without having to go through the turnstiles.

"Do we look that American that you recognized us the moment we came in?" Stella wondered out loud.

The young woman laughed. "I recognized you immediately from your dust jacket picture—your book. I've read it and enjoyed it very much. We've used some of the more colorful legends you've described in the educational brochure that we provide to the educators to distribute to their students before a museum visit."

"I'm flattered," she said. "Which legends did you choose to include in the educational brochure?"

"The Egyptian and the Greek legends are always a great hit with the young explorers, but we included a few of the Chinese and Indian folklore tales, as well," she said.

Martin Kirsch was a man of action. When his assistant ushered them into his office, he walked toward them with an outstretched right hand while holding something that looked like an artist's portfolio in his left one.

When they satisfied the social protocol, he said, "I had my staff prepare one of the workrooms down the hall. Beth's office is right next door. If you need anything, just let her know and she'll look after it."

Stella accepted the portfolio, gave the director a friendly nod and turned to leave.

"Dr. Hunter," Kirsch said, sounding hesitant.

She stopped and turned around.

"When I spoke this morning with Dr. Gorman, at the Smithsonian, he indicated that there was some urgency connected with this matter. However, the Smithsonian had the tracings of the original tablets for over twenty years now. In that time, they've been loaned out on exhibit to half a dozen museums, in the US and Europe. What's the sudden urgency regarding the inscriptions? Is there something amiss with the translation? I believe the Smithsonian had several experts work on translating from the original tablets when Mr. Friedrich first brought them to their attention."

Carter was about to reply, but Stella was faster.

"There may be some passages that were translated with skill but without intuition. Ms. Marshall said that the ROM has used some of the more colorful legends and folktales in their education brochures. It's really about my book. Some of my interpretations have come under fire by various academic factions back home. Initially, I wasn't going to get drawn into an academic war of opinions, but my publisher feels that I should at least cross-check and double-check some of my intuitive interpretations, for future considerations if they decide to make another print run."

He nodded. "Every time academics present their research and suggest that parts of it are defined by intuition, there will always be someone who'll want to challenge them. But the Friedrich Inscriptions deal exclusively with the Sumerian version of the Peacetaker legend. Why would anyone bother trying to turn this particular folklore into a controversy?" Kirsch asked, taking off his glasses and examining them.

To Carter, it looked like something a person might do when he didn't want to look directly at those he was addressing. Something was bothering Kirsch but he didn't want to be blunt about it.

Stella, however, decided to be blunt.

"Maybe because it's the only legend that keeps appearing in almost every culture and civilization that we have on record," she said.

"Yes, that is troublesome, isn't it?" Kirsch murmured, still toying with his glasses. "You've drawn a conclusion in your book that it's the product of human imagination and that we all tend to share the same dreams — and to some degree same nightmares."

"But you don't agree with such sentiments?" Stella

probed.

Kirsch finally lifted his head and stared at her. "I tend to disagree except when it comes to the Peacetaker legend." He leaned to a side and spoke to his assistant. "Beth, would you mind giving us a few moments here? I'll call you when we're done."

When the young woman left, Kirsch motioned at the sofa flanked by two lounging chairs. "Would you perhaps like to sit down? It might be more comfortable to continue our discussion seated."

"I'll sit down, Dr. Kirsch, if you have something to say that will knock me off my feet," Stella said, heading for one of the chairs.

"I do have something rather worrisome," the director admitted. He waited until Carter sat down in the other chair, then lowered himself on to the sofa, clasped his hands and leaned forward.

"We have the tracings on loan for a year and received them last November. They're usually out on the exhibit floor, in our Sumerian section. About a month ago, April 4th to be exact, there was a scuffle in the Sumerian exhibits. We had busloads of high school students doing tours that day. Several teenaged boys…I don't want to be ethnically biased here, but they were of Persian origin, though I'm sure all the young men were second or even third-generation Canadians. It's what figured in the police report that Beth brought me afterward. The boys were apparently members of some Persian gang. The kids started vandalizing the glassed exhibits, randomly, but later on when police took depositions from teachers and patrons who were also in the area, their vandalism turned out to be less random than one might have expected. Their goal appeared to be the Friedrich Inscription tracings on display in a glass case. One of the young men let it slip to the police that they were hired to steal them."

"Did the police find out who hired these boys to

steal the exhibits?" Carter asked.

Kirsch shook his head. "No. It didn't get any farther than that. I closed off that section of the exhibit for a few days, but since the Friedrich Inscriptions feature in our promotional brochures, I opened it again. Within twenty-four hours, the incident repeated itself. This time four street persons were arrested—all young men in their early twenties. No ethnic connection this time. Two men gave them fifty dollars each to get the tracings. The police weren't able to get any useful information on the pair from the young men. I increased security in the section, and while I allowed the artifacts to remain on exhibit during business hours, I took them home each night. I live north of Toronto, in York Region, in a suburb. I drive the 404 to Aurora and on the second day with that portfolio," he motioned at Stella's hand on the case, "beside me on the front seat, I noticed someone following me. I drive a BMW SUV, and another SUV—I didn't get the make—sat on my tail practically since I made it to the 404. When I pulled over to the right-hand lane to let it pass, it would pull right behind me."

"Did you tell the police?" Carter asked.

"Of course. They advised to use my chauffeur and Lincoln and get the truck's license plate."

"Did you take their advice?"

"Yes — and Mike, my chauffeur, confirmed that I wasn't paranoid. Whoever was in that SUV was clever. He never got close enough for Mike to catch even a scrap of the license plate. I called the police and for seven days after that we had police escort all the way to Aurora."

"Let me guess," Carter said. "No one followed you, or at least the police weren't able to pick out anyone attempting to tail you."

Kirsch nodded. "Very frustrating, Mr. Carter. I couldn't continue monopolizing the police, so I made arrangements for private security to take over their function."

"And?" Carter leaned forward, hoping that Kirsch would give him some lead, because even a Canadian license plate would be better than what he had so far—nothing.

"Beth wasn't able to arrange for the security patrol the next day. I figured that one day wouldn't matter all that much. Mike thought so too. That night, on my drive home, a half-ton pick-up truck tried to run us off the road. There was nothing accidental about its surge forward and then squeezing against the Lincoln. Thank God Mike's an excellent driver who knows how to handle a Lincoln on the shoulder and even in the ditch, which is where we traveled for some time before he was able to climb back out. Had I been driving my SUV, I wouldn't be sitting here, telling you this. Dr. Hunter." He turned toward Stella. "Why are people willing to kill to get the Friedrich tracings?"

She rubbed her nose, sighed and said, "The Sumerian version of the legend is perhaps the most thorough and detailed account of how the Peacetaker works. Lao Deng's scrolls from the Three Kingdoms period gives us the 'grooming process' of the Peacetaker, but the Sumerian account details all the pitfalls and defines all the conditions."

"Conditions for what, Dr. Hunter?" Kirsch asked, sounding baffled.

"That's what I'm trying to clarify, Dr. Kirsch," she said. "That's why I need to read those inscriptions in their original language."

Half an hour later, when she already sat hunched over a worktable, a headband magnifier on her head, holding another magnifying glass in her hand, Carter asked, "Are you trying to clarify conditions, or were you just giving him a diplomatic excuse?"

"Yeah," she grumbled.

"Well, which one is it?"

"A bit of both, I guess."

"What is it you're after, reading these…looks like someone took a chisel to a soft surface and kept stabbing it randomly until there was no space left."

"Repetitious use of strokes or circles defines numbers. The pictorials in combination represent objects or names. Around the third millennium BC, the cuneiform came to be written from left to right. The signs turned on their side. But this is older, by about a thousand years, so we have columns to be read from top to bottom."

"What is it you're after?" he repeated because he didn't want to hear a history lecture. He was more than comfortable to sit and wait in silence while she did her studies. At least he could use the quiet time to take stock of what slim leads they had.

"Ever heard of a blast radius?" she asked.

He leaned closer. "You're not reading that in there, are you?"

She sat back, flipped up the magnifying glass and regarded him the same way she did when he asked whether Gahiji was looking for a mythological deity.

"How large is that Cairo Stadium in Heliopolis?" she asked.

"It's a regular stadium. They hold world-class soccer matches there. Think any of our NFL football stadiums."

She nodded. "Right. Now, is it bigger than the Mall?"

"No," he said quietly, trying to catch what it was she was after. She must have seen he was struggling to understand where she was heading, because she took a glass paperweight that sat on the worktable.

"Imagine a large body of water, like a lake, then tell me what would happen if I dropped this in the middle of the lake from a height of about ten feet? And I'm not after the sound or splash."

111

"The ripple effect," he said.

"Actually, I'm after the waves moving from the source of impact in concentric circles. Do you follow?"

"Yes."

"Now, imagine a huge boulder, the size of a house, dropped into that lake. What kind of effect would you see then?"

"A mini-tidal wave swamping the lake shores."

"Yes. The impact would displace a correspondingly large amount of water that would rise out of that lake as a mini-tidal wave and head for the shore. So let's go back to the stadium and the Mall. We have two places of different size. The Peacetaker's effect in the stadium was like this paperweight dropped in the middle of the lake. The effect did not reach beyond and outside of the stadium. Yes, I know, there were more casualties, but that's probably because a stadium is a fishbowl environment and a lot of people were neatly packed into it. At the Mall, the Peacetaker's effect was like that of a huge boulder dropping in the middle of the same lake — it swamped the crowds from one end to the other, all the way down to D Street and north for at least a block or two."

In the plane, she'd spent five hours in silence sitting next to him, but it didn't mean she was idle. She'd shuffled through the reports that Saunders faxed to his house shortly before they left for Baltimore, and then she'd taken his laptop and kept surfing the Net for news reports on the Mall tragedy. Saunders kept emailing him more reports, and since he kept his email password written on a strip of tape affixed on the edge of the screen, she shamelessly accessed his Outlook.

"The magnitude of the effect may be different precisely because the two places were different," he said.

"The place or environment or landscape has nothing to do with the magnitude of the Peacetaker's effect. His power is such that he devours peace that lives in our minds.

He impacts on warm-blooded life, human or animal, make no difference."

"You mean he has no effect on cold-blooded species, like snakes?"

"Don't interrupt me!" She slapped his knee. "I'm struggling here to make some sense of it. The Nigerian tribes would send a Peacetaker to walk quickly through their neighbor's village under the cloak of darkness. Quickly is the key word. You don't want to lose your Peacetaker in the murderous frenzy he unleashes. Let's say an ancient tribal village took up about three acres. It might have maybe two hundred people. The village that sent the Peacetaker might be closer than the length of the Mall. Do you see what I'm getting at?"

"Are you saying that the Peacetaker's blast radius shouldn't be more than across a couple of acres and affect only about a couple of hundred people in any given appearance or transit?"

"If his blast radius was larger, the village that sent him would have been affected by his powers as well and there wouldn't have been anyone left to propagate the legend. Lao Deng found sixty dead monks in a relatively small temple. Throughout ancient times, the Peacetaker was used as the proverbial tool to light the fuse, not as a bomb that would obliterate everyone, far and wide."

"So you're saying that he's not a first-strike weapon meant to eliminate many different enemies at once. But his effect in Cairo and Washington was first strike."

"Two first-strike effects of different magnitude. That's what's so worrisome. Do you know why it worries me?"

"Tell me," he invited, because he didn't want to speculate about something he barely understood.

She stabbed her finger at the tracings lying on the worktable. "Because the old Sumerians say: *He devours peace as he walks amongst the men and his wake becomes quickly littered with death. If allowed to walk to where the land ends, the pathway behind him would be lined with limbs and still-beating human hearts.* The key word here is "pathway" and focal idea hinges on *if allowed to walk*. Which means I was right. There's always a controller nearby to remove the activator. In historical records, when it comes to the Peacetaker legend, his transits are more like appearances, never anything of longer duration. He walks quickly through a tribal village at night, a transit that would take maybe five minutes. Lao Deng believed he walked quickly through the Shan Tien Temple—a matter of couple of minutes at most."

"Well, he had to stay longer at the stadium and the Mall to leave behind the kind of destruction he did," he said.

"That's my point!" she exclaimed. "He *can't*. Or his controller can't *allow* him to make it a long walk. Especially in Cairo, if Gahiji were his controller, that greedy man especially would have made sure he didn't stray far from the exit. It would have been your regular cameo appearance, and then Gahiji takes back whatever amulet he's using to activate him and hustles the young man out and far away from the murderous frenzy. He doesn't want to lose his prize. He wants to collect his money."

"Are you're saying there should have been only a 'path' of violence left behind him?"

"He should not have been able to affect everyone in the stadium, that's for sure. A couple of dozen people at most and those would have been contained by the police. All through the history his power, its effect, has been quite constant—and limited by the length of his transit."

Even though she must have seen his grimace, she said she'd give him the Sumerian version of the legend.

"Enlil, considered 'the Father of the Gods,' was banished to the world of the dead by the assembly of the gods for having raped the grain goddess, Ninlil, his intended bride. He impregnated her, but she decided she liked him after all and wanted him to witness the birth of his child. Ninlil followed him to the underworld, but her foolhardy decision meant that their newborn moon-god, Sin, was destined to be imprisoned forever in the world of the dead. So Enlil and Ninlil mated again and offered their three future children to the underworld deities in exchange for letting the moon-god, Sin, ascend to the heavens in order to light the night sky.

"Ashkigal and Nephigal, Sin's two younger sisters, didn't overly mind being stuck in the world of the dead, but his youngest brother, Siphal, resented being a servant god of the deceased. He created a man with such terrible powers that his mere appearance would devour peace and good will, suck them right out of men's hearts and turn them into savage beasts. Sin's daughter, Ishtar, who threatened to smash the gates to the underworld and release the dead so they could eat the people and thus outnumber the living, gave the idea to him. Since Siphal's object of revenge was his brother Sin, the moon-god, the Peacetaker would make his appearance only at night so his power could affect the worshippers of the moon, causing them to kill or devour each other, thus replenishing Siphal's underworld kingdom while emptying Sin's ranks of worshippers.

"And there's another disconformity," she said. "The old Egyptians and Sumerians would only send the Peacetaker out at night, which made sense if you wanted to keep the identity of this special young man secret. The Chinese warlords, being hardier folk, might groom the Peacetaker in secrecy, but they'd send him out in daylight, as fitted their needs."

He could sit for hours studying pages and pages of warfare strategies or reams of new weapons' specifications that the manufacturers would include with each shipment, but history lectures tended to harden his cerebral mass to where it might look as if rigor mortis was setting in.

"I can see your lids drooping," she snapped at him when he said that lectures tended to put him to sleep. "But this is *important*. We have two very *atypical* and inconsistent Peacetaker strikes."

"Your knowledge of this deadly entity stops at about 600 AD. You said as much yourself. The ancient civilizations evolved into what we have to deal with today. Why not also the Peacetaker?"

"Because something that remains consistent for thousands of years, even if only in myths and legends, is not going to suddenly evolve just because it's born into twentieth century," she said irritably. "Besides, I think the Peacetaker falls outside of Darwin's theory of evolution."

"Mutations are a part of Darwinian theory," he said, just to show he could keep up with her—somewhat.

"Oh, he's not a mutation. Without his activating amulet, he would be as normal as any young man today."

"Then it's the amulet that has the power...."

"No. The amulet unlocks his powers."

"You know, Doctor, at this point I would be a lot happier if we were dealing with a 5,000-year-old mummy that came to life," he murmured.

"That is a myth, Carter. The Peacetaker is ugly reality."

He had had the foresight to bring along his briefcase, which meant he had his laptop. When she assured him that she wouldn't mind if he 'absented' himself in spirit so he could deal with his emails, he settled down to work

Reading one eyewitness report after another, a result of hasty depositions the Washington police managed to compile, as well as more formal estimates from the FBI agents, what she said about the atypical nature of the events kept nagging at him.

Her legends insisted that whatever tribe or ancient civilization had a 'special' young man, used him as a quick-strike weapon to instantly precipitate hostilities, but any further warmongering would be done by those with a thirst for blood and battle.

According to the Egyptian and Sumerian legends, he was created to plunder the ranks of moon-god worshippers, a handful of people on any given night. Throughout history, his effect at any given time scored against a couple of hundred people at most. Of course, if he were allowed to wander around for days, activated by his amulet, he would leave a path of destruction in his wake, but it would still be just a bloody path, not a stadium battleground and certainly not the Mall. The amulet was a tool of control, but only in terms of being an activator, a switch. Flick a switch and the effect hits within its controlled radius. Flick it off and....

"Stella." He raised his head.

"I'm listening," she said, not bothering to turn around from her tracings.

"In your myths and legends, whether he was released in daylight or at night, the Peacetaker's effect was controlled."

"The amulet only activates his power. It doesn't control its effect."

"I understand that part. What I'm trying to say is that in Cairo and at the Mall, the effect was as if it had no boundaries. In Cairo, it was contained to the stadium only because Gahiji would have quickly taken the amulet off the young man's neck or wherever he wore it. If he'd left it on, I don't think that effect would have stopped fanning out. And it was more or less the same situation at the Mall, except the controller was no longer Gahiji, and whoever it was must have left the amulet on longer than his predecessor. That's why the Mall was a boulder-dropped-into-the-lake effect, while Cairo was only a paperweight effect."

She finally straightened up and turned around. "I like that theory, Carter, save one pesky detail. There isn't a single reference in history—not in stone, not in clay, not on papyrus, not on a silk batik scroll and not on an iron tablet—about instant large scale carnage as a result of a Peacetaker's transit."

She returned to her perusal of the tracings while he tried to deal with his email but something was still bothering him.

"Stella?"

"I don't know," she grumbled, obviously trying to dazzle him with her psychic abilities because she answered his yet-to-be-asked question.

"Is that one of the things you're looking for?"

She sighed. "Yes, Carter. It's been bothering me for years. I've never found even a single reference to it. Not even in Lao Deng's account of the grooming process. The Peacetaker has to have a controller. There must be someone to outfit him with the amulet and take it off. So how does the controller safeguard himself from the Peacetaker's effect?"

Chapter Eleven

Toronto
May 6
Death of Muawiyah ibn Abu Sufyan
Prophet Muhammad's scribe

Beth came in just after one o'clock to ask whether they wanted to go out to lunch or have it brought in. "Brought in," Stella decided for both of them. Then, as if sensing that wouldn't have been his first choice, she explained that if they went out to lunch, the tracings would have to be stored in a vault and that it might take a long time to set up the workroom again. "I won't be finished today, so we'll come back tomorrow," she said, "but I'd like to leave before the museum closes."

Beth told them the ROM closed at six o'clock and that the Friedrich Inscriptions, these days, were locked up overnight in a vault.

"Dr. Kirsch used to take them home at the end of the day but it was a cumbersome practice. So we store them overnight in a vault under double lock. Once the timer is set, the vault can't be opened until Dr. Kirsch arrives in the morning and enters a counter sequence that releases the time lock," Beth explained and said she would have their lunch brought in.

After lunch, Carter felt lethargic and said he'd take a nap.

"Wake me up if you experience a brainstorm," he said, meaning it as a joke.

She, of course, took it literally.

"Carter!" Someone in the distance shouted his name then he felt something bounce off his chest.

"Wake up." She didn't settle for throwing things at him, but came to dislodge his feet from where he propped them up on a chair.

"Is it closing time?" he inquired, stretching and arching his back because sleeping with his head lowered while sitting in a chair with feet propped up on another chair was murder on his back.

"Soon, but I need to see Gahiji's cartouche again."

"I thought you were studying Babylonian bird-tracks. Aren't Egypt and Babylonia at least a Red Sea apart?"

"Were you always a bane of someone's existence, Carter?"

"Probably," he said, chuckling, but her question set him thinking. He had been one to Barbara for sure, and at least to a few of his training instructors…and maybe some of his teammates, maybe even occasionally to Saunders and a number of his other "temporary" bosses…when was the last time he went out with a friend for a dinner and drink?

"Carter—the cartouche, if you please—today?"

She sounded the way all women sounded to him—impatient and demanding.

"It's important," she said less irritably, "because if I don't get around to checking something I'll lose my train of thought."

"Don't you make notes?" he grumbled but was already opening his briefcase and taking out the plastic-covered serviette with the cartouche.

"Most of the time," she admitted, "but this time I don't want to because I'm not sure what exactly it is I'm trying to define."

He put the serviette on the worktable next to the tracings and pulled up a chair.

"Two squares stacked would be an image of a door, which stands for sound "p" but Gahiji drew them side by side. His double slashes have a right-handed orientation when it should be left. And the small bird, which can also mean a chick, has a mirror image. A single bird-glyph is a symbol for everything weak and bad, perhaps suggesting everything that doesn't deserve to survive, that should be exterminated. Two birds back to back then means the opposite—power, strength or shift in power, which happens in a war. I missed this back in Sunburst when you first showed it to me. I don't understand how I could have missed it." She kept moving her open hand in a circle over the tissue with the tracing of the cartouche.

"Well, you've spent the last year dealing with lawyers and trying to figure out how to get back at your husband. Your book's been out of print for more than two years. I literally appeared on your doorstep, out of nowhere so...." He let his voice trail off.

"Stop trying to dazzle me with how much you know about my personal situation," she snapped at him. "It's none of your business, anyway."

"It's what's feeding your anger, and anger is a doorway to hell," he said, repeating what Saunders's agent whispered on her deathbed.

"Jesus, we're all vulnerable," she said hoarsely.

"I was just trying to get back to our common purpose," he said, hastily, because if what Paige Smith whispered was true, then he'd had one foot across that threshold of hell ever since he could remember. "So what's so special about this doubling of everything?"

"That's it!" she exclaimed. "It's the duality that must be the key."

"What key?"

She shook her head. "I don't know yet but Gahiji knew exactly what he was doing when he drew this cartouche. How did you get it, and don't lie. It's important that I understand so I can figure it out."

He told her how Hurmutz, working as a waiter at a Lebanese restaurant in Cairo, was given a generous bribe to deliver a paper napkin with a hastily drawn cartouche to Nicola Moses when the billionaire was having lunch at his "roots" restaurant, as was his custom whenever he was in

Cairo.

"Gahiji gained entry into the restaurant disguised as an electrician. My man found him sitting on a crate, in front of an open breaker panel, not doing much of anything. He drew a cartouche on a serviette and asked the waiter to give it to Moses. My man made sure he gave him a stack of serviettes to make-up a harder surface. What you see here is an imprint in the stack left by Gahiji's pen," he finished.

"That explains a lot. Gahiji sketched the Peacetaker cartouche for me as well, in Dragonstar. He also used a serviette but no sooner he drew it and slid it in front of me long enough to see what it was, he crumpled it and I never saw it again."

"Was it the same as this one?" he asked, motioning at the tissue paper.

"No, it was a regular Peacetaker cartouche, with ten glyphs, all single-orientation and that's why the moment you showed me this one in Sunburst, I made the connection— obviously, too quickly. This one, because of its dual component, can be read both ways—the Peacetaker and the Peacemaker."

"Good and evil," he said.

"It's more like black and white, presence and absence. One does, one does not. The Peacetaker—and his controller. Gahiji not only found the Peacetaker, he found how the ancient controllers protected themselves from his terrible power. The fact that the Peacetaker legend is generously documented in many ancient civilizations means those who controlled him didn't hesitate to at least now and then advertise the terrible tool of destruction they possessed, but they kept the knowledge of how they safeguarded themselves from the effect indeed a secret."

"But it has something to do with duality, or opposites," he said.

"Duality more than the opposites, or maybe both—I don't know and the old Sumerians aren't obliging me with new knowledge either. Let's call it a day."

Chapter Twelve

The ten-minute walk to their hotel was a welcome exercise after sitting in a windowless workroom for hours. Toronto was having strange spring weather, too. The time and temperature sign above the gift shop showed it was just after six o'clock and the outside temperature was twenty-one degrees Celsius. Two days ago, the temperature at the Great Falls airport was twenty-one degrees, too, but the units were different, which, of course, made all the difference in the world.

"It's balmy weather and a beautiful evening, still plenty of light. Let's take a walk along Bloor Street. I haven't window-shopped in a long time," Stella said.

She didn't strike him as someone who'd like to shop. She was more the type to order things from a catalogue or off the Net, but he agreed. Not because the elegant display windows and well-lit, mostly empty stores beyond held interest but because he thought the two of them were a fairly unremarkable middle-aged couple—the type who wouldn't—and shouldn't—be noticed by most people. Much later, she reminded him that his scarred cheek elevated him into the 'extraordinary' category, but he argued that most people tended not to keep looking precisely because they wanted to avoid seeing ugliness.

A pair who behaved like a couple latched on to them moments after they walked out of the museum.

He made a sudden stop on the bottom of the stairs and irritably started searching his pockets.

"What did you forget now?" Stella demanded in a tone of voice that told him she knew or at least suspected his search had another purpose.

"My wallet. Did I give it to you?"

"No, and the last time you took it out was in the cafeteria. Did you put it down on the tray?"

"I'm sure I didn't leave it…" His voice trailed off.

He spent five minutes, with Stella indulging her passion for lecturing, slapping his chest, digging into his pockets and even turning them inside out.

"Well, let's march right back up the stairs and see if they let us inside," Stella said, grabbing his elbow and trying to turn him around.

His wallet was in the inner breast pocket of his leather jacket. He let her drag him up a couple steps, never stopping his frustrated search then halted so suddenly she stumbled. He grabbed her arm to steady her, saying, "I found it. It's wedged down inside the coat. The lining must have a hole and it slipped through." He offered her the jacket he held slung under his arm and used the motion to glance at the couple.

Stella pretended to search and 'find' the wallet too then expressed her wish to walk along the street and window-shop.

The couple in their late twenties were dressed in jeans and navy blue polo shirts. The "uniform" look gave an appearance of colleagues who worked at a club or some establishment that adhered to a casual uniform code. They could have been parking attendants, theater ushers or sales staff from one of the sportier shops, but their behavior was a little off. He noticed them the moment he walked out of the museum, two steps behind Stella. He heard them talk, but his pocket-search session on the stairs showed him that while they were engaged in a conversation, they weren't paying much attention to each other. He perceived their heads turning even as she searched his pockets. They walked down the stairs and talked at the same time but the hand gestures that normally accompany animated conversation were unnatural. The man's in particular were staged and out of synch with the woman's voice.

Once he 'found' his wallet, he grabbed Stella's elbow and forced her to walk beside him slowly, counting to see how long it would take for the couple who preceded them to stop and have an 'argument.' It took them ten seconds to do what he expected.

Stella took her time admiring shop windows, pointing at garments and accessories on the mannequins, while he played the part of a resigned male companion— nodding now and then without much enthusiasm.

It was only when she asked, "Are we still being followed?" that he grabbed her arm and, pointing at the light ahead, said loudly that they had to hurry to cross the street on green.

"Did we lose them?" she asked quietly, when they crossed to the north side of the street and turned to go back to Avenue Road.

"Point at as many shoes as you can behind this window and tell me how much you love them," he replied, lowering his head.

"This is David's. I don't think there's a pair of shoes in the store that's priced under three hundred dollars," she said.

"There's one, only hundred and seventy-five," he said, pointing at a pair behind the window and using the motion of pulling her forward to check behind them.

"That's only for one shoe. The other costs even more," she said, shaking her head and laughing. "I think we've lost our escorts," she said softly, also speaking to the ground.

She was right. The jeans-and-polo-shirt clad couple was gone—but a second couple took over. It was now getting dark so he couldn't see how old they were, but that's not what he was taught to watch for. It was people's behavior far more than appearance that gave them away. They could have been just another window-shopping couple, but their stopping interval was always within 'seeing' distance of him and Stella.

"Well, are you hungry yet?" he asked, raising his voice.

"Yes, let's eat. There's a nice restaurant on Hazelton. It's near the hotel," she replied loudly. When they abandoned window-shopping and started walking faster, Stella said, "There was no other answer to your question, was there?"

"You're getting very good at reading my tone of voice," he said.

"Who's following us, Carter, and why?" she asked when they sat down at a table the waiter hesitated to give them because it was in the back of the restaurant in a tight spot. However, it was a perfect place from where he could see everyone entering the eatery without having to watch his back.

"There's an Obelisk Meridian hotel in Toronto," he said.

"At the airport, but how would Moses know about me and you having anything to do with anything connected with him?"

"It's not difficult to buy excellent intelligence. All it takes is money. That's one thing Moses has plenty of."

"You're missing my point. How would Moses know what we were doing at the museum?"

"He probably doesn't know, but he suspects."

"Suspects what?"

He couldn't answer her. He had already involved her in issues that made even him uncomfortable. Moses had been his "target" for more than five years, although he wasn't the only contract he'd worked on during that time.

"It's you they're following, isn't it?" she said, putting down the menu. "They don't know about my connection to anything, yet, but you are a...a known member of the intelligence community?"

Moses had intelligence that rivaled and sometimes even eclipsed that of the US agencies. And there were always moles. Human nature remained constant, and there would always be people who'd do anything for money.

Carter was fairly sure that none of the official security agencies or police in any country he'd entered knew him to be anything else than what his passport and documents said he was. But these last couple of years, he grew less than certain that he'd managed to maintain such excellent cover where Moses was concerned. Hurmutz came to see him at the Maher Teaching Hospital in Cairo, when Carter could still only blink and feebly scribble on a piece of paper: *Get lost.*

If any of the nurses or doctors saw the scribble, they'd take it at face value but the rude order meant something entirely different to his operative. It was no longer safe to remain in the employ of Joseph Yassine. Back then, Carter was convinced that what happened at the stadium was a direct strike against the US, since their ambassador's wife and children perished in the tragedy, and that Moses had not only financed but orchestrated it. He was mostly right. The only wrong assumption he made was that what happened in Cairo was a result of a terrorist attack. The again, the Peacetaker was in the hands of a terrorist, and since he used him as a tool, it was a terrorist attack.

"You know what they say, Carter," she said, and he unfocused from reviewing the situation. "The devil knows his ranks far better than the angels know their numbers. The same analogy can be applied to an intelligence community—on a global scale. They know you—"

He interrupted her. "They don't know me, and I don't know them. It's a little more complex than heavenly analogies. Moses may suspect that I'm involved in the investigation of the Cairo event. But that's not something that would alarm him. Many of our government agencies are involved in that situation. Our ambassador's family perished as a result of a terrorist attack. John Ashcroft declared a war on terrorism therefore—"

"Ashcroft! Carter, the young woman at the hospital

said the young man's name was Ash-croft — Ashcroft. Don't you think that's a strange coincidence?"

He shook his head. "It's no coincidence. He gave the name they wanted us to hear. It was probably a message as much as a warning. We declared war on conventional terrorism, so they went shopping through their ancient history filled with myths and legends and came up with such an unconventional tool that no one in our country would believe it, even if we had proof, which we don't."

"Agent Saunders doesn't know the myths and legends premise, does he?"

"He suspects something extraordinary—I mean your presence would have told him as much; I don't normally drag along a university professor, and a controversial academic, to boot, on my fact-finding expeditions."

The waiter came and they ordered. They ate in silence and only when the coffee came did she speak again.

"If you're not such a well-known member of the intelligence community that you'd be recognized ten hours after you enter a country, who's following us and why?"

"Probably the same people who followed Dr. Kirsch up to his home when he was taking the tracings with him," he said.

"But no one except Kirsch and his assistant know we're here to look at the Friedrich Inscriptions."

"Someone in the museum could be an informer."

"So the people who are following us work for Moses."

"Probably. He has spies everywhere."

An hour later, when they rode the elevator to the sixth floor and walked halfway down the corridor to where they had adjoining suites, he said, "Don't let anyone in, no matter how they identify themselves. If someone knocks and says they have a message or it's the room service, I'm next door — bang on the wall or pick up a phone and call me—but don't open the door unless you hear my voice. Do you understand?"

She appeared to be fascinated by the plastic key-card she kept twirling back and forth.

"Stella!"

"I heard you," she said, not taking her eyes off the plastic square.

"What don't you like about what you heard?"

"Drama and paranoia. Maybe those people followed us because they were fascinated by your…facial injuries. Did you ever think that might be the source of people's morbid curiosity?"

It might have been the case with the restaurant waiter who kept sneaking glances at him even as he took their orders, but those who followed them kept trying hard to play the role of a self-involved 'couple.'

"I'll tell you something. Even if I had been wearing a ski mask, those people would have still followed us," he said harshly.

She laughed. "If you were wearing a ski mask, everyone and their policeman would have followed us."

He didn't want to frighten her in the restaurant and tell her that she was probably the target that their shadows were ordered to tail because it was her picture that figured on the dust jacket of the book that must have served Gahiji as a key reference, and that she was the only one connected to the Friedrich Inscriptions, once again through her book.

According to Hurmutz, Gahiji saw Moses at Papillon Blue on February 1st, only a month before the stadium riot. As far as Hurmutz knew, it was their first such meeting. It meant that Gahiji no longer needed money to fund his search for the Peacetaker. He'd found his legendary prize and the meeting would be about negotiating a price — for such a prize, but first Moses needed to be convinced that the Peacetaker could indeed cause the kind of mayhem and destruction Gahiji claimed.

The march organizers would have started the arrangements six months prior to the event, but Carter would have bet a bottle of Jack Daniels on the fact that Moses didn't come forward with an offer of sponsorship until a month before the event was scheduled to take place. His wife and daughters would have been scheduled to participate from the onset but he had to wait until the last moment to "cancel" their participation so as not to arouse suspicions. Between February 1st and March 2nd Moses would have had plenty of time to do a thorough background check on Fineas Zahur Gahiji. Even if the curator didn't tell him about his reference book, Moses would have readily connected the event at the Los Angeles conference where Dr. Gahiji sought out Dr. Hunter and the two had a "working" lunch in Hollywood at the Dragonstar.

"Dr. Kirsch is alive today only because of his chauffeur's excellent driving skills," he said. "Two and a half months ago, a Cairo stadium was littered with dead bodies. Three days ago, a large area of our capital city, perilously close to the White House, was left looking like a stampede of killer elephants made a transit—ten times. Now, get in your room and don't let anyone in unless you first notify me. Is that understood?"

She saluted and almost cut her forehead with the edge of the plastic key-card, then swished it through the reader, pushed the door open and, just as he expected, let it close behind her with a bang. He stood there, wondering what kind of relationship she had with the Dean and whether their marital union was periodically stressed out by a mutiny or at least a mini-revolution. Then again, it probably wasn't until the marriage started to dissolve that she stopped going to the hairdresser's, donned rumpled khakis and a lime-green sweatshirt, loosened the chain on her temper and no longer bothered to be diplomatic. Did she live all those years willingly encased in the socially-correct armor of an accomplished academic as well as a

Dean's wife? The picture on her book's dust jacket seemed to indicate that. How old was that picture, anyway?

He wondered what she'd have said if he insisted on searching her room first before letting her enter. Why hadn't he?

"Stella?" He banged on her door.

Five seconds later, she flung it open. "Is it morning already?"

"Did you check the room? Is everything all right?"

She made a small sound, like a floorboard creaking, and then still holding the door moved to a side.

"Well, is it bigger or smaller than your room?" she asked.

"I haven't..." He stopped because he felt, rather than saw, a shadow move across the dark glass of the balcony sliding door. The curtains were open. She had been inside long enough to close them, since the sixth floor wasn't overly high not to worry about visibility. She probably stood by the door all this time, reflecting on how they parted because the new Stella Hunter had only emerged from her academic and socially correct cocoon recently and old habits die hard.

"Stay by the door. Keep it open," he ordered quietly and advanced toward the balcony sliding door. Once again, he anticipated the movement a fraction of a second before it came and turned sideways, his shoulder leaning into the confrontation he expected. He grabbed the hotel directory lying on the round table just as the door panel slid along the track. Using it as a Frisbee, he swished it through the air at the midsection level and heard two quick spits. The drapes reduced the phone book's impact because the gunman was able to squeeze off two shots. Carter hoped Stella had remained where he told her to stand and didn't venture after him.

He threw himself forward, along the same trajectory as the phone book, because he knew the gunman's reaction would have been to seek cover and not to expose himself by stepping in front of the glass panel. His right shoulder hit against the edge of the glass frame, but his left hand found a forearm, fastened, squeezed, then wrenched it sideways. He heard a scream, then another gun-spit and then came the sound of broken glass. The intruder obviously wanted to shoot his way to freedom because there was nowhere for him to go on the small balcony strip.

Carter drove his knee into what he hoped was the man's groin. He must have succeeded because suddenly the weight of the man's body almost pulled him down. He listened for the telltale clatter of the gun on the concrete balcony floor. It didn't come. Instead, the weight that collapsed against him suddenly vanished and he felt a blow on the right side of his head. He drove his fist upward, as if punching the air, and winged his elbow just under the man's throat hollow then drove it in. The raspy chortle told him that the gun wouldn't be used again if the man were still able to hold it.

Suddenly, he heard crunching like that of ice cubes being crushed in a blender and a strange sound that could have been a kettle whistling. An odd shape came flying through the now glassless doorframe. Carter's instinct saved him from being in the vicinity of the object's impact. He threw himself to a side a fraction of a second before the bulbous missile hit the gunman's drooping head.

"That should teach you to respect old myths and legends," Stella said. She stood next to the sofa, shuffling her feet in the broken glass as she hefted in her hand what had to be a companion to the table lamp she'd just hurled at the intruder.

"He shot the bathroom wall with the mirror," she said, shaking the lamp at him. "Good thing I wasn't in the washroom. But that's what you get when you break a mirror—seven years of bad luck and it starts with instant retribution. Are you all right?"

He had expected her to call the police or at the very least hotel security, not throw lamps to where he stood along with the intruder.

"What if you'd have hit me instead of him?" he asked, nudging the man's still body with the tip of his shoe. He went to get the gun where it clattered on the cement, picked it up, slid out the magazine, cleared the round in the chamber and put it all in his pocket.

"I used to be a star softball pitcher in my younger days," she said, finally putting down the lamp in the middle of the glass-strewn floor.

"Younger is the key word here. I don't find that overly comforting. Did you call the police?"

"Why? Isn't this what normally happens to you when you stay in hotels, particularly in foreign countries?" she asked, crossing her hands on her chest.

"We're not in a foreign country. We're in our backyard," he said, walking back to the room to find the phone.

"Some Canadians would lynch you for expressing such sentiments."

"I avoid Quebec," he deadpanned, bending down to pick up the phone from where it had fallen behind the table.

"Carter!"

He straightened up and spun around in time to see what she was pointing at. The intruder's form was no longer lying on the ground. He only saw a shadow grab the balcony railing and swing over. By the time he ran to lean over the edge, he was able to only hear a dull thud as the man landed on the window-washers' platform below and just off to one side. Squeaking sounds told him the platform was on its way down. Pursuit would be useless. He'd have a car waiting to scoop him up somewhere nearby. The intruder had not gained entry through the door. He'd used the window-washers' platform, probably left overnight by the crew who would come to use it again in the morning.

He went back to get the phone.

"What are you doing?" she demanded, hands on her hips.

"Calling the police and the hotel security."

"Why?"

"Because my credit card has a limit, and I'm not authorized to sign for the amount that's going to be needed to cover the damages."

***

"Carter, I really need to talk to you before you book that flight," Stella said, tugging at his jacket sleeve just as he was about to step up to the counter and book their 2:00 p.m. flight back to Washington, having stood in line for better part of an hour. A few days ago, had anyone done this sort of thing to him, he'd have shot them on the spot — or at least ignored them and gone ahead with his purpose. However, the tide of events that brought her into his business sphere was brutal, therefore he should expect correspondingly brutal disruptions of all his plans and schedules.

With only a sigh and a pained smile, he motioned for the customer behind him to take his turn at the counter and allowed her to drag him to the lounge area. He already suspected she had another brainstorm, since she had announced in the morning that another visit to the ROM wasn't necessary and she could "divine" whatever else the Sumerian bird-tracks had to tell her from enlarged copies Kirsch's assistant gave her.

He was feeling contrary because last night the hotel management, the police and the hotel security were politely disbelieving that an intruder was responsible for the room damages, and he thought that he would have to defer to Saunders and have the Toronto police call the FBI agent, just to spare his budget.

Then, to increase his headache exponentially, Stella's unfortunate choice of words when she demanded,

135

"What, do you think we caused this damage on purpose and should be charged with mischief and vandalism?" had all three authorities contemplating exactly what she suggested.

The police did thoroughly examine the holes in the partition-wall but failed to find the bullets. The search of the balcony didn't yield casings either. He already suspected that the intruder was using prototype projectiles that had not yet hit the market, not even the terrorist kind. The Obelisk Corporation had a chemical fertilizer-manufacturing complex in Malaga, Spain, but rumors in the intelligence community had it that the ground underneath the factory buildings was hollow and was indeed another complex—research kind. The "ghost" bullet made of edible polymer would dissolve within minutes of penetration. Its outer coating, however, that permitted it to be fired without disintegrating, was supposed to be the scientific breakthrough.

Carter had time to give the gun he'd picked up on the balcony a quick scrutiny. It was a customized .22 caliber SIRIS, with a suppressor end cap that wasn't meant to be removed often. Obviously it was chosen because it worked well with a variety of ammo. He briefly considered giving the gun to the police, but the consequences could be a trip down to the police station and perhaps a much longer stay in Toronto than he originally planned. He decided against it and hoped Stella wouldn't feel righteous enough to mention it either.

The hotel manager, not wanting to attract negative publicity to his five-star establishment, finally relented and settled for accepting his guests' story — with a grain of salt. They were assigned new suites, on the twenty-fifth floor, which made him want to ask whether the hotel never washed its windows that high, and checked out mid-morning without further molestation.

However, last night he took out the gun and the magazine with three remaining cartridges and arranged them on the white pillow then took four shots from as many angles with his cell phone, forwarded the pictures to his email, then went to fire up his laptop. He was pleased to see the email already in his Outlook when he logged in. He forwarded the email to Saunders, with a brief message what it was about and also included the gun's serial number.

In the morning, he struck Stella speechless when, on their way to breakfast, he suddenly grabbed her arm and dragged her with him inside a tobacco shop. She must have realized that he wasn't desperate for a nicotine fix because after a while she came around to where he was "choosing" cigars and asked about his "shopping criteria."

"Height of the cigar box. I need one at least two inches deep," he said.

When they were checking out, he told the clerk to also add a FedEx International service to his bill. He slid the cigar box into the sturdy envelope, sealed it, filled out the form and thanked the clerk when she assured him that the courier would pick it up at noon with the rest of the FedEx mail.

"Did you actually courier a gun out of this country to ours?" she asked, half-mouthed, as they waited for a taxi to pull up outside the hotel lobby.

"What do you think?" he asked back.

"You're right. I don't want to know."

He wiped away a smile with the back of his hand, wondering what would have been her reaction if he'd told her that it was becoming an almost routine practice. Of course, he didn't just toss out cigars and put the magazine and the gun in the cigar box, then seal it. He went into the washroom and zipped out a portion of his leather jacket lining; the special fabric, made from lead-coated fibers that would hide the article nestled amongst a few cigars. However, couriered packages were seldom scrutinized to a degree that would require elaborate protection.

Once in a taxi and heading for the airport, he

relaxed, closing his eyes. The silence and his luck held all the way until he was next in line to be served by the ticket agent.

"You better have a compelling reason for making me lose my place in the line," he said, already resigned to hear another history lecture.

"The Peacetaker is in our country legally, and considering we haven't a speck of description that would at least let us look for him somewhere—anywhere—we're not going to catch up with him any time soon."

"I've heard this before," he said. "Tell me something that will make me feel better about giving up my place in line."

"Gahiji said he found the modern-day Peacetaker clue in Berenice. That was back in '98."

"If your visa's in order and you don't mind traveling light, I'm game," he said.

Once again, she stared at him as if he was her idiot-cousin. "I wasn't suggesting we go to Egypt or Sudan. Gahiji was with a team of UCLA archeologists, doing excavations in the region—spice and silk route."

"Well, I suppose it won't be overly difficult to find which group of California academics was excavating in Egypt back in '98. I'll get right on it when we land in Washington." He was pleased that she suggested something within a mortal's reach as opposed to her usual Herculean feats.

"What for?" she grimaced. "I know them all. There were eight in the original expedition but two have since died—natural causes; well, one was a natural causes—cancer, the other was I believe a traffic fatality. But that still leaves six archeologists to question."

"Ah," he breathed out. "You want me to book two tickets to Los Angeles. Why didn't you just tell me this when I was standing in line?"

"Because we have to go to another airline counter."

"Good point," he murmured, already looking around to see which way they should head in the never-ending terminal tunnel.

Chapter Thirteen

Los Angeles
May 7
Ancient Egypt: Horus hears the supplication of the god

An hour after Stella pulled Carter out of the lineup at the American Airlines ticket counter, they sat in the first-class cabin of Harmony Airlines flight 386 to Honolulu—with a requisite stop in Los Angeles. As luck would have it, it was the only flight out of Toronto with a stopover at Los Angeles and naturally, they only had two first-class seats available.

"At least we'll be able to work in comfort," she said, reaching for his briefcase with the laptop.

"I don't mind letting you use my laptop, but I'm just curious. Why didn't you bring yours—not even a cell phone?" he asked.

"Because then I would have to deal with all the calls and emails from my lawyers and from my...him, and the children, though the children's emails I don't mind all that much, unless they're fighting and squabbling."

"Why did your marriage fall apart?" he asked.

"Is this a test? Surely this information would figure in the background check you'd have done on me."

"I want your version."

"Bruce has always cheated on me, since the day we married. But we always managed to work it out. This time we didn't. That's all there is to it."

Dr. Bruce Hunter, age fifty-three, decided that he should celebrate being half a century old by giving himself a special gift — a trophy wife. Allison Grant was a twenty-two-year-old clone of every blonde pop star Carter had ever seen flash on his laptop screen on his way to serious news, and though she did study drama and literature, she didn't want to be an actress. She wanted to attend faculty parties and academic conferences where she'd mingle with the distinguished educators of such venerable institutions as Harvard, Princeton, and Yale in the coveted role of a Dean's wife. It wasn't until he read on page three of the report that Bruce Hunter's uncle on his mother's side recently passed away and left his nephew an impressive stock portfolio of several mostly Fortune 500 companies that Carter came to understand the young woman's "noble" desire to enter a state of matrimony with a balding and generally average-looking academic.

"Are you now trying to settle the custody of the children?" he asked.

"No. They chose to live with their father. The custody was never an issue."

"Did that bother you?"

"Maybe, but the twins are seventeen and want to attend Michigan. They like the prestige factor, having a Dean at their school for a father. The girls never lack for dates. The boy is fifteen and chose to stay with his father because he gets little if any supervision at all. I told him that if his grades start slipping there'll be hell to pay. He knows that when I finally resort to threats, I'm dead serious."

"So what is the...problem?" Suddenly he wasn't sure how to word it.

"You mean why we're fighting when all appears to be *fait accompli?*"

He nodded.

"We're fighting over my tenure—my job, my livelihood, my...well, everything that defines me in my academic life. He wants me to resign my teaching post and find a job—elsewhere—preferably very far away from Michigan. I said if a trophy wife is that important to him, he should resign his tenure and go work somewhere else. The money's not an issue for him. Two years ago, his uncle left him a fortune in stocks. He could probably buy a small

141

college, turn it private and be its king-chancellor."

"Why won't he?"

She laughed. "Bruce and I are where we are because we worked hard to get our academic posts. Neither of us bought our way into the academic ranks. He could be a chancellor of his own college, but everyone would know he'd be the king because he bought his crown. That's not what he wants. And if I resign my tenure, in today's poisoned environment—who's going to hire me?"

"Because of your book?"

"Not too many colleges or universities these days are brave enough to hire a professor encumbered with the kind of controversy that surrounds my book even today."

"But you appear to be right, and if we catch up with the Peacetaker—"

She cut him off. "We must or humanity is indeed doomed, not just here in our country, but world-wide. However, if we do catch up with this special young man, do you really think your employers will allow any publicity about him or his connection to these horrible events?"

"Well, let's not worry about that right now. We're getting ahead of ourselves. I don't think we've even made it out of Canadian airspace yet."

He put his seat into a reclining position, propped up his feet against the bulkhead since they were in the front row and said he was going to spend the flight productively—replenishing his energy.

"I'll wake you up if I have another brainstorm," she promised.

He pretended to be already asleep.

By the time they landed at L.A. International, she was not only able to track down all six archeologists but sent out emails and received a confirmation from Dr. Helen Brighten for a dinner-appointment for nine o'clock, at her home in Ocean Park.

Dr. Brighten was another member of the Baby

Boom generation. Her beachfront house off Pico Boulevard could have used a new coat of paint and maybe a two-day session with a carpenter to fix all things that creaked, like stairs, railings and even the door, but otherwise it was a very nice place with a spectacular view of the Pacific.

For someone who woke up every day to see the sand and sea, she was remarkably untouched by the sun. Carter looked at her left hand and saw her ring finger was bare, but there were still slight indentations in the skin from where the ring or rings used to be. The world was quickly filling up with people who didn't want to grow old together and opted either for trophy spouses or loneliness. He couldn't decide which of the two was a worse punishment.

Unlike many Californians, Helen Brighten didn't believe in ordering in and cooked—chicken and fish, seaweed salad and fresh mangos, alfalfa sprouts and diet mini-pita bread. He'd missed the in-flight meal because Stella didn't wake him up, so even the fuzzy bean sprouts looked appetizing.

"Oh, we had the most exciting times in Berenice, Victor and I," Helen said wistfully when she served green tea, steeped in a fat Chinese teapot and poured into tea cups that Carter hesitated to pick up because he wasn't used to drinking beverages out of thimble-size containers.

"Victor's my ex-husband, Dr. Mansfield," she hastened to explain when she must have interpreted his grooved forehead as confusion. "He's now up at UC, Berkeley Campus, teaching ancient history, his passion, while I am...."

"You're down here, at the L.A. campus," Stella helped out. She must have realized that his frown was due to many things, not just the miniscule teacup, and wanted to reach the key issue that brought them here as quickly as possible.

"Well, actually, I'm no longer teaching at UC. I'm now at Santa Monica College. It's really quite convenient, just up the street. I hardly need my car."

"But you're still the Near Eastern Languages and Cultures professor, right?" Stella asked.

Dr. Brighten appeared distressed then smiled and shrugged, saying, "No, not really. I'm teaching urban studies at the college."

"But you were a co-director of the '98 expedition to Berenice," Stella said, sounding dismayed.

"After Victor and I divorced, it just wasn't convenient to be teaching at the same school, on the same campus. At that time, we were both here, at UCLA, so I changed jobs," she explained haltingly.

Carter said, "But Dr. Mansfield is now teaching at Berkeley. When did he leave the L.A. campus?"

"Oh, about six months after our divorce. He got a very attractive salary offer, not to speak of the continued funding of the Silk Road field studies." She reflected on something, then lifted her head and smiled widely. "I got to keep the house. I love living within a breath-and-a-prayer distance of the sea."

"Well." Stella cleared her throat. "Maybe we won't have to take a trip up to San Francisco. Do you remember the Cairo Museum curator, Dr. Fineas Gahiji?"

"Oh, yes, very well. I strive to be courteous with colleagues, but Gahiji was like a bug that begged to be squashed—pestilent," she said, grimacing.

"That's Fineas, all right," Stella flashed Carter a quick smile. He knew by now that she wasn't predisposed to smiling at him if she could help it at all, so the smile had to be a warning to keep all 'Fineas-mentions' in the present tense. It would have been his choice, too. People didn't need to know Gahiji was dead.

Stella launched into an abridged version of the story of her ten-year association with Fineas, finishing, "He had input into about thirty percent of my book, and now he claims I misquoted him or misinterpreted his research information."

"I remember that water-well," Helen said. "It was large. Then again, it was a communal well that supplied water to what seemed like the entire nomadic community of Arab Saleh, so it had to have a large reservoir of water. The stone wall was about waist-high, maybe higher. Berenice was founded by Ptolemy II Philadelphus early in his reign, which ran from 283 to 246 BC. He named it after his mother Berenike, the most influential of Ptolemy Philip's wives. There were three stones with cartouches dating back to the times of Philadelphus, and some dating to times of Aurelius and Lucas Verus who ruled simultaneously between 161 and 169 AD. We also found an engraved image of Seraphis, the patron god of the Ptolemaic dynasty and of sailors and travelers, but Dr. Gahiji, oddly enough, was interested in a modern-day scribble. It was someone's attempt to desecrate the surrounding antiquity, but he seemed very excited by the mock cartouche."

Helen Brighten went on to tell them of her colleagues' displeasure at seeing a distinguished museum curator interrogating the locals about what they thought was graffiti.

"He took it seriously," she said, shaking her head, "as if he found a treasure map or a new curse that would make him the ruler of the world."

"Did you by any chance take a look at that mock cartouche?" Stella asked.

"Naturally it was a joke—someone's convoluted attempt to herald the arrival of the Peacetaker. Did he represent this find as genuine and you included its existence in your book?" She inclined her head at Stella.

"You haven't read my book?" Stella asked, pursing her lips.

"Once I started teaching urban studies, I sought to distance myself from my…passion," Helen finished quietly after a slight pause.

"I didn't mean it that way," Stella assured her. "But your assumption is mostly correct. I did include information Fineas provided that's now being questioned by my colleagues, and not just here at home. So, please, tell me everything you can remember about that cartouche and anything Fineas may have said and done at Arab Saleh."

"He bought a camel just so the merchant would talk to him. Then he bought a flock of sheep, for the same reasons. Then he bought six goats and pigs—well, I don't have to repeat myself—and then he gave them back to the merchants to slaughter and throw a feast. Not just the nomads in the village but everyone in Sudan, for all I knew. The crowds that came for the feast made Berenice look like it were staging a war campaign. We feared that if even one of the animals that parked at Saleh became spooked, we'd have a stampede that would pretty well obliterate all our work. Think dozens and dozens of nomads, arriving on camels, donkeys and horses—it was that kind of picnic. It lasted five days, and I would have welcomed such a wonderful assembly of nomadic tribes in linguistic and cultural terms, but I could hardly find someone who was coherent, because those who weren't observant Muslims were drunk, and those that were, were stoned out of their minds. I ended up talking to some missionary couple who was on their way to Sudan, just to distract myself from contemplating destruction of all our work."

"Was Fineas happy after the feast?" Stella asked.

"No. He was gloomy because the villagers wouldn't let him rip out the stone with the graffiti cartouche. But I think he did it anyway because the next day he was gone and there was a hole in the well wall. Of course, we had to pay to have it fixed or we wouldn't have been allowed to continue our excavations."

"Did you take a good look at that cartouche?" Stella asked.

Helen sighed. "Yes, long enough to ascertain it was just as I said—graffiti."

"Why would you say that?"

"Because whoever carved it couldn't remember his hieroglyphics and kept groping for letters to represent the sound. What I saw could be read as the Peacetaker or the Peacemaker."

"You've never seen a duality like that in a cartouche before?"

"Duality? More likely confusion, Dr. Hunter. You know the symbols we have to represent the male-female orientation—the circle with an upward pointing arrow and the circle with a downward slanted cross—that's the way it struck me. What surprised me was that Dr. Gahiji, someone who worked for the Cairo Museum, would be so enthralled by a bogus cartouche. I mean, otherwise, the man was very knowledgeable. You'd show him a crude carnelian or faience bead and he'd guess right within a year or so which Ptolemaic dynasty it came from. The others thought he was up to something, but I concluded that he was merely... eccentric," she finished.

"So you wouldn't attach any importance to this cartouche?" Carter asked. He expected Helen Brighten to respond quickly and was surprised to see her hesitate.

"The villagers were very pissed off when they found the stone missing. I got an impression that it was the graffiti they missed as much as the stone. I think it was something of a sacred mark."

"Did you ask them who made it?"

"The hand of god, of course," she laughed. "That's an all-purpose reply you get when the villagers either don't know or don't want to tell you."

"How long were you with your team at Berenice?"

"Six months."

"Did Dr. Gahiji ever come back?"

"No. He only came the one time and stayed a week,

and five days of that was howling celebration, so we got very little work done."

They stayed another fifteen minutes. Helen Brighten jotted down all the names, addresses and telephone numbers of her five colleagues who were in Berenice, including that of her ex-husband and told them to come back if they felt they still had to cross-reference something else.

When they already sat in the rental Grand Prix, Stella said, "Let's stay the night at the great splendor of the Beverly Hills Hotel. It's on Sunset Boulevard," she added because she interpreted his stony silence as lack of direction.

"Do you know how much the rooms cost at that place?" he finally demanded.

"No and frankly, I don't care to know right now. But consider this: royalty and world leaders call the place their home-away-from-home whenever in L.A., so it must be safe. And if the unthinkable happens, and we're attacked in our suites, we'll complain so loud and so bitterly that just to shut us up, the management will waive all charges."

He couldn't help but laugh. "Why didn't you employ this tactic in Toronto?" he asked.

"You don't know Canadians well, do you? You really ought to learn more about your unimpressionable backyard neighbors," was all she said, pointing ahead. "Sunset Boulevard and step on it, but keep it around the speed limit. I don't want to spend the night in local jail."

"Now, there's another safe place to stay tonight… free."

Chapter Fourteen

Garden City, Long Island
May 7
Roman Festival: For Maia and Bona Dea New Moon

Eunice Samuels found her shopping cart discarded in the far corner of the parking lot. The buggy had been pushed over the concrete edge and left teetering on the brink of the stonewall that divided the small strip plaza from the Save-On-Mart on the corner of Grant and Osborne.

"Thieves, vandals, hooligans," Eunice chanted, even as she struggled to drag the cart back on to the paved ground and make it sit right. How did they know to always take her cart? Why didn't someone stop them before they emptied it? Was there no goodness left in people's hearts? Was Long Island the Devil's stage now? Didn't anyone in the Garden City praise Jesus-Christ-the-Lord and walk in his footsteps, spreading the word of God?

"Vandals, young hoodlums, bad seed everywhere," she kept mumbling, shaking her head. She always found her buggy, but it was always empty. She pushed the cart down the road, still muttering. Now and then, when she saw a useful item, she'd make sure the buggy wasn't going to move, then go and pick it up. Nowadays people threw away so much it made her wonder what they kept in their homes. Were their shelves empty?

"Look at this, just look at this waste," Eunice said, holding up a discarded pop can. She put it to her ear and shook it. Empty. Well, she wasn't thirsty yet but maybe in a little while she might feel parched. She put the can in the buggy. It sure was a hot spring day. Should she take off her coat? But what if the vandals stole her cart with her coat in it? She patted her brown knee-length car coat up and down, grunting with satisfaction when she heard the rustle. Good paper, close to her body, kept her warm all winter long. But maybe it was too warm now. She stuck a hand inside her coat and tugged out a handful of crushed newspaper. She put it carefully in the cart and resumed her shopping expedition. Once on the Cherry Valley Road heading north, she decided to go to the Community Park. The shopping would be better higher around the Country Club, but that's where the vandals always stopped her and took away her cart, and then they would make her sit in a room until her children came to get her.

"Just look at this waste," Eunice said, leaving her cart to go pick up more pop cans, bottles, juice and milk cartons and good clean newspaper that someone just threw away. She resumed pushing her cart along the paved pathway until she reached the east parking lot. Here the ground was hard-packed gravel, and it became difficult to push her buggy.

Suddenly, she heard laughter and music. Was the church having a picnic in the park? One hand on the cart's handle, she shielded her eyes with the other, looking over the park. The misty distance seemed to move with colors, so the church was probably having their spring picnic. Her 'long' sight wasn't what it used to be though her 'short' sight was sharp as ever.

"I didn't bring any pies," she said, walking around the buggy and pushing aside the newspapers and empty cans. "Mildred will tell everyone that I'm cheap. She always had a mean mouth, nothing good ever came from it."

She gripped the handle again and pushed, but the cart wouldn't budge. Eunice rattled it, and then looked up to see a harlot's face. The woman blocking her path had painted her lips so bright red they looked like fat satin pincushions. She put flour paste on the rest of her face. Her aunt Clovis, God rest her soul, used to mix flour-paste and pat it on to Uncle Zeke's face before he went on stage.

Back then, a black man had to be made white before they'd let him on stage to stand and serve. Clovis always made sure she washed his white gloves too so Uncle Zeke would look smart in his role as a butler. It was different for Eunice. She got picked as an understudy for *Hair* and stepped on stage often enough to put it down on her resume. But her big break came in *Godspell*—and that's where this harlot must have come from—an audition, which meant she was her competition.

"You know nothing about clowning or pantomime or charades and you sure don't look like you can bend over backward like an acrobat has to. You ain't never seen a vaudeville, not like I have when Uncle Zeke took me backstage," Eunice said, rattling her cart and pushing it against the woman.

"Get out of my way, you cheap hussy. You don't have what it takes to tell the story of Christ. You may be dressed as a clown but you know nothing. You don't scare me 'cause there's no part in *Godspell* that's got your name written on it. Get, get out of my way, you harlot!" Eunice stumbled when the painted woman stepped aside and the cart surged forward.

"Thinks she's Mary Magdalene but can't carry a tune," Eunice mumbled, pushing her cart across the gravel with such force the stones kept flying all around. Suddenly she stopped, turned around and shook her fist at the woman, who stood where Eunice last saw her, in front of a dark truck but shielded her eyes as if looking for someone in the distance.

"If you're looking for my George, he ain't out there. He wouldn't be caught dead drinking and carousing with skinny harlots like you," Eunice shouted.

"Come *Jibreel*, come *ibn-alakh*, it's time, we must hurry," she heard a voice and saw the woman wave to someone.

"Uncle Zeke?" Eunice took a step toward the

woman, dragging her cart along. "Is that you, Uncle Zeke? I don't see any wheel. And what's this about even Allah? A proper Christian got no business to let the heathen name cross his tongue. Speak the Lord's name like your mama taught you." She shielded her eyes, staring out across the park. "And Matilda sure can't dance a jig. That woman's so fat she can only sit on a table. What are you doing here? Don't you know Aunt Clovis needs you back home? Her eyes are real bad and she might get hurt if you're not there to take her around. Uncle Zeke…?"

A sharp sound of a car horn startled her. She crossed herself, mumbling, "Dear Lord Jesus Christ, forgive me, but I don't want my children to find me before I'm finished doing my chores." She turned around and, pushing the cart with the weight of her body, hurried to the end of the parking lot.

She came to a steep grass hill and the cart's wheels became stuck in the turf. Eunice rocked it from side to side, hurriedly leaning over when the empty pop cans threatened to fall out. Then she tried pushing it again but the recent rain had left the ground soggy.

Eunice turned and walked along the crest of the hill, mumbling, "Vandals, hooligans, took my cart again but I'll be back. Just you'll see! I'll be back to take what's rightfully mine." She turned again and this time walked down the slope until she slipped and fell down. She scrambled on her knees. Just then a car horn blared again.

"I hear you, Lord Jesus Christ." Eunice remained kneeling, steepling her hands in a prayer. After a few seconds she sat back, patted the coat around her body and, tipping her head to a side, became very still, watching the road and the houses across the park on Hamilton and Concord.

***

It was the third time this week that Melissa Richmond took advantage of Jaycie Vasquez, using nothing more than a guilty smile and a quick hug to send her do her chores and walk the children at the same time.

"I made this appointment with the podiatrist months ago and just plain forgot," Melissa said, grabbing her car keys and purse in that all-assuming manner that the young teacher she hired to work for two hours a day with her six-year-old autistic son wouldn't mind spending two or three more hours, doubling also as her nanny and housekeeper.

"I forgot, but I know you don't mind," Jaycie mimicked the woman's patronizing tone as she walked along Grand Avenue, pushing a double-width stroller with the two-year old twins, while holding Casey's hand. She loved her work, loved trying to help children with disabilities, though working with autistic children was her specialty—and her college major—but she hated women like Melissa, manipulative and mercenary bitches who had a nose for people like Jaycie who couldn't say no.

"It's all your fault!" Jaycie stopped and rattled the carriage so hard the wheels bounced up and down as if the carriage was a trampoline. The twins screamed and started to cry. She let go of Casey's hand and the boy merely stood there, silent and unreceptive. Suddenly, a wave of such intense hatred welled up in her that she had to open her mouth and scream or she'd suffocate. Casey didn't even blink. She made a fist and punched him in the chest. He sat down more than fell and she bent over, feeling the urge to literally swoop down on him with crooked fingers and tear him to pieces. Just then the twins' screams passed into the high-pitched range, like a whistling kettle boiling. Jaycie turned and emptied her lungs of stale air in order to breathe in a fresh batch then pounced on the screaming children. *No more Jaycie-mouse, you cheap lousy bitch. It's time for Jaycie-tigress.*

And in the basement of number 67, the house she'd just passed, sixteen-year-old Tyler Madigan snatched the feebly glowing joint from his friend Joey's mouth.

"Always the first one to toke but never one to put up your share of the cost. What the fuck do you think Les does—gives it to me for free?" he snarled, because suddenly all those instances where Joey "forgot" to bring his wallet or left his money in his knapsack that he left in someone's car, compacted into such a ball of hatred and resentment, all he wanted was to kill him.

"Fuck you, loser. Who needs your shit, anyway?" Joey threw down the joint, stomped on it then spit at him. Before he could gather more spittle, Tyler's fist smashed him right between the eyes.

And just around the corner on Osborne, Jim Drake leaned on his horn, muttering curses. The fucking idiot in the car ahead of him thought the stop sign was a red light— or a parking lot.

He slid down the window, stuck his head out and shouted, "Move your pile of junk or I'm going to park your tail lights right on your fucking dashboard."

The driver of the blue sedan got out of his car.

Jim felt such an overwhelming hatred suffuse his chest he ripped open his shirt. Growling like a wounded animal, he leaped out of his truck. He turned and momentarily reached back inside to yank the tire iron out from under the front seat. Then he was ready. The fat jerk in a business suit approached him like a wrestler, hands raised and fingers crooked, hissing and grunting like a pig.

Jim drove the straight end of the tire iron right into the man's gut, feeling a warm sense of satisfaction when the metal rod entered the man's belly. But the flash of wellbeing was brief as if indeed it was a teaser, showing him how good it felt if he continued to deliver to fucking jerks everywhere what they deserved.

He turned around, ready for the next confrontation when a car that had been sitting at the stop sign across the road surged ahead, ramming into another car that stopped to block the intersection. Jim smiled. Both fucking jerks deserved to feel the metal in their gut — all the drivers on the road deserved to die. Then the roads would be just as they were meant to be, unobstructed by fucking bastards who should have never been born.

***

"Stella, wake up!" Carter shook her shoulder, wondering whether she had brought along a supply of lime-green sweatshirts as nightclothes. Last night, he'd compromised and agreed to go to the Beverly Hills Hotel. She, in turn, compromised and let him get a one-bedroom bungalow suite at six hundred dollars—the cost of two guest rooms would have raised more than just Saunders' brows.

Carter let her have the bedroom while he camped on one of the two fancy couches. The elegantly furnished suite made him feel like he was sleeping in a display window of some Beverly Hills furniture store that catered to royalty. He was used to standard hotel rooms where he could throw his luggage across one bed and stretch still fully clothed across the other.

Here, he had to let the porter carry his crush-proof nylon bag to the suite and even store it — which was the reason why it took him such a long time to find his chiming cell phone. He had no idea where the man had stashed his luggage in this decorator's showcase. He finally found it in a closet he'd thought was an ornamental wall panel, since everything in the suite seemed to be ornamental.

"Are you all right?" Saunders' anxiety-thickened voice said, when he finally fished out his work tool.

"Yeah. What's up?" Carter didn't want to get sidetracked into explaining why he let the cell phone chime until it went into messaging—three times—before managing to answer the fourth urgent chiming.

"Are you still in L.A.?"

"Yes."

"Where are you?"

155

Carter quickly glanced at the pager he also found in his bag. It was six o'clock in the morning and a Sunday. Was this a good time for explanations?

"We've stayed overnight at a hotel in Beverly Hills but I was going to book us a flight back...after breakfast."

"Fine, but right now I need you to get to the office over there as quickly as possible. Special Agent Masella's your contact and Agent Gordon will be ready with the conferencing set-up. I don't think either of them has been home in the last seventy-two hours. It's not a live session but both videos are current, just a few hours old. Listen carefully and make notes. Bring Doctor Hunter along. I'll clear her with Masella. How fast can you get there?"

Carter sucked in his breath. He was less than three miles away from the FBI headquarters on Wilshire. "About five, ten minutes."

"You're that close? Where exactly are you staying?"

Ah shit! "We were in Ocean Park yesterday, talking to one of the academics who was in Egypt six years ago, an archeological expedition. She had some interesting information regarding transients that passed through their dig site."

"Isn't that in Santa Monica?"

"Yes, sir, very close. I better get going if you want us to make it there before six-thirty," he said, flipped the cell phone closed and went to wake up his traveling companion.

"What time is it?" she asked, sleepy-voiced.

"Early and we have to leave, right now."

"Your credit card bounced?"

"Not yet. Saunders wants us to get over to the FBI headquarters on Wilshire. I didn't ask details but I guarantee you, it's important. How long will it take you to get ready?"

"What? I'm ready now," she said, sitting up,

stretching and yawning. He suspected that she'd just climbed into bed in her clothes—probably a result of Sunburst habit, since she made her 'recommended' sabbatical into a reclusive retreat.

"Well, then, I'll be in the lobby, settling our bill and having a cigar while the parking attendant brings around our rental limousine," he said and walked out of the bedroom.

"I don't understand how a man who has a sense of humor this early in the morning couldn't hold on to his wife," she yelled after him.

Well, she finally got something wrong. It was the other way around. Barbara didn't want to hold on to him because, as she threw it in his face, if eighteen years didn't melt his heart and coat him with at least a veneer of humanity, nothing could. He was a cold, unfeeling statue.

"So you *are* an FBI agent—undercover, right?" Stella asked, fifteen minutes later, when she lowered herself with great ceremony into the passenger seat because the doorman came to open the car door for her.

"No."

"Come on, Carter," her voice tinged with impatience. "We've now spent two nights in the same room. You could at least afford me some honesty."

"Two?"

"Sunburst."

"Ah, yes. But I'm not lying to you. I'm a contractor," he said. When he glanced at her, he saw her grimly set mouth, so he relented and went on to explain. The FBI's territorial jurisdiction was the United States while the CIA's ring of authority was outside the country. In the past, the two security agencies often clashed over the jurisdiction and territorial rights, particularly when perpetrators who wreaked havoc on the US soil moved beyond it. It was difficult for the FBI, having done much work chasing after them while they were in the country, to give up all such exhaustive work and pursuit just because the criminals fled beyond their jurisdiction.

"I 'bridge' between our security agencies, serving one then the other and sometimes all of them at the same time," he finished.

"So you really don't have a badge to flash and intimidate people?"

He laughed. "I have business cards that I hand out to people, and my social security number is in the Human Resources data bank at... well, currently Global Environics out of Toledo, Ohio—Timothy J. Carter, Senior Vice-President, Technology and Solutions."

"But that's not your real name," she insisted.

He didn't reply and pretended to be occupied glancing in the driver's side mirror. Not that there was anything interesting happening behind him but he wanted to discourage her from pursuing the subject.

"Actually, I'm getting used to Carter," she murmured when they entered the underground parking garage at 1100 Wilshire where the FBI had its headquarters on the 17th floor.

She didn't speak again until they were cleared all the way into a claustrophobic conference room with a table set up with a laptop and a mercifully large screen on the head wall. He introduced her to Special Agent Masella and Agent Gordon, nodded at the laptop and said, "Let's get started."

"This incident occurred yesterday, in the afternoon, between two and three o'clock, in a Long Island village—Garden City to be exact," Masella said and motioned for Gordon to start the video.

The five-minute video clip had to be filmed by a traffic helicopter newsman or even a policeman from a chopper, trying to get to the scene of what looked like one never-ending accident in the streets just east of the park.

Masella went toward the screen while Gordon froze

the image.

"This," the agent outlined the large area with what looked like a crowd, "is the Garden City Community Park. Yesterday afternoon, the Fraternal Organization of Garden City Benevolent Police and the Nassau County Police 5th Precinct were holding their annual spring picnic. The park was filled with police officers. Perhaps that's the reason why it took so long to respond to the violence that erupted in this part of the residential area." He outlined a sizeable wedge of house-dotted streets.

"There was no riot in the park? No disruption of the picnic?" Carter asked.

"This wasn't like the Mall event in Washington," Masella said. "The picnic was well attended but the celebration wasn't marred by a riot or any form of violence. The murder and carnage this time came from the households and the streets—traffic and pedestrians. More than two hundred cars were used as killing weapons. According to the last report, there were 165 dead, 22 of them children, and more than 150 injured... People simply went berserk and attacked each other, and I mean total strangers, friends or family members, all went insane in a span of about five minutes, though the actual violence lasted longer. After the Mall, we issued a bulletin, warning the public about holding large-scale celebrations in the open...but, how do you caution people about riots in their own homes or mass-road-rage?"

"Long Island," Stella spoke up. "Why Long Island?" Carter alone knew what she was wondering about and hoped that the other two agents would just take it as a civilian's shock and disbelief of what she saw. The aftermath had left the streets literally looking like a scene out of a demolition rally. Cars and trucks had collided at almost every intersection, leaving mountains of crushed metal. He could only imagine the cries that must have issued from underneath those heaps.

"We've checked everything," Masella said. "That area's not even on a flight path, so the possibility of some deadly aerial agent dumped over it is nil. There were no chemical spills, no water contamination or gas seepage. Nothing. New York had hazardous waste units on the scene, checking radioactivity levels. All normal. All the hospitals where the injured were taken for treatment have instructions to tell their labs to test for exotics, any substance they deem suspicious that shows up in a patient's blood- work is to be reported. So far, nothing."

"You think it might be an effect of some hallucinogenic drug?" Carter asked and hoped Stella would realize he was just observing protocol.

Masella outlined the residential grid again. "That's a large area for any kind of chemical substance to have effect, short of gas release, but like I said, the air tested normal. As far as we can tell at this time, 500 households were affected, some more than others."

"Was anyone not affected?" Stella asked.

The agent grimaced. "That's almost impossible to tell. According to those few depositions the New York agents were able to take from the injured being treated in hospitals, they don't know themselves what caused them to go…." he paused then finished, "homicidal."

"They only remember being so angry that if they didn't strike out at the nearest person, didn't try to kill him, they felt their head or chest would explode," Carter said, because that's what he'd felt back in Cairo. "And for a moment or two, to some of them, it might have felt like a self-preservation instinct, out of control, driving them to kill or be killed."

Masella agreed. "That's about the only common factor between the survivors of the Mall riot and Garden City. No one's rushing to issue press releases. We have no idea what to tell the people, how they should safeguard themselves from…" He shrugged, his voice trailing off.

"Sir." Gordon raised his hand then inclined his head at the laptop.

"Oh, yes." Masella reacted by telling him to shut off the video and run the second one but pause it for a moment while he explained.

"Saunders feels it's significant but he wasn't able to define just how. He felt you might be able to make a connection, if any," Masella said and gave Gordon a sign to start.

This time the video clip showed a standard conference room, almost a copy of the one where they sat, with an old lady dressed in a bulky brown coat sitting facing the camera but keeping her head lowered, while Saunders and a woman in her late thirties sat on either side of her.

"Tell us again what you saw, Mother," the woman asked, moving her hand along the tabletop in front of the old lady to catch her attention.

"I saw souls, crying and begging for mercy in Purgatory," the old lady said in a deep voice, so richly resonant Carter pursed his mouth. Many preachers who sought to hold their flock's attention from a pulpit would thank the Lord if he blessed them with such a penetrating and melodious voice.

"You told us you saw car accidents and people crying for help," the woman said, still moving her hand across the tabletop but slowly, hypnotically, in circles. "But that's after your buggy got stuck and you went to sit on the hill. What did you see before that, in the parking lot?"

"I saw the Devil. It was his work. I saw him. He didn't fool me with his harlot's face. She wanted my part in *Godspell*, you know." The old lady kept nodding as she spoke but she wouldn't lift her head. She indeed appeared to be speaking to her daughter's hand languidly moving in circles.

"Mrs. Samuels—Eunice." Saunders leaned forward,

waiting.

After a few seconds, the daughter said, "Mother, what did the Devil look like?"

The old lady suddenly raised her head. Carter made a soft sound of appreciation. Eunice Samuels was probably close to seventy but like her resonant voice, her beauty was ageless. Those who served the Egyptian royalty with mallets, chisels and stone-carving tools 5000 years ago would have clustered around her, imprinting her sharply defined almond-shaped eyes, high forehead and perfectly oval face into gold masks or stone walls. Her skin color was neither dark nor light but a sunlit combination of the two, like the ochre color of the sunset or the transparent bronze of the sunrise. Her hair was the only part that showed her age—and her mental condition. It was stringy, mostly white and unkempt.

"Like a harlot, sweetheart, like a painted harlot who came to tempt our Lord, Jesus Christ. I was in *Godspell*, you know, and your Uncle Zeke was in vaudeville when few, if any, black men were allowed on stage. Are you a stage actress too?"

"No, Mother," the woman said, with a forced patience. "I'm your daughter, Natalie, and this is Mr. Saunders. You sneaked out again when I was doing laundry and went…shopping. You made it to the Community Park, to the east parking lot, and you saw someone there. Who was it? What did he look like?"

"Child, it was your great-uncle Zeke. He wanted to show me the wheel but my eyes aren't what they used to bee. It was the skinny harlot. She made him forget the name of our Lord, Jesus Christ."

"What name did he say, Mother?" Natalie pressed.

"Even Allah, you know how the heathen talk and Matilda, dancing a jig, why that woman's so fat she—"

Natalie quickly rapped the table with her knuckle. "Mother, can you remember the exact words Uncle Zeke said?"

"He called them out—jig-wheel, jib-reel, come even Allah, jig-wheel, sounded like he was calling a dog. It wasn't Uncle Zeke, was it?" The old lady turned to her daughter. "It was the Devil."

"Yes, Mother," Natalie said and put her hand over her mother's, stroking it in the same circular manner as she table. She turned to Saunders. "She can't tell you anything else. This is all we were able to get out of her. The thing was that when she told us she sounded very lucid. I thought it might be important—"

Saunders interrupted her. "It is, Mrs. Brown, it is. Thank you for coming."

The headwall screen went blank.

"There are dozens of possibilities what those words might mean in any of the Arabic dialects," Gordon said. "Of course, the old lady's version might be so badly garbled that we might never be able to get a decent match. I don't think we'll get anywhere but we're trying phonetic matches down at the computer lab."

Carter nodded. "Let me know if anything promising comes up, like a name."

Gordon made a displeased sound. "We're never that lucky."

"Dr. Hunter and I are going back to Washington today, but can we use this room for a while?" Carter asked.

"You're welcome to stay," Masella said and both agents left the room.

Chapter Fifteen

Los Angeles
May 8
International Red Cross Day

"I think Eunice Samuels saw the controller at the Long Island park," Stella said when they were finally alone. "And whatever those words Eunice heard might turn out to mean in Arabic, I think the controller was calling to the Peacetaker, summoning him back from the park, or even from just the edge of the parking lot."

"I'm not dissing your brainstorm, Stella, but do you really think that in ancient times those who sought to use the Peacetaker to start a war would entrust his control to a woman?"

"I can't see the Chinese doing it but the Egyptians and Sumerians wouldn't be overly bothered by it. In fact, if that was the requirement, that's exactly what they would do."

"What about African tribes?"

"Some ancient tribes used to be matriarchal but I see your point. Still, it's hard to let go of the theory. Everything in the universe arises out of two forces—yin and yang—six astrological signs are masculine and six are feminine, energetic and magnetic. One of the functions of mythology is to supply symbols that carry the human spirit forward to counteract other constants that tend to hold it back. It's all about balance and opposition, and there's inherent duality in everything. There has to be a nurturing component to the aggressive nature..."

She continued her lecture with the passion he'd come to admire but for some reason admiration wasn't enough to stop his lids from creeping down, eyes wanting to close.

During his Special Forces training, he had stood all night waist-deep in a swamp, holding his rifle with both hands just above the water line, never as much as moving his eyes to track the slithering shapes, belligerent and even deadly. And while fatigue grew such that he wasn't able to feel any part of his body, not even those that come morning would be covered by leeches, he never took his eyes off his sergeant, pacing up and down on the strip of dry land, lecturing at the top of his lungs. And as long as the sergeant's lungs worked, his eyelids stayed open. But two dozen words into an academic history lecture or one of her one-sided debates and his eyelids lost discipline and behaved as if they were not a well-trained machine like all the rest of his body parts, but sissy punks who washed out the first week of the training camp.

"Carter!"

"Yes, ma'am."

"The controller is a woman. He has to be a woman."

His ears pricked. She sounded too sure to mix-up her pronouns. He decided to be plain. "I have no idea what you're talking about."

"It was a police picnic. They would have entertainment. Maybe a live band, maybe even singers and dancers—or mimes. Eunice Samuels saw a painted face. A harlot's face, she said. But I bet you anything that the face she saw was a theater mask."

"A female mask." He nodded.

"A man wearing a female mask. The Roman actors used them, the stage actors used them in Shakespearean times; so did Chinese performers. The old Egyptians wore masks not only for stage performances but to battle, or during exhibition combat in a palace."

"So you're saying that a female mask will protect you against the Peacetaker's power?" He must have sounded more disbelieving than he meant to because she rose, braced her hands on her hips and glared at him.

"We're dealing with a curse damning humanity for all eternity spun by a mythological demon. It produces a male child born during the night of the Blue Moon. When the child reaches adulthood, his power is activated with an amulet and as he walks amongst men, he devours peace, leaving them howling with murderous frenzy like primeval beasts. Which parts of what I've just said doesn't sound rational enough to you such that you can't believe the controller is a man wearing a female mask?"

"Well, what if it's cloudy during that particular night of the Blue Moon and the actual moon can't be seen? Would ancient folks have known then it was a night of the Blue Moon? I'm just trying to play the Devil's Advocate."

"An excellent point. We'll gloss over it. Not because it poses challenge for me, but because we have, once again, a more important puzzle to baffle us," she said with such candor that he raised both hands to show her he was capitulating.

"The Peacetaker's effect rippled away from the picnic grounds as if someone had put a barrier across Cherry Valley Avenue. I'd say it was literally cut off from concentric wave propagation and fanned into the residential streets southeast of the park," she said.

She was right. From what he saw in the first video, and according to what Masella said, the effect was as if someone had split a circle in half. It fanned southeast, into the residential area bound by West Hempstead and Westminster and infected more than 500 households and drivers and pedestrians who were out yesterday afternoon. At two o'clock on a Saturday afternoon, many residents of this laid-back Long Island village were out shopping and also at work, or the casualties would have been much higher than 165. Sixty percent of the dead were traffic fatalities, pedestrians run down by berserk drivers or other drivers who perished in the bizarre and gruesome "road-rage-duels."

"We have another atypical Peacetaker strike," he said.

"Yes," she said irritably.

"Any theory as to why?"

"No!"

He turned his head away from her and began to stroke his cheek because his scar was itching to a degree where it was becoming painful.

"I'm sorry, Carter," she said, her tone lifeless and with a tinge of defeat. "I mean, half the time I don't believe I'm chasing after a product of legends, and the other half, I'm worrying about every translation, every interpretation I make...am I being fanciful or intuitive? Did I miss something or am I not able to see the forest for the trees? Until you showed up in Sunburst, I thought Gahiji was a crackpot. An interesting crackpot, but definitely touched."

"How long was your lunch with Gahiji at the Dragonstar?" he asked, not turning around.

"Pretty long, a couple of hours, I think. He wouldn't take a hint that I wanted to go shopping with what little time I had left in Hollywood. He kept ordering coffee and dessert... finally, I grabbed the waiter when he was passing by and slapped my credit card down on his tray and said to settle the bill."

"So you must have talked a lot."

"He talked. I tried to encourage him to eat just to shut him up. Carter, I honestly don't remember anything else than what I've already told you."

"Would it help it we went to the restaurant for lunch?"

"No, Carter. I'm in no mood for food. Let's just fly out of here."

He rose and went to check with Gordon whether in the meantime Saunders had phoned or faxed any information that would give him a lead on a possible target.

"None of the seven Obelisk employees under

surveillance have left the L.A. area in the last forty-eight hours," Gordon said, his eyes going to the headwall where the surveillance map showed the target's current locations. "They were either all at work, where they were supposed to be, or home, once again where they were supposed to be. It's almost as if they had orders to follow their routine without any change whatsoever in the last two days."

They probably did. It meant that whomever Moses had installed as the Peacetaker's controller, was not a direct Obelisk Meridian employee anywhere within his US holdings. Who would Moses trust with this fantastic responsibility? A relative or just a trusted associate? The billionaire knew that any of his family members entering US would raise a red flag with the country's security agencies. Same held true for his executives. Would Moses just throw enough money at someone to do it? Could he have chosen an American?

While Carter tried hard to believe that the country's patriots far outnumbered traitors, his "reality" gene kept reminding him that the American fabric had become a cultural, political and religious mosaic tapestry. Ethnic roots coupled with a Swiss bank account stuffed full of money might easily corrupt a less idealistic citizen.

Just then Gordon's desk phone rang. He picked it up, listened for a few seconds then handed over the handset.

"It's Special Agent Saunders, for you, Mr. Carter," he said.

"What's the matter?" Carter asked. "Is my cell phone not good enough?"

Saunders heard him. "You don't bother answering your cell phone these days. Besides, I wanted to save you air-minutes and money," Saunders said crisply through the handset. "I knew you'd still be there. We've finished checking all B-1 and B-2 visas issued since March of this year. Lot of people came into US on temporary business or tourist visas but all those still in the country check out."

"What about those who left last night from New York?"

"Nothing. We don't even have a ghost or a shadow to chase after."

"Which means he's still in the country," Carter hissed, rubbing the back of his neck because everything in the vicinity of his scar suddenly hurt as if his skin was cracking.

"Who? Carter, you know that I don't ask too many questions when I see results but I'm having problems here with your oblique suggestions that this is all the work of one and the same terrorist. Did you pick up anything useful from the interview with Eunice Samuels?"

"Maybe, I'm not sure yet. You want it to stop, correct?"

"I want to apprehend him and his group!"

"That may not be possible, sir. Would you settle for stopping the terrorist activity?"

"Carter! I said I've never questioned your methods, or your creativity—FedExing me stolen weapons with prototype bullets that set quite a few technicians in our lab hopping from foot to foot—but are you actually suggesting that this sort of thing may be... continuing?"

"The gun was stolen?"

"Yeah, last year a dealer's shipment to a shooting range in upstate New York vanished en-route and is thought to have crossed the border to Canada. That SIRIS is an obsolete model, discontinued. The owner of the shooting range was getting a deal on discontinued weapon lines. The bullets, however, are something else."

Carter closed his eyes, holding back a sigh. So the gun was a dead-end too.

"Carter!"

"Still here, sir. And that reminds me. I'll need a firearm."

"Fine. Get one issued and sign for it. Do you have any information on where the next strike might occur?"

"No, sir." Stella couldn't figure out the reason for lack of consistency in the Peacetaker's effect and there didn't seem to be a pattern in choosing the sites either. And he just couldn't tell Saunders that he was chasing after a product of a 5000-year-old curse that featured only in legends.

"Mr. Moses sent his deepest sympathies to our nation's CEO, right on the heels of the condolences from the Egyptian President and other Middle Eastern dignitaries."

"The Peacetaker and the Peacemaker," he said, knowing Saunders would interpret it as sarcasm.

"What did you say?" He barely heard Saunders' voice it sounded so low.

"Nothing, sir, just frustration, that's all."

"Very odd, but that's more or less what Moses' sympathy message to our President said. ' Those who take peace away from the minds and hearts of American people.' Very odd that you'd summarize it that way."

Carter held away the phone so the agent wouldn't hear his furious snort. That smug son-of-a-bitch Moses was laughing even as he dictated his message….

"Is there anything else, sir?" Carter asked when he composed himself.

"No. I'll let you know if anything new comes from Immigration. Keep in touch. Now put back the agent on duty."

Carter waited while Saunders looked after protocol that would see him carry a gun. He thanked Gordon when the agent simply opened a desk drawer, took out a Glock 22 had him thumbprint a pocket-scanner.

"When you get yours again," Gordon said, "courier this one back here."

"Internal dispatch?" Carter asked, checking the two

magazines and wondering if he should ask for a holster or just stuff the gun in the back of his jeans and pocket the magazines.

"Sure, but FedEx is faster," the agent deadpanned.

"Right," Carter said and resigned himself to walk around with metal pressing into his back. He returned to where he'd left Stella in the conference room. When he opened the door, he saw that she appeared to be lost in thought but unfocused from her inward contemplation when he cleared his throat.

"Did you book our flight yet?" she asked.

"No, I'm going to do it right—"

She didn't let him finish. "Not yet," she said crisply.

"Oh-kay," he said carefully. "Where are we going?"

"Berkeley."

"We're going to see Dr. Mansfield after all?"

"No. I forgot something else."

"How long ago were you at Berkeley and what did you forget there?"

"The Hearst Museum of Anthropology."

"You forgot a whole museum?"

"No, just a crocodile mummy stuffed with Greek and Egyptian texts."

"It's a six-hour drive to San Francisco. You can tell me all about it. I'm sure it'll keep me wide awake."

Chapter Sixteen

San Francisco
May 8
Ancient Athens: Thargelia celebrating Apollo

For over an hour, as they headed north along I-5, Stella behaved as if there was a soundproof glass partition separating the driver and passenger seat. Carter couldn't tell whether it was nostalgia or whether she was trying to read between the lines, but she kept leafing through her book, reading passages in a whisper. Now and then, she'd tap the page with her finger while staring fixedly ahead, though there wasn't much to see on the Interstate other than traffic. It wasn't until he passed the exit for Bakersfield that she turned around with such force he thought he'd run over an old tire because the car seemed to bounce.

"There was someone unaffected by the Peacetaker's effect—Eunice Samuels," she said. "According to what her daughter said, the old lady sat on the hill overlooking Cherry Valley Avenue and watched drivers vent their road rage."

"Then it must be her mental affliction," he said.

"Yes, of course. What moon-god would want a feeble-minded worshipper? But if all the healthy worshippers were affected, then all that's left would be the ones like Eunice. Therefore, Sin or Set's revenge against Thoth was further layered—Set's curse would strike only healthy minds. And I think this would also apply to hospitals. Those already sick or disabled would be exempt from feeling the effect—the same principle would apply."

"This is very fascinating, Stella, but how can it help us in tracking down the Peacetaker?"

"Well, it eliminates quite a few places where he will *not* strike—mental asylums, hospitals, rehab centers and nursing homes."

"That leaves all the parades, festivals, fairs, assemblies, airports and transit system—"

She interrupted him. "Not the transit system. He wouldn't be able to get out of the chaos he caused. He'd perish with the rest of the commuters."

He sighed. "Yeah, I keep forgetting that he's a normal, mortal young man."

"He's as much a victim, Carter, as all those who perish under his effect," she said, voice hardening.

He knew what her campaign was about—charity and good will toward the one who took precisely those qualities away in others.

"Do you have any idea where he might strike next?" he asked to change the direction of the conversation.

"That's something else I'm mulling over. Why Long Island? Washington is almost self-explanatory. He killed a great many people practically on the White House lawn, but Long Island... Garden City? Why? What's there to wound?"

"People," he said.

"Then he should have made a cameo appearance in Manhattan," she said.

"Well, like you said, he wants a place that gives him a quick and easy exit. Can you see him getting out of Manhattan quickly enough, and I don't mean just street crowds but traffic."

"A crowded stadium during a game would be actually an ideal place for him to strike next," she speculated.

"Stella, if you think the FBI should issue a warning directive to people to abstain from attending games, then I'm afraid you don't have your finger on the pulse of an American sports fan. I'm not sure if a direct nuclear threat would be sufficient to discourage people from catching their home team on their turf whenever they can. Besides, he did a stadium in Cairo."

"You think he's calibrating sites? Carter, that's insane."

"Well, we now have three atypical Peacetaker strikes. You're telling me that according to legends, his effect should be consistent, but we have yet to see what your legends tell us we should expect, a ripple-effect with about a hundred-foot radius."

"Maybe his controller is not all that knowledgeable," she mumbled.

"What does he have to be knowledgeable about? You said all it takes to activate the Peacetaker is an amulet—like a switch, on and off."

"Yes, I can't explain the inconsistency. It's as if… as if…" Her voice trailed off.

"What? Finish it."

"Well, as if he had no control, but what's there to control? The Peacetaker doesn't control anything. The effect is a property of what he was born to do. That's all there is to it."

"Are we going to Berkeley to cross-reference more legends?" he asked.

She sighed so loudly that he took his eyes off the road for a second, looking at her. Finally, after another sigh, she said, "Not really. We're going to take a look at legends that I wasn't allowed to examine when I was doing research for my book."

"Your book came out almost four years ago. Weren't you still happily married back then?" He thought it was her husband who'd blocked her pursuit when he decided that he didn't want to grow old with her.

"Were *you* ever happily married?" she asked peevishly.

"I thought I was," he said softly after a few moments.

"Ah! You thought you were but your wife thought

otherwise. Since the communication between the two of you was probably a hell of a lot less than your business communication, you never found out what she thought."

"I wasn't home a lot. That part of my job's...well, it's what I do. But when I *was* home, no one else existed for me but my family. I thought she knew that, saw it. I guess I was wrong."

"How many members were there in your family?"

He chuckled softly. "You mean how many children do I have?"

"Yeah."

"Two daughters. The oldest one would have been eighteen this year and the younger one is now sixteen. She lives with her mother."

"Would have been?"

She was a quick analyst of diction. "She died two years ago of a heart attack."

"At sixteen!" He had heard the shocked exclamation often enough whenever he had to answer these kinds of questions. In that aspect, her reaction was just like everyone else's.

"She was obsessed with being thin and took drugs—over the counter, or ordered on the Net. She also smoked, drank and did other recreational drugs, like many of her peers and friends. She was petite, almost frail. She collapsed in a nightclub. The police took three days to contact Barbara, my wife...ex-wife, because Emily carried only forged IDs in order to get inside the club. And when she collapsed, her friends abandoned her. By the time Barbara made it to the hospital, our daughter was in the morgue. I was in South America, getting ready to come home. I arrived just in time to go to the morgue to identify Emily's body. Barbara was already there, talking with a grief counselor. I didn't see her again until Emily's funeral."

"I'm sorry, Carter. I don't know and don't want to

know what it feels like to lose a child. I'm sorry for your loss," she said.

Until he saw an exit for highway 46 West flash by, there was no sound in the car other than the steady hum of the tires on the road.

When he saw a sign announcing that they were leaving Kern's County and passing into Kings, he said, "I'm going to gas up at the next service station. It's your chance to stretch your legs, take a washroom break."

He felt more than saw her glance at the gas gauge. The needle sat at the halfway mark. She might think the break was for him rather than her. That was fine with him. But ever since they passed Santa Clarita, he thought they were being followed. Some drivers liked to sit on your tail if you were going above the speed limit, figuring that if a cop sat ahead, he'd nab the frontline speedster, and they'd have a chance to slow down. For a while he thought that was the case, but then he slowed down and pulled into the right-hand lane where there was no reason for anyone to follow him. The dark sedan slowed down as well and never showed any ambition to pull ahead of him

Well, let's see if the situation changes when we take a breather, he thought, craning his neck to read the distance to the next service station.

***

He got back on the Interstate and for five minutes he didn't see any cars that were *not* anxious to pass him. Then the dark sedan appeared behind him, still distant in his rearview mirror.

"When would you like to stop for late lunch?" he asked her, nodding at the dashboard clock that showed it was already one o'clock in the afternoon.

"Oh, give it another fifty miles so we're at least halfway there."

Five minutes later, when a large sign advertising the next major service center came into view, he said, "There,

176

the next fast food court is sixty-two miles." The sign advertised the ubiquitous companion of every global highway, McDonald's, and a couple of other food court style eateries.

She murmured that was fine then once again opened her book and resumed her mumbling study.

He afforded her ten minutes of peace then said, "If you thought you were still happily married when researching your book, why didn't Berkeley extend you the academic courtesy and let you study whatever it is they have that interest you?"

Not taking her eyes off her book, she replied, "Because I slugged the museum curator when she came to the east coast for a conference."

He worked his mouth to stifle laughter and when he felt reasonably composed he asked, "A difference of academic opinions?"

"A loss of temper and a momentary lapse of good judgment," she said.

"What did the man do to make you so angry?"

"She—Dr. Abigail McEwen."

"Correct me if I'm wrong, but didn't you say that traditionally, in the course of history and legends, women played the part of the Peacemaker, not Peacetaker?"

"I study legends. I don't live them."

"Really? What about the night spent at the Beverly Hills Hotel?"

He saw her hang her head and after a moment she burst out laughing. "I just wanted to do something totally impulsive, totally out of character," she said, still shaking with laughter.

He thought it was very much in character, considering that her "bird-of-paradise" house in Sunburst was a decorator's dream.

"So what did Dr. McEwen do to make you angry enough to slug her?"

"She slept with Bruce, in a hotel room two blocks over from where I was giving a lecture. Now can you see why that would make me angry enough to slug the bitch?"

"Definitely," he said, keeping poker face. "What was then the lapse of judgment?"

"I slugged her at a dinner reception in front of 350 academic colleagues."

His estimate of the situation would have been that it was a catastrophe, not a mere lapse of judgment, but this wasn't time to nitpick.

"Was Dr. McEwen unpleasantly surprised?"

"I imagine so, since inside my balled fist I held my car keys. I really didn't get a chance to explore her sentiments because the paramedics quickly carried away her limp figure, and I didn't see her again until I was in L.A., attending the Wasserdown Conference."

"Were you civil to each other at that conference?"

"More or less."

He was tempted to ask her what she meant by that and decided that maybe he too should do something totally out of character—graciously gloss over it. Still he couldn't help but murmur, "And we're heading to visit this... embattled museum curator?"

"She's not embattled anymore. Bruce dumped her too."

"Ah," he breathed out, finally understanding. "The two of you are finally and absolutely equal so there's no reason for continued animosity."

"Equal?" She snorted. "Hell, no! My PhD's much bigger than hers."

An hour later, when the service station sign came into view, he was still now and then shaking with laughter.

***

Stella wanted to eat inside at some food court buffet but McDonald's had windows.

"Go get your salad and join me in there." He

motioned at the row of window booths. She launched into another lecture, about good eating habits this time, but he wouldn't yield. He let her think he was a fast-foot addict and, after he bought his McMeal, he went to sit down where he could keep an eye on their Grand Prix. The parking lot wasn't crowded, but there were enough sedans for him not to be able to settle on any car as the one that was following them.

She was still in a studious mood and brought some local tabloid-style newspaper to read while she ate.

"I don't think he's going to strike next at some local fair," he remarked when she started running her finger down the advertisement page.

"There has to be a reason why he struck in New York as his second target after Washington," she mumbled.

"Major cities," he said. "That's where you get most press coverage as well."

"No, no," she kept mumbling. "It has to be something...something mundane and practical."

"Why can't it be just a matter of opportunity? Terrorists strike wherever and whenever they can," he said.

"I don't think opportunity plays a part in this, Carter. You're the expert on Nicola Moses. Is he the kind of man who'd leave something as hugely important as a new form of terrorism against our people to mere opportunity? The man's a businessman, above all else. Businessmen plan—everything. But you're a businessman too, so you should know this," she said, finally looking up at him.

He felt she was grasping at straws but didn't want to be rude and tell her plainly that while he couldn't deny the events in Cairo, Washington and Long Island, he kept struggling with the "cause" as documented throughout her legends.

"Businessmen also take opportunities when they see them," he said.

"Not Moses. These events were carefully planned using whatever opportunities he saw or came into his possession once Gahiji contacted him. Gahiji's dead, so someone else is controlling the Peacetaker, and they're following a plan that's so natural, so innocuous, that I just can't put my finger on it. Something concrete links Washington and Long Island, such that the controller was able to be at either place because he was *supposed* to be there. He didn't just choose the sites randomly. I'd bet anything the sites were chosen by Moses, based on the resources and information he had when Gahiji sold him the Peacetaker."

"Why?" he asked because he just didn't see any rigidly or even loosely planned scenario.

"Because the Peacetaker and his controller are in our country legally," she said, pushing up her brows at him.

"Are you suggesting these two are here on a business trip, on a valid B-1 visa?" Saunders already told him that all the business and tourist visas checked out.

She moaned and grabbed her head, forgetting that she held a fork.

"Ouch!" She glared at the plastic utensil then threw it down on the plate. "I'm trying to find a pattern here, Carter, because if I could latch on to it then it might provide us with much-needed clues to the identity of the controller and thus his tool."

He had already entertained an idea that the controller may be an expatriate American and told her, just to see what she thought of the idea.

"Would Moses trust an expatriate American to carry out acts of terrorism against American people?" she challenged him.

"He might, if he believes that everyone has a price and can be bought."

"Well, in your line of work you've probably seen only the worst of human nature. You might be right." She surprised him by giving some credit to his idea. He didn't think she'd even consider it because she was fixated on ancient legends and that was one thing American people didn't have—ancient history. At least not collectively as a nation.

"But that still leaves the Peacetaker's entry into our country legally a mystery," he said because that was perhaps the main reason why his own theory bothered him. An expatriate American, whether he was a businessman or not, might return home and it would be hell trying to track down such a man because thousands of Americans returned home every day on just as many flights across the country. It might be worthwhile to ask Saunders to check along these lines for anyone coming from the Middle East but that might only tie up a great number of FBI staff across the country. The controller could have come home from anywhere in the world. Heck, Moses could have flown his Peacetaker to Paris and "connected" him there to his controller.

"It's something…something that's been nagging me in the back of my mind," she mumbled, "but I just can't seem to put my finger on it. These strikes are planned. The plan fits in with who the controller is as much as what he does—legally in our country. The Peacetaker is…he is…" She stared at him, grimacing with frustration. "I have no idea what or who the Peacetaker is or how he's connected with his controller. Both of them are legally in our country, functioning such that no one has any reason to attach any suspicion to them."

"Maybe seeing Dr. McEwen will bring on a sudden flash of inspiration," he quipped and lowered his head so she'd not be able to see his smirk.

"She's a bitch," she said, sounding less venomous than her sentiments.

"Yes, you've told me that."

"But I wouldn't mind getting a job at UC, or even at

the Hearst Museum. I wonder if she'd give me a recommendation?"

Academics were a breed apart from the rest of the world's populations. Just then, he caught a movement in the parking lot and turned his head. A bus had pulled in for a rest stop and opened its doors, letting out passengers. He knew the bus would go park in the area reserved for commercial vehicles but while it stopped to let out the people, it was obscuring his view of their car.

"We should be going," he said, motioning at her half-eaten salad. "Take it with you."

She cored him with a harsh look, rose and said she was going to get coffee. He packed up the salad for her, took his tray to the disposal area and headed for the door just as the bus passengers arrived as an anxious crowd that wanted to gain entry through the narrow entrance all that once. For what seemed like eternity he had to hold the door open for the elderly church crowd, as was only too obvious from every set of hands he saw clutching a Bible, and when the exit was finally free he bolted outside. He knew it was only a matter of five minutes, but he didn't like to lose sight of their car.

"Are you all right?" she asked when she got in at the entrance since he pulled up to wait for her. She'd bought two coffees and for once her hospitality was much appreciated.

"Yeah, I'm fine," he mumbled, peeling back the lid portion and taking a sip.

"So, you just needed the exercise, and that's why you ran toward that bus? For a moment, I thought you were leaving me behind, aiming to take the bus," she said, also taking a sip of her coffee.

"Don't worry. In all my years, doing whatever I do, I have never left a traveling companion behind," he assured her.

She didn't need to know that he seldom, if ever, had

travel companions.

Chapter Seventeen

San Francisco
May 9
The Akhet eye pleases Ra

O nce again, Carter spotted the dark sedan five minutes after they left the food and service stop. It was just after three o'clock in the afternoon. Traffic on the Interstate was light.

All right, you don't want to pass. Let's see if you have the guts to keep up with me.

"Carter?" Stella used her "cautious" tone of voice when the speedometer moved past seventy.

"Uhm."

"I think I saw a speed limit sign back there and though it flashed by so fast the numbers were a blur, I think it said 55 mph. Of course, I wouldn't presume that your foot on the gas pedal has fallen asleep, but what if it did?"

"My foot's awake, the rest of me likewise."

"So you're just showing off your driving skill for me?"

"Nope."

"Was it the burger or whatever it is they serve under those golden arches?"

"Do you have a pen and paper handy?"

He heard her rummaging in her purse and when she gave a victorious squeal, he knew she found them.

"Ready and waiting," she announced.

"Just keep them handy."

"For what? Are you going to dictate to me your last will and testament?"

He couldn't afford to laugh because the speedometer was now heading for ninety, though the Grand Prix sat fairly solid on the road.

"You know, Carter, they do have speed-traps on this

highway," she said, using her ruminant tone of voice.

He hoped the nearest one was not too far ahead. The dark sedan showed guts, keeping up with him but just enough so it wouldn't lose him.

She glanced in the rearview mirror and started a countdown. "Five, four, three, two…one," she finished just as the sound of the siren erupted behind him.

He knew the routine, having used it once or twice in the last couple of years and braked hard. He slowed down sufficiently to be able to safely pull over and roll to a stop on the gravel shoulder.

"Keep that pen and paper ready," he warned her. He had to get out of the car even though it would be perceived as an act of aggression by the cop in the police cruiser that came to a halt about twenty feet behind him. He had to risk it because he needed to see the sedan's plates – clearly. The moment the cop's siren sounded the rest of the highway traffic behind him would slow down because it was a universal driver-reaction to police presence. The police officer was still ten feet away when the dark sedan passed by, doing the speed limit. Carter committed the car's license plate to memory and, leaning against the Grand Prix, he rapped on the window.

When she leaned over and opened it, he said, "Write this down, quickly," and then dictated the license plate.

"Sir, may I see your driver's license and ownership registration?" The cop wasted no time and launched right into protocol.

Ten minutes later, Carter climbed back in the car and passed the speeding ticket to Stella.

"We're out-of-towners, and because we don't have enough cash on us, he's giving us a break. The police station is five miles down the road. He expects us to reach it, doing the speed limit, in a few minutes, pay our fine, listen to a lecture and then we're on our way again."

"If this is a break from protocol, what's the usual…protocol?" she asked.

"It depends."

"On what? Aren't the road laws pretty much the same across our country?"

"You would think so. The end result is the same— you've got to pay the fine, but the means can be a little different. If you're driving a rental or your plates are out-of-state, you might be asked to pay cash on the spot. Cops tend to be very skeptical about promises to mail in a fine when you're back home, a thousand miles away. If you're short of cash the local law may give you a ride in the cruiser, behind the steel wire cage, to the police station where they have electronic means to make a payment. By then they'd have towed your car to the impound and you'll have to find your own means how to get to the impound and get your car out. Down south, close to the border, you might even spend a day or two in a local jail, just to adjust your perspective, and there are places in Vermont where speeding will not only get you a huge fine but community service and they don't care where you're from – you've got to come back to serve your community service or you'll be a fugitive in your own country. This was a pay-cash-on-the-spot scenario."

***

She kept staring at the speeding ticket as if it was one of her ancient rice paper scrolls. "You don't have five hundred dollars cash on you?"

"I do," he said, "but it's in the bag in the trunk— next to my gun. I also didn't want to waste time having the car towed and then paying the tow truck driver and the impound fee. Can you reach my laptop in the backseat?"

The nearest FBI field office was in San Francisco. He pulled up his address book, scrolled down until he found his "field contact," then asked her to dictate the license plate number to him. He sent the message, coded top priority, and then once again turned to her. "Is there a phone number on that speeding ticket?"

When she gave it to him, he called the police station five miles down the road and reported a stolen car, a blue Chrysler 300C sedan, late model with California license plates.

"The vehicle has been spotted heading north on Interstate-5, passing Train Junction, heading your way. The occupants of the vehicle are wanted in connection with the Washington riot at the Mall. This is Agent Darkwood, San Francisco field office," he quickly dictated Darkwood's phone number, adding that if the police needed to give pursuit, extreme caution should be exercised, and hung up.

"One, two, three," he started the countdown, watching her out of the corner of his eye. "Four... five." No sooner had he finished, then the police car that had remained on the gravel shoulder all this time screeched as it pulled on to the paved road and sped by them.

"Well, aren't we going to follow him?" she asked quietly.

"No."

"We're not going to pay that speeding ticket, are we?"

"It'll get paid, don't worry about that."

"You planned this way back...way back at the McDonald's, didn't you?"

He didn't answer her. He was waiting for a phone call.

"That's very clever, Carter. I didn't see it coming."

Over the year, on various jobs, he'd picked up a "traveling" companion but never one for the length of time he'd already spent with her. And while he did talk to those he took along because they were useful, he never shared his plans with anyone. This wasn't time to break a habit that had roots in security.

"My point is," she said, "that you planned this

meticulously, so why can't you accept that Moses plans so thoroughly that we can't see where the next strike's coming from?"

She did have a point, an excellent one; fortunately his cell phone chimed and saved him from capitulating. It was Darkwood, just as he expected.

He quickly re-confirmed what his message was about, asked him to pass on any information that the car license plate might yield, thanked him and hung up.

***

They rolled past Oakland just after six o'clock, heading for I-80 toward Berkeley. It was too late to visit the museum. On Sunday, it didn't open until noon and closed by five p.m.

"I've never been to San Francisco," Stella mused when the Golden Gate Bridge appeared in the distance. "Do we have to stay in Berkeley?"

Carter didn't reply but checked his mirrors. When he saw his opportunity, he changed lanes and took the ramp west toward the bridge he'd crossed often enough whenever a job took him to San Francisco but never, as far as he could remember, with a traveling companion. A week ago, if the job would have required him to be in San Francisco, he'd have headed straight for Holiday Inn or Grant Plaza or any Best Western — all perfectly good two or three-star hotels. But the Fate that marked his cheek with a rosette-shape scar had brought him to Sunburst, Montana—population 492 on the best of days—and old rules no longer applied.

"The Ritz-Carleton, Mandarin Oriental or Four Seasons," he said, "take your pick."

"They have Four Seasons here?" she exclaimed, delighted at the prospect of tempting Fate again.

"You don't believe in bad luck, do you?" he murmured.

"Oh, I see your point." Her enthusiasm paled. "Well

then, Ritz-Carleton it is."

Mutely he handed her his cell phone.

"A veritable bargain," he quipped when she told him that a double deluxe room at Carleton for one night would set them back mere 350 dollars. "I trust you reserved two?"

"When he was still just a teacher, my soon-to-be ex-husband used to consult for various corporate clients. His per diem fee was 500 dollars plus expenses and that was a long time ago. Surely we deserve to get a decent night's sleep—in safety?"

"Stella, American people are already not getting a decent night's sleep, worrying about their safety," he said, meaning it as a reminder of what her consultancy was about in the first place.

She took it as criticism. "I'm well aware of that, Carter, but if something happens to us, American people are not going to be able to sleep at all."

The Ritz-Carleton bordered financial district and was a 1909 Nob Hill landmark, but he always thought of it as in Chinatown.

"It looks absolutely fantastic," she breathed out when the elaborate hotel façade, with its majestic pillars came into view. "It looks better than Parthenon — before it was damaged by fire during the invasion of Herulians. It has not only the look but the feel of a sacred temple."

"I'm sure they have a replica of a sacrificial altar in the lobby as the ultimate crowd-pleaser. We'll sleep in the safety of our deluxe rooms but we'll eat tonight in Chinatown," he said, pulling under the ornate canopy portal of the historical building.

"You're a Philistine, Carter," she said, snorting and shaking her head.

He didn't know how to take that—as an insult or a compliment—so he didn't react but wondered how many guests drove under the portico in a rental Grand Prix.

***

The next day, Stella reached her no-longer-embattled academic colleague just after breakfast and managed to obtain an appointment for eleven o'clock at the curator's office.

"The museum's closed on Mondays and Tuesdays but she'll come in, just for us," she told him, handing back his cell phone.

Carter wondered whether his portion of psychological training needed a refresher course or whether he had spent his entire life misreading the female of the species. Over the years, he'd slugged many of his fellow men in the course of doing his duty—for his country and for himself—but he always assumed that those he'd left on the floor, cursing and spitting blood, would take a long time to come around to offering him a handshake if they crossed his path again, never mind going to such lengths as to come to work on their day off just to see him.

Half an hour later, when they stood in a small reception area and the young woman sitting behind her circular desk barely lifted her eyes when they entered, then ignored them entirely, he felt better about his grasp of female psychology and Stella's optimism bubble was about to burst.

"I'm Dr. Hunter and this is Mr. Carter. We have an appointment with Dr. McEwen just about now," Stella introduced them, using her official lecturing voice when the young woman refused to lift her head after her brief glance to check who was so rudely intruding into her domain.

"Hello?" Stella rapped hard on the assistant's desk. The sound produced the desired effect. The young woman raised her head, stiffening her back and staring at them with rigid hostility.

"You may wait for Dr. McEwen over there." She indicated with her eyes the Art Deco wood-and-chrome bench near the entrance.

"Isn't she in yet?" Stella asked irritably. She leaned over and picked up the small metal-framed moon-faced clock that stood near the telephone, thrusting it at the woman. "It's eleven o'clock. I spoke with her just an hour ago. She said she'd come in early to accommodate us."

"The museum's closed to the public on Mondays and Tuesdays, and otherwise our business hours are noon to four p.m.," the assistant said, her nostrils flaring.

"I'm not a tourist and this is not a visit," Stella said harshly. "We're here on business. Now, pick up that phone and tell the bit...your boss that we're here to see her."

"Dr. McEwen will come in at three o'clock. If you wish to wait for her, sit over there. If not...." Her voice trailed off and she shrugged.

Carter stepped up, holding his wallet. He rifled through his business card portfolio until he found what he was looking for, then placed the card in front of the assistant with a crisp snap.

"Just as Dr. Hunter said, we're here on business, and we have made an appointment for eleven o'clock with the curator. And while Dr. Hunter may be inclined to sit and wait hours for her colleague, the Justice Department can't waste time like the members of academia. You obviously knew we were coming, correct?" He waited, staring her down to confess. He knew her boss had phoned her and not only gave her instructions how to treat the "visitors" but also what their business was about. If their arrival were a complete surprise to her, she'd have asked questions. She might even have been alarmed because museum visitors would head for the exhibits, not the third-floor administrative wing.

"Sorry, Special Agent Saunders, I wasn't told—"

He interrupted her. "Special Agent Saunders is my boss, and that's his business card. Now, if you still have doubts about the validity of our appointment, pick up the phone and call his cell phone number. He's always on the other end."

"No, I'm sure that won't be necessary, sir. Dr. McEwen phoned...said she was detained and that you might be coming...I mean that Dr. Hunter was coming. How can I help you?"

"Did your boss tell you our objective?" he continued, allowing his voice to color with irritation.

"She mentioned you were interested in the crocodile mummies that came from the temple of Soknebtunis."

"The crocodile god, Sobek, was the patron god of the town of Tebtunis." Stella walked up to stand beside him. "I'm interested in all the papyri from the town that I understand you have here in storage."

"We have 21,000 fragments but most of the texts are now preserved and stored in the Bancroft Library. We only have a few dozen specialized..." The assistant's voice trailed off, her eyes widening with shock when she realized that they meant to see the fragments – all of them.

"The artifacts that came from the village and the crocodile mummies are on display but I'm interested only in the Egyptian-demotic text papyrus fragments that were found inside them, the ones that are here," Stella said. "I also know that those texts you have kept here are in storage or restorations."

"Yes, quite right, Doctor," the assistant replied, now very business-like. "Carl will take you down to restorations." She pressed a buzzer even as she talked.

Five minutes later, they walked behind the security guard and took the elevator down to the basement. Carl gave them a quick orientation tour of the area where the object of their interest was stored, in linen-lined and moisture-proof aluminum containers.

"The phones are there, there and there," he pointed in three directions at the wall-mounted phones, "but you can use one of these too." He handed Carter a walkie-talkie radio. "When you finish, or if you need something, just call and one of the security staff will either come and get you or bring you whatever you need. This is a restricted area and on a Monday, it's closed so no one will come in; that is, no one who's not authorized to be here should be here."

Carl also showed them a small kitchen and washroom, all within the "restricted" area for work staff's convenience.

Carter motioned at the ceiling where in a corner he perceived more than saw a camera. "This area's also monitored, right?"

"From the control room on the main floor," the security guard said, flashing him a brief smile. "That's for our staff's security."

Carter knew it was more likely to monitor the workers in restorations to make sure they didn't misappropriate a valuable article. He smiled and waved at the camera. When he heard a slight scraping sound, he knew the guard on the other end had panned close.

"We just need to look," he told the guard. "And we'll be careful with the artifacts. Dr. Hunter is an expert in this sort of thing."

Ten minutes after the guard left, Carter sat on a stool next to Stella, wearing latex gloves and a cheesecloth facemask. The mask was much welcome because he never liked the smell of antiquity.

"You mean the smell of all things dead," she said, using tweezers to lay the parchment scraps on the linen-lined work area under the high-intensity lamp.

"Musty smell of root cellars and garbage bins," he said, because to him the smell of blood represented smell of all things dead. The sickly miasma associated with rotting corpses stood in a category of its own.

"Well, you're right about that," she said, pointing at the half-dozen brownish fragments lying on the linen. "Because all these papyrus documents were essentially used as scrap paper, garbage, to stuff the mummified crocodile."

"You mean we're going through someone's 5000-year-old garbage?"

"Only 2000 years old. These come from the Ptolemaic and Roman times. That's about three centuries before the birth of Christ and three or four centuries after."

He felt she was quibbling over details in terms of human life span. But it was interesting to note that this "detecting" practice of examining someone's garbage survived to modern times.

"Did they really find 21,000 of these?" He carefully poked one of the earth-colored fragments covered with faded brownish script that even he recognized were no longer hieroglyphics. No sooner had he asked then he regretted it because he forgot that where history was concerned, any question, no matter how banal or innocuous, would result in a lecture—and his eyelids would start to close like a malfunctioning drawbridge.

Sure enough, Stella explained that around 300 BC the town of Tebtunis stood where today there was a modern town of Tell Umm el-Breigat. In 1900, Phoebe Hearst hired two British papyrologists to carry the excavations at the site.

"They found human and crocodile mummies, stuffed with thousands and thousands of scraps of these documents," she said, uncharacteristically cutting her lecture short.

"These aren't hieroglyphics. Is that a problem for you? What script is it? What's written on them?" He braved few more questions since her lecture was so brief.

She straightened up, put down her magnifying glass, and he knew he was in for another lecture. This one, however, kept him awake—and thinking—maybe because it dealt with language, since improving his means of communication, according to his ex-wife, was what he required foremost in order to better himself as a human being.

Demotic was known as the popular script, after Greek *demotikos,* which literally meant popular. It was developed from a northern variant of the Hieratic script around 660 BC. It was the language of legal and business documents and preferred script at court.

"It was used for writing business, legal, scientific, literary and religious documents. You read it from right to left, in horizontal lines." She moved her finger across the parchment. "They used ink and wrote on papyrus but Demotic inscriptions have been found on wood and stone. In Ptolemaic times, Demotic was generally carved in stone. You've heard of the Rosetta Stone?" she asked, looking at him sideways, waiting.

"Somewhat," he said, not wanting to lie.

"It's a stone inscribed in three texts, Hieroglyphic script, Greek and Demotic. The fact that all three languages, basically saying the same thing, featured in one place made it possible to decipher ancient Egyptian scripts. But around the 4th century AD, Demotic became replaced by the Greek-derived Coptic alphabet and then around the 13th century, it was replaced by Arabic. Back in March, was that your first time in Cairo?"

"I was on a business trip," he said, stifling a groan. "I spent my time there sitting in many reception areas, waiting to meet up with bureaucrats wearing dark suits, white shirts and red ties."

"No cultural visit to Cairo Museum?"

"What do these Demotic texts say?" he asked, not willing to be sidetracked into dangerous territory.

"A Copt served as the Secretary General of United Nations. There are tons of Coptic Christians in Cairo who speak Arabic but use Coptic in their religious ceremonies," she said.

"I wasn't compelled to visit a church either."

"You should have—instead of going to that

stadium. All right. The variety of possible readings from one Demotic sign is far greater than with any hieroglyphic sign. These texts," she once again bend over to study the fragments, guiding her magnifying glass over them, "appear to have been written with a reed brush but later on reed pens were used. It's more difficult to tell from the brush-strokes which consonant…it's like a person's cursive handwriting, messy."

"What *are* you looking for?" he repeated, trying not to sound impatient. The cheesecloth face mask made it hard to talk and its stringy fibers kept sticking to his lips.

She busied herself, picking up the parchment pieces with tweezers and replacing them in the aluminum container, then laying out a fresh new batch.

"Stella, what are we here for?"

"We're here to find fragments of a letter, written by a Lower Egypt temple priest to a colleague in the Fayum region, probably the nearby town of Hawara, thirty miles north of Tebtunis, in which he gives the tale of twin boys born on the night of the Blue Moon, who both tested as Peacetakers."

"Twins!" The mere idea of two such cursed human beings walking amongst mankind, devouring peace and leaving a trail of howling madmen made his breath stuck in his throat. "You don't think we have two such individuals in—"

She reached over and patted his knee. "Relax, Carter. I don't think modern humanity is doubly damned. I'm pretty sure we're dealing with only one such phenomenon, here and now."

Phenomenon would not have been his choice of name for a demon in human form, but he didn't want to lose his train of thought.

"I read your book just as I said, cover to cover. You never mentioned anything about twins."

"Because the bitch wouldn't let me take a look at

these texts. Malcolm Yarbrough, a papyrologist from London, told me about them and where they came from. He worked on contract for UC, translating some 2000 Greek texts and said that while he found only a reference to the twin Peacetakers, dating to around 200 AD, the older Demotic texts, dating from about 180 BC, were much more detailed. My grasp of Demotic is about as thin as this cheesecloth mask, but I knew that if I get a look at these fragments, I'd be able to muddle my way through it. Besides," she frowned at him, "there's no time to contract a translation expert. Malcolm said it was a chain letter—"

He interrupted. "A chain letter—the ancients already practiced this abominable form of spam, on papyrus?"

"The chain letter method of propagating information became corrupted into the hideous practice we now have only by the modern man. Back in old Egypt, it was a practical means to disseminate important information. The temple priest wrote the letter and sent it by camel courier to his colleague in Hawara with post-script instructions to keep passing it on until everyone learned this terrible news. They didn't have faxes, cell phones or real-time satellite imagery, but that didn't mean they weren't resourceful and strangers to teamwork," she snapped.

He spent what seemed like hours, sitting beside her, trying not to think about the doomsday scenarios that would play out in real-time if indeed two Peacetakers now walked the globe.

"Ah, I think I'm in the batch that belongs to the letter," she exclaimed when she started working on texts from a new aluminum storage box. "This is a horoscope, the twins' horoscope cast at the time of their birth, the night of the Blue Moon. Pity they couldn't just spell out the actual date and time. I'm so much more comfortable with ideograms than alphabet script."

Five minutes later, she assembled a dozen fragments and started humming as she guided her loupe over them.

"He who walks over his own footsteps," she murmured, "shall kill twice as many and no army shall stop his advent. He needs but air to breathe and ground to support his feet because his weapon is the curse of gods. This is it," she sighed and tilted her head back. He knew that underneath her cheesecloth mask she was smiling.

When she pieced it together, she pre-empted his skepticism by apologizing for her feeble translating skill and then gave him an abridged version of the tale that featured in the temple priest's letter.

Mneris, the keeper of the eternal light on the altar of God Sobek, was summoned by one of the local lords to witness what he believed was a crop-blessing ceremony. Instead, he found himself a witness to another ritual—a test of the four-year-old twin boys, born on the night of the Blue Moon, that would confirm their Peacetaker powers. The lord wanted an educated witness to confirm what he'd suspected since the twins' birth, but that didn't mean he planned to let him live post-witnessing the event. He had Mneris ambushed and stabbed as the priest walked to his temple. But Sobek intervened and nudged the blade that sought to pierce his devoted servant's heart such that the wound, while mortal, allowed Mneris to live long enough to reach Naremset, his trusted protégé, and tell him about the terrible twin-power that the lord was grooming until it could be unleashed and vanquish his enemies. The children were called Ir-Ra and A-Ra, meaning radiating and pure, respectively, but would be properly named when they came of age and settled their powers.

"They would be activated with an amulet carved in a likeness of Antaios, a double god," she said, "and though the symbol of the two falcons would be made of gold, one bird's eyes would be black onyx, the other's blank. The elder twin would walk first, with his younger brother following in his footsteps, ten paces apart. It was judged to be an ideal distance for the effect not to overlap but rather reinforce such that it would spread over two villages...and we're back to the Nok tribal village scenario covering three or four acres," she finished, clasping her hands and resting her forehead against them.

"I gather we're back to square one," he said cautiously in case she became angry.

"Two Peacetakers were expected to wipe out two villages at once. Considering that the neighboring village would be just down the road, we're nowhere near the Mall effect, not even the Long Island effect. And no one talks about inconsistency. That's what's so damn strange!" She smacked her fist down on the table, setting the reddish pieces dancing on the white linen background. For a moment, they looked alive to him, as if her anger indeed had the power to energize them.

Briefly, he wondered whether she hadn't come here simply because five years ago she wasn't allowed to study these ancient texts and now that she had an opportunity and knew his authority would let her see them, she grabbed it out of pure academic curiosity.

'No!" she said vehemently, as if she read his thoughts. "I really expected to find at least one reference to erratic application of the power, even a mention of a random strike, but there's nothing anywhere that would explain what's happening in our country."

He wasn't bothered by the Peacetaker's erratic performance as much as he was by the fact that he had no means to even guess where he might strike next because "next" was part of Moses's meticulously worked out plan, just as she said earlier.

"I know you think that because I'm a scientist, I'm obsessed trying to explain deviations occurring here and now in an experiment that has been performed many times throughout history with great consistency," she said. He began to wonder whether she indeed didn't have marginal psychic powers and was able to catch fragments of his thoughts.

"Are you?"

"It bothers me, bothers me a lot, Carter, but there's nothing obsessive about my worry. I feel that if I could explain why his power performs differently in our times, I'll be able to give you some direction what kind of man to look for."

He must have looked skeptical because she rose and took a couple of steps backward, facing him.

"Do you have a gun that you've owned for a long time and have... used, fired many times, always with the expected, dependable results?"

He had an arsenal of such weapons back home in Arlington, so he just nodded.

"So how would you feel if one day this gun mis-performed?"

"What do you mean?"

"Didn't fire, or fired when you know you haven't squeezed the trigger."

"I'd have it serviced."

She grimaced. "Right. You're a practical man. So let's say you have it serviced and it works fine, once or twice, then misfires or even fires such that it injures your hand."

"I'd scrap it and get a new weapon."

She smiled. "Naturally, you're also a logical man. But what if the fate of humanity depended on you continuing firing that gun? Wouldn't you tense up just a little each time you knew you had to squeeze the trigger and stave off whatever enemy wanted to vanquish humanity? Wouldn't you regret, each time you had to fit your finger behind the trigger that you didn't pursue the gun's 'faults' until you unraveled the mystery?"

She was devious in making her point.

"After all," she resumed, "if with your next squeeze of its trigger the gun explodes and takes you out, who's going to continue protecting humanity? We may not know where his next strike's going to happen, but we should at least have an idea how *far* away we need to be not to become its victims."

Chapter Eighteen

San Francisco
May 9
Going forth of Nit along the river

Carter called the security desk and the guard came to get them, collected his walkie-talkie and ushered them outside.

"Don't you even want to pay your colleague, the curator, a brief courtesy visit?" Carter asked as they walked across the parking lot, heading for their car.

"I'll send her a thank-you note," she said snappily.

"She did let you take a look at those texts," he said.

"Only because of your FBI authority. I should have known the bitch was laughing at me when she said she'd make an exception, just for me, and come in early for an appointment," she grumbled.

Just then he heard someone shouting her name and turned around. A kid was running toward them, waving one hand while holding what looked like a stack of books under his arm.

"Dr. Hunter, Dr. Hunter!" The student skidded to a halt on the wet asphalt since it must have rained while they were inside. "Dr. McEwen sent me to ask you if you would be kind enough to autograph these copies of your book. It's for our library," he explained haltingly, still catching his breath. He dumped the books on top of the nearest car trunk and fished out a pen from a pocket of his jeans.

"Come on, be gracious," Carter said because she was glaring at the kid. "It's only four books and it's for the library."

"Yeah, well, give me that," she grumbled but took the pen the kid offered and set to work, autographing the copies of her book. She tried to put the pen down but it seemed to have stuck to her fingers. Finally, she shook her hand and it fell down on the open book. She closed it with a snap, trapping the pen inside and thrust the book at the kid, "There. Tell Dr. McEwen that I appreciate her academic generosity, and I'll be sure to mention her in my biography."

"Sure, thanks," the kid said, gathering the books and rushing back to the museum.

"We're not flying out today, are we?" she asked, when he pulled out of the parking lot.

"It's after four o'clock. I doubt we'd be able to get a flight out, which is just as well because we need to stop by the field office. I need to find out if Darkwood got anything on that license plate. Here." He handed her his cell phone. "Call the Ritz and tell them they'll have the pleasure of our company for one more night."

She told him to drop it in her lap and started licking her fingers.

"What are you doing?"

"That kid must have a ton of candy or chewing gum in his pocket. His pen was all sticky. My fingers are practically glued together."

"Use a moist tissue. There should be some in the glove compartment. Car rental companies put them in a kit," he advised.

"Real gooey," she kept muttering, and continued to moisten her fingers with the tip of her tongue, wiping them into a tissue she found in her purse.

The San Francisco FBI field office was on Golden Gate Avenue. They'd make it in twenty minutes, half an hour tops. It was only four o'clock but it was also Monday and considering what was happening in their country, the FBI staff most likely hadn't been home all weekend. Would Darkwood have gone home?

"Stella, if you've finished using the phone…Stella!" He didn't bother checking his mirrors but yanked the wheel to the right and braked hard until the car came to a stop.

She was leaning forward, hands clutching her throat, mouth open as if trying to speak. Except her eyes were already rolling back in her head as she fought what looked like an acute asthma attack.

"Epi… epi…" She choked off the rest, wheezing and gasping for air. "Epi… nephrine."

"Epinephrine… where is it?" He climbed over the console, grabbing her shoulders and trying to hold her upright.

"Pur—" The rest was cut off by such a wheezing gasp for air he knew he didn't have time for more questions. He grabbed her purse, turned it upside down and shook it empty into her lap. The yellow plastic tube fell out. He cracked it open, shuffled backward then pushed her against the window so he'd be able to give her the needle in the hip or at least some place where he wouldn't have to worry about hitting a vein. He yanked out her sweatshirt, pulled down her jeans and jammed the needle into the soft part of her hip. He emptied the epinephrine in controlled manner, all the time conscious of her now limp form. Not letting go of her arm, he felt with his other hand for the cell phone. He found it wedged between her knees, flipped it open and stabbed 911. He had no idea what street he was on but described what he saw out the windshield and the dispatcher told him that the ambulance was on its way and to stay on the phone.

She asked him to describe what he gave her.

"Adrenaline shot, epinephrine."

"She will start to convulse very soon. It will look like a seizure but it's a normal reaction after administering adrenaline…"

***

At the Bates Medical Center, Carter never left Stella's side, not even when the emergency room doctor asked him to give his patient some privacy. He just flipped out an FBI badge that was legally his while working for

Saunders, and said he would turn his back if privacy was an issue but he wasn't leaving Dr. Hunter.

They flushed out the adrenaline, once it did its job and saved her life, and by nine o'clock the doctor said the patient could be safely discharged.

"I'm all right, Carter, I really am," she said, sitting up and balancing herself on the bed with both hands by her side. "I'm tired, so maybe we'll skip that visit to the field office, but otherwise I'm fine."

When the doctor asked him whether he knew what she had ingested, he couldn't think of anything but she was able to push the words out.

"Peanut... allergy... acute... mere contact with products that came in contact with peanuts..."

That's when he remembered that this information figured in her 'bio' that he'd read but obviously didn't attach much weight to this particular entry in the health category. An hour later, when she said she was feeling almost normal, she told him that as recently as a year ago, her peanut allergy was just severe but each attack afterward became more and more acute until it turned into a life-threatening allergy.

"If I as much as touch something coated with peanut oil or that was mixed with peanuts, I'm dead in the water—so to speak. That kid's pen was sticky. He must have had a melted peanut bar in his pocket. I licked my fingers and two minutes later—well, you saw what it's like. I bet you that woman gave the kid a peanut bar, maybe even stuck the pen into it to make real sure... Carter, the bitch tried to kill me."

He thought it was a very remote possibility that her academic rival knew about her peanut allergy, or that she'd be that clever as to use it as a weapon. Academics exchanged business cards, not detailed bio-sheets containing private and personal information. People like him and Nicola Moses did those types of things. He walked some distance away, though still able to keep an eye on her, and called information, then asked to be connected to the curator's home phone number.

"Dr. McEwen didn't send the kid with books for you to autograph," he told her when he finished speaking with the academic, who must have been dealing with her family because in the background he heard a man's voice yelling at the dog to stop barking.

"Sure she did." Stella refused to believe him. Then again, it was probably more satisfying to think that her old rival was still so embattled that she'd go to such lengths to revenge herself on the colleague who slugged her, rather than consider the dismal possibility that a total stranger wanted her dead, for no other reasons than those that featured in her book.

"I'll have Darkwood send an agent over to question Dr. McEwen in more detail, but I believed her when she said she did no such thing. Stella…"

She grabbed his forearm. "I know what you're going to say, but if it's no longer safe for me to tag along with you, where would I be safe?"

"I hate it when you make sense," he mumbled and pulled up a chair.

The irony of the situation was that they certainly couldn't go to the police with their suspicions, and he couldn't even involve the FBI, because it was just like she said a while ago. The two of them were the only people in the country who believed in the Peacetaker legend and knew who was behind the acts of violence at the Mall and Long Island. He'd let Saunders think that he was tracking a new terrorist cell that somehow managed to establish itself in the US, and that Nicola Moses was financing their terrorist activities. Saunders believed that the Cairo incident was the billionaire's retaliation against the Egyptian government for some business hardships. Carter let him think that situation was an example of the age-old tradition of offering your enemy a handshake with one hand while the other holds a knife poised to stab him in the back. Moses kept privately nurturing his Lebanese roots while he faced the rest of the world from behind a wall papered with money. When he shook hands with political dignitaries of any country, it was a business handshake, and politics were part of the scenario only in terms of economics.

Carter had tried to trace that all-assuming phrase that people who gave him information invariably tacked on to their report: 'Moses has political ambitions.' However, no matter how much information he compiled on the billionaire, he couldn't pinpoint the time or occasion when Moses actually expressed the exact same sentiments. He concluded that it was probably a result of some newspaper reporter's speculation, and Moses saw it as something that suited him because he could use it as another screen. After all, if the public believed that a wealthy man had political ambitions, those who sought to chronicle such man's business dealings would not connect him to any criminal activity. Political candidates for any prestigious office could indulge in hypocrisy and under-handedness, but not terrorism. The problem was that Carter couldn't pin down exactly what political office Moses aspired to other than being a puppet-master, the controlling force behind some politician. While today Moses used an Egyptian passport, up until about six years ago, Moses traveled on a British passport and no one in the world would have dared to invalidate it. His father was a British-born Lebanese and even served in the British Desert Patrol in North Africa.

After the war, Moses' father established himself in the country of his forefathers as a restaurateur and vintner. His wine export/import made him a wealthy man, the kind who could afford to send his children to Oxford. In 1968, the newly graduated twenty-two-year-old son of a wealthy Lebanese merchant opened "The Obelisk," his first Levantine-flavor restaurant in London. After that, backed by his father's money and his own success, Moses quickly made inroads with not just restaurants, boutique stores and wineries but also hotels and resorts all over Europe. His three younger sisters eventually joined the 'family' business as they came of age and finished schools.

Then, in the seventies, when Lebanon became established as a haven for terrorist groups, Moses urged his father to liquidate his business interest and perhaps transfer them to Egypt or across the Mediterranean into Greece or Italy. In spite of Palestinians from various factions kidnapping wealthy Lebanese for ransom or killing them outright, the elder Moses accomplished the transfer of his business interests to Egypt and then to Italy without difficulties. He left Lebanon in 1976, just around the time when the Lebanese Ambassador Edward Ghorra was pleading with the UN General Assembly to help his country, ravaged by PLO thugs and brigands. However, in April 1982, Avram Moses was diagnosed with terminal cancer and expressed a desire to "walk the ground that echoed with the footsteps of his forbearers for hundreds of years."

The PLO situation in Lebanon was by no means calmer, but foreign members of the press kept fearlessly visiting Beirut and even ventured further inland, to get eye-witness accounts of the PLO atrocities, so the elder Moses made it a patriarchal wish to visit the land of his forefathers and hold a traditional family-gathering ceremony to pay 'homage' to his country, since he obviously realized he'd never return again.

Some 18,000 PLO terrorists were still camped throughout Lebanon when Avram Moses chose to hold his family function the first week of June of 1982—just when the Israeli Defense Forces attacked in retaliation for the earlier attempt by a terrorist group led by Abu Nidal to assassinate Israel's Ambassador to Great Britain, Shlomo Argov. The PLO responded with a massive artillery and mortar attack on the Israeli population of Galilee. In response, the IDF moved into Lebanon to drive out the terrorists in 'Operation Peace for the Galilee.'

It was never determined whether Avram Moses, his wife Miriam, their three daughters, a daughter-in-law, two sons-in-law and six grandchildren perished in the Israeli gunfire or in the PLO artillery and mortar attack. The bottom line was that in a matter of twenty-four hours, Nicola Moses lost his parents, sisters and his wife and two sons, aged nine and seven. The forty-strong private security force that Moses dispatched to protect his family members perished as well, doing their duty. The thirty-six year-old millionaire survived only because a business deal kept him an extra day in Rome and he was waiting for his corporate jet to come back from delivering his wife and children to the family celebration and pick him up at the Fiumicino Airport.

Moses allowed himself only one public criticism of the event that robbed him of his family. Two weeks later, when the former US Secretary of State, Henry Kissinger, defended the Israeli operation by saying: "*No sovereign state can tolerate indefinitely the buildup along its borders of a military force dedicated to its destruction and implementing its objectives by periodic shellings and raids,*" he gave an interview to a Washington Post reporter, bitterly accusing the US of standing shoulder to shoulder with murderers of women, children and innocent civilians.

Carter had found the microfiched newspaper clipping in the Washington library archives, after searching for months and months for any evidence that Moses, at one time or another, harbored something less than warm feelings toward the USA. He thought that Moses' sentiments, at the time, might have been a product of grief, because that's the first thing people struck by tragedy sought to do — find someone to lay their blame on, as if that would ease their sorrow. Surely, Moses, an Oxford-educated businessman, would have realized that it was the PLO terrorists who ravaged his country and slaughtered thousands of innocent civilians, while the Israelis were the proverbial 'liberators'?

Over the years, as Carter kept adding to the information database he was building on Moses, what bothered him often enough was the fact that Avram Moses was able to transfer his business interests from his PLO-ravaged country without obvious difficulties. He kept trying to find even a slight reference to the son either "paying" for such favors or being in outright collaboration with the PLO leadership. Moses' hospitality interests elsewhere on the globe prospered no matter what was happening to global economies. Rising interest rates didn't seem to affect his holdings and neither did stock market fluctuations or oil prices. The Iran-Iraq war of 1980 didn't seem to affect his Middle Eastern business interests, and those it did affect caused no hardship ripples down the Obelisk Meridian Corporation. Was Moses' business strategy indeed based on "sleeping with the enemy," whoever that enemy happened to be, in order to safeguard his business ventures?

Saunders believed that Moses' hatred of United States led back to the IDF attack on Lebanon that saw his family perish, but Carter didn't think it was that simple. It had been said that very few wealthy men gained their wealth honestly, and even though Moses started his entrepreneurial career bankrolled by his father's money, he must have run into some bad luck or made bad investments that would see him recoup or minimize his losses with less-than-honorable measures.

Like an honest but desperate businessman who gets in bed with the mob to save himself from bankruptcy, Moses might have grabbed an opportunity to become a financier of various terrorist factions in exchange for protection of his business holdings from the said terrorists.

And there was another, psychological component to this strategy. Rich men, when they amassed so much wealth that ten lifetimes wouldn't be enough to dilute their wealth, tended to grow bored with run-of-the-mill business deals.

Sending his condolences to the US President, and expressing his shock and outrage at the alleged terrorist action in Washington, would be just the kind of 'high-stakes poker game' that would appeal to Moses, knowing full well it was his initiative behind such atrocities. Maybe Moses' political ambitions were to destabilize any and every country he chose with the kind of terrorist activity that no one could trace to its source. Having a tool like the Peacetaker certainly made Moses a member of the same country club that boasted membership of gods who featured only in Stella's legends.

Chapter Nineteen

San Francisco
May 10—12
Day of purification of all things

MAy, like any other month in San Francisco, was a busy tourist season. The Ritz-Carleton reception desk clerk was only too happy to take back one of the rooms when Carter asked if that was possible, since Stella agreed that perhaps tonight he shouldn't leave her side.

"Carter, thank you for all your help today," she said when he settled her in the double bed and went to the seating area where he'd set up his laptop on the coffee table, with a carafe of coffee and a bottle of spring water since he planned to work for a while before retiring.

"You're welcome," he said, not lifting his head.

"You don't like it when people reach out to your…human side, do you?"

"I have a human side?" he murmured, pretending to be occupied by what was happening on the laptop's screen.

"It's buried, but it's there; so is your sense of humor, though that comes out to play more often than your human side."

"I'm willing to listen to your insights on the Peacetaker and where he might strike next, but I'm not going to listen to psychoanalysis," he said.

"Do you ever see your daughter?"

He mis-hit a key and had to delete all the way to the beginning of the message just to gain time. The loud tapping of his finger on the keyboard didn't deter her.

"Well, do you?" she insisted.

His ex-wife remarried quickly enough after their divorce became final and moved with her new husband, a rancher from Texas, to Merickville, just outside of

Houston. Katie went with her and other than her phone call on January 2nd of this year to wish him a Happy New Year, he hadn't talked to her in five months and hadn't seen her in couple of years. He kept telling himself that he didn't want her to see him scarred and was waiting until the doctors could smooth out his cheek, but he knew that was only an excuse.

"She's a teenager, has her own crowd to keep her busy down in Houston," he mumbled.

"Of course," she said in that horribly false tone of voice people used when they wanted to disguise their sarcasm. "Just like Emily. Why don't you call her now, just to see how she's doing? Teenagers like that, even if it looks like they don't."

He stopped typing, grabbed his cell phone and tossed it to her. "Here, you call her, name's Katie Rose-Jean." he quickly dictated the number, "and then you can tell me how much she liked it."

He felt her staring at him but wouldn't raise his head to look at her. He was busy, working and the saving-her-life part of his duty was over.

He heard her clicking the keys and thought she was just goading him. But when she said, "Is this Katie Rose-Jean?" he snapped his head up, staring at her, disbelieving that she'd called his bluff.

"Hi," she said, "you don't know me but my name's Stella Hunter. I'm a teacher of medieval history at University of Michigan, but that's not the issue. I'm calling you because I'm sitting here in a hotel room in the Ritz-Carleton in San Francisco, watching your father work in the sitting area. I'm his business colleague, not his girlfriend, and just a few hours ago he saved my life. Would you like to hear more?"

Half an hour later, she was still chatting with Katie while he kept sneaking looks at her, tightening his lips so as not to laugh as he listened to what even in the FBI circles would have been a thorough debriefing—of both parties. Finally, when she slung her legs over the bedside, he rose and came to get the phone because he knew his daughter wanted to talk to him.

"Yes, Katie, it's the same Dr. Hunter who wrote the book," he said and spent more time than he probably gave her in all her sixteen years, talking to his daughter about legends, museums, hotels and lastly, Hollywood and Beverly Hills. When he hung up, feeling oddly mushy inside, he said, "Tomorrow, we'll have to go shopping, probably in the Union District. She wants a souvenir from San Francisco that she can wear and show off to her friends."

"Perfect," she declared. "I need a few new sweatshirts too."

She settled back in bed, this time climbing under the covers and made an effort to show him that she was going to sleep. Just as she plumped up her cushion for what he hoped was the last time, he said, "Stella, thanks. It was the nicest thing anyone has done for me in a long time."

"Aw, shucks, it was nothing," she drawled. "The kid actually sounded very intelligent and her interest in my academic subject was quite genuine."

He shook with silent laughter, then settled down to deal with his email.

Saunders's update was thorough—and empty of leads. The FBI's linguistic human and electronic experts kept mulling over Eunice Samuels's versions of what she heard the Devil say in the parking lot. And while quite a few words came reasonably close to sounding like "jig/wheel," none of them were revealing in terms of connectivity to the suspected terrorist activity.

Then again, people who spoke their country's language and its many dialects would invariably color it with accent of their region. Statistically, such variety of pronunciation increased the odds of matching up "jig/wheel" to some relevant expression. When it came to deciphering "even Allah," the experts unanimously agreed that since "iben" meant son in Arabic, Eunice probably heard: "Ibn-Allah," which meant "God's Son." And any name coupled with "ibn" would mean that man's son. Would the man who controlled the Peacetaker refer to him as 'God's Son' or even his son? It didn't seem likely.

"No, no," he sat back, mumbling. "I'm looking at it from a wrong angle...or rather, I have to examine it from a different angle." Moses might have been doing it for a batch of the most complex reasons in the world—or simply because he could—but the same motive and motivation didn't have to apply to the controller... and most likely not the Peacetaker either. Stella was right about that. The controller could be a man waging *jihad* or whatever motivated his revenge, and Moses would have selected him precisely because a fanatic was best suited for his purpose. The controller was Moses' mule and the Peacetaker was the proverbial grunt who did all the work.

"It has to be like that," he whispered, but deep down he knew that he wanted it to be this way because it also meant the controller was not an American. He shook his head to banish his inner critic. An American, even an expatriate, would not use an Arabic expression when calling someone; much less call him "Ibn-Allah." Such practice, however, was common in the Moslem culture where traditions and formality went hand-in-hand. An Arab would naturally greet a visitor to his house with the words, "Welcome to my humble home, Ibn-Ahmed," or Ibn-Ali or Ibn-Salekh...

He leaned forward, put his hands on the keys and wrote down the product of his mental analysis. Even if he wouldn't share them yet with Saunders, he had to get his thoughts down such that he could save them. After a while, he sat back because a new thought sought to undermine his conclusion.

How could a Middle Eastern fanatic with a cause gain legal entry into US? Especially in today's jittery atmosphere, all foreigners entering country on a visa would be scrutinized to death. And didn't Saunders say as much already? All the holders of B-1 and B-2 visas currently in the country checked out.

What about those who were in the country on student visas?

No, he shook his head. The controller and the Peacetaker had entered the country no earlier than the last week of April or even the day before the riot at the Mall. The foreign students would be either still writing their exams or have already left the country if finished. Any student entering the country at the end of the academic school year would be rigorously questioned as to his motives for such unconventional practice.

What if Moses chose a student who remained in the country after his semester finished, either doing graduate work or...?

"No good," he sighed and closed his eyes. It was plausible, but then how would Moses have managed to get the Peacetaker into the US—legally? The Peacetaker and his controller had to come into the country together, legally. Who or what could they possibly be?

"Ghosts!" he heard a moan from the bed and opened his eyes to see Stella sitting upright. "Carter, you've been moaning and mumbling for hours now. Give it a rest. There is an incredibly deluxe comfortable double bed right over there." She stabbed her finger at the other bed. "Stretch out, count to ten, count sheep for all I care, but go to sleep."

Five minutes later, he was under the covers, the pillows on either side of him since he preferred to sleep "flat"—one of the enduring legacies of his military career.

**

In the morning, they checked out of the Ritz-

Carleton, and as he drove along Market Street, heading for the FBI field office on Golden Gate Avenue, he saw a café and pulled over. While Stella went to the counter to get their breakfast, he found a table, sat down and called Darkwood.

"Good timing," the agent said. "Have your breakfast, and by the time you come in, our guests from the Chrysler 300 should be here. They've spent a weekend down in Patterson. The local police held them for us in detention until we could bring them up here. That's not to say I've been idle all weekend. Their names are Hamed Amzine and Brahim Amzine, cousins from Rabat."

"Moroccans?" Carter mumbled, though it shouldn't have surprised him if they had been Australian Aborigines. Indeed, Moses had cast his business nets all over the world. Just last year, Moscow celebrated its first opening of yet another crowd-pleaser, catering to the needs of the common man — the Obelisk-Slnechnij, a five-star ultra-deluxe hotel that boasted security that would have made the historical KGB green with envy.

"They're here on a student visa, valid too," Darkwood said. "They're scions to the mercantile and shipping empire of the Amzine family back in Rabat. Both young men are business majors at UC, though their rightful domain is the LA campus. And guess what explanation they gave the Patterson cops for following you on the Interstate?"

"Tell me," Carter said because the agent's tone of voice told him that guessing would be unproductive.

"They're great fans—though not yours."

"Ah," he breathed out, understanding. "They're Dr. Hunter's fans."

"Yeah, this celebrity status is a dangerous thing, my friend. They said they recognized her in LA."

"We were in Santa Monica… and Beverly Hills, but who's quibbling," he murmured.

Darkwood cleared his throat. "Well, if that's the case, their story might even check out. They said they saw her on Pico and Lincoln and tried to follow you there but lost you. Then they picked you up again at the Beverly Hills Hotel and tried to get to see Dr. Hunter, get her to autograph her book for them—by the way, they carried a copy each; now that's being a real fan—but the staff at that hotel are apparently Nazis and wouldn't divulge any information about their distinguished guest, much less allow them to pester her. So being determined and impulsive young men, when they spotted you again the next day leaving the hotel, they took off after you."

He didn't think he'd find too many young college students who'd be determined to spend their weekend hounding an academic for an autograph, but this was California, and what might stretch imagination and credibility back east might well be a norm here.

"Carter?"

"Yeah, still here. They're clever."

"Meaning they gave the Patterson cops the real story, the truth?"

"Yep."

"Very clever. Give the true story that will withstand all scrutiny by the authorities but the motive...ah, that's something else. We can't question their motive since, after all, they confessed to being impulsive. I'll see you when you get here," Darkwood said and hung up.

He debated whether he should tell Stella about her "fans." Would it upset her... frighten her more than she already had to be? Last night in the emergency room he realized that Moses upstaged him when it came to being analytical. He'd picked a detail that Carter missed or glossed over in Stella's background check and used it so cleverly that no one could connect anything to anyone. Unknowingly, Stella came in contact with a substance coated with peanut oil or peanut butter and nearly died of anaphylactic shock. Accidents like that happened all the time, particularly to people with life-threatening allergies. He knew better, and Stella knew too, even if she wouldn't openly admit it, that it was no accident.

Once Moses had connected Stella to Gahiji, Carter knew her life was in danger precisely because he'd meant to eliminate all people who might as much speculate about the Peacetaker's existence. Gahiji lived for three weeks after the "demonstration" of the Peacetaker's power at the Cairo stadium. Were Stella's days also numbered?

"The police picked up the people in the car that followed us on the way up here," he said when she brought coffees and what looked like brunch—a tray full of croissants, bagels with cream cheese and finger-sandwiches.

"Kicking and screaming or refusing to talk?"

"Neither," he said and told her what Darkwood said.

After breakfast, he headed for the field office and reconsidered. Perhaps for once something else—or someone else—should take precedence.

"Did we forget something at the hotel?" she asked, when he made a left turn on to Geary Street.

"Who knows how long we might be at the field office. We're expected whenever we arrive, so I thought we'd attend to some shopping first." He knew she'd be pleased but he didn't expect her to squeal with delight and clap her hands together, like a little kid.

An hour later, he looked like a model husband—both hands full of shopping bags, pockets bulging with gift boxes, and once she even made him hold a bag in his teeth while she "made space" in the other for the purchase. She chose an "attitude" T-shirt for Katie that said on the front: *Obey Me.* When he wondered out loud whether the skimpy article would fit, she rolled her eyes and said that his daughter was size four. He'd listened to their conversation last night and knew that such personal information as height, weight, hair color and tone of make-up were discussed in great detail so he yielded.

"She'd love this too," she said, holding up a white sweatshirt, with the Golden-Gate Bridge logo and *San Francisco* embroidered underneath. Then she chose a black Hilfiger tank top, two more white T-shirts bearing their celebrated designers' logo, what looked like a large silver-pyramid studded wallet but what she said was a "neat purse," and a pair of Versace sunglasses.

"Two hundred dollars for those horn-rimmed glasses?"

He must have raised his voice beyond her tolerance because her nostrils flared and she asked, "How many daughters do you have?"

"But they look like something I used to wear when I was still in high school," he sought to placate her.

"Ever heard of history repeats itself?"

He sighed and blinked in acquiescence.

"What about your sweatshirts?" he asked, wondering whether he shouldn't walk back to the car with the parcels that weighed down his hands better than a rifle.

She made him walk down another half a block before she saw an article that 'called out to her'—in every color of the rainbow.

When the sales clerk rang up her purchases—six sweatshirts that he felt she'd chosen not as much because she liked their color but because she liked the exotic names assigned to each color–Magnolia Blossom, Cerulean Blue and Magenta Red– she started humming a tune from *West Side Story*.

"Your husband is so helpful," the sales clerk said, handing over to him the first shopping bagful of sweatshirts.

"Yes, he's a treasure," Stella said. And when the sales clerk walked away to attend to packing up the rest, she finished softly, "but that's because he's not mine."

"I bet you all women say that—about somebody else's husband," he murmured, glaring at her. She bit her lip but couldn't hold it in and burst out laughing.

Although she declared that their shopping was done, she insisted they cross over to the other side of the street as they made their way back to their car.

"You know, I think this is my first shopping expedition where I've been neatly fitted into the role of a stereotype and didn't even see it coming…Stella?" He became aware that she was no longer walking beside him and turned around. She stood in front of a store window, staring with such rigid attention that she looked transfixed. He walked back to see what had such hypnotic effect that she didn't even react to her name.

It was a bookshop that also sold posters. The books on display were in the lower part of the window and she was staring at something higher—one of the colorful Walt Disney posters.

"A lad in, a lad in," she kept repeating. "That's what Paige Smith kept saying. Aladdin, a Walt Disney cartoon classic." She raised her hand and traced the outline of the cartoon character in the poster, shown sitting on a flying carpet with the young princess beside him. "She wasn't saying "a lad in anything," Carter. She was saying "Aladdin," which makes a hell of more sense because the Mall demonstration was a festival with a fantasy theme. The man she spoke about, the one she talked to, was dressed as Aladdin."

"Yes, that's probably more like it," he agreed, though he couldn't see how that helped their situation.

"He came dressed in a costume," she said.

"Unless it was something he rented from a costume shop, we still don't have anything that we could start checking," he said. But he wondered whether it wasn't a lead, no matter how slight, and whether he should ask Saunders to check all costume rental places in Washington to see if anyone had rented an Aladdin costume a day or two before the festival.

"Maybe, but something else is bothering me. I can't put my finger on it. He came to Washington ready to make an appearance at that demonstration that was really a fantasy festival. Would he have brought an Aladdin costume with him?"

"You said Moses plans every detail."

"Yes, but would he risk something like that? I mean, there's always a chance customs might ask the visitor or a businessman to open his luggage. May is not a festival season and Washington's not New Orleans. A businessman with an Aladdin costume in his suitcase would be well remembered by the customs officers; a tourist likewise. Paige also said something about a sword and magic. So the Aladdin she saw must have had a sword. That's definitely something customs wouldn't have allowed into the country."

"What are you trying to say?"

"He put together his Aladdin costume and most likely got dressed in it—in someone's house, in the Washington area. He's here to visit someone or he's staying with someone...could even be a relative."

Someone visiting a relative—now, that was something worthwhile to pursue. It reduced the number of visas Saunders would have to check by at least fifty percent because only the visitor's visas would have to be checked all over again. And if they eliminated all the "pure" tourists who were visiting without having friends or relatives in the country, the work could be even further reduced.

Since the Aladdin poster "called" to her with such strong voice, he agreed that she should buy it and keep it for further inspiration.

"You must think I'm insane," she murmured when they got back in the car.

"No, Stella. I don't think you're insane," he said,

smiling.

"I mean about buying six sweatshirts in every color of the rainbow."

"I used to have two dozen T-shirts, all the same color," he deadpanned.

"Army green," she said, chuckling.

"Mottled," he said. "Camouflage."

Chapter Twenty

San Francisco
May 10—12
Netjer of the Month Payni: Horus

"We've questioned them apart and together. They're sticking to their story," Darkwood said, leaning against the wall with the one-way observation window. "Now we've left them to mull things over, talk it over between themselves, but they're smart that way too."

Carter knew the two young men, light-skinned but with that crisp-textured black hair that defined their North African ancestry, would have been, if not trained, then at least rigorously coached by those who sought them out for the shadowing job. They might have even done it as a favor to a countryman, or as something they had to do in order to gain advantage for their families back in Morocco. They probably didn't do it for money, since that's one thing they didn't lack. Was there a cause involved? Probably, but he doubted that it would be connected to the Peacetaker. When it came to his "human walking weapon," Carter felt that Moses would be extra secretive and wouldn't want to take too many people into his confidence.

The cousins sat facing each other across the table, their hands clasped and in sight. They didn't even attempt to communicate with looks, merely sat there, heads lowered—silent.

"We're going to have to let them go," Darkwood said in resignation. "We can't even charge them with mischief. It's not a crime to be a fan, at least not to a degree they claim to be. Following someone because they wanted their autograph is...." His voice trailed off.

"Why would two business majors be interested in ancient history, legends and folklore of long-dead civilizations?" Stella sounded preoccupied..

"Where one's heritage is concerned—" Darkwood started.

Stella cut him off. "But they're not Egyptians. Are they Moslems?"

"Actually, no. The Amzine family is Byzantine Christian. We can't connect them to any terrorist group, never mind activity."

"Byzantine Christian," Stella said, stretching the words. Carter stifled a moan because he felt a lecture coming on. However, she surprised him and spoke to Darkwood. "Do you have those two copies of my books these boys carried?"

"Yes, of course. We've examined them and found nothing suspicious."

"Can I have them?"

"Dr. Hunter—" Darkwood started, but once again she cut him off.

"These young men thought it was worthwhile to pursue me for four hundred miles just to get me to autograph a copy of my book. Don't you think they deserve to be rewarded for being such ardent and devoted fans?"

Five minutes later, Carter watched as Stella entered the gray-walled room.

"Ah, so these are my fans," she exclaimed, no doubt for the benefit of the cousins as much as the agent who opened the door for her. She stopped at the head of the table where both men would be able to see her. Whatever they expected to happen next, Carter saw that the appearance of the book's author in the flesh was not even a distant consideration. From the way they stiffened, heads raised, they had to be in shock.

"How do you do? I'm Dr. Stella Hunter and, according to the FBI agent who rudely interrupted my meeting with my colleague, Dr. McEwen, you two went to some extraordinary trouble to get me to sign copies of my book." She put down both books on the table.

"Dr. Hunter," the one Darkwood identified as Hamed jumped up and gave a good performance of a startled fan. "We never... I mean I never... so sorry but when we saw you down in LA, I said to Brahim... gosh, it's great to see you in person."

Carter couldn't remember the last time he heard anyone say "gosh" and tipped his brows at Darkwood, who regarded him back with the same skeptical eye-squint.

Stella pulled up the last chair in the room and sat down to an animated chat with the two business majors. She quizzed them on everything, indeed like a professor interviewing potential graduate school candidates to take on as their supervisor. They were the kind of "hired help" he would have liked to find more often—the type who study their assignment in detail, then bury themselves in the part. When she started asking them questions about her book, they were quick with answers. They'd read it, cover to cover, just like he did, but their understanding of the academic material seemed to be a notch above his.

She'd asked what they wanted her to write as a dedication, wrote it and signed both copies, thanking them for their support and interest in her subject. They never saw it coming.

She rose and offered them a handshake when suddenly she saw something that made her lean toward Brahim. The young man stiffened with surprise.

"Why, that's an Our Lady of Maronite medal," she exclaimed, fingering the gold medallion she'd plucked from under his partly open sport shirt, though it couldn't have been that visible. "You're Byzantine Christians?"

"Ahem, well, yes, of course," Brahim stammered, managing a grimace at his cousin, who looked alarmed.

"It's so nice to see young people upholding religious traditions of their forefathers," Stella gushed, motioning with her other hand to Hamed. "Let me see yours? Is it the same? I teach medieval history, but you know that. Byzantine period is of particular interest to me. Where do you go for services in Los Angeles?"

"Ah…" Hamed looked trapped.

"Oh, no! Don't tell me you're hypocrites who like the look and feel of gold but hold little respect for the religious meaning of this." She gave the gold medallion on Brahim's chain a slight yank. "You *are* observant Byzantine Christians, correct?" She'd brought out what Carter knew had to be her ultra-harsh "discipline" tone of voice.

"Of course, we go every Sunday to Our Lady of Mount Lebanon Maronite Cathedral," Brahim said quickly.

Stella let go of his medal and patted his chest. "Good. Glad to hear that you're not blasphemous. There's a beautiful icon of Our Lady Maronite in the Kidane-Mehret Catholic Church in our capital. And the design of our Lady's Maronite Church down in Austin, Texas, was inspired by the ruins of St. Simon the Stylite, which is in the area that's now known as north Syria. You know the Syriac theology, spirituality and liturgy developed according to biblical themes rather than philosophical thought." She went on, holding both students captive with her voice and lecture as much as their uncertainty what it was about. Carter, however, knew that every word of her lecture was meant for him, and it was the kind once again that kept him not only awake but analyzing even as she talked.

Father Maron was a priest and hermit who walked the land once traveled by Christ's Disciples, Peter and Paul. He converted an old pagan temple that stood on the banks of the Orontes River into a church and spent his life teaching about the faith and tending to people. It was said he had a gift of healing and wise counsel. Later on, nearly a thousand monks followed in his footsteps. They became the early followers of the lifestyle that became known as

227

Maronite. The Maronite Community became established as an organized church in Lebanon, the third geographical center of influence for Maron's family of faith. The Maronite Community consisted of several religious orders of monks and sisters and today Maronites were Catholics of many nations and diverse cultures.

"I'm sure you know that today, the Mother Church is in Lebanon and daughter communities exist in every nation of the world. So, *Beit Maroun*, sons of the house of Maron, do not spent your Saturdays as autograph-hounds so you won't have to spend your Sundays—your day of worship—in jail. But it's good to have fans." She patted Brahim's cheek in a motherly way, repeated her parting gesture with his cousin and walked out of the room.

"I was awake all through your lecture," Carter greeted her with those words when she came back. "What was it all about?"

She walked over to the table and leaned against it, suddenly looking tired and dispirited. "Carter, it's an ugly thing to say, much less to speculate about it, but I think Moses is using his church—churches all over the world, wherever they happen to be—as something else than holy shrines, though I'm sure the clergy wouldn't be a part of his schemes. Just like the special young man, they too would be only his tools."

And when he continued to stare at her, she shook her head. "You do know that Nicola Moses is a Byzantine Christian, a Maronite?"

He knew that Moses was a Christian, and used his religion as another screen. Who would draw a connection between mostly Moslem-terrorist groups and a Christian financier? But Carter didn't know the details of Moses' faith, because it hadn't seemed to matter. Apparently it did.

***

"Sir, it might be worthwhile to check with the Archdiocese of Washington." Carter raised the scrap of paper where Stella wrote for him the name of the church in south Capitol area and read off what sounded like "cheese-write" but what she said was actually a language of the Axumite Kingdom. He continued, "It's a parish for Ethiopian and Eritrean immigrants. Check their affiliations too."

"What would I be checking for, Carter, illegal immigrants, refugees?" Saunders asked impatiently.

"No, sir. Overseas guests who are legally in our country." Carter paused because it was just as she said—an ugly thing to consider, never mind talk about. Saunders must have realized what had stopped the conversation.

"Priests, friars, brothers, monks, missionaries, nuns?"

"Not nuns. But all the rest, yes, I guess, but just as sources of information. "

"Who are we looking for, Carter, and don't give me another diplomatic excuse."

"Two people."

"Male, female?"

"Most likely both male. One would be probably age eighteen to twenty-five, the other is an unknown variable but he too would be male. They would be together, companions, friends, that sort of thing. It could be a student-teacher type of relationship or even relatives; one older, the other younger."

Saunders made a swooshing sound of appreciation. "You've been busy. That's good, because I was just starting to wonder...very well. We'll pay a visit to the south Capitol area, and we'll be very diplomatic. Anything else?"

"The same diplomacy should be employed when you send someone to visit the Maronite church in Bethesda."

There was a moment of silence then Saunders asked, "Is there any particular reason why you're fixated on

Eastern Catholic sects?"

"Religious orders are notoriously charitable. Their members do God's work all over the world. But sometimes even God's servants fall prey to the Devil's schemes."

"Did you have a near-death experience? What the fu...heck are you talking about?"

Carter knew it had to be Stella's influence that lately he tended to use analogies instead of just saying plainly what was on his mind.

"It's just a theory, sir," he said, "but it's possible that Moses might be using his religious affiliation to bring the kind of people into our country that shouldn't be here."

"Sometimes I wonder whether *I* should be here. Carter, what *are* you saying?"

"Members of various religious groups work, sponsored by their own church or in conjunction with other charitable organizations, all over the world. Often such staff will stay for a few years in the field before coming home. Who's to say that the American priest or monk who went to Africa or the Middle East is the same American citizen who returns?"

"You think Moses has smuggled a couple of terrorists into the US as priests returning from abroad?"

"Well, think about this scenario. If Brother John, sponsored by his Washington church, went to Sudan to work at one of the field camps, it wouldn't take long for him to start showing ravages of such an existence. A robust, healthy man left and a lean, cadaverous man comes back — who's going to question him at customs about the lack of resemblance on the passport? He's a cleric who's also a teacher or even a doctor and his life's purpose is helping those less fortunate than him. He's spent five years in a famine-stricken region—get my point?"

"Yes. Now I know what kind of questions we ought to be asking. So whatever holy ground we desecrate with our presence, we're working on a premise that the clergy's not part of this alleged deception, correct?"

"Absolutely." Just then his cell phone whirred, which meant he had a message.

"Keep in touch." Saunders heard the echo of the sound and rang off.

"There's something else, something else that's just not coming to me," Stella said, waving a hand in front of his face.

"You've already helped a lot," Carter told her and raised his finger to show her he was listening to a message. It was from Helen Brighten. He'd left her his Timothy J. Carter business card, which meant she would have gotten his voicemail. Then again, all his business cards, except the one he flicked down in front of Abigail McEwen's assistant, had a phone number that would go into voicemail messaging. And when a message clicked in, his cell phone would let him know. No one, other than his "contract-boss" had means of direct access to his cell phone number. If he called the person back, and they had call-display, it would show them the exact same number they called and left a message. The world of communications was made to deceive.

"What is it, Carter?" she asked him when he lowered the cell phone and kept staring ahead.

"Well, it's here." He quickly tapped into his voicemail and handed her the cell phone. "You listen to it. Actually, I think it's meant for you."

"Odd," she murmured when she finished listening. "I didn't think there was any other source in existence that mentioned the Peacetaker legend. Is it possible that I could have missed something?"

It was possible, but now that he'd gotten to know her, also very unlikely. Helen Brighten said that after they left, she called her ex-husband and chatted with him about the good old days in Berenice and the strange cartouche that Gahiji found on the stone that he stole from the well wall.

Dr. Mansfield mentioned a graduate student, doing his doctorate in cultural anthropology, had just come back from spending six months with an international archeological expedition to Saqqara. Helen managed to contact Jason Barron and he confirmed that he had a portfolio of pictures that he was still working on. They were taken at three of the five rock-cut tombs of priests from the sixth dynasty that served in the mortuary of King Pepi I. The colored reliefs depicting lives of the high officials were well preserved—and so were the three rather unusual cartouches that appeared to be markers or titles of a story that might be found elsewhere in the labyrinthine necropolis. Two side-by-side drawings were actually a mirror image of each other. The third one, Jason thought, contained a title: The Peacetaker.

"Saqqara—that's fifteen miles south of Cairo," Carter said. "The souvenir shops are full of postcards of the newly discovered necropolis stuffed with tons of mummies. But I didn't see any of back-to-back cartouches."

"So you have done some sightseeing when you were there." She flashed him a nasty smile.

"The Egyptian people spent the last hundred years selling key-chain pyramids and talking about Nefertiti, so when something truly new comes out of the ground, the whole country, I suspect, not just Cairo, is flooded with fresh souvenirs," he said, adding "Which part of Dr. Brighten's message struck you as odd?"

"The one about contacting her ex-husband and chatting about good old times in Berenice," she said.

He would have thought it was what she said in closing, that they should go see Jason Barron and could find him on one of the few privately owned digs, in Monticello, Utah, doing excavations of the large pueblo-style Anasazi settlement known as the Montezuma Village.

"You don't think there's a rather large interest gap

between people who lived in North Africa four thousand years ago and those who lived in the canyons of the San Juan River just a few hundred years ago?" he asked.

"The ancient Anasazi lived from around 450 AD to 1350 AD and then vanished," she said, absently tapping a straw against her nose. "And they still haven't found the tombs of the first two kings of the sixth dynasty in Saqqara, so there's a unifying theme if you want, but this graduate student's a cultural anthropologist. He's not an archeologist. He studies drawings and writing of any kind to learn what each society that made them lived like, on a day-to-day basis, then he'd seek to correlate cultural practices between various ancient civilizations to show that people traveled and kept in touch since the dawn of time."

"We're *not* going to Utah," he said, waiting for objections.

She was becoming unpredictable. "I don't think we should, but what we should do, Carter—or rather what you and the FBI should do, is send someone right away to check on Helen Brighten."

"Right," he breathed out, stifling a curse because she was actually starting to think like he used to.

Chapter Twenty-one

Carter asked Darkwood to call the office down in Los
Angeles and arrange for the local police to check on
Helen Brighten.

"They're sending two of our agents right away,"
Darkwood told him when he got off the phone. "If police
assistance is required, they'll call them." Carter thanked
him and went back to Stella.

"I'd like to wait until they check up on her, make
sure she's all right," she said, pre-empting his question.

"There's an American Airlines evening flight, at
6:15, non-stop to New York," he said. "We can spend the
night in New York City and take a morning flight to
Washington. Or we can wait until the morning and take a
10:15 Delta Airlines to Washington with a stopover in
Cincinnati. All the direct flights to Washington are booked
solid for the next three days."

"We can't go back to the Ritz?" she said, looking
crestfallen.

He suppressed a smile. "No, but the Holiday Inn
here is very nice."

She nodded and smiled so briefly it looked like a
grimace. "There's something here, Carter, that just doesn't
feel right."

He looked around the office.

"No, I don't mean right here, in this place. I mean
about the nature of the Peacetaker's effect. Paige Smith
back in Washington said, 'A lad in—Aladdin.' A young
man dressed in Aladdin's costume, which I suppose is
natural since the Mall event was a festival-demonstration
with a fantasy warrior theme. But why dress up in a
costume to begin with? The Peacetaker and his controller
just had to make a brief appearance to unleash the effect…
or did they?"

"What's really bothering you, Stella?" he asked.

She threw her hands apart. "I don't know, any more, how this Peacetaker effect works, Carter. I thought I knew it all, documented it and analyzed it in my book, but nothing that features in my legends bears out what's happening here and now. According to Lao Deng, the Peacetaker took out a temple and sixty monks. We're talking a few hundred feet at best. According to the Sumerians, his effect struck a village. We're talking a dozen houses, a small compound. Twin Peacetakers, walking tandem ten paces apart might affect two neighboring villages, a few acres at best. The African tribes used him to start a tribal war by wiping out their neighbor's village; once again, we're talking a couple of acres here. But our twenty-first century Peacetaker's effect is huge— and totally unpredictable."

"Are you saying that our modern-day Peacetaker is *not* the product of the legends?"

"That's the problem, Carter. He should be – he *must* be! Otherwise there's no explanation for what's happening in our country. Gahiji was particularly interested in the scope of the effect. All through our lunch he kept coming back to this subject. I told him about the Tebtunis texts I wasn't allowed to see. I expected him to get excited about the prospect of historical reference to twin Peacetakers. He wasn't. He kept coming back to the range of the effect and what did I think it might be, as if he expected me to say that with time and history it would grow."

"Legends tend to grow in scope and color with time," he said.

"Yes, but not the effect that has been consistently documented throughout history. I have a horrible feeling that I'm not seeing the forest for the trees."

Just then his pager whirred to signal that he had a message.

"That was Saunders," he told her when he finished listening to the message. "Agents are on their way to check out the Maronite church in Bethesda and the other one in the south Capitol area, but he called both congregations and spoke to the resident pastors. Neither congregation has any overseas visitors, though both religious communities have quite a few members working in overseas missions. They'll keep checking," he said, because she hung her head in defeat. "And that was a good lead, Stella," he said, raising his voice. "From now on, the FBI will keep a closer watch on members of the Maronite church community, country-wide."

"So I gave the FBI a reason to harass members of a religious community," she said, groaning. "How is that a good lead?"

"Someone like Nicola Moses, who doesn't hesitate to use members of his own religious community to do his dirty work, must be, if not apprehended, then at least discouraged from such a hideous practice. Those two students you've just seen may have been recruited with ideologies or something else, but the fact remains that Moses used them. The FBI will be careful dealing with the Maronites, but what they seek to do is actually good for the faithful members of the community. They'll stop Moses from using them as his tools. And those who've already fallen under Moses' influence... Well, they need to be stopped."

"So our religious link is a bust," she said, rising and stretching because they'd sat for hours now, and even he felt as if he'd just put in a regular work day at the office.

"Maybe not," he said but knew she'd hear the lack of conviction in his voice. "The Peacetaker and his controller had to be staying somewhere, with someone in the greater Washington area. Same for Long Island... what are you doing?" Even as he spoke, she rose and walked over to an empty desk with a computer.

"I just want to use the Net, to check out something," she said, nodding at the workstation.

"Sure, go ahead," he said, even though he didn't feel he had the authority to give such permission.

"Well, Moses may be using his Maronite community as a handy pool for contractors whenever he needs someone to do something in our country, but the religious link's a bust. There's no Maronite church in the New York area. The closest one is around Buffalo and there's another one in Connecticut and a couple in Pennsylvania."

"Carter!" Darkwood called, and he looked up to see the agent waving to him.

He squeezed Stella's shoulder. "Try not to break into any classified databases or documents," he said, then went to see Darkwood.

"Wilshire crowd's wondering how come we seem to be ahead of them," the agent said quietly.

It was Tuesday and Helen Brighten was expected to teach her eleven o'clock morning class at the Santa Monica College. When she still hadn't showed up at two o'clock to teach her next class, and phone calls to her home weren't picked up, her department head, John Sterling, contacted the Santa Monica police and asked them to check on a staff member who couldn't be reached. The police found nothing suspicious around Dr. Brighten's beachfront house, but no one answered the doorbell either. They did detect a smell of gas, which gave them a legal reason to break down the door and enter, cautiously. Ten minutes later, the utility emergency crews were on the scene, having first turned off the gas, and the coroner's staff was packing Helen Brighten's body in a plastic bag.

"They're treating it as suicide," Darkwood said. "Signs seem to point that way. Sterling told them she was still under psychiatric care, being treated for depression and other symptoms arising from her recent divorce, and the fact she gave up her UC job, though he said she maintained that was voluntary. But the odd thing is that the woman had everything ready for a workday at the college. Her lunch was made and sitting in the fridge. She was dressed for work, had put on make-up and her briefcase was by the front door, with all her lecture notes and materials for the entire week ahead in it."

Wordlessly, Carter nodded and walked back to where Stella sat at the workstation. He repeated verbatim what the agent just told him, not knowing what else to do to soften the impact.

"Oh, God," she moaned when he finished and put her head down until it came to rest in her lap. Her shoulders shook from the sobs. He pulled up a chair and did what he hardly remembered ever doing for his wife — gathered her into his arms and stroked her unruly hair, gently rocking both of them back and forth, not saying a word.

Sometimes the only comfort a person needed was to be held. It was a very human thing to do, and for some reason, it felt more right to him than any other thing he'd done in a long time.

***

They stayed the night at the Mandarin Oriental Hotel, in the financial district and the bay view, deluxe room with a king-sized bed—for her—and a queen-sized pull out couch—for him—cost 350 dollars per night. He hardly blinked as he handed the check-in clerk his Platinum AMEX. The card gave them a "correct" identity in the clerk's eyes—wealthy eccentrics who didn't care about their outward appearance, but drew the line when it came to their sleeping comfort and luxury. He checked in his "*au courant*" identity as the Senior Vice-President of Environics, out of Toledo, Ohio and let the clerk assume Stella was his partner; to further define what kind would have been rude, and rudeness had no place in hospitality industry, especially at a hotel with Asian management. They had dinner in the opulent dining room with multi-tiered chandeliers illuminating the elaborately arranged seafood on their gold-trimmed plates. She'd found a white-linen shirt and black cotton pants to wear to dinner.

"Good choice," he quipped, wanting to relax her because she looked gloomy though her mood was understandable. "Just make sure you sit down quickly in case they mistake you for one of the service staff."

Finally, she laughed.

They made a pact not to talk about "work," his or hers, and spent the dinner talking about the rest of the world.

"Bruce liked to spend every Christmas someplace other than home. Academics have a lot of holiday time between semesters, so one Christmas we'd spend in Aruba, another in Cuba or the Dominican Republic or down in the Florida Keys, but a few years ago, for whatever reason, he decided that we should have a European Christmas, not our usual warm-land vacation," she said.

Carter thought it was odd, since Christmas was the time of year people liked to spend at home, with their families.

"Oh, Bruce is Jewish and we'd celebrate Chanukah with his folks in Lansing, but Chanukah is often offset from the Christian holidays, so come December 20th or so, we were off for another exotic land."

"Aren't you Jewish, too?" he asked, because he'd assumed it from his Bette Midler comparison.

"I'm Presbyterian, or at least my aunt and uncle raised me in my parents' faith because it seemed like the proper thing to do. My uncle was Anglican but turned a Jehovah's Witness, and my aunt—my mother's sister—joined him in that faith, but they thought they would do the "right" thing by me. Don't you already know this, since you've done a thorough background check on me prior to coming to visit me in Sunburst? Are you just keeping up your end of the conversation?"

"My background check on you concerned your

current status as it further pertained to the key issue that brought me to Sunburst—your authorship, your book. Your past or religious affiliations didn't play any part, so I had no reason to check them out," he said, grinning.

"I'm just wondering whether there is anything you don't know about me yet," she murmured.

"You mean did I discover any nasty secrets about you?"

"I don't have any skeletons in my closet," she laughed.

"That's precisely what I discovered," he deadpanned. "You're a 'True-Blue' American."

She laughed. "Oh, I'm an American, but I'm a little more colored than just true-blue. I was born in the Philippines, but…" Her voice trailed off, and her face settled into that rigid expression of someone listening to a voice no one else could hear.

"Stella, what is it?" He leaned over and put his hand over hers.

"The religious connection," she said in a far-away voice. "It has to be a religious connection." She snapped out of it. "I think I've just figured out how the Peacetaker's in our country—legally. I was born abroad, in a village near Bambang, about four hundred miles north of Manila where my parents were missionaries, but I'm an American—and I entered this country at age three as an American. The Peacetaker was very likely born abroad and his parents were either relief workers or missionaries or affiliated with some other charitable organization. Carter, do you know what this means?" She snatched her hand from under his then gripped it, squeezing with impressive strength.

When he continued to stare at her, she gave an impatient snort. "Carter, the Peacetaker is an *American!*"

Half an hour later, he was calling Saunders from their suite on the thirty-eighth floor.

"It's very important, Vern," he said. "But have your

people check how many American citizens, born abroad—anywhere in the world, but main focus should be on African and Middle Eastern countries—have returned to the US, or have made their first official entry into US, since March 3 of this year to…well, present time for simplicity's sake."

"Carter, Africa and the Middle East are full of our diplomats who raised truckloads of children born abroad without the said family members ever having entered our country," Saunders moaned.

"You're not listening, Vern. I said those who came back or came into our country for the first time but were born abroad and yes, that would include all adult offspring of our diplomats."

"You're not doing some academic research of your own, Carter, are you?"

"I don't think we're looking for an adult son of our diplomat but one never knows, and caution is seldom misplaced."

"Then who or what are we looking for?"

"Missionaries, relief workers, those who work with global charitable organizations and their adult male children."

"Why are you fixated on the sons of our people who do God's work all over the globe?" Saunders groaned.

This was a perfect opportunity to tell Saunders exactly who or what was behind the riots believed to have been set off by terrorist groups or at least a terrorist cell, but the agent's tone of voice told him that the man was stressed out. It meant he was being pressured by his bosses to deliver some tangible news or information that would lead to, if not arrest, then containment of the said terrorist activity.

"Because whoever it is, is in our country legally by virtue of being an American born abroad and those people fall into very specialized categories," he said and closed his cell phone.

"Will you ever tell Agent Saunders the truth about the cause of these riots?" Stella asked from the depths of the palatial room, though she could have even been in the washroom; the echo was the same because everything was "suite" size.

"Yes—when I'm ready to retire."

***

In the morning, just as Carter was deciding between a noon and an afternoon flight back to the east coast, the room telephone rang. Since he was busy with his laptop, Stella picked it up. After a while, when he didn't hear her voice, he turned around to see her listening with a frown. She put down the phone and looked at him.

"Better not book that flight yet. That was actually Agent Darkwood. It seems Abigail McEwen called Agent Saunders—you left her assistant his business card—asking for you, then me, and he passed on her call to Darkwood...anyway, we're invited to visit my esteemed colleague at her house in Kensington. I understand she has a spectacular view of the Wildcat Canyon Regional Park. She told me that at the Wasserdown Conference in LA, bragging, no doubt."

"Are you sure you want to—"

She cut him off. "I wouldn't miss it for the world."

He had a standing arrangement with the car rental company to leave the car in San Francisco at the airport, so there was no rush to return the Grand Prix, and flying out on Thursday actually suited him better because there might be openings on one of the non-stop flights to Washington.

When he told her what the plan was, she shook her head. "We can't stay another night in this place. I'm starting to feel guilty about hundreds of dollars being spent...well, frivolously. We'll camp at the Holiday Inn tonight."

He didn't argue. She'd probably change her mind

again anyway.

"Is anyone following us?" she asked as they headed up I-80 to where the reception desk clerk said to take the exit for Albany, then weave their way through the residential streets to Kensington to Los Altos Drive, which ran along the edge of the park.

He'd been checking his mirrors since they left the hotel and if anyone was following them, they were either very good or got lost in the heavy traffic.

"The museum's closed Monday and Tuesday, but it's Wednesday," he said. "How come Dr. McEwen's home and not at work?"

"She called Agent Saunders from work because the two FBI agents who were waiting for her when she came to work this morning must have asked disturbing questions— and brought up my name. You were right. I don't think she sent that kid with copies of my book for me to sign. He was probably just another handy tool for someone who's connected to Moses."

"Stella, if she doesn't bring up the subject, it might be better not to mention it," he said.

"Right. So, what do you think she's remembered that's so important she's willing to have me as a guest in her house?"

"And that might be another subject that should be off the conversation list," he said, glancing at her.

"Oh, you mean I'm not to ask her whether six years ago was the first time she slept with my husband?"

"That's exactly what I mean."

"Don't worry. I'll be very professional."

"That's what worries me. We can't return the car to the rental agency with a body of a museum curator in the trunk."

She was still laughing when he turned into a circular driveway, paved in faded red cobblestones.

"Looks like a fancy motel," she said, getting out of

the car and looking around. The motel effect was mostly due to an extended entranceway and the Mediterranean arches. The white stucco bungalow with a red Marlee-tiled roof sat on top of the hill. Up here in San Francisco, the desert effect was much less pronounced than in Los Angeles. The house was screened from its neighbors by mature pine trees, and the raised island in the front had flowering shrubbery surrounding an ornamental pole with a lantern. He saw a couple of token palm trees down the street, but they were nowhere near as tall as those that swayed in a gentle breeze over Los Angeles streets.

"You must be Dr. Hunter and Mr. Carter. Come in, come in," said a man in his fifties, wearing rimless glasses and dressed in a male-version of Stella's favorite loungewear—a light brown sweatshirt and khakis. He opened the door wide as if indeed it was his way of showing just how welcome his guests were.

"You must be Frank," Stella said, offering the man a handshake. "I'm glad I finally got to meet you. Next time Abigail heads for a conference on the east coast, you have to come."

"Dr. McEwen." Carter hurriedly offered his hand to the man because he didn't like the 'flavor' of Stella's invitation.

"Oh, I don't hold that title." The man shook his head, smiling. "Abby's the only PhD in our family, though soon enough we might have two. Our daughter's just started hers, down in San Antonio. She's an environmental engineer, with a MBA and—"

"Frank!" Abigail McEwen came from the back of the house, wiping her hands into a tea towel. "We're very proud of Priscilla, but Dr. Hunter and Mr. Carter aren't here to flip through family albums. Let's go in the green room. I've set up for lunch. Nothing elaborate." She flapped the towel at Stella. "Well, come on. The least I can do is offer you some refreshments."

Stella had to nudge him in the arm to move. He couldn't take his eyes off Abigail McEwen, wondering whether some aerial agent didn't affect his vision. If Stella donned white Capri pants and an orange off-the-shoulder T-shirt, put on high-heeled strapless sandals and went to a good hairdresser, she'd be Abigail's twin. Is that what Bruce Hunter saw—a style-conscious copy of his wife?

The hostess sat them down at a glass-topped patio table in an atrium-style room just off the kitchen and for the next half-hour, they were simply guests who came to lunch. Then Frank McEwen brought coffee and suddenly the atmosphere hardened in spite of the sunshine streaming in through the thin-weave window blinds.

"It's really Frank's story," Abigail said, nodding at her husband, who thanked her and said he'd first give them the background history of the issue so they'd understand its source.

Frank McEwen was an antiquarian and, like his wife, traveled a lot. He worked on contract for various private foundations and academic institutions as well as corporate and individual clients. His specialty was tracking down ancient manuscripts and first editions of literary merit.

"Shakespearean works, political and economic treatises, philosophical and even medical collections," he said. "Actually, volumes dealing with alchemy are the most interesting—"

"Frank!" Once again, his wife sought to stop what she probably knew could turn into a passionate lecture.

Frank apologized to her. Carter almost expected her to admonish him not to digress again. It was as if the curator's doctorate title indeed established her in the role of a disciplinarian, while her husband settled into the role of an adoring pupil. The two were such polar opposites. She obviously favored bright, dazzling colors, while he preferred washed-out beige comfort. Her personality was sharp while his was like that of a weak, over-sweetened tea—mild.

Frank resumed his story.

Peter St. James was another antiquarian, but he specialized in tracking down religious texts for his academic and corporate clients. Five years ago, Frank McEwen ran into him at the Blessington Book Auction in London. He was surprised to see St. James because had he known his friend and colleague was in the country, he'd have looked him up. But Frank heard that he was down in the southern Mediterranean region, in the heel part of the boot, somewhere between Brindisi and Taranto. St. James told him that Principessa Alteolani just wanted an expert to do a free cataloguing job of her ancestral journals and papers, and that her great-great-grandmother's love letters were of little interest to him. He'd cut his 'consultation' visit short and headed to Paris for his quarterly meeting with one of the assistant curators of the Louvre Museum, since he was on contract as their 'expert-at-large' of religious scripts and texts.

"Peter said that no sooner had he arrived in Paris than the curator told him that he had to postpone their meeting because the field team out of Sorbonne, working in Aube, found several crates filled with texts in an armariolum, a small book-room in the monastic cloister. He invited Peter to come along because any discovery at the site of the ancient Clairvaux Monastery is exciting in academic terms," Frank McEwen said, glancing at Carter, no doubt to see whether the only non-academic at the table could follow the conversation.

Carter gave him an encouraging nod to show that nothing that had been said so far fazed him.

"But there's a prison on the site of the Clairvaux Abbey," Stella said. "And after the 1971 revolt, where a nurse and a prison guard were murdered, the French government suspended all academic work permits on the site. Six years ago, one of my doctorate students, doing his dissertation on the Cistercian monastic order, wanted to only take pictures at Clairvaux and he was almost shot."

"I guess that's why the Louvre curator was so excited, because the Sorbonne team actually held a valid three-week permit to dig and search in the central and west part of the grounds. That's how they found the armariolum. It was just up from what used to be the undercroft of the monks' dormitory. Peter was at the Blessington Auction because the Sorbonne and the corporate sponsor who funded their research put up four texts that came from the Clairvaux book-room for auction. Peter said his hasty visit to the Champagne region proved to be most fortuitous. The Louvre and the university kept most of the purely religious texts, but the curator gave him a scribe's diary—he called it a modern-day version of a tabloid—written in Latin. It chronicles a period in the Abbot's life, from 1121 to about 1128, when he started performing miracles." Once again, McEwen looked at Carter.

This time, he just sighed and shrugged to show that while he heard every word the man said, he shouldn't assume that strings of such words made sense to him.

Suddenly, Stella turned to him and took his hand, squeezing. "Bernard of Clairvaux was a knight by birth and Abbot Sugar of St. Denis in Paris entrusted an army to him on the Crusades. I encourage some of my gifted doctorate students to believe that Bernard of Clairvaux was Sir Galahad and send them on a quest to prove me right or wrong, doesn't matter which, as long as they produce a sharp dissertation. Among other things, Bernard was the driving force behind the Council of Troves, who provided the Knights Templars with the Latin Rule, and he was also a monk who happened to have founded the Cistercian monastic order."

When he continued staring at her, she sighed and said, "Benedictine monks? St. Bernard, rings a bell?"

"Of course. Why didn't you just say so," he said gruffly but knew she'd see that his eyes were laughing. Then something occurred to him. "Wasn't the Benedictine order founded by St. Benedict?"

She rapped her knuckles on the back of his hand. "No. He only wrote their rule—its prologue and seventy-three chapters—commonly known as RB. It spells out basic virtues a man should have—humility, silence and obedience. It also gives details of common living and sharing. Many a broken marriage today would still be intact if the partners had only taken trouble to learn the ins-and-outs of St. Benedict's Rule." She let him ruminate on her lecture and turned to McEwen. "What's in the tabloid/diary that would interest me?"

The antiquarian resumed his story. His friend Peter immediately set to translate the Latin text of the diary and, when finished, he sat back reflectively, much puzzled how such a fanciful tale could have indeed been written by a monk. Brother Lucien, the scribe at the Clairvaux Abbey, was inspired to become Abbot Bernard's unofficial biographer when he heard that clergy in Paris had already started this noble pursuit.

In 1121, after Bernard restored speech to a relative who had been struck dumb, and the following year when he cured several people at the church of Foigny by blessing them with a sign of the cross, the news of the miracle-worker abbot spread like wildfire. In 1123, while passing through a hamlet of Carmel, on his way to Paris, Bernard asked his driver to stop the cart so he could say a quick prayer at the roadside shrine of the Virgin Mary, where he found a young woman, weeping so bitterly that he became alarmed. He comforted her with spiritually uplifting words until she calmed down and told him about her great sorrow. Her betrothed, a young man named Gaspard, had asked her to cut off his feet to stop him from doing great evil. He told her that it was the only way to break a curse. If he could never, ever walk again, the Devil couldn't use him to sow misery and sorrow amongst the people.

"Cut off his feet?" Stella echoed disbelieving, looking at Carter. He stiffened his back, hoping his poker face wouldn't betray what flashed through his mind. Since they were drowning in legends and folklore, and neither category figured on the FBI list of identifiable terrorist causes, to suddenly hear something so utterly normal, felt like a breath of fresh air to him. While undeniably drastic, the solution was actually quite practical… if painful. Hell, if that's what it took to stop the Peacetaker…

"No," Stella said, her eyes narrowed by an angry scowl. "We'll let Frank here finish the story."

Bernard, too, was alarmed by such a drastic solution to what he figured had to be the young man's spiritual torment and wanted to know whether a gentler approach wasn't possible. He sat down on the grassy knoll and coaxed the story out of the anguished girl. Gaspard was a foundling, left in a ditch by what the villagers believed were a band of Gypsies. The village blacksmith and his wife found the newborn infant on the night of the full moon, the second such moon in the month, and being childless, took it as a Lord's sign that they were meant to raise a child after all. The couple found a strange ornament in the baby's swaddling blankets; a cat's head carved out of black stone. They hid the ornament and when the boy turned ten, they wanted to give him something special for his birthday so they brought out the stone and the blacksmith was about to put it around the boy's neck when the cat's eyes flared red.

Being able to read and interpret not just godly signs but those of the Devil, the blacksmith quickly put away the ornament but each year after that, on the boy's birthday, he'd repeat the ceremony—and the cat's eyes would flare with Devil's fire. When the boy turned eighteen, the ritual that both the son and the father came to regard as a light family tradition, changed. The cat's eyes remained black but shone above the polish of the rest of the stone surface.

And that's when young Gaspard's troubles began. He'd walk through the village and horses would rear, roosters would get in a fight, dogs would growl at each other and cats would hiss and swipe their paws at hands that fed them.

"He only had this effect on animals?" Stella asked, this time turning to her hostess for answer.

"Apparently so." Abigail nodded. "A few weeks after Frank told me about it, I had a reason to contact Peter St. James, museum business, and it occurred to me to ask him to send me a translated version of the Latin text." She stopped and moved her head uncertainly from side to side.

"Oh, go on," Stella said, sounding disgusted. "That was about four years ago, right?"

"Could have been a bit earlier, I don't recall," Abigail said, fingering her wedding band and the diamond ring.

"Fine," Stella snapped. "It was five years ago, just after I contacted the Hearst Museum, asking whether they'd let me study the Tebtunis Demotic texts and whether they...whether *you* knew about any other source of the Peacetaker legend. I was finishing my book and yes, I could have used this biographer-monk's translated text—it could have added even more controversy to the book since the Clairvaux text is basically the latest information we have on record. I used what I had at the time, the 6th century Roman reference."

"I'm sorry," Abigail said, still fiddling with her rings.

"It doesn't matter now. As it turned out, there was more than enough controversy in the book as it is. Was there anything in the text as to why Gaspard only affected animals, not people? Surely that wouldn't have stressed him out to such an extent that he asked his girl to cut off his feet?"

"Frank, may I?" Abigail looked at her husband, seeking permission to continue.

"Of course, dear, by all means." He smiled at her. Carter felt pity and admiration at the same time for the mild-mannered antiquarian. Did he know of his wife's affair or affairs? And if he did, how did they manage to work out their marital problems such that today he was able to adore her with his eyes and smile? Maybe he didn't know. Sometimes it was better to take some secrets to one's grave.

Abigail McEwen resumed the story. Her version was more technical, drier and devoid of the color Carter had come to expect in legends.

Gaspard was a bright man and quickly figured out the cause of animal unrest he left in his wake and took off the amulet. However, while he was in control of his actions during the day, at night someone or something kept draping the amulet over his neck, and soon villagers began to find not just their domestic animals slaughtered but wild life as well. They believed a hellhound came to ravage their village because the dead animals were torn apart, with bits of flesh missing. However, they never could find any fang or claw marks. Indeed, it looked as if the animals had simply turned on each other.

Then one morning, Gaspard woke up on his straw pallet, found the amulet around his neck, went to take it off—and couldn't. Either his fingers slipped, the stone danced out of his hands and through his fingers, or the leather strap wouldn't slide off his neck. Frightened, he ran to find his girl and, much to his relief, she was able to take it off. That's when he told her the story and the curse that came with the amulet. She took the ornament and threw it in the water-well. The next morning, Gaspard found the amulet around his neck and when he went outside, all he could hear was crying and lamentation. Three villagers who went to the well to draw water ended up fighting each other over who should go first and two were now dead while the third one was receiving his last rites.

The frightened couple ran away and buried the evil cat's head in the forest. The next morning, Gaspard woke up to feel the cool silk of the polished stone against his skin. His fear intensified when he saw his pointed-toed shoes, *pigache,* were not just stained but soaked with blood and his stockings were torn. Outside, villagers were already talking about Aubert the woodsman who went to check his traps. They found him dead, an axe buried in his head. His son, who had accompanied him lay nearby, dead of deep cuts and slashes to his head and chest with the said axe.

Gaspard ran to his betrothed and asked her to cut off his feet. She told him to hide in the hayloft and went to seek spiritual counsel from the Virgin Mary.

"Bernard had a solution that worked, right?" Stella asked. When Abigail didn't reply, Stella pointed her finger at her. "Don't tell me that part of the text was either un-translatable or missing or…"

"He was a miracle worker," Abigail said. "That's why the friar wrote down the story. Bernard told the cart driver to turn around, took the girl and they returned to Carmel to find Gaspard in the hayloft. Bernard watched as the girl took off the amulet then he performed an exorcism on it, right then and there, in the barn."

"Just like he exorcised flies out of the Foigny church?" Stella raised her brows, smiling. "It didn't work, did it?"

Carter passed a hand across his mouth to wipe out his smile. Stella was getting to know her ex-adversary better and better.

"No, it didn't," Abigail admitted.

"But something else did, which made the friar document the story as a miracle," Stella maintained.

Abigail pursed her lips. "Well, most Latin texts

aren't overly difficult to translate and besides, Peter's a very talented linguist. It didn't work because after Bernard resumed his journey, the couple went about their work but come next morning, the amulet was around Gaspard's neck and two more villagers were dead. That's when the girl ripped the ornament from her young man's neck and ran— all the way to Clairvaux Abbey where she pleaded for audience with a monk—any monk—and Brother Lucien just happened to be the one who opened the tradesman's door and let her into the kitchen yard, which had a smithy right next to it. I imagine this time the girl gave him an abridged version of the tale, though she probably mentioned Bernard and that his 'miracle' cure didn't work. Brother Lucien saw his opportunity to leave a mark in history. Underneath his monk's robes he was a practical man. He took the girl to the smithy, told her to place the amulet on the anvil and with one swing of the blacksmith's hammer, the black obsidian cat was smashed to smithereens."

"Exit curse and Gaspard and his betrothed lived happily ever after," Stella finished.

"That's not in the original text or the translation, but I imagine that would have been the case," Abigail said. "Are you working on a second volume to your *Ribbons of Truth?*"

Stella's smile grew wider.

"I'll have Rita, that's my assistant, put together all the material I have back at the office and I'll ship it to you...well, will next week be soon enough?" Abigail asked.

"Thank you," Stella said. "I'll remember Berkeley and the Hearst Museum on my dedication page."

Chapter Twenty-two

Miami Valley, Ohio
May 14
Thoth appears with Shu to bring back Tefnut

Louise Norton was just about to spin the right wheel of her wheelchair to bring it around so she could get back behind her table when a strong gust of wind rustled the heavy-gauge plastic cover she had just finished tucking around the edges.

"Oh, dear," she murmured when a corner of the plastic sheet flapped over, exposing a whole tray of her homemade chocolate, walnut and maple fudge. Most folks had finished setting up their stalls but a couple of latecomers, like Jonah Drake, who'd been bringing his seeds and grains to the Miami Valley Arts and Crafts Spring Fair ever since Louise could remember, and Hal Biddle, whose dusty stuffed critters never changed either, were still rattling and shaking things, raising dust. She couldn't have grit falling down on her fudge.

What would a customer think if her smooth-as-butter fudge melted in his mouth, only to leave behind sand grains and dirt? She'd already used the sewing weights her late mother, God rest her soul, left her along with heavy metal parts from the old Singer machine to hold down the corner of the plastic tarp. Maybe she should have done what her granddaughter, Melissa, advised and put her fudge squares on trays with see-through plastic covers that could be taped shut. But then her table would look like one of those supermarket food stands, and that's not what the people wanted to see when they came to a local fair.

"Why won't you let me staple it down, Grandma?" Melissa had asked when she came this morning to set up her stall.

Louise was already worried that an eggshell bit may

have slipped into a batch of her walnut fudge when Melissa insisted on cooking her breakfast while Louise fussed over her fudge, packing it into shoe boxes such that even a single square wouldn't end up with a broken corner. To have to worry, all through the fair, about those little bits of steel finding their way into her fudge if someone pulled the plastic harder than they meant to, would just raise her blood pressure. Then that young Oriental doctor, who took over Doctor Palfrey's practice when Gerald died, would wag his finger at her and tell her that if she didn't take her medication as often as he insisted she take it, she'd not see her eighty-third birthday.

She wheeled herself closer to the side where her fudge squares lay exposed and, leaning forward, tucked the plastic under the layers of old Dayton Daily News that kept the moisture away from her goods.

"Are those fudge squares as good as they look, Aunt Louise?" Hal Biddle walked across the aisle.

She pretended not to hear him though there was nothing wrong with her ears. He was her best friend Charlotte's boy, a cocky whippersnapper, but that's not why she disliked him. Charlotte and Bill had had him when she was past forty and, since he was their only child, they spoiled him rotten. Charlotte passed away a couple of years ago, and he hardly shed a tear at her funeral. At the wake, all he did was complain that she'd sold off the land she'd owned near Trothwood and used up all the money on doctors and drugs—and what good they did her anyway?

He was a selfish, mean-mouthed youngster and now he was a forty-year-old moocher who thought everyone ought to just hand him everything he asked for. He worked for the city, fixing roads, and bragged about his hunting, fishing and trapping skills.

No one ever could rightfully tell where exactly he went hunting and fishing, not even his wife, but he always brought back another critter to stuff and add to his collection that now sat across from her stall, propped up on crates and tied to perches. He was the reason why Melissa wouldn't stay and help her at the fair. She said what Biddle did to birds, squirrels and fish was cruel and inhuman. Last year, he'd brought a dozen stuffed rats and sold them as a parcel. Some folks were just shortchanged in a lot of ways by the Good Lord when he made them.

"Morning, Harold," Louise said when his shadow fell across her table with the fudge. It was a beautiful May day that felt closer to summer than spring. It would have been perfect if not for the occasional gust of wind that tormented her so much.

"You gonna let me try one of those, auntie?" He poked his finger into the plastic.

"Shoo, Harold, shoo. Don't you poke your dusty fingers into my fudge." She pushed his hand away. "You want to taste my fudge, you come back with two dollars, like any other customer."

"You're getting to be a cranky old lady, Louise," he said and walked back to his stall.

"Is he bothering you, Aunt Louise?" Stanley Ford called out to her. He'd set up his rifles and antique carbines next to Harold's stuffed animal menagerie. He was another one she'd known from birth, her friend Martha's boy and she, too, was gone, God rest her soul in peace. Stanley was a mechanic, a fixer, who served in Vietnam. That's where folks said he got a lot of his guns and knives that he brought to the fair every year and hardly ever sold any of the nicely polished weapons.

"He's a pest," Louise called out to Stanley. "Just like every young whippersnapper who brings stuff here they otherwise keep in a garage. This ain't no garage sale, you know. Why don't you make something, instead of bringing those guns and knives?"

He shook the rifle that looked mostly made of fancy polished wood and said, "This is not just craft, Aunt

Louise. This here is the finest Remington 7600 pump action rifle in the State. Any deer that pokes its head out of the woods is a dead duck when a hunter carries this, right, Hal?" He shook the rifle at his neighbor who grunted something that Louise couldn't hear.

She waved her hand at him and rolled her wheelchair backward, then fitted it behind the table with her goods. When she was still able to stand behind her table, before the first hip replacement, she'd take a deep breath every five minutes just to be able to draw in the smell of pies and home-made baked goods. Today, if she'd tried something so foolish, she'd only get a mouthful of dust from Harold's stuffed critters.

She looked at the kitchen clock that Melissa left for her on the box next to the table and saw that it was almost ten o'clock. Folks should have finished setting up and the parking lot should be filling up with people, locals and visitors. When she found out that this year's fair was not only postponed to Thursday, a regular workday to boot, but also going to be held in the parking lot next to St. Luke's Church, instead of its usual place in Belmont Park, she almost cancelled out. The fair's theme and meaning no longer held true if the event wasn't held on April 16th, Wilbur Wright's birthday. It was as much a local event as it was the birthday celebration of Dayton's famous historical figure.

"The Department of Building Services hasn't even started cleaning up all the garbage that's been illegally dumped in the park," Melissa told her. "That's why they won't let the fair be held there this year. It's just not safe or even sanitary, Grandma. There's been a lot of illegal dumping going on in Dayton, and I'm afraid that the rest of us have to pay the price for the polluters. And I'm sure folks won't mind celebrating Wilbur's birthday a bit late. It's the thought that counts."

Louise remained skeptical but she didn't want to

argue with her granddaughter. Now, she had the open field behind her that the wind blew across, and while she didn't mind the Lord's House on one side, the other end of the parking lot ended in a blank wall of industrial storage buildings.

"A local fair held in a parking lot," she murmured. "What is this world coming to?" Just then, she heard a commotion down by the entrance where the quilters and linen crowd had set up their stalls. It meant customers had arrived.

An hour later, she still sat behind a mostly full table. She hardly had a reason to open up a new box.

"It's this place," she murmured. "Whoever would think of coming to a fair that's set up in a parking lot? Folks used to swarm into Belmont Park, and not just locals, either. I should have just saved my money this year and not come." She looked down to where Maggie and Liz had their quilts hanging on clotheslines and Leticia had had her son-in-law set up metal shelving for her jams and preserves. A bunch of folks were walking around, but nowhere near the crowds that she remembered from previous years. Suddenly she became aware that someone had stopped in front of her table and turned her head.

"Well, hello there, young man," she said, smiling because the child looked frightened. He was oddly dressed too, in a faded red-and-blue checked short-sleeved shirt. Today, children dressed in T-shirts and sweatshirts, not something that even she would have donated to charity back in the fifties. He had a bunch of polished rocks and gold ornaments threaded on black leather straps hanging around his neck.

Ronnie, her grandson, God rest his soul in peace, collected rocks like a magpie. She was always checking his pockets, emptying them of rocks and pebbles before she walked him and Melissa to school. And if God had not slept that awful, awful morning when a man who ought to have known better and didn't, pressed his foot hard down on the gas pedal in a school area. She shook her head to banish the terrible memory.

The child stood there, as if mesmerized.

She motioned at the ornaments. "Did your parents buy you those down at the rock-man's booth?" The 'rock-man' was a relative newcomer to the fair, having first set up his stall only a couple of years ago. She'd had Melissa wheel her by his table just to see that what Mary and Alice told her was true—the man had not only polished rocks in every color, but cheap watches and socks and postcards and all kinds of junk-store nick-knacks that didn't belong at the fair.

The boy continued staring at her as if he had fallen asleep with his eyes open.

"Here, I'll let you taste my special chocolate fudge," she said, leaning forward to reach the front row where she'd always set up the favorites.

The boy took a step backward.

"Don't be afraid," she said, leaning back and pushing the wheels to get out from behind the table. "I just can't reach the piece that has your name on it. What's your name?"

"Ash… Ash…" the boy pushed out the word with difficulty.

Louise stopped rolling her wheelchair and stared at him. "You all right, child?" she asked, motioning with her hand for him to come toward her. "You look pale."

The boy's forehead was beaded with sweat and it wasn't that kind of sweltering day. "Ash," the boy said again as if he couldn't breathe out the rest.

Louise lifted her head to see if indeed ash and dust weren't falling down. Last year, that fool Trevor who owned a deli in the Sweetston Strip Plaza had brought a barbecue to cook and sell his homemade sausages. By noon, ash and soot had covered her table. If not for the tablecloths that Melissa brought when she came to check on her, the last three boxes of her fudge would have been ruined. She didn't see anything flitting about or falling down. When she sniffed the air, it smelled all right, though that horrible mustiness that always wafted from Harold's critters was quite nasty today.

Louise reached down and brought out a bottle of spring water from the cloth pouch Melissa made for her wheelchair. The child looked parched. Maybe he needed a drink more than a fudge square. She wheeled herself closer to the boy, holding out the bottle of water.

The child didn't back away this time but he wasn't reaching for it either.

Louise took his hand and gave it a slight tug so she wouldn't frighten him even more. "It's all right, child. Come here. This old lady won't hurt you." With her other hand, she fished out a Kleenex from her cardigan pocket and gently dabbed at the boy's sweat-beaded forehead.

"You're burning up, child." She clucked her tongue, looking around to see if his parents weren't around but no one seemed to be looking for anyone. Just then a loud crash from across the aisle startled her into exclaiming, "Dear Lord Jesus! What's happening now?"

Even as she spoke, a wooden crate smashed down just a couple of feet from her wheelchair. Louise grabbed the boy and pulled him into her lap. All around her buckets, cans and wooden crates bounced, spilling their contents. She pressed the boy's face into her shoulder, shielding him from what looked like a rain of farming tools that came flying at her. Out of the corner of her eye, she saw Harold throttling Jonah, all the while growling at him like one of his critters must have when still alive.

Everywhere she looked, folks were grappling with each other, ripping and kicking apart their merchandise. Harold slammed Jonah's head into a sack of grain and kept pushing as if he meant to drown him in the seeds. Stanley was brandishing his rifle, smashing folks who came near him with its butt-end with such force she heard bones breaking. She felt moisture rain down and prayed to the Lord it was just syrup and juice, not blood.

"Jesus Lord, protect us," she moaned, shielding the boy's head and pressing him into her shoulder so he'd not have to see the madness or hear all the screaming and growling that went on in the parking lot. What was happening to the folks of Miami Valley? Why was Stanley smashing a stranger's head with a rifle butt? Had Letitia gone mad, smashing jars filled with her preserves over every head she could reach? Where were the police, since they usually sent a patrol car or two to drive by the fair?

Suddenly, a white-faced apparition with huge flaming-red lips swooped down on her out of the melee of flying crates and human hands brandishing knives and slashing everything they could reach in an insane frenzy to shred, gouge and rip everything apart.

"Jibreel, Jibreel! Come ibn-alakh, come, we must go." The apparition had human hands that reached after the boy she held in her arms. The claw-like fingers gripped the boy's shoulders and tugged so hard the boy's head snapped back and forth like a doll's.

"Devil be gone! You can't have Ronnie. I won't let you!" Louise shouted and started to cough because her lungs weren't used to such harshness and the air was filled with grit.

The creature's hand fastened on the stones and ornaments around the boy's neck and yanked so hard that once again the child almost flew out of her arms.

"Our Father, thou art in Heaven, banish this foul creature…" Louise prayed just as the boy's head suddenly reared as if he'd just awakened. The creature shook the hand holding the stones and the leather strings danced in front of Louise's eyes like writhing snakes.

"Jibreel, let's go!" This time the creature grabbed

the boy's shoulders and yanked him out of her embrace, momentarily holding him off the ground then released him, grabbed his hand and dragged him down toward the quilter's stall.

"Stop, stop, you foul monster!" Louise shouted, hand outstretched and reaching after the child dragged by the unholy creature. And just as she gripped the wheels to move after them, a hand holding something came at her, smashing whatever it was in her face.

***

Three miles south of Miami Valley, at the Park Hill strip plaza in Oakwood, Yakov Stremskij kept rocking back and forth, waiting while the clerk kept examining a perfectly good pay check from the Marfa Brothers Wholesale Distributors that Yakov collected this morning for his two weeks' work. His bank wanted to put a hold on it but he needed to pay off Effrem or the "*svolosch*" wouldn't give him back his car. The CashMart would have been his last resort because he couldn't afford to lose a "*kopeyck*" of the money but no one else would cash his pay cheque.

"It's good, it's good," Yakov grumbled, banging his fists on the counter to show the rat-faced guy he was in a hurry.

The clerk refused to lift his head from scrutinizing the cheque. He'd already put it under his blue-light machine and rubbed it with some sticky shit until Yakov thought the paper would tear.

"Get your ID ready," the clerk said, dipping his hand under the counter and bringing out a large magnifying glass.

"ID?" Yakov smashed his fist down on the counter. "Your fucking sign says you cash cheques, no questions, no fucking ID." He felt anger well inside him, almost as if someone had put a boiling pot of borscht in his gut.

"That's for our folks." The clerk leered at him.

"Your kind's gotta show they're parked in our country legally."

Yakov felt as if the boiling pot in his gut turned into a volcano. He roared and grabbed the guy's scrawny neck, squeezing until his eyes bulged.

"*Svolosch*," he ground out then yanked the guy's face forward and sank his teeth into his nose.

Half a mile south, on East and Fair Hill, Shane Andrews let go of the handle and jumped off the garbage pick-up truck. It was his first day working with the broad and they were already an hour behind schedule. If he didn't need this fucking job, he'd have told Morris back at the compound to shove it up his ass when the foreman came out this morning to choose his first victim—the sanitation worker who would be saddled with the first woman the Conley Garbage Disposal Services hired, doing their part for equality and all that shit.

The scrawny broad looked like a gust of wind might knock her off her feet, never mind lifting a fifty-pound bag of garbage and tossing it in the back of the truck. He was right. Ten minutes into their route, she'd already dropped two bags, spilling garbage all over the sidewalk. He wasn't going to clean it up and had to settle for waiting while she did, one stinking piece after another. It made them lose fifteen minutes. Next street over, she couldn't even lift a half-filled plastic bin and more garbage spewed into the street. He thought of telling her to go sit next to the driver but then he'd have to do the whole five-hour route by himself.

"Well, aren't you going to help me?" The bitch stopped, turning around. "I've been doing pretty much all the work myself, and this is supposed to be a team effort, right?"

Help her? Shane felt such a suffocating wave of fury suffuse his chest he thought it would start caving in any moment.

"I'll help you," he growled and strode toward her. Before she could scream, he smashed his fist into her face, caught her limp form and carried it without as much as leaning for counterbalance to the dumpster part of the truck. He tossed her inside, returned to the curb, picked up the garbage bags and tossed them down on her then banged on the side of the dump truck to let the driver know it was "good" to start flipping and compressing the load.

A mile further south in Kettering, a police cruiser pulled up in front of Ho-Sing's Custom Jewelry store. Constable Josh Lum got out and looked around. The store glass front window was intact. There weren't any teenagers lurking around and everything looked peaceful and in good order, which meant that the proprietor had once again abused his right as a merchant and citizen and pushed the "panic button" because he "thought" he saw someone outside his store, casing it for a job. It was the third such occurrence this year, and Lum resented being the one saddled with the "false alarm" calls simply because of his Oriental heritage. There wasn't anything wrong with Sing's English, even though he liked to garble his speech whenever Lum arrived with a partner.

He walked into the store and Sing's hand-waving gesture, coupled with a rapid salvo of Cantonese told him it was just as he suspected—another frivolous alarm. For some reason, the sight of the proprietor's moon-face, split in a wide smile, made Lum furious. His anger mounted with each step taken toward the glass counter and the elderly man behind it.

"This is not what it means to exercise your rights, sir," Lum said, feeling as if steam was about to rip off the top of his head. His hand automatically went to his side, unclipping the leather strap and drawing out his weapon. The smile on the proprietor's face vanished. A torrent of Cantonese spilled out of his mouth, but Lum didn't latch on to the meaning though he was fluent in the language.

"And this is what happens to those who abuse them," he said, squeezing the trigger. The sound of the shots seemed to act as a release valve because the pressure in his cranium vanished just as the top of Sing's bald head dipped below the counter.

At just about the time Sing's body landed on the floor, further south, about a mile from the jewelry store, in Whites Corners, Claire Vanier stopped listening to her boss's "explanations" why she didn't get the promotion and would have to spend another year as a bank teller, instead of training to become the loan officer. She knew he gave the job to Marsha because he was fucking her.

"I know how you must feel..." Some of his words suddenly broke through the haze that seemed to coat her eyes as she stood in front of his desk, in his office with the doors closed, which was always a bad sign.

Her eyes fell on the chunk of green marble with an inset pen and pencil, the last Christmas management's gift to the jerk. She snatched it and quickly ran around the desk then smashed his face with the rock.

"Now you know how it feels, don't you?" she said, breathing hard. Just then a scream sounded from outside. She bashed the jerk's drooping head again, tossed the rock in his lap and walked for the door. She opened it and the computer monitor screen that someone must have ripped out from a teller's station and flung at the door smashed her face.

At about the same time Claire's lifeless body settled on the floor, Officer Joe Burdock was heading west on Interstate 675. He took his eyes off the road for a moment to see the exit 4B flash by then turned back—and saw a pall of smoke rising in the air. It seemed to hang over the eastbound lanes. He reached for his radio to report what might have already been reported and to see if much police assistance would be required on the scene of the accident.

And south of the Interstate, those Americans who

could afford to take a nap on Thursday afternoon, slept well.

Chapter Twenty-three

The late afternoon Delta Airlines flight to Washington was somewhere over the Midwest when the hostess switched on the TV, tuned to some local newscast station.

Thirty seconds later, Carter found himself wondering whether he should call Saunders and ask him to use FBI authority to arrange an unscheduled stopover for Flight 8699—somewhere close to Dayton, Ohio. Cincinnati would be good. Then again, Cincinnati and every other airport within a twenty-mile radius would be swarmed with the FBI and police air traffic.

Over the last couple of weeks, he only had time to scan the daily news whenever he opened up his laptop, but even a cursory look was enough to see that people were panicking. The FBI spokesman, Connelly Dwight, offered only platitudes in his press sessions. Carter felt it was a tactical mistake. It left the media free to speculate about the cause and motive for "The Mall Madness," as the newspapers dubbed the tragedy, and the "Long Island Homicidal Frenzy," as they called the other event.

Dwight should have been briefed better and the committee that wrote his press release should have first drafted a list of "causes and motives" for the tragic events, prioritizing them from "least alarming" to "panic-setting." The FBI spokesman then should have offered a couple of causes and motives from the top of the list. It would have given the media something to focus upon while the FBI continued their investigation.

But without anything definite to latch on to, the media started offering possible causes—chemical and biological warfare, a deadly airborne virus accidentally released by a secret government laboratory in Maryland, mutated Mad Cow disease, poisoned food on Washington supermarkets' shelves, contamination of water supply and even aquifers, abandoned transit tunnels all over America teeming with aliens and their chemical laboratories, a mysterious plume of gas discharged from an alien craft in Earth's orbit that was actually meant for the White House and missed by a few thousand feet—all sensationalistic and therefore very profitable in terms of newsprint sales.

And while a few conservative newspapers allowed their reporters to speculate about possible terrorist action, those who read such newspapers normally just scanned the headlines and headed for the business section. At least he used to, since business and economics were most often the underlying causes of mayhem in the world. In metaphorical terms, if politics were a human body then business and economics were its vital organs

He kept his head tucked between his shoulders, watching one 'on-the-scene' reporter after another give commentaries to the police and medical work that went on in the background. Suddenly he felt Stella's hand settle on his and turned his head. She was saying something. He pulled down the earphones because he wasn't in a lip-reading mood.

"He struck at a local fair," she said quietly.

He remembered her saying something like that earlier, though at the time it could have been just sarcasm.

"Your prediction was right," he said.

"Yes but it's something else. Let me have the laptop."

He watched her call up a map of Dayton, Ohio, then zoom in and start pointing with the mouse arrow at the names of communities mentioned by the news reporters: Oakwood, Kettering, Whites Corners.

"Here," she said, pointing the mouse at the red line of Interstate 675. "This is where the southbound effect stopped or played out. I didn't hear any reports of an outbreak of madness in Belmont or Shakertown. None west of Interstate 75 either. It affected a long strip about half a mile wide at best; in geographical terms certainly a ribbon of madness that ended at I-657."

"Another atypical strike," he murmured. They didn't need more puzzles. They were still trying to make sense of what they had.

"And a bad one," she said. "His effect this time was like a plume, indeed wrath of a vengeful god."

"Stella, maybe you're trying to fit something into a logical pattern that doesn't lend itself—"

"History repeats itself—or it should," she snapped.

"Keep your voice down," he cautioned. Even though, once again, they were in first-class, every seat around them was occupied. "When we land in Washington, you go collect our luggage while I go book us the first available flight to Cincinnati."

Trying to call Saunders first would probably be unproductive, since he was most likely already in Dayton along with every available FBI agent from Indiana, Kentucky, West Virginia, Pennsylvania and Michigan. While Saunders had managed to contain the agency's involvement in Washington to his jurisdiction, the Long Island event became a community job. The Dayton strike would bring in other security agencies as well, because now not just the peace of mind but also safety of every American citizen was at stake.

They landed at Dulles just after nine o'clock and there was no flight out for any parts of Ohio before morning.

He watched her wheel the cart with their bags toward him and knew she'd read the dismal news from his expression.

"We could..." he said just as she began to say exactly the same thing.

"You go ahead," he told her.

"Drive," she finished.

"You've read my mind," was all he said, turning

and heading for the Hertz Car Rental counter. He could have gone home to get his SUV, but the way he felt, he didn't want to lose a moment. It felt as if he wore a leash and a hand kept yanking it if he as much as thought of heading anywhere but Ohio.

When he left the Spur part of the interstate where it became I-270 North, he asked her whether she'd mind driving for a while. "After we make it to I-70W, we'll make a quick pit stop and then you can drive for couple of hours."

"No problem," she said. "I've always wanted to drive a Lincoln Navigator. You rent such interesting vehicles."

"It's the only thing they had ready to roll," he said.

"It rolls like a tank. It should have a mow-down grille."

"What?"

"You know—the chrome bars up front."

"I've never heard it called a mow-down grille."

"That's probably because you've never spent much time driving around with a woman."

***

"Washington, Long Island, Dayton—what connects these places?" Stella kept musing out loud while he kept moving his head, trying not to get caught too often in the headlights of the cars heading east.

"Geography," he mumbled. "They're all American towns."

"No. Geography plays no part in this. Something connects these three places, either ideologically, politically, economically or…."

"Or what?"

"Practicality. He had a reason to be at each of these three locations."

He grunted. "So we have a practical human demon, that's just great."

"Carter, he is *not* a demon. How many times do I have to repeat it? Without his activating amulet, he's a normal young man and no, if and when we find him, you will not entertain cutting off his feet."

"If we find him, Stella, did you ever think what might happen to the two of us?"

"If his controller doesn't outfit him with the amulet—nothing. The controller's the one you need to stop. The Peacetaker is being victimized. He's—"

"If you're going to say 'blameless' I'll pull over and let you out. You can walk to the nearest service center."

"He's an American, Carter. I bet you didn't count on that. Once his controller drapes that amulet over his neck, the Peacetaker becomes a sleepwalker. And I'd bet anything that when the amulet's taken off, he doesn't remember a thing. Would you kill an American, Carter? He's probably a son of people who represent American values all over the world better than anything that's written or said by our Ambassadors. He's being used to terrorize his own people. If you're in a killing mood, kill the one who's controlling him and forcing him do it."

He had always suspected that she'd agreed to come along precisely because she believed that she could protect the Peacetaker, stop the law from taking the shortest route to a common goal.

"Carter?"

"Look, Stella, when I get this Peacetaker in my crosshairs, I might not quickly squeeze off a shot but you should know that someone like me, a contractor for government agencies, can't afford to worry about collateral damages."

"How many people did you kill as a matter of your job, Carter?"

"The ones I know of?"

That shut her up for the next ten miles. When the sign announcing the next service center flashed by, he offered her a truce. "Stella, I was in the army, Special Forces. I trained to save lives—and kill; both functions are required of a soldier."

"I'd like to think we're heading for the saving scenario," she said quietly.

"Every soldier thinks that way until the time comes to switch to the other mode—to save more lives. Do you know what I'm talking about?"

"Kill one to save many."

"Better than what he's doing—killing many."

She was silent for a long time then said, "You know, Bernard of Clairvaux was a mediator in his time. He helped to bring about the healing of the papal schism that arose in 1130 with the election of the antipope, Anacletus II. He spent eight years traveling back and forth between England and France, working for peace and reconciliation among the nobles. He rose off his sickbed and went into Rhineland to defend the Jews against persecution. He became known as the Peacemaker."

"But the mythological demon's curse proved to be immune to Bernard's exorcism," he said. "Brother Lucien's practical approach worked much better."

"Perhaps that's all it takes—to destroy the amulet— the Peacetaker's activator."

"I'm not going to promise anything, Stella," he warned.

"Carter, being a military man, would you destroy a gun if no one can make bullets for it?"

"It's still a weapon."

"Yes, I keep forgetting that you're a practical man. But we have a human being used as a weapon. Would you still destroy it if it could no longer be armed?"

He still had almost a five-hour drive ahead of him. To reply, one way or another, might see him nod-off at the wheel if she launched into one of her lectures, this time ideologically slanted.

"The service center's coming up. We'll switch after we gas up," he said.

Chapter Twenty-four

Miami Valley, Ohio
May 15
Month of Epipi begins: Festivals of Het-Hert and Bast;
Great feast of the Southern heavens

The Miami Valley Hospital looked more like a maximum-security prison after a riot than a hospital. Every doorway was policed by one or two officers, and clusters of patients in wheelchairs and those able to walk and wheel their intravenous stands were outnumbered by blue uniforms.

He spotted Saunders just down the corridor, talking on his cell phone, when they walked out of the elevator. The agent raised his hand and waved them over, not interrupting his call.

"Dr. Hunter." Saunders nodded at Stella when he flipped the phone shut. "Glad to see you're still with us."

"We keep meeting in hospitals," she murmured. "That's not a good thing."

"You're telling me," Saunders agreed. "This way." He motioned further down the hallway. "It's probably nothing, but at this point we don't have..." His voice trailed off when the two police officers, flanking the door, moved to block it.

"Come on, guys," Saunders growled but the policemen wouldn't yield. He flipped a badge out of his pocket, held it crack-close to their faces and grumbled something when they stepped back.

"Paranoia in the police ranks—and ours," Saunders remarked softly when Carter stopped beside him.

"How many dead?" Carter asked.

"At last count, 235 men, women and children perished at the hands of their fellow men, and I mean that literally. No one's immune from the madness, not even

274

police officers. One cop shot a storeowner point-blank and can't tell his fellow officers why. A local newsman managed to break through the police barrier at the fair and interviewed a few of the injured while they were waiting for ambulance transport. Someone mentioned that they were possessed by madness—so possession is the latest story circulating on the cause of this tragedy," he finished.

"Carter?" Stella said in a quiet voice, and he knew she thought this was his opportunity to expand on that 'possession' theory, maybe take it as far as ancient curses, but he just couldn't bring himself to broach the subject.

He blinked at her and shook his head. She understood, but he saw she didn't like his procrastination.

The hospital room was a ward, normally shared by four patients, but they'd squeezed in two more beds. Only one relative per patient was allowed in the room, but in their case, the floor head-nurse made an exception.

"This is Melissa Norton," Saunders introduced a young woman with eyes almost swollen shut from crying. "She's the patient's—Louise Norton's—granddaughter. I know this is a bad time for answering questions, Ms. Norton, but what your grandmother told you might be important. I'd appreciate it if you could repeat it to Carter and Dr. Hunter here."

Melissa Norton leaned over her grandmother's diminutive form, once again almost obscured by all the life-saving apparatus, and kissed the bandaged face with tubes leading out of the mouth and nose areas.

She straightened up, holding in her grief because her shoulders shook from the effort. "They said she might lose her sight. That's if she lives. With elderly patients, there's always a worry about secondary infections, pneumonia…I should have never left her alone. I should have stayed with her. My dust allergy is not life-threatening, and I could have just worn a mask. Charlie— one of the police officers outside—said Hal Biddle suffocated Jonah Drake by holding his head in a sack of grain feed. Then someone stabbed Hal with a pitchfork, and someone else then split *his* head with an axe. Stanley Ford shot people…Grandma never believed his gun collection was real. Maggie Grace is dead too. She was hit with a glass jar so hard… the doctor said Grandma's lucky to be alive." She covered her face with both hands, sobbing.

The male nurse came inside, since he must have been hovering nearby to make sure the police didn't stress his patients to where it would endanger them even further. "Maybe you should conduct your business outside."

"No, I'm fine." Melissa dropped her hands and shook her head in a way to show she was composing herself. "Thanks, Ahmed, but I won't leave Grandma."

The nurse checked his patient and said, "She might not show it, but she can hear you. And if she doesn't like what she hears…" His voice trailed off.

"All right, Ms. Norton, tell us again what your grandmother said," Saunders said, turning to the nurse. "It might be a good idea for you to stay until we're done, make sure the patient… Mrs. Norton is not disturbed. Stop us if you see anything… bad," he finished.

Melissa Norton told them that she had arrived at the Church of St. Luke parking lot seconds after the first ambulance reached the site of the riot. A policeman wanted to turn her away, but she gave him the slip and ran around the other side of the church to the new Miami Valley Arts and Crafts fairgrounds. She heard screaming and crying, sounds of breakage and even shots, but managed to block it out because her goal was to reach her wheelchair-bound grandmother and get her to safety. In the back of her mind, she registered that people went berserk and were killing each other with whatever tool they could get their hands on, but her mind was focused on her granny—and it was filled with fear, concern and love for her grandmother and nothing else.

Stella glanced at him when Melissa came this far in her story. He nodded to show that he understood her silent message. By the time Melissa made her way through the battling fair merchants, the Peacetaker was either gone or— if his controller didn't get him away in time—he no longer wore his activating amulet, because Melissa's mind wasn't affected by the madness.

She found her grandmother in the shambles of her stall, lying next to her wheelchair, bloodied but moaning. Some of the "blood" turned out to be strawberry jam preserves, but Louise suffered more than just facial cuts from glass. Four of her ribs were broken and one might have caused further internal damage. Melissa never left her grandmother's side, and as she rode with her in the ambulance, Louise wanted to talk.

She told her that a Devil's foul creature with a white face and flaming red lips attacked her and snatched "him" out of her arms just before the outbreak of madness at the fair.

"She spoke in fragments," Melissa said, moistening her cracked lips with the tip of her tongue. "Much of what she whispered doesn't really make sense. I mean about the Devil snatching my late brother out of her arms."

"What about your late brother?" Stella asked.

"Grandma used to walk us to school when we were children. A speeding car plowed right into the crossing guard and caught Ronnie, my six-year-old brother, too. Grandma held him in her arms until the ambulance arrived. He died on the way. She always brings it up when she's warning me to be safe. I think that part may be just her memory, but I believe she held on to someone, tried to help, and it was a stranger with a painted face or..." She stopped and glanced at Carter.

"A scarred face or facial deformities, like mine," Carter supplied in a business-like voice to show her that the issue of his facial scarring wasn't a sensitive point.

"Sorry," Melissa said quietly.

"It's all right. Go on," he urged her to continue.

"She said the unholy creature cursed her and wanted to drag her to hell, screaming 'Jibreel, Jibreel, ibn-alikht, come, come we must go.' He stretched his claws—"

"Excuse me," the nurse adjusting the patient's intravenous tubes turned around. "What did you just say?" he asked, facing Melissa. "It's all right, just repeat it," he urged her.

When she did, the man shook his head. "He wasn't cursing your grandmother, Ms. Norton. He was just calling to his nephew, Gabriel, to come. Jibreel, Jibreel, come ibn-alakh—it means Gabriel, Gabriel, come, nephew. Your pronunciation is a little off, but what you said is certainly no cursing. If I heard the speaker say it, I'd be able to tell you whether it's Saudi or Egyptian, or some other local dialect."

Even as the orderly spoke, Carter stared at the man's nametag: *Ahmed Jabrr'Jabal*. This American citizen, or at the very least landed immigrant, certainly knew what he was talking about.

"She also kept saying something about ashes, or ash, but there wasn't fire at the fair. It was all just people, fighting and trying to kill each other," Melissa said when they walked out of the room.

"Thank you, Ms. Norton," Saunders told her. "You have my business card. If you remember anything else, please don't hesitate for a moment to call me. I wish your grandmother a full recovery."

"Now we have a name and a link between the two men we're looking for," Carter told Saunders when they were once again outside in the hallway. "An uncle and a nephew, though they may not necessarily be related."

"You're splitting an infinitive," Saunders snapped.

"Is it that bad?" Carter knew the pressure on Saunders, already great after the Mall event, would have increased to where the FBI Director didn't want to hear another "creative" explanation as to the cause and its perpetrators, because the White House didn't want to hear more platitudes. They wanted results.

"We trod carefully in the Maronite religious community, but there were still complaints—all the way to the Director and to the press. A few of our statesmen serving abroad have already called the State Department to inquire why the FBI's focused their interest on their adult sons born abroad but very much true-blue American citizens. I thought we were looking for foreign nationals, Carter, not home-grown terrorists."

"They're probably not home-grown in the pure sense of the word, but one or both of them are most likely Americans."

"Carter, something has been bothering me ever since you planted this idea of riots without a cause being orchestrated by terrorists, foreign or home-grown—their numbers. While the FBI's looking for an organization, or at least a group, you're looking for two men. How can two men be responsible for what's been happening in our country?"

"It doesn't take much to start a riot," Carter said, knowing it was a feeble excuse.

"I would agree, Carter, if we were down in Colombia, or in any of the African countries where military juntas stage revolts on a weekly basis. But this is America in the twenty-first century! I can't even remember the last civil rights march that disintegrated into the kind of riots we're seeing now—in three places separated by much geography. Americans who live in places like Dayton or Long Island, or even Washington, might expect to become casualties of traffic accidents, but not to be killed by their friends, neighbors or family members during a local arts and crafts fair."

"Keep your voice down," Carter cautioned. "This is

a hospital."

"That's my point, Carter! These last couple of weeks I haven't been able to get *out* of hospitals, doing my job. An agent I mentored down in Atlanta for years bit through her partner's jugular—literally. A babysitter strangled two-year-old twins, a cop shot a store owner he's known for years, hundreds of drivers turned our highways into trash compactors, and you're operating on a premise that two men are somehow responsible for this outbreak of madness?"

"We're looking for an uncle and nephew, possibly named Gabriel," Carter said, knowing that once again this was neither time nor place for myths and legends. "The name Ashcroft figures in there too, though I don't know how. These two men entered our country sometime between March 3rd and May 2nd, the day of the Mall riot. They're still in our country. One or both are American citizens, born abroad. You now know everything I know," he finished with a lie he felt was not just justified but necessary, considering the circumstances.

"Do you think this outbreak of madness has anything to do with the Air Force base here?" Saunders asked.

"Is that the latest worry that fell into your lap?"

"The question's been asked from the place above the Mall five minutes after we got the news. Wright-Patterson may not be a sexy target, but it is one of the largest and most important Air Force bases we have in the country. Would it be prone to this... attack of madness?"

Carter could just imagine the worry in the White House and the Pentagon when it came to "extrapolating" where the next outbreak of madness might score. An Air Force base would be a nightmare. Hell, if one of the "madness-stricken" pilots took off in a C-21, a military version of a Learjet, he wouldn't need rockets to threaten those below. His afflicted mind would probably see him point the jet's nose down and head for the target, civilian or military—the pilot wouldn't care, because he wouldn't know what he was doing or why.

However, if Stella was right and the Peacetaker's connection was through religious channels, the chances of striking at a military base were slim. Besides, visiting a military base would not be a "natural" thing to do for the Peacetaker's controller... if Stella was right. Although Carter didn't feel fully convinced, she was, and he assured Saunders that Wright-Patterson was safe from the outbreak of madness.

Saunders waved a hand at him, looking resigned, not reassured. "It's three o'clock in the morning. Go get some sleep. I'll see you...whenever. Dr. Hunter." He nodded to where Stella hovered, some distance down the hallway and walked away.

"Saunders's right," he said when they walked out and headed for the hospital parking lot filled with so many police cruisers it looked like a depot. "We've driven all night to get here. Let's get some sleep."

"I'm bone weary," she said, "but I'd like to cruise around the neighborhood of that fair, if you don't mind."

"Tomorrow morning..."

"Now, Carter. There's something here that's familiar."

"Familiar? This is Dayton, not exactly a preferred vacation spot."

He yielded because the place wasn't too far away from the hospital. The entire block where the church sat seemed to be blocked off with yellow barricades and police tape. She said that the owners of the stores in the strip plaza would see a sharp drop off in their business for weeks to come if the barricades and the police tape didn't vanish quickly enough.

He disagreed. "American entrepreneurial mentality," he said when she asked him why. "I bet you anything that when all the grief plays out, this place will become another tourist attraction. This is the birthplace of aviation, first solo instrument landing, world altitude records—what happened at this local fair will join all those other historic events and their corresponding shrines in a great alliance of the tourist attractions, featured in brochures produced by the local Chamber of Commerce."

"Shrines?" she murmured, sounding perplexed.

"Just an expression."

"Shrines, shrines," she kept repeating. "And alliance... shrines and alliance... oh my God!"

"What is it?" He made a quick right-hand turn and stopped just a few feet short of a yellow barricade, cutting off the entry into the church parking lot.

"Shrines and alliance," she said, smacking both hands down on the dashboard. "Why didn't I see it before? That's why this place feels... sounds familiar. The Christian and Missionary Alliance—my parents were members, both of them attended Nyack College; in fact, that's where they met, in Nyack, which is thirty-five miles north of New York City. It's their *alma mater*, and there's a Nyack in Washington, just up from the Mall, on North Capitol Street, which brings us here, to the Nyack campus in Miami Valley, where they did a year of graduate studies before going to the Philippines. I think I have a photo of their graduating class back in Sunburst, taken here at the Oak Ridge campus. Aunt Hazel made an album portfolio of all their...where are we?" She turned to him, eyes skipping between him and the windshield.

"Off Main Street," he said, since technically speaking, they were in a parking lot of a strip plaza adjoining the Church of St. Luke.

"The campus here is just north of Interstate 675, west of Oak Ridge. That's certainly within visiting distance of the arts and crafts fair. I mean we're talking five miles here, at most. And since the fair is an annual spring event, it would have been well advertised. I bet you anything they're staying at one of the guest cottages on campus reserved for missionary staff that come back for a short period of time, for whatever reasons."

He glanced at the dashboard clock. "Well, we can't pay them a visit at this time of the morning. At this point, we have a name and possibly a family link between the two individuals. It shouldn't be that difficult to get the college dean to answer our questions."

"Director of Extensions, not dean, since this is an off-shoot of the original college in Nyack, founded in 1882."

"Well, let's find lodgings, and we'll see in the morning whether your brainstorm was brilliant or bust," he said, shifting to drive and turning around to get back out on the street.

"Son-of-a-gun," he said ruefully when not even half a mile later the much welcome hospitality sign appeared. "Holiday Inn, just what we ordered." He meant to draw out her comment, wry or sarcastic, but for once she remained silent.

"Stella," he said when he parked the Navigator. "We're getting very close, but we're not there yet. It's no use to spin scenarios, try them on for size."

"I won't let you kill him," was all she said and got out of the truck.

Chapter Twenty-five

S tella started calling the college at eight o'clock in the morning. It wasn't her first attempt, either, because when Carter knocked on the door and she let him in, he saw her dragging the phone cord while trying to keep the receiver stuck to her ear.

"Let's have breakfast," he said when she threw the phone receiver on the bed. "It's too early. College is like any other business that functions nine to five."

All through the breakfast, she kept asking for his cell phone. Finally, when he saw it was after eight-thirty, he gave it to her. She waged a war with the administrator on the other end and, according to her grimace when she handed back his cell phone, lost it.

"Director Burgess will see us at two o'clock. Her commitments won't allow her to see us earlier," she said.

He wondered whether she was that impatient or just bothered that her name and academic title didn't prevail over the commitments.

"Did Agent Saunders check in with you lately?" she asked when the hostess brought their coffee.

He sipped coffee, sorting his thoughts, because if he told her the truth she might take it the wrong way or overreact. Saunders didn't have to check in with him or pass on any information that the FBI would have obtained on its own. His contract with Saunders was the only legal bridge that spanned between their respective functions. Without that bridge, Carter's job title fitted into a less flattering category: Mercenary for hire.

It's what quite a few of his buddies opted for when they retired from the Army. Such vocational choice wasn't driven by the popular reasons the media kept feeding to their readership—combat, bloodlust, money—but rather practicality and economy.

Why waste all that Special Ops training and

experience on serving as bodyguards to the Hollywood crowd or checking private and commercial security systems when one could still serve one's country, albeit from the shadows?

His wife preferred to believe what she read in the newspapers and tabloids, not his version of the truth. When he retired at thirty-seven, she'd already planned out his new career path, Security Officer for Commodore Industries. He didn't want to wire circuits or adjust security cameras at parking lots filled with bulldozers, tractors and front-end loaders.

She said that her uncle, the Supervisor of Security staff at Commodore, would retire in a couple of years and he could have his job. He didn't want anyone else's job, no matter how good the benefits. He wanted to remain in his own, on his terms.

Six years later, when she shouted at him across the hallway just as he was ready to leave on another overseas assignment that she just wanted him home with her, to be there each and every morning when she woke up, he wondered why she wasn't so plain back then when he took his own path to job satisfaction.

He knew today that back then, he had a choice: renege on the assignment and stay home with Barbara, or carry out his obligation. In a sense, his choice gave her the momentum to make her own—to dissolve the marriage. A year later, Emily's death just speeded up what he knew couldn't be stopped. Six months later, just as Emily's headstone went up, he signed the divorce papers.

The next morning, he was at Dulles, heading for another 'business' meeting in Istanbul. In retrospect, he decided that jobs that brought him to noisy places like airports were what he wanted after all, because all the noise and hubbub around him was energizing. Just being there, part of the crowd, gave him a rush, a sense of immediacy, even urgency, that he was going somewhere, doing something.

But occasionally, like now, when Stella's question forced him to see his job from an unflattering angle, he knew that he craved the noise of a busy airport because it drowned out the voice in his head that insisted he had made a very bad career choice. The worst part was that he knew his country had not asked him to sacrifice his family and the choice had been entirely his own.

"There are certain contractual obligations on both sides, Stella," he said, "but the truth is that Saunders doesn't have to share information. If the FBI gets a lead and it proves to be a hot one, I'm afraid we'll be left out of the loop."

"Really?" She sat back, eyes narrowed.

"I'm afraid so."

"Do you trust him?"

He leaned forward, almost knocking over his coffee cup. "Who?"

"Saunders."

Now that was an interesting question that seldom if ever crossed his mind. He laughed. "I have no reason to suspect he's anything but an upright lawman of our country."

"So he would have told you the truth about the results of questioning the members of the Maronite community and checking visas and such shit?"

"Yes."

"But only because the investigation didn't uncover anything suspicious."

He smiled with his eyes, keeping his mouth straight. "You're getting to understand the rules of the...contract." He substituted "contract" at the last moment. What he wanted to say was that this is how the game was played between those who had badges and those who didn't.

"But if we find something, if you get a solid lead, you're expected to notify Saunders immediately, right?"

"That's right."

"I'm glad you're playing the game and I'm just an impartial observer," she declared, and asked the hostess for more coffee.

After breakfast, he decided to drop by the hospital. Maybe Saunders's people had found more survivors who'd noticed something or someone odd in their midst before they went berserk.

"Sir, if your facial injury's more than twelve months old, we'd really appreciate another blood donor." A Red Cross worker blocked his way just as he turned to see whether Stella followed him.

The hospital parking lot had been turned into a blood donor clinic, with white tents set up as far as he could see. Many cots were occupied, but many more were empty. It made him feel guilty because he had to refuse.

"Sorry, but I've had a blood transfusion just over two months ago," he said.

"Well, then I'm afraid we can't use you, sir." The woman moved to let him pass.

"I'm healthy and injury-free," Stella said from nearby.

The Red Cross worker rushed over to her new donor.

"Go, go. I'll be all right here. Where am I going to go with a needle stuck in my arm?" Stella waved him away.

He took a couple of steps but for some reason his feet felt oddly heavy, as if they didn't like to move in the new direction. Truth was that even though the parking lot was filled with police, medical staff and people wanting to donate blood, he didn't feel comfortable leaving Stella alone.

He turned around and walked after her to one of the tents they'd set up. He hovered nearby, not wanting to crowd while another Red Cross worker filled out a form and only when yet another staff member, a lanky man dressed in jeans and cowboy boots made her lie down on a cot, did he come around.

"Are you a volunteer with the Red Cross?" Carter asked the man who was fiddling with the tray on the small portable dolly next to the cot.

"Yes," the man mumbled, not turning around.

"Where is your name tag?" Carter motioned with his eyes and shook his head at Stella, who'd already rolled up her sleeve to wait.

"Sir, if you're not donating blood, please wait outside for your companion," the man said, turning his head but only in profile.

"Where is your name tag, sir?" Carter's voice hardened. "I want to see some identification before I let you attend her." He purposely identified Stella with a generic pronoun. Most people, including the Red Cross staff, would have assumed that Stella was his wife. It could have been just a diplomatic sort of thing to say— companion—but the man said it all-assumingly, as if he knew that to be the case. He didn't even say partner, which would have been another good diplomatic choice people would use when unsure of the couple's relationship. However, since Carter had hovered nearby when Stella was answering questions to satisfy blood-donor protocol, he'd heard what the worker asked. Marital status didn't figure in the blood-donor questionnaire; at least not here in an emergency situation. The volunteer wanted to know if Stella's blood was "good" in medical terms, not whether she was married.

"Sir, please wait outside. We have an emergency situation..." The man's voice trailed off even as Carter moved toward him. Suddenly, just as Stella sat up on the cot, the man shoved the dolly against it and bolted, leaping over the empty cots and zigzagging between those that were occupied with people giving blood.

Carter ran after him, all the while conscious that he

couldn't make it into a reckless dash that would see needles ripped out of people's arms and apparatus overturned or smashed. Once outside the tent, he saw the man running alongside a moving black pick-up truck with the passenger door swinging open. The man managed to grab hold of the door, swung himself into the truck then the vehicle sped off.

Carter returned to the tent.

"The man who just ran out of here," he addressed the volunteer who was doing the initial screening. "Do you have his name?"

She shook her head. "We've had so many volunteers in the last twenty-four hours that it's almost impossible to keep track of them."

"I suggest you strike the word 'impossible' from your list, ma'am, and make sure each of the Red Cross volunteers carries proper identification—and corresponding medical accreditation," he said and walked to where Stella sat on the cot, frowning.

"Did you just need the exercise or was it more serious?" she asked.

He didn't reply but motioned at the nurse, wearing the usual hospital whites with a nametag and a stethoscope around her neck.

"Would you mind checking whatever supplies are on that dolly, see if there's something that shouldn't be there."

The nurse picked up a blue paper packet with a top torn off and a partly exposed syringe.

"That's the problem with volunteers," she said, holding out the syringe to make her point. "Many have good intentions but little if any medical training. What was he going to do with this, draw 10ccs of blood?" She set to do the job, using a needle with a plastic knob that fitted into an intravenous tube leading directly into the collector bag.

Carter sat next to Stella, watching her blood course

through the plastic tube. When she finished doing her duty, he handed her a bottle of orange juice with a straw.

"What tipped you off—the needle?" she asked, sipping the juice.

He hadn't seen what the man was doing on the tray because he'd had his back turned.

"He called you my companion. Most people would just assume you were my wife or would have said "partner." But when you're shadowing someone, those who give you such orders would say: Male target and his female companion." He paraphrased a little for her peace of mind. Because those who would have given such orders would have said: Female target and her male companion.

***

Director Burgess saw them at precisely two o'clock, even though they arrived fifteen minutes early for their appointment. She was one of those women Carter thought would always looked competent, no matter what clothes they chose to wear. She had on a navy-blue suit and a white silk blouse with a string of pearls around her neck. However, even if she'd put on one of those skimpy T-shirts that Stella had bought for Katie and tight jeans with silver studs, she'd still have walked with purpose on her three-inch heels. Layers of make-up wouldn't erase that determined expression that said: There's no question I can't answer, no test I can't ace. He wondered if such women knew or even cared that nothing short of reincarnation would give them a dose of sex appeal.

Stella, once again dressed in her politically correct black khakis, white shirt and a beige linen blazer that looked "stylish" with all its creases and crinkles, had more sex appeal than the college director.

She shook their hands, invited them to sit in chairs facing her desk and settled down to business: What did they want from her? He couldn't catch her even once looking at his scar. All her looks were direct, true eye-to-eye contact.

He let Stella talk, since she'd made the appointment and the college was her parents' alma mater. He noticed the director glancing at Stella's empty 'wedding ring' finger and his matching empty digit and suppressed a smile.

When Stella paused, he flipped out his wallet, extracted his United Global Press business card and placed it in front of the director. While her competent expression didn't change, he did notice that she smiled more often, listening and nodding her head.

When Stella finished, the director looked at him and asked, "You are then Dr. Hunter's assistant?"

"I'm a freelance photographer and a journalist, but I'm also available for consultation. I met Dr. Hunter at a booksellers' conference in Michigan. When I'm not in the field, I do background research for clients like her."

They'd settled on a story that Stella said might even "come true" if she lived long enough to return to Sunburst. Since she'd already made her reputation as an author of a controversial academic book, Stella decided that her next project should honor the memory of her parents. She planned to write a book about missionaries and other members of charitable organizations that did God's work all over the globe.

An academic colleague in Washington told her that two members of the Church and Missionary Alliance had recently returned from Africa, having also worked in the Middle East, and to seek them out, for surely they would be willing to share their experiences with someone writing a book about people who didn't seek limelight or praise.

"Dr. Schram thought they might be staying at the Nyack College, the Miami Valley Campus," Stella said.

"I'm afraid we don't have anyone like that staying with us," Dr. Burgess said, tapping a finger against her cheek. "The cottages are unoccupied. Our graduates can be found working at missions all over the world, and our staff members may accept an occasional developmental rotation to teach in Africa or the Middle East, but none who are currently away are scheduled to return for some time."

"What about additions to your staff?" he asked.

"Oh, well, there's Father Malcolm, on rotation from Port Elizabeth Presbytery, South Africa. He joined us last September. There's Claire Petty, she transferred from the New York campus in December and that's about it, Mr. Carter."

"Would you know if any of your staff members have visitors from overseas, relatives, friends…?" Carter asked.

Once again, the director shook her head. "I can't be one hundred percent sure, Mr. Carter, but we are a very close-knit group here, in Miami Valley, which means that I would have heard if one of our staff had visitors from Africa or anywhere else. The topic would have certainly cropped up in our staff lunchroom."

"What about your students? Do you have someone who enrolled just recently?"

"Mr. Carter, it's the end of semester. The last enrollment was in January. We've had some student transfers from New York and Washington, but only in September, at the start of our academic year. None, to my knowledge, are foreign nationals."

"We're looking for American citizens," Stella spoke up.

"We do occasionally get a foreign student from Asia, Africa or the Middle East but most of our foreign students come from Holland, Germany, Scandinavia and England. However, like I said, currently I'm not aware of any recently enrolled foreign students, not even any with dual citizenship."

"What about your non-academic staff?" He knew that Stella would be even more frustrated than he was because the religious link was quickly dissolving with each minute spent talking to the college director.

"I'm afraid that's of no help to you at all. All our non-academic staff are local people, from Dayton. I think there might be a caretaker who's originally from Cincinnati but he's lived in Dayton for a number of years."

"The college has stringent admission requirements, right?" Stella asked. When the director nodded, she continued, "So, as the head administrator, you would have reviewed most if not all the applications per any given academic year."

The director sighed. "I see what you're after, Dr. Hunter, and I'm sorry to disappoint you. I can't remember even one of our students having already spent time in missions or as a relief worker anywhere in the Middle East. Of course, some of our students are mature students when they seek admission and those would have field experience, whether with the Peace Corps or with the Red Cross, but in the last two years, none of the applications that crossed my desk offered this particular qualification. When you phoned for an appointment and told me who you were, I took the liberty of searching our alumni archives. Your parents, Herman and Ulrike Warner, obtained their graduate accreditation in Christian Work and Counseling in '56 prior to being posted in the Philippines; more or less what we group today under the Missiology and Theological Studies. Your father's field experience with the Red Cross, during the Korean War, features in his records, but it wasn't the reason why he gained admission to college. He was an excellent and dedicated student; his academic record certainly reflects it."

"Thank you," Stella murmured, looking uncomfortable.

"I'm sorry, Dr. Hunter. Particularly this academic year, none of our first-year students have prior missionary or any other volunteer relief work experience that was gained anywhere but within the United States."

They didn't have any reason to disbelieve her or not

to trust that what she told them was less than pure truth.

"She's not hiding anything, Stella," he said when they left the college campus, driving back to the Holiday Inn. "She's a capable administrator who knows what's going on in and around her institution. I'm disappointed, too."

"The religious link is a bust," she mumbled.

"Probably."

"We've got nothing. We're back to square one."

"We've got a name and a possible familial association. Gabriel is not an overly common name. The FBI has resources to keep checking visas and citizenships of recent arrivals in our country. I'm sure they'll get a lead soon."

"I thought the lead was supposed to come from us—from you."

Yes and no. His contractual obligation to Saunders was investigating Nicola Moses' terrorist affiliations in terms of financing their activities on US soil. The Justice Department had their eye on Moses' piggybank, those funds that resided in US banking repositories. They couldn't touch his US holdings, because most, if not all, had US-partnership affiliations. And besides, they provided employment to thousands of American citizens who would not be happy to find themselves jobless, or at the least have their job security threatened.

Moses, however, was also a very crafty businessman. While his non-US holdings were encumbered with a certain percentage of debt necessary in every large-scope investment, the debt-equity ratio of all his US holdings was much, much higher. It meant that while Moses' Obelisk Corporate logo figured in a company ownership portfolio, bank financing or American private investors underwrote most of such company ownership. While he owned the Obelisk hotel in Monaco outright, the Obelisk Palisades in Los Angeles had a list of fifty private investors and two major US banks.

Carter had told Saunders that the only thing that belonged to Moses, as far as his US business holdings were concerned, was the billionaire's signature in a glossy program commemorating the opening of the said enterprise. But like most men whose signature becomes more powerful than the person behind it, Moses had to keep a certain amount of reserve in US banks because if he didn't, those whose job it was to make sure that people didn't just use the country's resources to make money that was then siphoned out of the country, would long since have cried foul.

The Justice Department wanted a good reason to padlock Moses' US cash reserves. Proof that the billionaire was financing terrorist activities on US soil would have been an excellent reason. The problem was that all Carter had managed to get in five years was 'solid' suspicions, not solid proof.

"Carter?" Stella's voice made him shake his head to banish reflections. "I'm not really hungry, but we should stop somewhere and eat, or I'll get nauseous. Maybe a mall or something; I don't want to eat at the Holiday Inn."

Parkwood Mall was a typical windowless, Lego-style conglomerate of retail stores and food courts, according to the forest of advertising signs posted along the edge of the parking lot.

"Perfect," she said but there was no energy in her voice.

They walked quietly, side by side, like a couple heading for their first session with a marriage counselor.

"What would you like to eat?" he asked when she sat down at the first unoccupied table she saw.

"You choose," she said uncaringly.

He came back with two daily specials from A Taste of Japan and two iced teas.

The beef and shrimp teriyaki was decent, but it

didn't deserve to be savored for as long as she played with it. He gave her ten more minutes of prodding the rice with her fork and toying with the bean sprouts, then said, "Let's take a walk around the mall. Sometimes it's easier to think on your feet."

"What's there to think about?" she murmured darkly but rose and followed him.

It was late Friday afternoon, but the mall wasn't crowded. There was nothing else to study but display windows.

"There must be another connection between the three sites," he mused when he judged she was ready to listen because shop windows didn't hold much interest for her, either.

"Maybe, maybe not. I don't know anymore, Carter, what to think, never mind offer suggestions. Washington, Long Island and Dayton—they could have been random picks. Maybe you were right back there when you said I was trying to apply logic to situation that's not logical. I was so sure about the religious connection, and I was wrong. Then I was so sure about the missionary connection and the college...same thing. What's left?"

"Stella, I'm not saying this just to cheer you up, but for some reason I feel that the religious and missionary connection still applies, just that we're not looking at it right or we're missing something."

"If that was true, your boss would have already come up with a name, or even a list of names, before the Dayton strike. You said the FBI has resources. How many American missionaries, or even relief workers, could have returned to the United States in the last eight weeks—a hundred, two hundred? And we're only interested in males, so that cuts down that number at least by half. How long would it take for the FBI staff to check out one hundred people across the country?"

He saw her point. In an emergency situation such as

now, the FBI didn't need elaborate permissions from the country's executive seat or the lawmakers. When the order came from the top, every able-bodied agent would be assigned to the task. If anything, once the subjects were located, the operation would have been carried out simultaneously across the country in a matter of hours. And if necessary, the local police enforcement would have been brought in to speed up the identification and questioning of targeted individuals.

"Not long, Stella." He decided to be truthful. "The FBI would have finished checking out all such identified subjects within twenty-four hours."

"I was so sure," she murmured, "so sure about ribbons of truth woven into the myths and legends. What if all of that's wrong too? What if those who criticized my book and panned it were right? What if Leandra Franmore and all my colleagues who said..." Her voice trailed off. She stopped and tilted her head to a side, staring at a display window of what looked like a shoe store.

He looked up to see the store's name: Kiddie Kobbler.

"I don't think they would have your size in there, Stella," he said, hoping to find her humorous vein.

"They wouldn't, would they?" she mumbled and took a couple of steps toward the display window then stopped and rocked herself back and forth.

"Stella, are you all right?" There was no one around to witness her strange behavior, but it didn't mean he wanted to see her rock herself into a trance.

"Back in the hospital, what did she say?" Her voice came misty. He didn't like that either.

"That the Devil snatched her grandson..."

"No, no. The other hospital, Paige Smith. She said Aladdin—a lad in sneakers and stars. White, red, gold—Carter?" She stopped rocking herself, turned and grabbed his hand then raised it, guiding his index finger to point

297

where she wanted it to point.

They moved closer to the display window that was set up with children's shoes resting on slanted platforms at various levels. She was pointing his finger at a white child's sneaker with red piping trim and gold stars. And while the footwear might have appealed to tomboys, the manufacturer's target consumer was definitely a young boy because the sneaker was the kind one might see on a cartoon hero—a fantasy warrior.

Suddenly, the pressure around his finger vanished. He turned his head in time to see Stella drop down as if her knees suddenly gave out. He bent down to help her rise but she resisted until he let go. She remained kneeling, hands around her body and rocked back and forth again.

"No, no, no," she moaned softly. "No, no, no. You didn't do it. You couldn't have done it. You didn't..."

He knelt down beside her, worried that the stress of these last few days might have caught up with her.

"Stella," he said, putting his hand around her shoulder. "Get up before the store clerk sees you and calls 911."

"Yes, call 911, all over the world," she said, leaning against him. "He did it, Carter. The fucking son-of-a-bitch did it!"

"What are you talking about?"

"That!" She jabbed her finger at the white sneaker with red trim and gold stars. "Don't you see, Carter? The bastard activated a child! The Peacetaker is a kid!"

While he saw the mercenary aspect of such action and understood how it would upset her that Moses wouldn't hesitate to use a child to perform acts of terrorism in the United States, he thought she should have been relieved to figure out yet another piece of the puzzle.

"Carter, there are rules," she moaned and finally allowed him to help her stand up. "The fucking bastard even hand-wrote an annotation in my book; you showed it to me, page 324. ' While the Peacetaker may be activated at age four for the initial test, he cannot - *must not* - be activated again until he's eighteen-years-old.' Remember the Latin text from Clairvaux—the blacksmith tried to put the amulet around child-Gaspard's neck but the cat's eyes flared red. It was a warning."

"A Devil's warning?" In his limited experience with the Devil, Carter wouldn't have thought him capable of such courtesy.

"Mythological demons were not stupid, Carter," she said in a voice he very much welcomed back. "They wouldn't just fling curses left and right, without rules and solid knowledge of human biology. A curse without a fail-safe system could wipe them out too."

She'd finally said something he understood only too well. "What do you mean, without a fail-safe system?"

"A child can be activated for a test only once, at precisely age four, to determine whether he possesses the Peacetaker power or not. He must not be activated again before age eighteen, precisely because he's a developing child, which means his physical, spiritual and mental energies are unsettled—unpredictable. It's absolutely *forbidden* to activate a child again before he turns eighteen, because you may not be able to deactivate him even if you take off the amulet."

Chapter Twenty-six

In a matter of minutes, a mere emergency situation in a country changed into a global doomsday scenario.

Stella marched back to the food court area and once again sat down at the first empty table she happened upon.

"I corresponded with Gahiji for ten years," she said, "and when I finally met him, I disliked him at first sight. I couldn't figure out why. Now I know. The fucking bastard! The lousy opportunistic weasel...with morals thinner than rice paper. I can't believe he did it, Carter. I still can't." She kept smacking her fists against the plastic table, shaking her head and snorting.

Carter wondered whether Gahiji would have told Moses about the pitfalls of activating an immature Peacetaker. Then again, if the curator was only after money, he couldn't wait until his 'discovery' turned eighteen. Most likely, the billionaire didn't know he was buying a weapon without a fail-safe system.

"Stella." He put his hands over hers. "Now more than ever I need you to become the woman whose picture is on the jacket of your book."

She stared at him then asked, "What are you talking about?"

"Oh, right," he said, sighing. It never occurred to him to consider that the picture was another publicity feature, suggested by her agent or publisher. While she might even have occasionally dressed to look like an academic matron, such apparel couldn't hide for long the personality—and the person—who'd been his partner now for nearly two weeks. He should have realized as much the moment he walked into her remodeled house in Sunburst.

She'd learned to play different roles as demanded of her by her job and her husband's, but that's not to say she buried herself in any given role for too long. In Sunburst, she didn't reinvent herself as someone she used to be. She just didn't bother bringing along the various masks she had in Michigan. She left behind her, in the matrimonial home, the collection of faces the world expected to see as a poignant reminder to her husband that such variety comprised their history together, and that he was giving up not just an accomplished woman but a partner who had worn those masks gladly—for him and their family.

"I'm calm," she announced. He saw she finally latched on to his meaning.

He was skeptical because she still kept tapping her fingers on the table but he was a gambler — and sometimes even won.

"What exactly are the consequences of activating an immature Peacetaker? Be specific."

"From all my research, and as far as I know, no one's done it. Not the Egyptians, not the Sumerians, not the Chinese nor Indians, nor Greeks. The African tribes worshipped their Peacetaker like you worship your gun and laptop. The Romans were arrogant but not stupid, and the Byzantine folk could not only read the Devil's warning signs but heed them. Every culture in our history that contains the Peacetaker's legend in its folklore held great respect for the power such a man possessed, so there's no reference in any script, ancient or modern, to anyone activating the Peacetaker before his time. There are, however, warnings—chiseled in stone, brush-stroked on rice paper and written on calfskin with reed pens. Those who seek to unleash the power before its receptacle has ripened, will suffer the wrath of Set, or Siphal, if you prefer the Sumerian version, and wither."

"That's it—just wither?"

"Wither is an all-purpose word with many applications and interpretations. Set left it vague on purpose. It's more ominous that way. The offender can't take any steps to protect himself from a curse whose effect he doesn't understand. It could literally mean wither as in age prematurely in a short span of time; or it could mean parts of your body will wither, or even your vital organs."

"What do *you* think it means?"

She laughed. "You're getting to know me, Carter. I'm not sure whether that's good or bad. I found an inscription on a stele that came from the temple of Kôm-Ombo — that's in the Aswan region, close to Berenice— that dates from about second-century BC. Ptolemy Philomentor started building the temple and his successors kept adding to it. It's actually two temples; temple of Sobek, the crocodile god and temple of Horus—"

"Stella!"

"The inscription translates 'withered' to mean pitted sandstone. A stone that has undergone much weathering, though sandstone is technically a sedimentary...."

"Stella!"

"...rock. How did you ever survive your formative years, those spent in school rooms?"

"I joined the Army right out of college."

"My, I'm impressed. I'd have said grade school. I also found another inscription on a stele from the 18th dynasty, circa 1200 BC, attributed to Merenptah's *hem-netjer*, a traditional title for a priest in ancient Egypt. Stop glaring at me. You're not falling asleep. That's my sign to be expansive. The stele is from the Amada Temple in Nubia. Merenptah, who was the son of Ramesses II, spent most of his adult life as a General in his father's army. Since Ramesses lived to a ripe old age, and ruled as pharaoh for fifty-five years, he outlived most of his throne-worthy sons. Merenptah is thought to be his thirteenth-born son and apparently the only one left to ascend to his father's throne when the old man kicked the bucket at eighty. And if you believe anything that's chiseled in stone, then Merenptah had a Peacetaker to assist him in his war campaigns. He was a very successful soldier but a rather mediocre pharaoh. The priest, Ahsarun, was either commissioned or compelled to chisel a warning into stone of what consequences awaited the wretch who activated an un-ready Peacetaker."

While Carter tried hard not to glare and even managed to blink to hurry her story along, she was in her element. Ahsarun must have had a direct pipeline to the gods, because he detailed such dire consequences. The offender who would place the hammered-gold moon amulet around the child's neck before the child's eighteenth year had come would have light fade from his eyes until these became like dry clay. Inert. His throat would grow parched and no amount of water would soothe his thirst. His lips would grow pale like sick worms, or—depending on the translator—turn black like asps. Unlike such living slithers, they would not remain supple but acquire coarse texture like that of a poorly crafted stone statue.

"And last but not least," she said, using her index fingers to conduct an invisible orchestra, "his testicles would shrivel and fall off."

He must have looked stunned, because she poked him with a finger.

"I'm awake. What a horrible curse. It almost eclipses that of the Peacetaker." He saw her squished-eye smile and groaned. "You made that last bit up, didn't you?"

"Somewhat," she admitted ruefully, turning serious immediately. "But ultimately that's what would happen, because with each transgression, the effect would intensify until the offender has turned to stone, essentially becoming a stone statue, his own unholy memorial—testament of his crime."

"This is pure lore and legends, right?" he tested.

"Well, other than the Biblical reference of Sodom and Gomorrah and Lott's wife turning into a pillar of salt, I haven't been able to find even one mention in any literary works left by civilizations preceding us of this curse actually kicking in. It could be just pure folklore. Then again, until you showed up in Sunburst, I thought that Gahiji was a crackpot and the Peacetaker was just a product of folklore."

"Now, tell me about the malfunctioning fail-safe system."

"Like I said, a growing child's energies fluctuate precisely because everything is still developing and nothing's settled. Activating a child then means the Peacetaker effect would be unpredictable, which explains why we have three atypical strikes. If Gahiji was the boy's controller back in Cairo, then he would have known how dangerous it was to activate the boy, so he wouldn't have kept the amulet on him for long. He also would have expected to remain the controller, so he knew he'd be activating the boy more than once in a fairly short span of time. What had to be a very short activation in Cairo affected the entire stadium. Indeed, it must have looked like the effect was not petering out. That would have alarmed Gahiji and set him thinking that maybe he should ask Moses for more money. That could be another reason why Moses got rid of him."

"And with the curator gone, there wasn't anyone else who'd understand the consequences of activating an un-ready Peacetaker," he said.

"This is just my own interpretation, Carter, but if a Peacetaker is activated before he turns eighteen, the effect might not stop at all. If it does, then it's chalked up to luck precisely because of unpredictability. Same thing applies to the next activation. So far, we've been lucky three times. I have no idea why, but I can tell you that where ancient curses are concerned, mortals' luck tends to run out very quickly. It's very possible that the next time the controller threads the amulet around the boy's neck, the effect will not cease to propagate—at all."

"And it won't stop unless the child perishes in the mayhem he unleashed, right?" he tested.

"I don't know," she said, looking away.

"Stella, believe me that it would be the last resort. I don't even want to entertain the idea of having to kill a child but…"

"I don't *know*, Carter. That's the truth. There's no reference in any historical record I studied to anyone activating the Peacetaker before maturity. We're talking here about fourteen years in a child's life during which time he's constantly growing, changing…it's not possible to predict anything. I don't even know how many variables would come into play. It could be that a six-year-old's not physically and mentally strong enough to produce the kind of effect that would sizzle from coast to coast but an eight-year-old might well be capable of unleashing such a cataclysm."

He wondered why she picked those two particular ages as her examples.

"Because he's either six or eight years old," she snapped at him, tugging at her hair in frustration.

"How do you know that?"

"Paige Smith talked to a child. We've established that much. A teenager wouldn't be caught dead in that kind of footwear, much less wear an Aladdin's costume."

"But why six or eight?"

"Because he would be born either in 2007 or 2009. The last Blue Moon occurred in 2012. He's not three years old. But before that, there was Blue Moon in 2009 and in 2007. Though I lean more toward '07. Gahiji spent years searching for him and two years ago when he approached me at the Wasserdown Conference in LA, he couldn't sit still. At the time I thought he was just a nut-case, but now I realize he had already found the child—and tested him. That's why he was excited. The conference was in January 2012 so four years back would take us to November 2008. But there was no Blue Moon in 2008—there was, though, in June 2007. That's when the Peacetaker would have been born."

"Why would the boy be born in '07?" He didn't understand where she was getting her inspiration.

"Carter! Haven't you heard anything I've said since we left Sunburst? We've agreed to follow the Egyptian conventions because that's what Gahiji followed. At the conference in January 2012, he had already tested the boy and confirmed his powers. The test can be done only once, at age four, so go back four years from 2012 and you're in 2008. But that year there was no Blue Moon. So a year back takes us to 2007 when there was Blue Moon in June and that means Gahiji must have tested him in June 2011, just in time for the conference six months down the road. There were only seven Blue Moons in the last fifteen years. Considering we're dealing with a child born in the last ten years, I'd put my money on June 30th, 2007, the second full moon in that month—hence the Blue Moon."

"Jesus, Stella." He moaned even as he flipped out his cell phone to call Saunders.

***

Carter didn't even bother going to his room when they got back to Holiday Inn but walked into hers and camped on the bed, cell phone to his ear, checking his messages.

"It'll take a while, because he could have entered the country at any airport that lands international flights," he told her when she faced him, hands braced on her hips, "but the FBI will make sure it will be given top priority. What is it?"

"I need your laptop."

He flicked his key-card at her. She caught it and opened her mouth to say something, reconsidered and left to get the computer.

"I want you to unlock this folder," she said when she booted it up and brought up a menu. The folder, *Moses*, contained five years of work he'd compiled on the billionaire.

"May I ask what you intend to do?" He knew he'd let her have it because like Saunders, she was an upright academic who'd not abuse any secrets he'd unlock for her perusal.

"What I do best, research," she declared, thanked him when he entered the password that unlocked the folder, then took the laptop and went to sit on the other double bed. He knew what was in the folder, having read the material often enough these past five years. She couldn't possibly find something that would have escaped him.

"Why don't you just ask me what it is you're after? It'll give me an opportunity for once to give you an extended lecture."

She shook her head. "You're probably so familiar with what's inside this folder that you can't see the forest for the trees. But don't feel bad. I'm like that, too, when it comes to my work. Take a nap. I'll wake you if I have another brainstorm."

Chapter Twenty-seven

Carter dreamed he was in the morgue again, looking down on Emily's body. Suddenly her hand jerked and rose, grabbing his forearm, pulling him down, toward her face. The bluish mottled pallor of death began to fade, but the color of life didn't rise to warm up the skin and once again make it supple. Instead, her skin turned parchment-like, with spider-vein cracks.

"Daddy!" She yanked him toward her. "What's happening to me?"

"Carter, wake up!" Stella shouted, practically in his ear.

He struggled to sit up, feeling sluggish, as if he'd aged a hundred years in his sleep. "I'm up. What is it?"

"It's morning, that's what it is. We've got to move."

"Why?"

"Because this Holiday Inn's slated for demolition and the wrecking crew's here."

It took him a few moments to digest what she said. "You're either high on something or you've not slept at all and are on your second wind," he said, stretching and moving his head from side to side to exercise the stiffness in his neck.

"I might have nodded off now and then because you keep such boring information on the man. His holdings, their financing, the new and old business deals, the partnerships, real estate properties—the man owns a luxury cruise ship, for crying out loud, but you're interested in technical specs of the craft; nothing about its luxurious appointments and amenities. He holds meetings with presidents, but you're interested in where and why and what kind of security there is, not what such luminaries talk about. He has a wife and two daughters, and possibly a mistress in every port, but you dismiss it with a post-script note."

"Moses works hard at projecting an image of a devoted family man. It's very unlikely that he *is* such an upstanding Christian, but he's never been connected to any sexual misconduct scandal in public," he said.

"You suspect him of financing various terrorist activities, not just in our country but elsewhere in the world."

"That's the part of my Moses-portfolio I was hoping you'd leave alone."

"If I had left it alone, I'd have missed a very interesting article that explores Mr. Moses' humanitarian side." She grabbed his chin, squeezed it, no doubt to make sure that rigor mortis hadn't set in yet, then hopped over to the other bed and brought back his laptop.

In 1999, nine sub-Saharan countries declared HIV/AIDS to be a natural disaster in their countries, therefore requiring emergency response. Granroy Stewart, the President of the International Federation of Red Cross and Red Crescent Societies, issued a worldwide appeal for funds to bolster primary health care, not just in the said countries but the rest of the African nations. Nicola Moses, on behalf of the Obelisk Meridian International Corporation, pledged twenty million US dollars to the Red Cross African relief.

"With a little catch," Stella said, pointing at the laptop's screen. "That the Federation is able to raise an equal amount in donations from all over the world, thus matching his generous contribution, dollar for dollar. Not too many news reporters ferreted out this little qualifying condition — but one did. Your friend, the late Bastiat-award winning journalist, Pascal Giroux. The Red Cross fell short that year by ten million. However, good sport that he is, Mr. Moses just smiled, said shit happens, and donated a full pledge. Mr. Giroux, no doubt overwhelmed by the billionaire's generosity, decided to probe further into the matter. He was never allowed to publish this, was he?"

Once again she poked the laptop screen with her finger, tapping a headline that indeed never featured in any global newspaper. Pascal had sent him the investigative article he wasn't allowed to publish. It detailed an interview Pascal held with Dr. Haig Baladha, a senior health officer with the International Federation where he told Pascal that the original "contractual" stipulation was observed and Moses donated only the exact sum raised by the Federation—just under ten million. However, as far as all the watchdog agencies whose job it was to track such things knew, Moses donated the full pledged sum.

"That's how Mr. Moses finances various terrorist organizations without having his financial deals overly scrutinized," she said, prompting him with her eyes to nod. "After all, what banking institution or government would scrutinize a Red Cross charitable donation?"

"He's clever," Carter said.

"He's a murderer, Carter, because Dr. Baladha died three days after he talked to Pascal, from a bee sting—an acute allergic reaction. Moses just loves these 'natural causes' deaths, doesn't he?"

"Those who do his dirty work are certainly experts in allergies," he said, wondering where she was heading.

"And in 2000, Mr. Moses, through the United Middle Eastern Meridian Relief Fund pledged—and delivered—a two-million US dollar donation to the Red Cross/Red Crescent Society for meningitis vaccination in Sudan."

"Moses likes changing strategy. It's one of the reasons why it's been so difficult to obtain solid proof rather than just what's in the folder—suspicions."

"He may like changing strategy from one charitable deed to the next, but there's something he likes well enough not to change at all—the Red Cross organization. His Meridian Relief Fund deals almost exclusively with the Red Cross/Red Crescent societies, world-wide."

"Stella, the International Federation of Red Cross is a very solid and highly respected relief organization that—"

"I don't doubt it, Carter. I wasn't suggesting any improprieties that way; at least not in terms of the organization as an entity."

"Then what are you suggesting?"

"A healthy orchard will produce beautiful and delicious apples, but also a few rotten ones. And those are the ones Mr. Moses seeks out."

"All right—so where does this rotten-apple-in-a-barrel analogy take us?"

"The corner of Hilldale and Watermain, in Kettering."

***

The American Red Cross Dayton area chapter offices were located in a low-rise commercial building that looked like a flagship of the small business park occupied by insurance companies, real estate brokers and law firms.

"Who are we going to be this time?" Stella asked him when they were still in the parking lot.

He flipped out his wallet, rifled through his business cards and, when he found what he was looking for, he gave it to her.

"T. James Carter, Private Investigator, Washington, DC?" she read, sounding perplexed rather than dismayed.

"We're on contract to Catholic Social Services of Washington, trying to track down a child, male—age nine, born June 30th, 2007—believed to be traveling with his uncle, who is the child's only surviving relative but who doesn't officially have custody of the boy."

"Good thinking." She nodded. "We don't want to give them an impression that it's a kidnapping, just an ignorant relative who didn't square things with social services prior to taking his nephew. We don't have the child's full name."

"We'll dance across that minefield if and when the

time comes."

"They'll ask us why we're looking for the boy at the Red Cross."

"Because his uncle is a Red Cross employee, Washington Chapter."

"We need an international connection."

"He's an emergency and disaster relief worker, but his home base is Washington."

"We don't have a name for this relief-worker uncle."

He stopped. "Do you want to go back to Parkwood Mall, sit down at one of the food court tables, drink a dozen coffees and brainstorm a new scenario?"

"Let's just wing it," she said, walking in to the building.

Five minutes after the receptionist introduced them to Kevin Baird, the Director of the Emergency and Disasters Relief Section, they found themselves standing in a minefield. The fourth floor office was a totally open-concept environment. Carter didn't see even a low partition, never mind a door. It was Saturday, but every desk had a body sitting behind it, most of them busy with phone calls or computer work.

Baird wanted to know the uncle's name so he could serve them efficiently—by searching the Human Resources database—worldwide.

"John Ashcroft," Stella finally said, when the silence was becoming not just uncomfortable but ominous. Baird quickly entered the name then wanted further details. Birthdate, Social Security Number, last residential address—everything short of Mr. Ashcroft's visa number.

"We don't have much information on the boy's uncle," Carter said, "that's why social services are looking for him."

"But surely if he's a Red Cross employee—"

Carter cut him off. "He has been overseas for an

extended period of time, Middle East, working with emergency and disaster relief groups at various locations but his last confirmed residence is Cairo."

"When did he return to United States?" Baird asked, no longer eager to keep entering information.

"According to the Washington Chapter, he was scheduled to return in mid-April but for various reasons postponed his return until the end of the month."

"Are you saying, Mr. Carter, that our Washington office doesn't know the date their employee returned to United States?"

"Yes." He decided to be brief even though he knew it would result in even more controversy.

"I'm afraid that's not possible. The Red Cross organization takes its responsibility to its employees most seriously. If one of our employees doesn't arrive back home at a specified date, we immediately begin to track him down. I'm sure you realize that considering the fact our staff most often works in disaster-struck areas where hundreds and thousands have already perished, we can't afford to be lackadaisical concerning their whereabouts."

"Do you have anyone at this office, sir, who has recently returned from Africa or Middle East and has an eight-year-old nephew?" he asked, voice hardening. He knew that at any time he could shackle him into very quick co-operation by flipping out the Department of Justice business card, but he didn't want to play that ace just yet.

"No." Baird, too, was no fool. He wouldn't suspect that his visitors had harder affiliations with the government than just social services, but he probably thought they were nosy reporters.

"Did an employee from one of the New York Red Cross chapters arrive here, at this office, in any capacity in the last week?"

"No."

"How about from Washington?"

"I'm afraid not."

"Did you have any visitors at all in the last two weeks?"

"Of course," Baird declared in that false tone of voice meant to be sincere.

"Names, please."

"Ellen Dufresno, counselor. Miriam Thaw, health and safety, Ming Ha Cheng, public relations and Jennifer O'Neil, administrative supervisor."

"What about your volunteers?"

"I could sit here all day and rhyme off names, Mr. Carter, but I'm afraid it would be a poor use of my time. We have an emergency situation in Dayton. We're busy, in case you haven't noticed." He swept the office with his hand. "And most of our staff is where they're needed the most—running a blood donor clinic at the Miami Valley Hospital, counseling survivors and bereaved, those who lost loved ones, and generally coping with many emergencies that arise out of events like the one that struck our community just two days ago. Why don't you drop by the blood-donor clinic, have a chat with our volunteers, debrief them if you must, and in the process perhaps leave a pint or two of your blood behind for their trouble? Good day, Mr. Carter, Dr. Hunter…is that an honorary title or are you a medical doctor?"

"There's nothing honorary about my title, administrator," Stella said, breathing hard. "And we've already visited the clinic. Carter can't donate blood because he's had a transfusion just two months ago. but rest assured that I donated enough for both of us. Good day, Administrator Baird."

When they were outside in the hallway, Stella yanked his sleeve. "He's hiding something."

"No, Stella. He's just pissed off because he suspects we're not who our business card says we are."

"Who does he think we are, for God's sake?" she

exclaimed.

"Probably reporters who came to sniff out something, anything, about what happened at the local fair."

"I'm pretty sure he's hiding something," she maintained.

"He just doesn't want to compromise his organization in any way," he said.

They waited for the elevator and just as the light above turned green, someone called out to them.

"Mr. Carter, ma'am." A young woman came running down the hallway. "Let's go downstairs," she said and hurriedly walked into the elevator.

"I'm Felicia Corazon, a trauma counselor. Mr. Baird is just in a bad mood. You have to excuse him. We've had our budget cut back...anyway, I'm not sure whether this is the man you're looking for, but we did have a male visitor from overseas, though not the Middle East. He's from the International Federation, someone fairly high up because he's in fundraising. He came Tuesday. I just caught a glimpse of him because Kevin took him right away to the boardroom, that's down on the third floor, for a meeting with the rest of our directors. Our fundraising efforts these past couple of years have been rather dismal. I'm sure that economic factors play a part, but back in January we got an email from our national headquarters in Washington that fundraising experts were scheduled to make rounds of chapters and asking management to indicate when it's their preferred time to have these consultants come in."

'Did you get the man's name?" Carter asked.

"Well, that's the reason why I was eavesdropping on your conversation with Kevin. He introduced the man to us as Ernest Bourgawich, a Dutchman from Geneva, but the boy called him "Uncle Kraft," which seemed odd, but I thought nothing of it until you came this morning."

"Are they still here in Dayton?" he asked, already flipping out his cell phone.

"No, maybe," Felicia said and motioned for him to put away his tool. "That's not all, Mr. Carter. I wouldn't be here, telling you this, just because you pissed off Kevin. I think the boy's sick; so is his uncle. I work only Tuesday, Wednesday and Friday. Tuesday, I had a full schedule, no break in my appointments or I'd have looked after the boy while his uncle made the presentation. But I was busy, so one of the volunteers looked after him and I just saw him briefly. He was pale, but when I touched his forehead it was hot. He hardly spoke, couldn't even say his name, but his uncle said he had developmental disabilities and that his name was Ashton."

"But you don't think the boy's disabled in any way?" Stella spoke up.

Felicia grimaced. "I'm a trauma counselor; I work with traumatized *and* disabled children all day long. That child was sick, and it's probably not your run-of-the-mill cold or flu. His pupils were dilated too; made his eyes look like chunks of coal, and they were actually blue. His uncle must have some kind of skin disease, fungus or something, because he practically lathers corrective make-up on. He almost looks like someone who's undergone facial skin grafts."

"Give me a physical description of both and make it as detailed as possible," Carter asked.

"I only saw the uncle once, briefly, when Kevin introduced him. I saw the boy twice, when the volunteer came to take him away and when I went to the washroom. He stood in front of the water fountain, watching the water splash as if that was the most fascinating thing in the world. But when he took a drink, he started to choke. That's when I went over to help and noticed his dilated pupils. Mr. Bourgawich is about five feet eight inches tall, skinny, not just lanky, because the suit jacket hung on him as if it was a hand-me down but it was good quality. I have no idea whether he's ugly or handsome because he puts so much paste on his face. For the same reason, it's hard to tell his age, but I'd guess about thirty-five, forty. His hair is dark, crisp with a lot of flex but not curly. His hands are ten shades darker than his face. The boy's fair complexioned to begin with, which makes his pallor look almost ghostly. He has blue eyes, a slight build and is about four feet tall, maybe a bit taller; hard to tell."

"I hope you're taking detailed notes." Carter turned to Stella, who had fished out a pen and a small yellow notebook while the counselor talked. He heard her mumble something and suppressed a smile. He thanked the young woman when she raised her hand.

"We *are* investigators, Ms. Corazon," he said, "but our employer is the Justice Department."

"That's good." She smiled, continuing. "Because while you were talking with Kevin, I logged into our global personnel database. I have clearance because I spent sixteen months in the field, working with an international team of trauma counselors at Chernobyl, and also in Kosovo. There's an employee named Ernest Bourgawich, a senior fundraising officer, with the International Federation, the Red Crescent arm of the organization, and according to the assignment sheet, his home base is Cairo. Now, the International headquarters is in Geneva, so he *could* have arrived from there. But there is no employee with the Federation or the American Red Cross named Kraft."

"Now that is very interesting," he commented. "Would you know where Mr. Bourgawich and his nephew might have gone after his presentation here?"

"They came back Wednesday morning, briefly. That's hearsay, because I didn't see them, and then left. But Mr. Bourgawich is an international fundraising expert, so I figure he would head to Ann Arbor."

"Why?" Stella spun around with such force the notebook flew out of her hand.

Felicia moved her head from side to side, "Well, it's just my feeling, but if I was a senior officer in the organization, that's where I'd go; I mean, it's an opportunity."

"Why?" Stella insisted.

"Because the week-long twenty-ninth session of the International conference of the Red Cross and Red Crescent starts today, at Ann Arbor. I think today there will be only preliminary sessions held all over the campus. The main conference kick-off isn't until Monday. I think the hot issue will be the admission of Israel's Magen David Adom into the Red Cross organization."

"Oh, my God," Stella breathed out, pressing a hand against her mouth. "That's what happens when you're excommunicated. I'm out of touch. Carter, let's go."

"Thank you, Ms. Corazon. You've been very helpful, and I hope you won't suffer any consequences because of it," he said, even as Stella picked up her notebook and once again started scribbling.

She walked toward what she must have perceived as the door but what was a wall.

"Stella," he raised his voice before she made a painful acquaintance with the hard surface. She looked up from her scribbling and readjusted her feet to point in the right direction.

"Mr. Carter," the counselor called after him.

He turned around. She approached once again to speaking distance. "This is probably not related to anything you're investigating, but while today there's no Red Cross employee named Kraft in our human resources database— not based in Cairo or Geneva or here, there were actually three Krafts with the Peoria, Illinois Chapter of the Red Cross in 2004. Two of them, a married couple, Lucille and Andrew Kraft, left in 2005 with a relief team to work in the famine-stricken regions in Sudan, while Andrew's brother, Martin Kraft, joined them a year later. The Kraft couple died of cholera and yellow fever within two weeks of each other in 2009, but Martin Kraft, well..." Her voice trailed off.

"Well what?" he prompted her.

"Back there," she raised her eyes toward the ceiling, "Kevin was telling you that the Red Cross never loses track of its relief workers, no matter where they happen to be, which is ironic, because as far as the Peoria Chapter's concerned, Martin Kraft's still missing."

Chapter Twenty-eight

The traffic on I-75, north and southbound, was light. Back in Dayton, at the Holiday Inn, Stella started an argument as to why Carter should let her drive. Since he'd planned to let her drive in the first place, he quickly cut her off and said that was just fine with him.

"I have work to do," he said, climbing into the Navigator on the passenger side.

Initially, she drove at the speed limit, but eventually the speedometer needle inched upward. When he glanced over and saw it nervously jiggling around seventy, he said, "It's only two hundred miles to Ann Arbor. We'll be there in three hours, but that might not be the case if you keep testing your luck."

She turned on the radio and ignored him.

However, when the exit for Wapakoneta flashed by and she saw a police cruiser, attending to another speeding driver in the southbound lanes, she slowed down. She turned down the radio volume and after a while said, "You won't find it there."

He had his laptop on his knees and held her book open, flipping through it, now and then reading a passage over and over until he was sure he understood it.

"Won't find what?" he tested.

"The reference or details about the consequences the one who activates an unready Peacetaker will suffer. I couldn't even mention the steles from Kôm-Ombo and Amada temples without obtaining a ton of permissions from various British and Egyptian academics, as well as the British Museum. Malcolm Yarbrough obtained copies of the inscriptions for me. If I had as much as mentioned a detail from those inscriptions and referenced it in footnotes, I would have compromised him. He's an expert in ancient languages, has a PhD from Oxford and consults for various museums and universities. He also has a noble title, earl of something."

He let her chat, because that way she wouldn't be tempted to speed. She'd met Malcolm Yarbrough, Earl of Cranston, in London, when her husband was attending a conference and she came along to keep him company — and to sneak away and do her own research, when Bruce Hunter was attending presentations. While "browsing for inspiration" through the British Museum, she spotted Yarbrough's name beside a translated Latin text and impulsively sought him out at his Chelsea residence.

The academic from Oxford and the academic from Michigan forged an instant friendship. They had so much in common. They both loved horses and rode them like the ancient knights at jousting tournaments, with total disdain for broken bones and how long these took to heal in middle-aged people. Yarbrough's forte was ancient Greek and Latin, hers hieroglyphics and Demotic script. Together, they were a tower of knowledge few, if any, expert could uproot. He was an atypical Brit who loved coffee. She was a typical American who wished for an extra faucet on her kitchen sink that would dispense nothing but excellent, hot black coffee. They were both occasional drinkers but when the occasion called, they would have a Glenlivet on the rocks — no other form of water. And neither cared for austere décor or austere art.

"The man sounds like he's your soulmate," Carter remarked, stifling chuckles. He also wondered whether she'd indulged in something more than just pure academic friendship with the British linguist.

"Oh, you should have seen his townhouse in Chelsea," she said, sighing wistfully. "It was a positive anarchy of colors. Pink silk cushions and lime-green tassels on full-length burgundy drapes. Persian rugs and Aubussons, marvelous artworks. He had a Gauguin hanging right next to Monet, and you can't imagine the effect. It was like living in your own museum."

"Well, if you'd stop feuding with your husband and get down to serious business, you could be a free woman in a matter of couple of months," he remarked. "Then maybe you could reconnect with Dr. Yarbrough, give your relationship a new twist."

"Get real!" She started laughing.

Something occurred to him. He put down the book and started tapping the keyboard. If Dr. Malcolm Yarbrough, a Lord no less, was such a distinguished fellow academic, he'd be easy to find on the Net, since he probably had his own website, being a consultant and all.

"Your matchmaking talent sucks," she said. "What are you doing?"

"Trying to inspire you," he said and clicked on the first subject line since all the words in the string figured in the brief summary. "Dr. Malcolm Yarbrough, the Earl of Cranston, will be remembered for his contribution to the academic...Jesus!" He sucked in his breath when he realized he was reading an obituary.

"What is it, Carter?" She reached with her hand and turned the laptop such that she could see the screen though the print was too small to read from such distance. However, Yarbrough's picture with bold black numbers beneath it—*1967-2015*—was more than revealing.

"He's dead, isn't he?" she asked quietly.

He turned the laptop back and read the rest of the obituary. Lord Yarbrough died of acute asthma attack at his home in Chelsea, in those wee hours of the morning when the butler slept soundly and on the particular night when he gave his nursing attendant a night off.

"Malcolm's asthma wasn't that bad," Stella said. He glanced at her and saw her bite her lips. "His nursing attendant was his companion, his partner. Malcolm was gay. He was old-fashioned and not inclined to come out of the closet, hence the nursing attendant solution. I don't even think he really had asthma, but he had to have some ailment to justify a live-in male nurse."

"I'm sorry, Stella," he said obliterating the image of the late linguistic expert.

"Thank you. Carter?"

"Yes?"

"Moses is untouchable, isn't he? Our government will never be able to make anything stick. He's too powerful to harass, so all our law enforcement agencies can do is watch him in such a way that he knows he's being watched. Besides, he doesn't have to enter the US to look after his business interests. He has more than enough people to do it for him."

It was pretty much what he had felt even before he accepted the assignment.

"There are ways to remove anyone, Stella, no matter how powerful or how well-protected he is," he said.

"I was hoping you'd say that. I can hardly wait to read the news about Mr. Nicola Moses—dying of natural causes."

***

They gassed up just after the Findlay exit. She didn't want to waste time having late lunch or early dinner, but he insisted. "It'll give me a chance to check if anyone's following us," he said, though he didn't think anyone was tailing them. But he knew she'd accept that as a good reason to eat and take a break.

"Take your foot off the gas. We'll be there in plenty of time," he said when they got back on the highway and she started testing the speedometer again. "The symposium doesn't really start until tomorrow. Tonight it'll be mostly shaking hands and cocktail parties. I don't think Mr. Bourgawich will attend any of them, even if he could find a babysitter for his nephew."

"Your cell phone's been awfully quiet today. Shouldn't Agent Saunders call you, if only out of professional courtesy?" she asked.

That worried him too, and she didn't even know that when he'd checked his voicemail, there were no messages either. When Saunders stopped calling him, it meant the FBI had its own lead and it was probably better than his. After all, he'd upheld his end of the contract and passed Saunders every new bit of information they managed to pick up.

Saunders now knew what to give his agents as a starting point: Ashton or Gabriel Kraft, born June 30th 2007, somewhere in Africa or the Middle East but an American citizen by virtue of his parents being Americans. The boy had entered the US around or before May 2, arriving from points unknown, in company of a male adult, representing himself as the boy's uncle and likely traveling on a US passport, under the name Martin Kraft.

Carter felt the man would have entered the country on Kraft's passport and once safely past customs, he'd assume his other identity as a fundraising consultant with the International Red Cross Federation, Ernest Bourgawich, a Dutchman arriving from Geneva. At least that's how he'd represent himself at the Red Cross headquarters in Washington.

There was a small risk that someone at the headquarters would seek to confirm with Geneva that their expert had arrived. Then again, Moses planned in detail, just as Stella said. If someone from Washington contacted Geneva, they'd just hear what they expected to hear—that their fundraising consultant, Mr. Bourgawich, had indeed been dispatched to train the American Red Cross staff at its various chapters.

Did Moses indeed recruit a senior Red Cross officer into his scheme? Carter didn't think it likely. Which meant the real Bourgawich, based in Cairo, was still there, though not walking around. His body would never surface, because the Sahara was notorious for keeping what men like Moses liked to bury in its sands.

Pascal had told him that nomads who lived in peripheral desert regions had witnessed on quite a few occasions a helicopter hovering just ten feet above the sand, and though they couldn't see clearly for the mini-sand storm whipped up by the craft's rotors, they thought it dangled a rope that someone used to climb down, carrying something, then a while later the figure would climb back again and the chopper would roar away. Being children of the desert, they knew that what it swallowed was not meant to be brought up again and never bothered to investigate the spot. Pascal said that a hundred years from now, when a new wave of reality shows focused on recreating history, some Hollywood-style caravan would wind its way across the sand dunes and come upon bleached human bones.

At least Pascal's were resting in his beloved homeland. Carter made a mental note to visit Pascal's grave the next time his job took him to Lyons.

Was his cell phone indeed silent because Saunders had already found Kraft/Bourgawich and was even now interrogating him in a windowless room with a team of FBI brass watching from the next-door conference room? If so, what would Saunders ask him? After all, Saunders didn't know anything about the mythological aspect behind the riots. He would also not know what to make of the child and why Carter gave him such information in the first place. He might assume that the adult was using the child as a screen, since people were less inclined to be suspicious of strangers with children.

He should have waited another day before passing the information on to Saunders. If the FBI already had Kraft/Bourgawich then they'd question him about his partner, since Carter told Saunders they were looking for two adult males. The man's credentials would be solid in his Bourgawich identity. Moses would have made sure they were.

The boy's presence could be easily explained as a

charitable gesture, a humanitarian thing to do for a member of the Red Cross organization. When the boy's parents died in '09, his uncle took care of him, continuing to work in whatever capacity Martin Kraft joined his brother and sister-in-law in Sudan. A few weeks ago, Martin Kraft also died, and for a while the boy was cared for by nomads until a relief Red Cross worker spotted him and passed on such information to Cairo headquarters, where Mr. Bourgawich immediately made arrangements to return the boy to his homeland.

If the FBI questioned him as to why he then entered the country on Martin Kraft's US passport, Bourgawich would feign surprise: What US passport? Then he would implore them to look at the passport they'd have confiscated upon detaining him to show them what they surely knew already? His Swiss or Egyptian or even Dutch passport would be duly stamped by US customs to match the date and all other customs' information in the boy's passport. Surely the FBI was mistaken?

Saunders would then bring in someone like Felicia Corazon, a children's counselor, to talk to the boy...

"Carter!"

"What?" He snapped his head up.

"You're not just mumbling to yourself; you're having an argument with yourself and a fairly loud one. It's possible that Saunders might have already found the controller and the boy, but I don't think so."

"Why not?"

"Because Bourgawich or Kraft no longer looks like his passport photo. He's probably neither Bourgawich nor Martin Kraft, but no matter what he looked like when he entered our country, he no longer resembles that man. Even if Agent Saunders obtained a picture of Ernest Bourgawich or even one of Martin Kraft, I don't think the man who's the boy's controller resembles any of them. He no longer resembles himself."

"What *does* he look like?"

She glanced at him briefly. "I can't be sure."

"I'll settle for an educated guess, Stella."

"Well, if the curse I said has never kicked in throughout history did happen to kick in here, in the twenty-first century, he either looks like a sandstone statue or a skeleton."

"Neither is a very mobile entity, Stella. Why are we rushing to Ann Arbor? Why aren't we calling roadworks or sanitation department to see if their crews haven't picked up a skeleton or a sandstone statue somewhere along this highway?"

She laughed. "It might be one of those slow curses."

"I'm still listening, though your credibility with me is starting to erode, just like sandstone."

"He may eventually become a living skeleton or a…"

"Don't say it," he moaned.

"…a mobile statue, but since we're making history here because everything's happening for the first time, it's possible the curse is affecting him in stages. One transgression might well mean only his face will be affected; two and it's down to his neck and shoulders, three and we're down to his torso—well, you get the picture."

"I wish I could say yes, Stella."

"Felicia Corazon said the suit jacket hung on him as if it was a hand-me-down but it was a good suit. I'd go for the living skeleton version. Of course, it could be a combination of the two. His face could become like pitted sandstone while below the neck could be living skeleton."

"And you wanted me to tell Agent Saunders what we're dealing with?"

"Don't you think he'd have believed us?"

"He loves his job, Stella, as much as you love yours. There are many other things to undermine his sanity, like his director, the people above the Mall and on the Hill, even those in the Pentagon, not to speak of the human criminal element in our country. It would be sadistic to undermine his sanity further with mythological demons and curses that boomerang against those who seek to undermine our country's stability by sowing madness amongst our populations, turning them into living skeletons or mobile statues."

"You're a wuss," she said, chuckling.

"I don't want to spend the rest of my life being debriefed in a padded cell."

She drove for a while, chuckling now and then while he returned to his laptop. He had planned to test his hacker skills on the International Federation's human resources database to see if Bourgawich had a photo on file, but now it seemed useless.

"Carter, do you realize that the two of us are quickly becoming the only people in the world who know of the Peacetaker's existence?" she asked in a dry, constricted tone of voice, which meant she was thinking about Yarbrough and the many other colleagues whose names figured in her book; either as reference sources or cited quotes. Moses had the resources to see they all died of natural causes, if that's what it took to blanket the Peacetaker knowledge.

"I could ask Saunders—"

She interrupted him. "And ask what? These people are all knowledgeable about the Peacetaker legend as it figures in the folklore of various ancient civilizations, and though they don't believe in ribbons of truth in such legends, their lives are in danger. Protect them."

She was right. At the very least, Saunders would think such a request frivolous, an indulgence or maybe even a joke.

"We have to hurry, Carter. If he's indeed in Ann Arbor, that's where he must be stopped."

He agreed with everything she said, except the

"hurry" part.

"Stella, you're doing almost eighty. Take your foot off the gas," he warned.

"A jerk's been sitting on my tail since the last exit," she said. The Navigator kicked ahead as if the gas was indeed a needle in its fetlock.

"Switch lanes. Be courteous and let him pass." He couldn't remember when, if ever, she drove in the right-hand lane, as if the left lane had a higher speed limit. He looked in the side-view mirror. The black pick-up truck swung into the right-hand lane and steadily gained on the Navigator.

"Step on it," he said crisply. "And whatever you do, don't let him pass."

"What?"

"Don't take your eyes off the road. Keep changing lanes such that he's always behind us. Do *not* let him pass, understood?" He knew what the "right-lane-pass" strategy was about. It wasn't him they were after. First they'd annoy the left-lane driver by tailing him to see whether he'd take the bait and speed up. When that worked, they'd catch up once again but this time they would swing into the right lane just long enough for their target to see they intended to pass on the right. If the driver were like Stella, he'd surge ahead again, not wanting to let them pass in any lane. They'd play this game as often as the traffic permitted until the driver capitulated and pulled into the right lane to let them pass. And that's all they waited for. They wanted the driver in the right-hand lane, nicely lined up with the truck's passenger side as it matched speed with the Navigator for a couple of seconds it took for the passenger to aim his gun at the driver.

"They're gaining on us," she grunted.

"Cut him off. Do whatever it takes but keep cutting him off. Do not let him pass." He wanted to change seats with her but the speedometer needle was hovering close to a hundred. Did he dare…?

He turned around to see the traffic situation behind them rather than to see what the black pick-up was doing. There weren't any cars as far as he could see. He turned around. The road ahead was clear too. It was a light traffic day. He took his gun out, unclicked the safety and said, "I want you to do precisely what I say when I tell you to do it."

"Fine."

He watched the truck the in the side-view mirror. "Switch lanes. Now!"

She changed to the right lane smoothly.

"Brake hard, hard!" he shouted. She brought the Navigator to a stop that would have seen both of them sail through the windshield if not for their seatbelts. The black pick-up truck swished by them in the left-hand lane.

"Change seats," he shouted, but she was attuned to what was going on and scrambled into the backseat. He leapt into the driver's seat and gunned down the gas pedal. The Navigator's rear wheels kicked up gravel as the truck spooled off the shoulder and practically leaped on to the highway again. He didn't bother changing lanes and caught up to the pick-up just far enough to be able to stick his hand out the window and shoot its tires.

"Don't look back," he said because he never did either. The screeching, thudding and crunching noise was more than enough to tell him what happened to a truck traveling at hundred miles an hour when two of its tires suddenly blew.

"Can I come up front now or do you want me to stay in the backseat for the rest of the trip?" she asked.

It was possible that Moses would have a back-up crew on the road.

"Make a decision before we pull into Ann Arbor," she said when he remained silent. "We've only fifty odd miles to go."

"Come on up front," he said. "That was good job of parking on the shoulder you did back there."

"Thank you for saving my life again," she said, pulling on the seatbelt.

"You're welcome, but honestly, Stella, I do *not* want to be the only person left on this globe who knows of the Peacetaker's existence."

Chapter Twenty-nine

It was just after two o'clock in the afternoon when Carter made it through the I-475 loop. Traffic became heavier as transport trucks out of Toledo streamed onto the highway, heading for 23-North that would take them across the state line into Michigan.

Half a mile after he crossed the state boundary, Stella bounced in her seat as if she was trying to leap through the windshield and shouted, "Take the next exit. Take it!"

The next exit, a mile ahead, was for Lambertville, a bit of a detour he didn't want to make right now. They were about forty miles away from Ann Arbor. Whatever her emergency, surely it could wait?

"Take the goddamned exit!" she yelled at him when he passed the first one.

He glanced at her as he made a lane change since Lambertville had two exits. She sat very rigid, her profile hard, and though she must have felt him looking at her she didn't turn her head. He looked at her hands and saw she was braiding her fingers but there was nothing playful about the game.

"Stella, are you all right?" he asked as flatly as he could manage.

"Of course I'm all right. Stop asking me. Why can't you men ever listen and just do what the woman asks? Why does it always have to be a third degree? What can't you just…?"

"The exit's coming up. There," he said even as he turned the wheel to make the ramp that would take them east, toward Lambertville. "What should I be looking for?" he asked, keeping the same cautiously flat tone of voice.

"Find a store, any store that sells clothing. Why do I have to be the one to think of everything? Why can't men keep track of details? Why do women have to be the perennial secretaries, keeping the family on schedule, looking after medical and dental appointments, shopping for groceries, picking up dry cleaning? Why can't men pick up their own dry-cleaning? Why does it take half as long for a man to get tenure as it takes for a woman? Why can't the fucking jerk take his tenure and get a job somewhere else? Why is it always the woman who must yield and give up everything....?" All through her rant, she kept braiding her fingers, stopping only occasionally to crack a knuckle with a sickening snap that told him her mind was somewhere else than her body.

All through the four-mile detour, she kept flinging her questions at the windshield as if indeed she was somewhere else, not a passenger in a truck.

He stayed quiet and only when he saw what she asked him to find, did he say, "Gino's Clothing Emporium is in this plaza. Will that do?"

"What?" She snapped her head around. He only pointed with his hand at the department store in the plaza.

He parked the truck and followed her to the store. She walked as if he didn't exist, not even bothering to hold the door for him or turn to see if anyone was following. He caught up to her halfway down the aisle.

"Stella, what are you looking for?" he asked, grabbing her arm, prepared to restrain her if she became violent.

"What?" The sudden stop seemed to have awakened her. "Carter, where are we?" She turned her head, looking around. "What are we doing here?"

"We're in a clothing store. You asked me to find one for you. This is it." He released her.

"Clothing store, clothing store," she repeated, mussing her hair. "What do I want in a clothing store?"

"I don't know," he said mildly, knowing that guessing might set her off again. Just then he heard a muffled sound of a siren outside; either the police or firefighters were approaching the plaza. The sound grew louder as its source came closer and then once again receded into distance. For some reason, he found it worrisome, though certainly fires or other emergencies in and around the town would be nothing unusual.

"Clothing, clothing... masks! That's it, Carter. We need masks. I'd been meaning to ask you back in Dayton to stop somewhere and find masks but it slipped my mind," she said.

He looked around. It was doubtful they might find any kind of a mask in the store since it was a regular department store, filled with clothing racks and bins with lingerie and socks.

She turned and passed a hand across his face before he had a chance to move out of range. "Mask or shroud to cover the face."

"Wait here," he said when something occurred to him, and he walked back to the sales counter.

"What do you want?" the sales clerk, a teenaged girl, no older than sixteen, asked rudely. While she held her cell phone, she wasn't using it, so he wasn't interrupting her chat with her peers or boyfriend. There was no reason to be so rude, especially to a customer who had not yet spoken.

"Do you have any balaclavas left?" he asked.

"What?" the girl asked in a high-pitched voice. "Are you some kind of pervert? You look like a pervert..."

He slammed his hand down on the counter. The sound produced the desired effect. The girl jumped backward, looking startled.

"Ski masks," he said, watching her. "Those hats you pull over your face. Do you have any left?"

"It's May—" the girl started mildly enough.

He cut her off because he knew it would not last long. "I know what month it is, but do you have any hats like that left from your winter sale?"

She raised a hand, pointing to the far end of the store. "If there are, they'd be in the last call sales bin."

He thanked her and rushed back to where he left Stella. Five minutes later, a plastic bag in hand, Carter dragged Stella out of the store. The sound of sirens in the distance rose once again, this time lasting a lot longer than he found comfortable.

"Put it on," he said, tossing the bag to her and turning the key.

"Are you out of your...?"

"Put it on!" He used his military tone of voice, harsh, crisp and uncompromising.

She obeyed and a few moments after she put it on, he heard her chuckling. Soon she was laughing so hard she doubled over as much as the seatbelt allowed her.

Well, laughing insanity was probably better than snarling insanity.

"Carter, do you realize," she pushed out between bouts of laughter, "that if someone sees me looking like this they might call it in and we'll have police after us in no time? What's happening around this place? Why are so many sirens going off?"

He didn't reply but kept checking his mirrors to see if a police car or firefighters were closing on him. When he made it to the ramp that would take him back on 23-North, he had to squeeze left to be able to get on the highway. A truck and two cars were involved in a collision on the curved part of the ramp. While a police cruiser was already on the scene, the officer seemed to be more interested in an animated discussion with what looked like the drivers and passengers. Carter could only afford to glance at the group but it was enough to tell him that soon the forceful hand gestures might turn into something else than just signs of a heated discussion.

He felt Stella staring at him but didn't turn his head.

"He can't be affecting people down here, forty

miles south of Ann Arbor," she said haltingly.

"You said the next time he's activated the effect might not stop at all."

"But why would he activate him now? The conference really doesn't start until tomorrow."

"I don't know, Stella. Things have been going wrong all along."

"But forty miles… it can't be. Maybe he's not yet in Ann Arbor," she said, wringing her hands.

He knew what she worried about. Her family and her children lived in Ann Arbor. If what he'd already seen and experienced with her earlier reaction, the teenager's hostility and the multiple-car accident on the ramp was indeed a result of the effect streaming from the Peacetaker in Ann Arbor, then by the time they made it there….

He found he didn't want to think through such a possibility.

Thirty seconds later, the possibility hardened into a fact. He had to slow down and concentrate on maneuvering the Navigator between cars surging forward to ram the vehicle ahead of them and those already victims of fender-benders though still moving ahead. Accidents happened all round him, and it wasn't a result of the domino effect.

"Carter?"

"Quiet, please. I need to concentrate if we're going to get out of this alive." The transport truck in the right-hand lane had surged ahead, literally driving the pick-up truck ahead of him into the sedan ahead of the pick-up. Carter moved on to the shoulder as far as he dared and pressed the gas to get away from the mass collision he knew would result because there were other transports closing on them from behind. The police cruiser and the firefighters didn't get very far, either. He glimpsed an overturned fire truck in the ditch on the other side, with the police cruiser lying on its side. He couldn't afford to take a longer look but felt that those who lived would be now at each other's throats. The sound of crunching metal, screeching tires and the sickening thud of impacts, over and over, made him feel like he had fallen through a time fabric into a war zone, driving an army truck carrying the wounded and those whose bodies would come home in sealed containers.

"Carter!" she screamed when a burning wreck of what could have been an ambulance loomed in their path. He wrenched the wheel to the left and ended up in the ditch that as far as he could see was still unobstructed. Perhaps because the madness-stricken drivers would not seek to escape but rather compound the situation, the ditch was still passable.

"Carter?"

"Not now, Stella." Some parts of the ditch had steeper slopes. He had to concentrate on keeping the truck level so it wouldn't overturn, because if that happened, they were dead.

"You're not wearing a mask, and you're not affected. Why?"

"I don't know." He kept glancing at the road above to see whether it might be safe to climb out of the ditch for a while.

"The southbound traffic's flowing normally," she said. "The effect has a narrow range, maybe not much wider than this highway."

He didn't dare to take his eyes off the ditch ahead but felt that she was right. While the southbound traffic would not be flowing normally, since people would invariably slow down to see the mayhem happening in the northbound lanes, the sound of collisions and crashes seemed to be confined to the northbound lanes.

"Carter!"

"I see it." He brought the truck sharply to climb the left side of the ditch, since not too far in the distance, a couple of cars were nose down in the ditch while their drivers were grappling on the ground. Stella yelped when something bounced off the truck's hood.

"It wasn't a body," he assured her. "Just a gas can."

"Left again!" she shouted.

This time he almost had to climb the slope into the southbound lanes to avoid a pile of crushed metal and bodies dancing between the wreckage, locked in mortal combat, while more bodies lay in the ditch, some still moving.

Just as he was inching up the right slope to get a better view of the road ahead, an explosion rocked their truck.

"Keep going. It was behind us," she told him, checking her side-view mirror.

An overpass bridge came into view.

"Read the sign," he asked tersely.

A few moments later she said, "West Albain Road."

"Next?" He decided to chance it again and climb the right slope to see what was happening on the highway.

"Dixon, we're heading for Tecumseh Junction."

Suddenly he became aware that the noise of collisions had faded. He glanced at the southbound lanes. The traffic had almost stopped, but not because of accidents. A police cruiser suddenly swung out of the lane and headed toward him, cutting in his siren.

"Bad idea, buddy," he murmured. "Don't head this way. You'll become another statistic." He considered blocking the cruiser's path but what would he say or do then?

"Carter, Carter, it's petering out. Look!" Stella's voice decided for him. He wrenched the wheel to the right and climbed out of the ditch and into the left-hand lane. The bridge overpass with the road's name *Tecumseh Street* came into view. The road ahead was totally empty, all the mayhem left behind.

Stella ripped off her ski mask. "I'm all right," she

said after taking a couple of deep breaths.

Just then two helicopters swooped down so suddenly he wondered where they came from. One headed along the southbound highway, while the other passed overhead. He pulled on to the shoulder, jumped out and ran to the back of the truck. Stella must have figured out what he wanted to do because she opened the hatch-door with the remote. He found the flares in the emergency road kit but these were meant to be put down on the road, not fired into the air, and that's what he needed to warn the chopper heading into the war zone.

"Damn!" He slammed the gate shut.

"Carter," Stella came around, "are you all right?"

"Fine. I'm not affected, just frustrated, that's all."

Just then the regular splat-noise of the chopper's rotors changed into labored chugging He didn't want to look but out of respect for those about to perish in the craft, raised his head just in time to see the craft nose-dive into the road already littered with metal and bodies. He didn't even have the mental strength to swear.

He raked his fingers along the side of the truck, craving punishment of the sound when Stella put her hand on top of his, pressing it down.

"Carter, I'm sorry, but we have to go back."

***

"He's east of the northbound lanes," she said. "Once again, it's an irregular plume, just like in Dayton. He's not in Ann Arbor. He's somewhere nearby, maybe there." She pointed eastward, where he saw houses, so it was probably a small town, Dundee.

"If he's there, Stella, then the whole town would be affected. I may be immune from the effect and the ski mask protects you as well, but neither of us is immune from the killing frenzy that still might be going strong in that town. There are only fifteen cartridges in my magazine, and I might not get a chance to reload."

She pointed at the town again. "That's where we have to go to look for him. I don't think the whole town's affected; just a narrow strip, a few hundred feet at most."

"A few hundred feet *is* the whole town, Stella. At least let's wait until it subsides."

"Carter, that's my point. It is *not* subsiding. It's streaming from him, in a plume that may widen with time, and it's not subsiding. It's spreading southward from here and grows in strength as it moves. It affected me just before Lambertville, but only to a degree where I felt anger welling up inside me. I bet you anything that now the effect they're feeling in Lambertville is no longer just mounting anger but madness. It builds in stages precisely because it's time-dependent. Remember what I told you in San Francisco, at the Hearst Museum? If allowed to walk until the land ends, the Peacetaker would leave behind him a path littered with bodies. He's not walking now. He's parked somewhere in that town, and he's activated. The effect is streaming from him continuously and will not stop. Carter, do you hear me? It will not stop..." Her voice trailed off.

"Unless he's stopped, which means there may not be any other way but to eliminate him." At the last moment, he substituted a more pedantic word for "kill."

"Let's just go," she said, evasive as always and climbed back in the truck.

"Put on the ski mask," he said, checking the road to make sure nothing came at them.

She was quiet for a long time then said, "No, Carter. You need a sensor."

He was already on the exit ramp that would bring him on to Riley Street but braked hard to a screeching stop. He turned his head, tilting it such that she wouldn't miss the significance of his scarred cheek.

"We've just been through a war zone and though I certainly wouldn't want to take away from the horrors happening on that highway, it's just traffic accidents in comparison to what went on in Cairo. Do you want me to tell you what I remember of what went on at the Stadium?" He afforded her two seconds before continuing, "An eight-year-old stabbed her mother in the face with a burning candle. The police were equipped in riot gear and carried bamboo rods with sharpened ends. They skewered people with those bamboo spears—in the eye, in the leg, in the chest—wherever they could stab them. A woman half my size bit right through a man's jugular. It rained blood. All I saw was crimson haze. I crushed someone's head with my hands. The eyes literally popped out of the head. I think it was a woman. I've thirty-six stab wounds; the most serious were in the shoulder, stomach and in my left thigh. The rod that pierced my throat went right through my cheek. For a microsecond, I felt pain but then it vanished, replaced by fury such as I never felt in my life, and I'm a soldier, Stella, have been practically all my life. I saw the coroner's report on Pascal. He couldn't find a significant bone in his body that wasn't broken. You only saw twisted metal back there with a few bodies rolling on the ground." He jerked his thumb at the rear window. "There were no vehicles at the stadium, Stella, only people, killing each other with their bare hands and anything else they could reach. Now, put the mask on."

When she obeyed, he nudged the stick shift into drive and made a right-hand turn on to Riley Street.

"Felicia Corazon said that both the boy and his uncle were sick," she said after a long moment of silence. "That might be the reason why they stopped here. Maybe the uncle is too sick to drive, maybe the boy's too sick..."

"If he's sick, Stella, the sickness is not incapacitating the effect. You know better than anyone else that the effect won't stop until the one who's causing it is dead."

She moaned but said nothing.

He drove slowly, checking his mirrors. The street appeared to be deserted. That could mean the effect had already scored against the people—in their homes—and since there was no one to call for assistance, given the situation south of them and a general state of emergency that would be upstate, those who were clinging to life would probably die alongside those already dead. He kept checking for any sign of movement, even a cat, but everything around was quiet; nothing moved. He came to a stop sign, made a right-hand turn on to Custer Road and cruised eastward. The mostly white houses sat to the left and right, like plastic pieces from a game. Inert.

"Do you remember what Frank McEwen said about the young man, Gaspard?" she asked, a little too dry for his liking.

"Legends and folklore are your forte, Stella, not mine," he said.

"Gaspard didn't have a controller; or rather his was a mysterious force that kept putting the amulet around his neck when he fell asleep. But when he woke up in the morning, he was able to take off the amulet—until one morning he couldn't. That's when he ran to his betrothed and told her about his plight. She was able to take it off. Maybe that's the case we have here and now. The controller can no longer take the amulet off the boy's neck."

"More the reason to eliminate both of them," he said tersely.

"You're missing my point, Carter. The girl loved Gaspard. That's why she was able to unshackle him, so to speak. The controller's using the boy to sow terror in our country. There lies the difference. That's how it must work precisely because those who would activate an unready Peacetaker would seek to use a child only for their own gain, and that's forbidden. Set was the god of the underworld, an equivalent of Hades, not the Devil."

"The ruler of Hell by any other name," he said, not bothering to take the cynical edge off his tone.

"Anger *is* a doorway to Hell, but not for children, Carter, precisely because they are still developing and nothing is set yet in their emotional make-up. The boy's a victim. He needs our help. Kill the uncle, if you must, but—"

"There," he interrupted her when he spotted a house with its screen door askew and what looked like a couple of bodies lying on the bottom of the stairs. He quickly looked to see if he'd find a matching scene on the other side of the street. She must have realized what he was checking for because she pointed ahead. The two cars that had pulled up to the gas station were wedged together, their drivers lying across the hood of the first one, not moving.

"It's affecting only the south side of the street," she said. "He must be somewhere... there!" He saw it too, a motel sign just off the side of the road adjoining a small strip plaza. A scream rent the air and a woman staggered out of a convenience store, clawing the air with her hands. She didn't have a face or, rather, everything from the shoulders up was covered in blood. Someone else came through the door. It was hard to see whether it was a man or a woman but Carter saw the baseball bat even before it rose in the air and came down on the woman's head.

The soldier in him fought with the contractor, on a mission that didn't allow deviation from his path of purpose. The soldier had many memories of scenes like this one, never on US soil, always in some foreign land where political cause, race or religion was behind such madness. He liked to think that on any rescue mission, he'd saved more lives than he extinguished in the process of helping civilians out of the conflict. But who was the enemy here?

He forced himself to stare ahead, at the parking lot in front of the motel, where he saw some movement.

"Oh, my God! It's him, it's the boy," Stella said in a

strangled whisper.

He leaned toward the windshield to be able to see better and caught something out of the corner of his eye. He wrenched the steering wheel to the right, bouncing over the concrete curb even as he ducked what she threw at him — her ski mask. He had to split his attention between her and the small figure, staggering across the parking lot, about fifty feet down near the end of the motel. If he gunned down the gas pedal, and kept adjusting even as the truck sped across, he'd put a stop to all the madness in seconds.

"Nooo!" Her scream almost deafened him, it was that piercing. He knew she'd try to wrestle the steering wheel from him but he didn't expect her hands to fasten around his neck with such strength he choked. She was strong; then again, those driven by madness had madmen's strength.

He elbowed her out of the way but didn't know where his elbow hit. For a moment, the pressure around his neck vanished then she came back at him, doubly strong. He banged his head against her, sideways. That gained him another couple of seconds of air. She kept screaming, which was perhaps worse than choking him. His vision turned grainy.

No longer able to distinguish any movement against the gray cement of the parking lot, he elbowed her again, this time keeping his arm winged and steering with one hand. She must have let go of his throat because air rushed into his lungs just as she threw herself on the steering wheel. His foot stomped on the brake by reflex and the Navigator skidded to a halt.

Finally able to use both hands, Carter grabbed Stella's body lying across the steering wheel and yanked her upward, tossing her against the passenger door. He felt with his left hand on the dashboard for the ski mask, grabbed it and, not caring which way, pulled it over her head and then looked out the windshield.

The boy stood about thirty feet in front of the truck, swaying back and forth, as if he couldn't decide which way to fall. He seemed to be wearing a bunch of rocks and ornaments threaded on strings around his neck. They bounced and swung from side to side as he swayed.

Carter took his foot off the brake and pushed the gas. The truck surged ahead.

"Carter, for the love of God… he's a child!"

He blinked and took his foot off the gas. The image of Emily's bluish-mottled face flashed behind his lids before it changed into an unrecognizable mound of torn flesh. Pascal. His foot found the gas pedal. He was barely aware he made the decision. Once again the SUV jerked forward.

"He's not a terrorist, Carter, and this isn't a battlefield," Stella's whisper made his foot on the gas pedal jerk—but not move away. Instead a force over which he had no control kept pushing down his foot such that the truck now moved without the stopping jerk-motion.

"He's a victim, just like you—and me," she rasped.

The force made him stomp on the gas as if it was a brake.

"Carter!"

He heard the angry roar of the truck's engine, saw a blur of red-and-blue checks out of the corner of his eye as it flashed by his side window and then the Navigator's nose ploughed into the wall. The air bags deployed on both sides. He sat there, feeling vaguely threatened by the white balloon pushing in his face and turned his head to see Stella. However the passenger side was empty, the air bag hanging limply from the dashboard.

He beat back the air bag with both hands until it subsided and threw his weight against the door. He got out, momentarily disoriented, but his land-legs came back quickly enough.

He turned and saw Stella, still wearing the

balaclava, supporting the boy with one hand while holding a bunch of rocks and gold ornaments dangling on strings in the other.

"Is it over?" he asked, keeping his distance.

She raised her head then ripped off the ski mask, staring at him for a few seconds. "Yes." Her mouth tightened into a grim line. "The bastard put every single amulet that featured in history as the Peacetaker's activator around his neck."

"Is he alive?"

She cradled the boy's head in her lap, stuffed the amulets into her jacket pocket then stroked his forehead.

"We could use an ambulance, but considering the situation I don't think we're going to get one to come out here any time soon. He needs to rest. One amulet, the right one, activates him, but the rest literally drain his life energies. Carter," she raised her voice, eyes pointing behind him. He turned his head to see something that looked like a walking suit with a scarecrow's head flap out of the last cabin. He drew his gun out but hardly took a step when she called out to him again.

"He may be a living skeleton or a mobile statue, but be careful. I can't be sure about this particular interpretation…"

"Don't tell me, Stella," he moaned. "The curse also made him immortal."

"No, you idiot," she said in a tone of voice that told him more than anything else he saw that she was indeed all right. "He just might possess the strength of ten men — living men, that is."

"That's just great, Stella, just what I needed to hear. Stay put. I'll be right back."

Chapter Thirty

Carter reached the far edge of the motel and flattened himself against the wall. Gun held in both hands, he inched closer to be able to look around the corner. He blew a breath of surprise when he saw open space. The motel backed on to a wide stretch of grassland with a clump of bushes cutting off the view of the highway. He didn't see any movement in the bushes, and the grass field was empty. Yet the man had disappeared around the corner just seconds ago. He couldn't have possibly moved so quickly as to have reached the distant line of pine trees that fringed the southern end of the field?

Could he have doubled back and entered one of the motel units? Carter took a couple of steps and looked down the row of back doors. None were open. If anything, the unkempt grass growing all along the wall meant the motel guests seldom, if ever, used the back door. He raised his head and stared at the line of pine trees in the distance. Their formation looked too artificial to be a natural occurrence so it was probably a windbreak wall, and that could mean a dwelling nearby.

He headed across the field, gun held pointed at the ground. If the man did come up from behind he'd hear him approach, because the dry grass crackled underfoot as he walked. And if he suddenly rose from somewhere ahead of him, well, his reflexes were still good and he'd squeeze off a few shots that ought to stop the wretched creature. Stella said he'd have the strength of ten men, but he was still mortal.

Turning his head now and then to make sure that no one surprised him from behind, he walked quickly across the field but didn't even catch a movement of some small creature burrowing underfoot. He came closer and saw that the line of pine trees ran uninterrupted to where he felt was a house or some kind of commercial structure. From the

347

dirt-brown background, he picked out stone slabs that were not a natural occurrence but had to be quarried because he saw evidence of cutting. When he came across scaffolding and a wheelbarrow encrusted with cement, he knew he was right. A few minutes later, when he pushed through the dense branches to emerge into a work yard, he swiped the sweat off his forehead just to make sure it wasn't marring his vision.

"What the fuck?" he murmured, looking over the piles of stone slabs, bags of cement also piled on wooden skids and statues of angels in various degrees of decay, or finish, as he quickly realized when he walked over to one polished slab of dark stone and saw it was a headstone, a grave marker.

Just then he heard a low threatening growl and turned, gun held ready.

"Great," he murmured, staring at the animal that had to be a mix of Rottweiler and maybe black Lab. The dog growled again but didn't advance. He didn't want to shoot the dog, but if the animal attacked him, it would leave him no choice but to at least wound it to stop its charge. He knew the dog might react to even a slightest movement so he cautiously inched his hand with the gun until he had the dog's shoulder in line.

"Don't make me do this, buddy," he said softly, maintaining eye contact with the dog.

"Yo, mister, put that gun down." Suddenly he heard a shout practically in his ear and jerked his head. "Down, Cerberus, down, boy." The man slapped Carter's shoulder even as he walked around to face him, stopping next to the dog who flopped down on his belly when he heard his master's command.

"What are you doing here on my property, threatening my dog?" the man demanded, bracing his hands on his hips. He was dressed in dust-covered blue overalls and carried a roll of duct tape in his hand.

"I think it's the other way around," Carter said, sliding the gun into his pocket but keeping his hand there as well. "I'm looking for someone—"

The man cut him off. "Aren't we all? I can't even get a signal on my cell phone, never mind get a live creature to tell me what's going on out there." He motioned in the direction of the highway. "Sirens have been going on and off for hours now. There's smoke yonder, too," he thumbed over his shoulder, "a pall over the highway; must have been one heck of an accident...is that gun real, mister?"

"Yes. I'm a cop, a federal agent. What is this place?" Carter asked.

"Well, where you're standing, it's Dunning's Monuments and Stone Garden, but yonder there," once again he thumbed over his shoulder, "at the end of Custer Road's our Dundee Cemetery."

"So this is commercial property," he murmured, looking around and finding the army of stone angels and patron saints in various states of completion disquieting.

"Commercial property's all that rightfully fits next to a cemetery, mister," the man said, snapping his fingers at the dog. The animal rose, then started licking his master's hand. "Sure as my name's Al Dunning, folks around here aren't anxious to build their house next to a graveyard, if you know what I mean."

"It's usually the living who cause problems, not the dead," Carter murmured, searching with his eyes for any sign of movement amongst the stone army but everything was still.

"Ah, a federal agent with a sense of humor," the man said, chuckling. "Now that's something you don't get too...you have a badge to show me who you are, mister?" He slipped in his question so glibly at the end that it was Carter's turn to smile. He fished out his FBI badge and let the man study it, while he continued to look around. Carter wondered whether the man's question finally came as a result of his scarred cheek.

"I guess you're not going to tell me what's going on, right?" The man nodded at the badge.

"No, Mr. Dunning. I'm sure you'll read about it in the papers soon enough, but I'm really looking for someone who might have run over here and could be hiding on your grounds... somewhere," he said.

"Do you have something from this fellow?"

Carter blinked, shaking his head.

"That's too bad, because Cerberus, here," he patted the dog's head, "could sniff him out for you in a flash."

"Cerberus?" Carter glanced down at the animal wagging its stubby tail, no doubt in response to hearing its name.

"Sure thing. I named him after the guard dog of the underworld in Greek legends," the man said.

"You know about Greek legends?"

"Mister, you have no idea how much good stuff there is in legends. Mine is the only headstone business in five counties, so I make a good living, and folks are always scratching their heads, asking me for suggestions about what to put on the headstone. A lot of good stuff figures in those legends, and when you chisel it into the stone, it makes history come alive, if you know what I mean."

"I sure do, especially about history coming alive. Now, would you mind if I took a look?"

"I'd be happy to give you a tour of Dunning's Monuments and Stone Garden," the man said, snapping his fingers at the dog to follow.

Escorted tour was not what Carter wanted but there was no way to refuse. After thinking about it for a few seconds, he decided that the owner of the stone garden would know not only the likely hiding places, but also all the pitfalls around his grounds.

An hour later, when he felt the tension in his neck

from craning it to look behind every stone work and every messy pile of stacked materials, Carter knew more than he felt any man needed to know about the heavenly aspect of designing gravestones.

Al Dunning was just as adept at giving lecture-tours as Stella. Carter learned that Dundee folks preferred to erect the statue of St. Francis for their male departed loved ones and Virgin Mary for their female deceased. Michael the Archangel was the favored angel statue for youngsters' graves while babies were generally given guardian angels, mostly Gabriel and Raphael, but sometimes a cherubim choir would be commissioned for the child. Dunning had a warehouse full of molds and could produce a concrete statue in a week. The marble ones were special order and took a month to make.

"You've got to be real careful with marble, because it's brittle and can crack on you just where you don't want to have a seam. But if the figure's nearly finished and I get a crack in limbs or torso, I glue it neatly so you can hardly see the joint then offer the family a discount, 'cause I'm an honest businessman. Granite, however, is a whole new ball of wax, if you know what I mean. That's for gravestones, and most folks choose the obsidian black because it shows gold lettering real—"

"Mr. Dunning," Carter interrupted. "Is there any other place you can think of that a man would hide in?" He blinked, trying to hold back a sigh of frustration. The owner had taken him through the grounds, pointing out a stone figure here and there then telling him its 'saintly roots' and who commissioned it. They toured the open-sided warehouse and Carter looked behind every skid stacked with cement bags, every pile of tools and boxes, every forklift truck and front-end loader, finding nothing but dust and stone chips. They toured the workshop where Dunning and occasionally one or two helpers cut and polished the headstones and poured cement into molds to make statues.

The place was dusty like everything else around but empty of human presence. All through this, the dog had padded after them, quietly and unobtrusively. That told Carter better than any heat-scanner that there was only inanimate matter wherever he looked and not even mice were brave enough to invade Dunning's garden of stone.

The owner scratched his head, looking sheepish. "Well, no, Agent Carter. This is my business but I don't live here. My house is a couple of miles back there, when you get off the highway. You figure he could be hiding in my truck?"

Five minutes later, when they had searched the Ford pick-up and Carter had even climbed underneath the chassis to make sure no one was "hanging" there for a ride, he knew it was futile to continue his search.

Well, if the curse was one of those "slow-but-sure" retributions, then it was only a matter of time before the boy's controller would... what? Silicify or turn to stone, as Stella suggested, or fall apart, a rattling skeleton? Either possibility was not something a rational man could discuss with his employers. He gave up speculating about it, thanked Dunning for the tour and headed back toward the motel.

Just as he passed the point where he first met Cerberus, he caught a motion out of the corner of his eye and turned. Could it be that one of the half-finished statues...?

He drew the gun and slowly approached, looking over the concrete figures. By now he knew that the still-featureless face on a statue that wore a flowing gown such that its folds looked tubular in the concrete, would become Archangel Michael, and the neighboring cement cast would emerge as Virgin Mary from underneath Al Dunning's sander and chisel. The two other casts were 'spoiled' saints that Dunning said he didn't scrap because he wanted one of his helpers to 'train' on them.

Did anything in this stone forest move or was it just his overheated imagination?

Nah, he decided. It was time to get back to Stella and see if she'd managed to raise anyone on the phone to come and help the child.

He lowered his head, pushed away the pine branches to cross to the other side and walked out into the open field again. He quickened his step, and as he rounded the corner of the motel, he fully expected to see, if not Stella still cradling the boy in her lap, then at least the Navigator. However, the asphalt strip fringing the motel was completely, totally empty.

***

Carter couldn't remember the last time he thumbed a ride. The novelty of the experience was still coursing through his head when the trucker let him out at the gas station on Liberty Street.

The trucker was friendly and curious. He asked what happened to Carter's cheek. He gave the man the "tumbling tools in a garage" version and it seemed to be the right tale because it kept the trucker busy, telling him about his own mishaps with work tools, all the way to Ann Arbor. Carter also couldn't be bothered to make up elaborate stories about why he was walking on the highway shoulder, thumbing rides. When the trucker had pulled over on the shoulder, he'd walked up to the rig, opened the door and said, "My wife drove off in our car. We were heading to Ann Arbor, to visit her folks. I'm trying to catch up to her."

The trucker laughed and motioned for him to climb inside.

The gas station had a small coffee shop. Once Carter called a taxi, he went to sit with a cup of coffee and wait for his cab.

"Thirty-six Danbury Lane, it's in Foster," he told the cabbie when the man asked for his destination.

"Sure thing," the cabbie said then tapped the

dashboard radio. "Can you believe what's been going on...?"

The last thing Carter wanted was to start a discussion of what must have been keeping all the media in a state of emergency right across Michigan, so he just raised the rolled-up newspaper he'd picked up at the coffee shop, indicating that he preferred to catch up on dismal news in private.

His dossier on Dr. Stella Hunter contained not only her Ann Arbor address, but also a picture of her stately red-brick-and-stone mansion.

"That's it," he said, leaning forward when he saw what had to be the biggest house in the neighborhood, though the rest of the properties were equally proud, with sweeping manicured lawns and mature trees lining the cobbled driveways. He spotted his Navigator sitting where she must have left it in her flight, right under the portico with its stone pillars.

He told the cabbie to pull right behind the Lincoln, paid him and got out, waiting until the cab left before he rang the doorbell. After all, he knew that the day couldn't end without he and Stella having a confrontation. Even as he pushed the button, he wondered what had been Bruce Hunter's reaction to the sudden appearance of his estranged and embattled wife.

"Hello, Mr. Carter. Please come in," he heard and blinked in order to focus on the elderly woman dressed in a frilly apron over a black maid's dress, holding the door open and smiling at him. She continued, waving him inside, "They're expecting you. This way, please."

"They?" he mumbled, walking inside and growing aware of many voices, murmuring in the distance.

The woman nodded and motioned for him to head down the hallway toward what could be a kitchen or at least some kind of entertainment area.

It was a kitchen, though its size suggested a medium

dining hall, and the moment he stopped on the threshold, the voices died down. The rectangular oak table was set with dishes and cutlery. The full breadbaskets and two large salad bowls could mean two things. If the diners observed European customs, the dinner was over. If they held to American tradition, the dinner was just starting.

He quickly looked around, using his intuition to assign identities. The balding man in rimless glasses sitting at the head of the table was Bruce Hunter. Sitting on his right was what Carter's army buddies used to call a 'gorgeous bimbo,' and across from the future Mrs. Hunter sat a teenager with a shaved head that made his orange stubble cast off a halo. He had to be Stella's son, Adam. The two curly-haired girls sitting next to each other at the end of the table closest to Carter had to be her twin daughters, and the soon-to-be-ex Mrs. Hunter sat across from her twins, her hand draped over the chair where her young guest sat, still pale but no longer feverish, because his blue eyes were clear though they widened when they settled on Carter.

"We're having a family dinner. Do join us, Carter. In fact, I was hoping you'd be able to make it, knowing that you're a man of limitless resources," Stella said, motioning at the chair next to her, which would put him at the other end of the table, facing Bruce Hunter down its length.

"Yes, please do sit down, Mr. Carter," Allison Grant said huskily, smiling at him, and patting the air to show him she wanted him on her eye level. For a moment, he felt he could almost grasp what it was that made Bruce Hunter turn disloyal and trade his wife for this blonde-haired vixen, then he shook his head to banish such ignoble sexist speculation.

"Mom's been telling us some pretty weird shit about you," Adam said, leaning over to be able to see Carter.

"Repair your language, mister!" His mother's wrath

whipped at him.

"What's there to repair? It ain't broken," the boy sassed back and quickly lowered his head, shoulders shaking with laughter.

"You would do me a great honor if you joined us for dinner, Mr. Carter," Bruce Hunter said, sounding as stilted and formal as Carter imagined him to be.

"Well, it's been a long day, and I am hungry," Carter said, not sure whether he should smile or bow, then sat down.

***

Young Gabriel Ashton Kraft spoke accented English and liked being fussed over by young women. After dinner, Stella asked her daughters to help the boy with a bath, then find him some of Adam's clothes that might fit. Allison said she'd go with the girls and help. Carter glanced at Stella but she didn't seem to mind her 'replacement's' presence nor her initiative.

"I have work to do, but I'm going to take a break and watch the news," Bruce Hunter said. "There are terrible things going on out there, absolutely atrocious."

"Go with your father or go do your homework." Stella glared at her son.

"Oh, Mom, why do you always have to be such a Nazi?"

"A Nazi? Did you say a Nazi?"

"Oh, all right. I'm going, I'm going," the teenager said, raising his hands and backing all the way out of the kitchen.

"Stella," Carter started when he was sure her family was out of earshot.

"Did you catch up to the controller? What did you do with him?" She was quick, trying to derail him in his purpose.

"Stella!"

"No, Carter. I won't let you or your employers take

him. Never, do you hear me? Never!"

"Stella, he's a—"

"Child." Once again she cut him off. "And more important, he's an orphan who doesn't have a soul in the world to care for him."

"He's a Peacetaker, Stella, and you of all people should realize what that means."

"Without his activator, he's a child as normal as any of mine... well, as normal as any child his age."

"What did you do with the amulets you took off his neck?"

"I tossed them down a well."

"Stella!"

She leaned back, grimacing. "I'm not lying to you. But it was actually an open manhole back there near that motel. I threw them down, heard a splash—and good riddance. Carter, nobody should have those amulets, and I mean absolutely nobody. Not the good guys and not even the government guys whose job it is to make sure things disappear and never surface again. Where the Peacetaker's activator is concerned, I don't trust anyone."

"Which amulet was his true activator?"

She laughed. "Come on, Carter, I'm not going to tell even you."

"But you know?" he tested.

She shrugged. "I guessed—but I could have been wrong. Believe me, at the time, all I was concerned about was getting those fucking things off his neck. They were killing him."

"Stella, you can't—"

She interrupted him. "Yes I can, Carter, and you can help me so that I'll be able to look after Gabriel, legally, as his appointed guardian. Even as we headed up the highway, with all the madness and explosions behind us, Paige Smith's voice kept coming back to remind me that anger is a doorway to hell. That's why I came home...well, at least it *used* to be my home. The point is, I realized that I couldn't continue dealing with my marital situation with anger. It's a blazing doorway to hell, and these last few weeks, both of us have seen what it means. That's why I came here, even though I knew Allison was here and so was Bruce. I came home to my family to ask for help when I needed it. Bruce chose the young twit over me, and that'll always hurt, but I've accepted it and let go of my anger. I won't pretend that I'm fond of the bitc...*tart*, but I can sit down to dinner in her company and actually enjoy a family gathering—with my children and young Gabriel beside me."

"What am I supposed to tell Saunders?" he groaned. The pulse started drumming in his temples when he thought about his contractual obligations. He grabbed his head and pressed his palms against the sides. Predictably, she wouldn't allow him the comfort of the pressure and grabbed his hands then forced them down on the table.

"Plenty," she said, daring to smile at him. "I haven't been idle while waiting for you to find your way up here, you know."

"Dare I ask, Stella, what you've been doing?"

"Thinking," she said, her smile widening.

Chapter Thirty-one

Sunburst, Montana
December 18
Set goes forth.

It was a week until Christmas, and Montana was having its usual December weather. The temperature hovered around 20 degrees Fahrenheit and the wind blew indifferently at six miles per hour, with only an occasional angry gust as if it wanted to make a point that the snow fences along I-15 were just a placebo for the weary drivers heading for the Alberta border.

Carter stopped at Tickle Gas because the low-gas light had been on for the last ten miles. He tapped the horn twice and waited for the noise to bring results. A few moments later, a figure dressed in an orange survival suit came out and walked around. He lowered the window before the man tapped on it.

"Evening, sir," he said. "Fill her up, please."

"Sure thing, mister," the man said, craning his head to look inside. Carter accommodated him by leaning back in his seat.

"You've got yourself a real good truck here, mister," George Tickle said, smacking his lips in appreciation as he kept looking at the Range Rover's dashboard with its ambitious navigation layout.

"It's a rental," Carter said.

"Don't matter where it comes from, it's still a real piece of outdoor truck," Tickle said, shaking his head. "Where'd you rent it?"

"Great Falls, at the airport."

"Didn't know those rental outfits had decent trucks like this," Tickle murmured.

"I called ahead and requested it—reserved it," Carter said.

"That's real smart." Tickle nodded, then shuffled away to serve the customer.

Half an hour later, Carter brought the Rover between two looming snow banks and squeezed it into the driveway that could have used more vigorous shoveling. The citrus yellow house shone in the moonlit darkness of the clear, cold night. He spent five minutes changing his footwear, pulling on sensible boots that reached up to his knees, struggling into his parka and finally getting out of the truck. He carried his hiking boots in one hand and his briefcase in the other, intending to change footwear on the verandah, while he waited for the house owner to answer the door. There was still no outside lighting, but the moonlight was enough to show that the porch was now screened, so that only a little snow had drifted inside. He wondered why Stella didn't put up Christmas lights. As he drove through the town, he saw that nearly every house was dressed in garlands of holiday sparkle.

Hand planted on the wall for support, he changed into his dry-land boots, then rang the bell. A few moments later, when no one came, he tested the screen door. He turned his head, wondering whether he shouldn't go and rap on the window, but a better idea might be to get back in his truck and honk the horn.

He took a step backward when suddenly the yellow-painted front door swung open.

"Evening, ma'am," he drawled, tipping his fingers to his forehead.

"Whatever you're selling, I already have it," she said, laughter churning in her voice.

"You can never have enough peace and goodwill on Earth," he said.

"Ain't that the truth? Glad to see you found your way up here again, Carter." Six months ago, when he last saw her, he promised to visit her again, soon. She knew he'd come—just not when.

"Well, aren't you going to invite me inside?"

"Just a moment," she said, then her dark outline disappeared. He was starting to wonder what was the matter when suddenly his surroundings flooded with such brilliance that he dropped his boots and his briefcase.

"All the lights still on one switch?" he murmured, rubbing his eyes. He remembered the brightness when he had first came to see her. But that had been back in May, before she had a reason to decorate her house, bushes, hedges and the two pine trees standing in the front yard with garlands of Christmas lights.

"Merry Christmas, Carter," she said, and then she grabbed his parka sleeve and pulled him inside. "It's our first Christmas as a family, and we want everyone to know it," she said, pulling him along.

"Stella, you've got to call that electrician and insist he rewire these lights," he said, shrugging out of his parka. "I'm sure that every time you click that switch, somewhere in a control room an alarm blares and the operators scramble to reroute power before Montana experiences a massive blackout. I can't imagine what your electrical bill must be every month."

"I've called the hack, gave him a piece of my mind, and he's coming back in January to do just that. Gabriel, Gabriel!"

The crashing sounds of what had to be a video game came from somewhere between the Christmas tree sprinkled with flickering lights and the lime-green sofa. Slowly, as his eyes adjusted to the subdued lighting, he was able to pick out a small figure sitting cross-legged on the sofa while two more sat on the floor, hands busy with the video game controls.

"Gabriel, come say hello," she said, snapping her fingers at the boy who ignored the invitation for a few moments then handed the controller to one of his friends and slid off the sofa.

"Hello, Gabriel. You've grown taller," Carter said, smiling and feeling slightly uneasy because he still felt awkward around young people.

"Hello, Mr. Carter," the boy said with only a faint trace of an accent. "Zee said you'd be coming to see us. I have lots of presents under the tree."

"So I see." Carter craned his head, waiting to see if the boy would turn his as well, and when it worked, he quickly opened his briefcase and took out a festive package. "And here's another one for you to put on that big pile you already have." He gave him the present and smiled when the boy puffed out his cheeks.

"Thanks," Gabriel said, "it's a video game, right?" He shook the package that was the size of a large book.

"You'll find out come Christmas morning," Carter said. He'd bought him two video games and one computer strategy game, knowing Stella would insist the youngster sharpened more than just his dexterity. "How's school?" he asked.

"Okay. Stan and Mark are in my class," the boy said, turning to look at his two friends who were oblivious to everything but what was happening on the large TV screen. He knew the boy wanted to rejoin his friends so he let him go, and followed Stella to the kitchen.

"Zee?" he asked when she busied herself setting the table.

"Auntie. You're staying overnight, right?"

"Won't it be a bit crowded?"

"There are two bedrooms now up in the loft. Down here's all yours," she said, chuckling.

He tipped his head in the direction of the video game activity. "How's he doing?"

"Really good. The first week of school was a little hard for him, but I had a chat with his teacher. She helped him put together an ice-breaking class presentation about Africa, what his family did there as Red Cross relief workers and missionaries. After that, we've had friends over almost every day. In fact, we've had to make up a list of rules about friends and video games. He's learning to skate and wants to play hockey. None of my kids were into sports when they were growing up. I'm kind of looking forward to sitting in cold arenas, shouting encouragements with the rest of the parents."

"You've given up looking for another academic post?" He knew she'd resigned her position at Michigan, and though it surprised him that she'd give it up that easily, he knew that once she made up her mind, she wouldn't regret it.

"I'm doing research for my sequel to *Ribbons of Truth*. I owe a blurb on the dedication page to Frank and a very small one to Abigail."

"How are you set for money?" he asked. She'd given up her costly bitter divorce battle with Bruce, but he didn't know the final financial arrangements.

"I'm set for life." She laughed.

He arched his brows. "Did you already get an advance?"

She shook her head. "Bruce decided to share the bounty his uncle left him, within reason, of course. He's still a multi-millionaire but I'm very comfortable—and happy," she finished with a whimsical smile and a glance at the video-playing crowd. "Thanks, Carter."

"What for?" he asked, pretending not to understand.

"For Gabriel, for not pestering me about the activating amulet, for a month of scintillating company and dark adventure—for my sanity."

"I didn't do much—"

She interrupted. "Yes, you did. You stretched the truth to a degree that might be called...well, we won't go there. After the initial visit from social services, I haven't even had a phone call to check on Gabriel. He's thriving up here and I feel as if I had a new lease on life. I talk to my kids at least every couple of days. Allison sends me recipes by email and Bruce talked with Clarkson, my old department head, to see whether he'd put my *Ribbons of Truth* on the required course-reading list. If someone would have as much as whispered last year that I'd be sitting down to dinner in Bruce and Allison's company—at the same table—I'd have mowed him down with my car."

"Anger is a doorway to hell," he murmured.

"And the Peacetaker's controller was holding it wide open," she said, nodding at him. "Did the FBI ever find him?"

"If it's as you'd said back then, the curse would have done its job by now," he said. He'd felt guilty that the FBI would waste manpower looking for a phantom terrorist, but it was the only way to safeguard Stella and the boy—and his own sanity. There was sufficient truth in his report for Saunders to accept it at face value.

The Red Crescent office in Cairo confirmed that Ernest Bourgawich was on their staff, but further inquiries into his whereabouts revealed that his Cairo colleagues believed he was in Geneva, while Geneva staff believed he was in France. When the French office couldn't trace him either, the Cairo police opened his file as a missing persons case.

In September, Stella had sent him an email. Young Gabriel knew his parents had died when he was just a toddler, but he didn't know where they were buried. It was a good possibility that it was somewhere in one of the famine-stricken regions in Sudan, but even that was more Stella's speculation than the boy's own recollection. However, he was very clear on the issue of his uncle. After his brother and sister-in-law died, Martin Kraft and his young nephew ended up in a coastal mission in Port Sudan. About a year and a half ago, Martin Kraft had a visitor.

Gabriel's description of the man matched Gahiji down to his gold-rimmed glasses, though the man introduced himself as Sayed Hakim. The boy said his uncle Martin liked Hakim because Hakim promised to make arrangements for the two of them to come to visit him in Cairo. Then Martin Kraft fell ill. Hakim wouldn't let the boy see him because his uncle was infectious. Gabriel never saw his uncle again, though Hakim eventually told him he had died. He took Gabriel with him to Cairo where he "found" him a new uncle and asked him to also call him Kraft. Gabriel's description of his new uncle didn't come even close to the real Bourgawich, who was as expansive in girth as his name suggested.

Carter struggled for two days, tossing around the information in his mind so that what went into his report to Saunders would not lead to the boy in any other way but what he told the FBI agent about him. The child was a victim—a tool the terrorist had used to gain entry into the US. Since Nicola Moses was behind the acts of terrorism on the US soil, it would have been his people who'd found an orphaned American boy in a coastal mission and quickly seized the opportunity to use him, much like any other citizen would use a passport.

After the dinner at her Ann Arbor home, Stella did a lot of thinking—and a corresponding volume of talking. However, even had she kept her sales pitch terse, Carter would have agreed that the two of them should remain the only people in the country who not only believed in the existence of the Peacetaker but also knew who and where he was.

He suggested in his report that the fake Bourgawich was a member of a cell with international roots, though he didn't implicate the Red Crescent or Red Cross societies in any way. Once again, they were just vehicles that Moses used to carry his vile terrorist scheme. He let Saunders assume that Bourgawich made contact with cell members in each of the cities where the riots happened. This was the part that made him cringe each time he thought about it, because it meant that the FBI would commit considerable resources to flush out the others. However, when he weighed the consequences of the law enforcement agencies and their corresponding bureaucratic bosses on the Hill learning about the Peacetaker's existence against the waste of discretionary budgetary funds, it was no contest.

Stella was right. Myths and legends should be thought of as products of people's dreams. It was what helped them to cope—without anger and friction. He didn't put it in his report, but he told Saunders that very likely Moses' chemical warfare lab in Spain had made a breakthrough and his terrorists had conducted field tests in Cairo and then on US soil, with an aerial agent that turned people into homicidal maniacs. The FBI agent was skeptical but Carter inclined his head and said, "Is your lab still puzzling over those organic bullets I've FedExed to you?" And when Saunders whistled, he knew this part of the story was on solid ground.

"Have you watched the news these last few days?" Carter asked, when Stella came back with a pot of coffee and faded earthenware mugs.

She poured him a cup. "Not really. My big screen TV's down here, where it's of most use—Gabriel and his friends—and when I'm working with my laptop, I spend my time productively, doing research."

"Just as well, then, that I brought you a handful of news clippings," he said, reaching for his briefcase. He took out the folder with the photocopied pages of various global newspapers and slid it along the table toward her. "I don't think your productivity will suffer if you take a look."

A few minutes later, she looked up from reading the many versions of the same alarming story, smiling. "I hope our Justice Department gives you a generous Christmas bonus."

He pursed his mouth, frowning. "Why would they do that?"

Two weeks ago, Jean-Baptiste, Vicomte Fou de Dardaniel, held a huge reception at his ancestral chateau in the village of Bades-Chabanel, fifteen miles south of Perpignan. The event celebrated the opening of a vineyard that would add a proud new label to the wines of the Languedoc region. Five hundred of Vicomte's closest friends and business associates gathered for three days of indoor and outdoor festivities. Every one of the sixty-two bedrooms in the chateau had been opened to accommodate overnight guests, many of whom had also invested in Vicomte's new venture.

The tragedy struck on the second day of celebrations, during the lazy afternoon hours and just after a round of wine-tasting ceremonies. A group of guests that included Chevalier Robichaud, the French President's cousin, Charles-Pierre Awad, the man responsible for the French chemical industry being the fifth largest in the world, Lucas C. Bedlam, the US detergent baron, Lord Carmichael, the British newspaper magnate, Honorable Simon Talbert, the Belgian financier and Mr. Nicola Moses, accepted Vicomte's invitation to tour his stables. Jean-Baptiste had just purchased a new racehorse and wanted to show him off to his friends and associates.

When Mr. Moses stumbled for the second time as he walked across the grounds, his bodyguards grew concerned and suggested that he turn back and get some rest. Their employer refused, but when he stumbled for the third time, one of his bodyguards helped him sit down on the grass while the other took out his satellite phone and summoned the billionaire's personal physician, thirty miles away, on the yacht anchored in Port-Vendres. Moses had undergone a full physical just days prior to attending the celebration. His security staff knew he was in splendid health. Even before the bodyguard finished the call, his employer went into anaphylactic shock and thirty seconds, later breathed his last breath.

"The autopsy results were inconclusive, but the medical examiner found three small puncture wounds, two in the fleshy part of the deceased's neck and one behind his left ear, consistent with an insect sting—a wasp's sting?" She looked up at him, grinning.

He played along, saying, "Insect stings are harmless to most people, but to those with acute allergies even a mosquito bite can prove to be deadly."

"Back in San Francisco, I was in splendid health, too, when I accepted the pen sticky with peanut butter," she said musingly.

He nodded. "I know, Stella."

"So—did you bring back any wine samples from the Languedoc region?"

"I wasn't invited to the grand event," he said, shaking his head.

"But you were in France?"

"Lyons. I spent a long quiet moment at Pascal's grave."

The End

About the Author:

I have several "hats" in my closet, and all of them fit, at one time or another. I'm a writer, an engineer, an academic, an administrative assistant, a wife, a mother and an only child who took care of her parents until they passed away. I can't remember time when I did not write – something, anything – though I didn't get serious about publication until about 15 years ago. Between 2001 and 2005, I've published several literary short stories in various lit-magazines in US and Canada. Then I decided to concentrate on writing novels. I write mystery, romance, suspense, thrillers and fantasy.

My published works are:
"The Cracked Shadow," a paranormal mystery-romance,
"Cold Scheme," a romantic suspense
"Sweet Poisoned Wine," a romantic suspense,
"The Flaming Tiger," romantic thriller
"Burning Spiral," a fantasy/suspense,
"The Heirloom," fantasy thriller coming in 2015
"Mistress of Deceit," romantic suspense in 2015
"Thy Killer's Keeper," fantasy-thriller coming in 2015
"The Witches of Calamora," fantasy-sci-fic YA coming in 2015 (Wee-Creek Press)
"Garland of Pleasures," fantasy erotic romance, coming in 2015
"Ribbons of Death," suspense thriller with romantic elements, coming in 2015

Social Media Links:

Website: www.editapetrick.biz

Twitter: https://twitter.com/EditaBoni

Goodreads:
https://www.goodreads.com/book/show/17714335-cold-scheme

Blog: http://knotsinromance.blogspot.ca/

Cold Coffee Café:
http://coldcoffeecafe.com/profile/EditaAPetrick

Facebook: https://www.facebook.com/EditaPetrickBoni

Made in the USA
Charleston, SC
27 July 2015